THE BELONGING

ALSO BY KATHERINE GENET

The Belonging

KATHERINE GENET

Wych Elm Books

Wych Elm Books

Otago, NZ

www.wychelmbooks.com

contact@wychelmbooks.com

ISBN: 978-0-473-54448-5 (softcover) 978-0-473-54449-2 (ePub) 978-0-473-54450-8 (Kindle)

For Valerie, my traveling companion.

1

SNAKE DOES AS REQUIRED AND BRINGS MORGHAN TO ME.

It is time for her to see, to see without misunderstanding, why the veil is coming back down.

And what is at stake.

These human ones, they know the veil is shredding and are afraid – and well they should be careful. But they don't know that they feel fear for the wrong reasons.

It must come down. Things must return to the way they were, long ago. So long ago now, that none of them remember.

Which means that I must make her reach back to me, make them all, her, and the others – you, if you are one of them, reach back to see.

It is time.

She has been here before, flown here on the wings of her Hawk, come to this Isle of Healing where she has danced under Grandmother tree, tied boons to her limbs, and leaned against the warm and ancient stones of the circle here, but she has not seen the extent of this place. Nor its full purpose.

This time, she comes not on wings across the ocean, but Snake has swallowed her, travelling fast and deep, through the ancient tunnels that link all our worlds. Down and down the wide, obsidian steps.

I expect her to be out of breath when she transforms back from Snake, but she is good, my other self, and stands poised, looking at me, her wolf – our wolf – pressed to her side as he always was to mine. Our great protector. Our great reminder.

I turn to lead her, wordless, because she must see for herself.

And I hope she is strong enough to survive the seeing.

We go through the Hall of the Ancestors, and I feel her gaze upon the great stone statues of our gods. I am used to their shadowed gazes and lead her without stopping out into the light of day.

The trees stare down at her, uncurling their twiggy knuckles and she lifts her face to see how high they rise. Her astonishment shimmers in the air but I do not slow. These trees breach the sky and hold up the roof of the world. They are our history keepers and their spirits are tall and old and proud.

It is the view from the clifftop that I want to show my visitor in her modern clothes, a silver oak leaf and acorn on a chain around her neck, along with the egg, of course. She has long claimed that symbol, without being fully aware of its importance. I would marvel that she is me and I am here, but I am used to such things and it has been a very long time since I walked upon the Earth as she does.

Will she be strong enough to see this? To understand what I am showing her? Yes, I am all but sure of it.

Although living with it will be the trial. Because things must not merely be endured, but changed. She must change it. She and her Grove and all the other Groves, and every individual besides who thinks and cares.

It is miraculous that my Grove continues. The one I started all those millennia ago, during the time of the Great Turning.

When the way was lost.

I quit my own brooding thoughts for we are here now, Ravenna of the Grove, Lady of the Forest, Lady of Death, and Morghan Wilde, who does, and must, along with others, with each of you, claim the same titles. Lady of the Wilderness, Lady of Life.

Her gaze has already turned towards what I have brought her to see.

I spread my arms wide. Look, I gesture. Look, and understand.

She looks, the breeze pushing her thick hair back from her face, and I stand while her grey eyes take it all in. She understands in moments. I see it there in her face. The anguish.

But still. Understanding it is not breathing it, living it. Above all, it is not acting upon it. Which is what is required.

She stares across the water and I follow her gaze. Her world is over there, and I can feel the weight of its darkness from here. For it is dark over there. From our viewpoint, the sun does not rise there anymore, and the sky is a torment of thunder and lightning, despite the brilliance of the noonday light here on our Isle.

But there is still hope. It is not too late. We have not left it too late to act. Her world spills forth a glitter of golden lights from the darkness; not however, the lights of a million cities shutting out the shine of the stars, but the lights of a billion good souls. Souls who hope and dream and still, deep inside them, reach for us.

Altogether, it is a criss-crossing map of light and dark, a map of chaos, beautiful and deadly.

There is a sound below us and she drags her gaze away from the sight across the churning ocean to the gentling lap of water at the bottom of our cliff. Her hands are clenched fists. The bow of a boat grinds against the sand of the cove. I watch as she watches, silently, as the people on board are helped to shore, their legs unsteady, eyes wide like those of panicked deer.

Now she turns her gaze to myself, and I can see from the pain in her expression that she understands what I am showing her. The world over there, the lost ones being brought ashore. There is knowledge in her eyes, in the tightening of the skin around them. In the press of her lips together.

And then she surprises me, when I thought I could no longer be so startled. With a quick movement, she steps forward and into myself and I am me and I am her, and she is herself and also me.

I let her look, for what else is there to do? And perhaps looking will sustain her as it sustains the rest of us.

I look with her, for what she sees with new clarity is what I am used to, and although it never dulls, I admit it gives me a quickening of delight to see it through her unfamiliar eyes for this moment.

4

She turns us from the sight over the sea and looks instead over our land. I know she is seeking for a moment the far reaches of it, and she is right and also wrong. A flash of understanding. Yes, it is an island upon which we stand. The Isle of the Dead. The Isle of Healing, but it has no real borders. The seas surround us, and yet, the trees and meadows are endless. The Summerlands stretch onwards from it.

And all is alive. I feel her gasp at the sudden clarity with which she sees the truth behind everything. The way the very air hums with the web of energy that crosses it in an endless stream of knowledge, of understanding, of information. Life. The web is the lifeblood of all the worlds. It cannot be broken, but it can be forgotten. Not here, but over the sea, in her world.

She shifts my gaze from it and looks at the trees instead, at the stones, the blades of grass, each alive, aware, part of the world.

I hear her sigh at the beauty of it, at the vividness of the colour, of the way the energy permeates everything.

And then she is standing again in front of me, and one hand touches the egg on the chain around her neck with its leaf and acorn. Down below us, on the shore of the cove, the refugees are being given each an egg.

An egg to represent the soul.

I take a breath and look back out over at the far world. I would whisper to you all there, if I could.

I would tell you that there is a web binding us. That you must take the egg of your own soul and crack it wide open.

And reach for us.

2

MINNIE SHIVERED, CROUCHED BETWEEN THE LOW BRANCHES of the elder tree, and tried to tuck her cloak tighter around her knees. It was only made of fleece, the cloak, and she wished she'd been able to buy the wool one, like Morghan's and some of the other's.

At least her own was black though, like a proper witch's. And she'd get a wool one soon. Hopefully.

She had a view of the cave from here, and shook her head, wondering what the woman was doing in there. Morghan Wilde. Minnie had made sure to learn the names of everyone she thought was part of the coven or grove or whatever it was.

Morghan Wilde was the priestess, Minnie knew, but what she didn't know was why she'd gone into the cave, and what was taking her so long in there. Minnie had already seen inside it, on one of her many explorations, but she didn't know what it was used for. She'd tried to come up with ideas about it, but it was only big enough in there under the heavy old stones to sit and do what? Meditate, she guessed. Or pray. Did witches pray? She wasn't sure, didn't think so.

It wasn't big enough to do magic in, that was for sure. That she knew. And besides, you needed tools for doing magic. An altar – she was setting one up at home, in her bedroom. In the wardrobe, to be exact, so that Tiny wouldn't mess with it, because of course, Tiny messed with every-thing. But she had one started anyway, and so what if it was just a small table that her Gran had had a pot plant on? Her Gran hadn't noticed it was missing, or if she had, she'd not said anything. And the pot plant was all right on the windowsill instead. Probably got better light, for that matter.

She had a candle in a terrific candlestick she'd found at the junk shop. It was silver, she reckoned. Or maybe just silver plated, but that didn't matter when you were starting out, did it? Of course, what with being in the wardrobe, she had to bring it out to light it, but she was seriously considering bringing the whole altar out into the bedroom, and just threatening Tiny if she dared touch anything on it.

Her mother would be easy to deal with if she wanted to complain about it. Minnie would just tell her to go mind her own business and she'd scuttle outside to suck on a cigarette the way she always did, pushing her lank hair back from her face and squinting down at the ground.

The candlestick had ivy and grapes twined around it. The guy in the shop had said it was Victorian, which made it really old. It was part of the reason why she'd only been able to afford a fleece cloak, not a woollen one, but Minnie guessed she didn't really mind, because the candlestick was really cool, and just right.

What else did she have? She comforted herself thinking about her altar while waiting for Morghan to come back out of the cave. It was better than thinking about how her right foot was going numb from the cold and from not moving for like an hour or more. What was Morghan Wilde doing in there?

Minnie shook her head. She'd been watching Morghan on and off for a couple weeks now. Since she'd learnt who she was. In a little while, not this time probably, but maybe next time, she was going to step out from behind the trees and talk to her.

Minnie's throat went dry.

She was going to ask to join the coven or grove, or whatever it was. She belonged with them, she was going to say. She might just be a beginner witch, but she was a witch all right. She knew it in her bones. Was there such a thing as a bone witch, she wondered? She'd been trying to figure out what sort of witch she wanted to be, but there were too many to choose from. She didn't fancy being a kitchen witch or whatever. She hated cooking.

She'd tried telling her Gran about being a witch, when her Gran had asked why she was dying her hair black, but her Gran had threatened to totally flip out, and so Minnie had lost her nerve. She guessed she was still in the witch's closet.

That made her stifle a laugh and think about her altar again.

She needed an athame. That though, she'd have to order online, she reckoned. Even if they could go to Banwell

– and they couldn't because her mum was totally freaked out about the virus – she didn't think she'd find one there. Not even in the cool junk shop where she'd got the candlestick.

She needed a job so she could save enough money to buy an athame and the other stuff she needed. Like, a scrying mirror. They were cool. She wondered what she'd be able to see in one of those. Someone on Etsy was selling black obsidian ones, and Minnie was almost in a fever of need for one every time she thought of it.

And a chalice. She needed one of those.

Not to mention candles, and essential oils, and like, all the rest of it. You couldn't be a witch, not really, if you didn't have the right tools. Everyone needed tools, right? No matter what they were doing.

But she didn't have a job. Her mum didn't even have a job anymore; that was why they'd moved to Wellsford eight weeks ago to live with Gran. Minnie would have thought it was really shit, and she had to begin with, especially as her mum and Gran never stopped fighting, but there was one thing about this place that made it okay.

And that was Wilde Grove.

And Morghan Wilde.

Minnie remembered the Halloween bonfires. Samhain bonfires, she corrected herself carefully. It was Samhain, the most powerful date on the witch's calendar. Morghan – Minnie let herself use the woman's first name, because soon they'd know each other well, she thought – had been pretty fab up there on the stage. Minnie had taken in every detail of what Morghan had been wearing, the way she looked. She'd had a long red dress on, pretty simple, really, and

Minnie had wondered if she ought to take up sewing. Her Gran had an old sewing machine no one was using. It might be cheaper to buy material than something already made. Minnie filed the idea away for later and tried shifting again where she crouched, careful not to make any noise.

She couldn't help the low groan anyway. Her foot really had gone to sleep and now it was all pins and needles and awful. She gritted her teeth and considered leaving her hiding place and going back home. She could go to Haven for Books instead and lurk there for a while, see if they had anything new.

Maybe if she was real brave, she could ask for a job there. She was trying to get up the courage to do it. The woman who ran the place was American and had a great accent. She was pretty nice too and didn't seem to mind when Minnie came in just to have another look around without buying anything.

Minnie was pretty sure Krista – that was her name – was part of the coven as well. Part of the Wilde Grove coven.

She'd wanted to follow them the night of the bonfires too, when she'd seen them all start to leave, but her Mum had stopped her, insisting they all stay together, and that Minnie watch Tiny and Robin.

She'd burned all night wanting to know what they were up to in the woods.

She rubbed surreptitiously at her ankle. Her sneakers were almost worn out. She'd try to find a pair of black boots when it was time to replace them. That would totally be better than just another pair of cheap, no-brand tennis shoes.

Anyway, she'd ended up doing her own ritual that night.

Once Tiny was asleep, she'd lit her candle – not in the wardrobe, obviously – and done what she could. One of the books on witchcraft at Haven had a page on Samhain in it, and she'd secretly taken a photo of the page with her phone, and she'd done some of the things it suggested, doing it at midnight in the room she shared with her sister. It had been a bit spooky, if she was honest, but thinking about it still gave her a thrill, and she knew what had happened there in the corner of her room had been a sign.

A sign that she was a real witch.

That reminded her, she needed some tarot cards too. It was all very well doing the candle thing, and she had to admit that worked better than she could ever have imagined, but she wanted some cards too.

Being a witch was getting expensive. She wondered if she dared steal a pack from Haven.

If she didn't get a job there, that was.

Maybe she should ask her father about that. See what he had to say. He'd probably say it was okay. He was being surprisingly cool about stuff like that.

There was movement across the clearing and Minnie narrowed her eyes, peering out from her hiding place. About time, she thought, desperate to know what Morghan Wilde had been doing in there.

MORGHAN BLINKED AGAINST THE DIMNESS AND TIGHTENED her fingers into a fist in the dirt. She closed her eyes again, but the vision was still there, and she panted in the darkness of the cave, trying to gather the shreds of her wits about her. The air tasted of soil and chilled against the hot skin of her cheeks. She groped for the covering over her eyes and tore it from her head, squinting against the shadows.

She was on her hands and knees. Somewhere during the travelling, she had moved from her calm sitting position and now a stick dug into her knee. She shifted slightly, raising her head, breathing deep and slow, getting her bearings.

The cave was small, made who knew how many thousands of years ago, a sheltering of stones big enough to sit in.

Big enough to crouch on hands and knees panting for breath, still seeing stars.

Still seeing the yellow firefly lights of one world, and the web of the other.

Morghan pressed a hand to her chest, willing her heart to slow, to stop its loud pounding in her ears. She leaned forward and touched the dirt of the cave floor again, flattened her palm against it, then sank down and put her forehead there, closing her eyes.

The web. She'd seen it so clearly, looking through the other's eyes. Were there even words to describe such a thing? She groped for them, knowing that if she could find words for it, she could begin to process it, find her way back to it, let it sustain her. The glimpses she'd had of the web before paled into insignificance with how it had been to see through the ancient one's eyes.

She'd seen the expression in those eyes. Those deep, dark eyes. The expression that demanded she live with what she was being shown, across that sea, in the world where she lived, her world – live with its reality, so that she could...

Do what?

Morghan's hands tightened in the dirt. How could she possibly do anything about this? The task was too big. Too much for one person.

Too much.

She could not reverse centuries of wrongness. Could not take humanity back to where it belonged, to the understanding it once had, needed again. She was one person.

What could one person do?

She felt the cliff's edge under her feet. Felt the chasm between the two worlds. It split open her chest and left her gasping, her body heaving against the cold stone of the cave, shuddering on her knees in the dirt.

It was a chasm that had never been meant to exist, not in this way.

And how could she live like she always had, now she had seen? Had seen the world through the other's eyes, the true brilliance of it, the sheer life of it, where everything in it had consciousness, where everything contributed to the web. She would spend the rest of her life seeking to touch that again, no matter how fleetingly.

And the web itself. She didn't know what to call it but the web, because it spread out over everything, seen and yet unseen, filaments of energy connecting everything, all carrying so much information.

None of it negative.

So much love.

Morghan wept, her face in the dirt. This was what had been lost. This is what humanity had turned away from, forgotten. What they had chosen darkness over, become entangled in.

When she was hollow of tears, Morghan opened her eyes and lifted her hands to push her hair back from her face. It had come loose sometime during her travelling. She crawled from the cave and stood on legs that wobbled beneath her. How far she had gone this time. She'd never been so deep down into the Otherworld. And Snake had taken her so quickly, she'd not had time to look around, to slow and take it in. He'd simply swallowed her, then rushed off through the Wildwood, and down the great black stone steps. She frowned for a moment at the eye-covering in her hand, then shoved it into her pocket and took a step forward.

She knew this clearing like the back of her hand. Better, in fact, because age was changing her hands, wrinkling the skin to a crone's, darkening them with age spots. But this clearing changed only with the seasons. Past Samhain now, the grass was wet underfoot with discarded leaves, and the trees stood bare in a circle around it, shivering in the breeze that whispered of winter's coming embrace.

But she could barely see it. Turning her head, Morghan looked, eyes wide open, and yet what she saw wasn't the small clearing, the stones of the cave at her back, the trees leaning towards her with their great twiggy heads bare.

What she saw was the hill-top where she'd been in her journey. She shook her head. That wasn't right. This one wasn't on the Isle of Healing. She was back, standing above the world she lived in, the view of her vision reversed. She lifted her hands and held them to her cheeks. Above her, the sky screamed over her head, a great chasm of sky torn by lightning.

The veil.

Eyes closed, fingers digging into her skin, she stood high above everything, and around her the sky raged, and she teetered on the top of her hill, looking around, mouth open in a scream that echoed the roar of the thunder that shook her where she stood, and when she looked, she saw that the veil between the worlds was coming down.

She saw a vision of the Shining Ones – the goddesses and gods and ancestors and the faerie, and the spirits of those humans who touched and yearned to touch the web. They shone, and their numbers were great, but all around them were swaths of writhing, flocking darkness and Morghan flinched. Here were the restless and trapped soul aspects of humanity's own dead. Those who had not died well. Those who had not been sung on their way.

Those who did not believe in the singing.

She staggered, caught in the vision of the screaming sky, in the air that churned with the unveiling. Then forced her eyes open, looking for the familiar clearing in the Grove.

'Morghan?'

Morghan swallowed, tried to focus, lurched sideways, off-balance. A hand clasped her elbow, steadied her.

'Clarice,' she said, and her tongue was thick in her mouth, her throat dry.

'Are you okay?'

How could she answer that? She laughed and shook her head. 'Far from it,' she croaked.

The hand moved, and Clarice lifted Morghan's arm, draped it over her own thin shoulders. 'The Queen summons you,' she said. 'I'm to bring you to her.'

The ground swayed under Morghan's feet, and she could feel the wind swooping and screaming around her as though she stood still on the clifftop, watching the battle scene that was the earth.

Swallowing, she shook her head. 'I don't think this is a good time,' she said.

Clarice's hand was warm against her own. Warm but firm. 'I'm sorry, Morghan,' Clarice said. 'But you don't have a choice.' Then, because her stepmother staggered against her as if drunk, her eyes swivelling in her head as though she was not seeing what was in front of her, Clarice asked. 'Where have you been? What did you see?'

Morghan swung her head from side to side. 'I saw what we are facing and the choices we must make to save it all,' she said, her words slurred. 'And I do not know...' She swayed where she stood, found her voice once more. 'And I do not know how we are to do it.'

Clarice tightened her grip on Morghan, one hand around Morghan's fingers against her shoulder, the other gripping Morghan's waist, holding her upright. 'The choices?' she asked.

Morghan's eyes slid closed and she breathed deeply in, filling her lungs, and holding the cold air inside before letting it out, slowly, steadying herself. She took her own weight but kept her hand on Clarice's shoulder.

'The veil is being brought down,' she said.

Clarice looked at her, lips pursed, delicate white brows twisting in a frown. 'What? All at once? That will cause complete chaos!'

'Hmm,' Morghan said, and felt for a moment the humming touch of the web around her like an alternate reality. 'Not all at once. It has been happening for some time already, I think.' She paused. 'But even a slow thinning has consequences.'

Clarice stared at her, unable to think what to say. Her mind hunted for the meaning of what Morghan had told her. She spent her days going back and forth between the realms, spending as much time with the Fae as she did with her own family. But there was a reason there was a border between them, was there not? That for each, the other was behind the mists. 'What does this mean?' she asked at last.

Morghan took another deep breath. 'It means either the hope of the world, or that madness of many sorts is coming,' she said, pressing her fingers against the fine bones of Clarice's shoulders. 'Let's go and see what your Queen has planned, shall we?'

3

BURDOCK'S EARS TWITCHED, THEN TWITCHED AGAIN. HE wrinkled his snout, not wanting to wake up. He was comfy where he was, curled around himself on his nice soft bed that his person had brought upstairs and put right by the fire. He was toasty as a marshmallow.

But there was that sound again. Just a slight noise, and he lifted his head. Then gave a low growl deep down in the back of his throat. It sounded like someone was outside – and an actual person too, not just one of those pesky birds that were forever teasing him.

He uncurled himself and sat up, glancing over at his mistress under the covers of her own bed. He sniffed, but she wasn't having one of her dreams that smelled of iron-cold water. She was just regular dreaming. His ears caught another sound, and now he was sure. Someone was prowling around outside. How dare they? Didn't they know this was his place? His and his new person's?

'Woof,' he said, and then repeated it, louder. 'Woof!' His

toenails scrabbled on the floorboards as he dashed down the stairs to the front door, in full throat now.

Erin sat up blinking, her body rigid with the sudden shock of waking. She glanced towards the window, but it was barely light out there. Not that that meant much, since the sun was late in rising these days, and even later in making an appearance over the Wellsford hills.

She groped for her Grandmother's dressing gown, shivering as she pulled it on. She hardly touched her own clothes anymore. They were still in the suitcase in the spare room, but not on the bed anymore at least. She'd shoved them into the small wardrobe in there.

Burdock was going crazy downstairs, and Erin snagged her phone from the bedside table, flicking the screen on, looking for the time. Just gone 8am.

'I'm coming, Burdock,' she said, stumbling down the stairs while trying to both knot the dressing gown tie around her waist and open up the phone app, just in case she needed to call the police. Or maybe, she thought at the bottom of the stairs and heading for the door, pushing Burdock out of the way, maybe the video recorder would be more useful. The nearest police were probably in Banwell, after all.

Burdock shoved the door open and dashed from the house, his chest vibrating with his deepest bark. He'd been right, he thought – there were people here, men here where they didn't belong.

'What are you doing?' Erin cried from behind him. She hurried forward, phone still in her hand, holding it out in front of her like she really was going to take a video. 'What are you doing to my car?'

The man who had been bent over at the back of her little Mini slowly straightened, eyeing Burdock warily. He spoke out of the side of his mouth – god he hated it when they had dogs. Still, at least he'd been warned this job that the dog was huge but harmless.

'Got a warrant to repossess,' he said to the girl standing there in a red dressing gown, eyes wide with shock.

Her mouth fell open. 'What?'

At least she had her hand on the dog, and he, giant beast just like the kid's father had warned, was staying put. Had even shut up the barking.

'Repossessing your car,' he said, spelling it out to her. He glanced over at Russell, who hung out the driver's window of the tow truck and shrugged back at him. They'd hoped to get the car and be gone before the kid woke up.

'I heard you,' Erin snapped. 'But it's all paid for and everything. You've got the wrong one.'

This was a shit job, even for them, Baz decided. A guy having his own daughter's car repossessed, now that wasn't really cool. What had the chick done to tick off her rich old man? Baz scratched his cheek and eyed the dog again. Whatever it was, he was inclined to come down on the girl's side. The dad was one of those pompous jerks who thought they were better than you just because their wallet was fatter.

Not for the first time, Baz wondered if he was in the right line of work. Seemed to him, he was always taking cars and shit away from the ones who needed them the most.

He sniffed. A job was a job though, and he wasn't getting paid to question the whys and wherefores of anything. He was getting paid because he had a knack for breaking into cars and hustling them away before anyone noticed. And at least he was doing it legally these days.

She sure was cute though, standing there in her dressing gown, the big hairy dog beside her. Baz glanced at Russel again and straightened his shoulders. In a moment, he'd finish hitching the line to the sweet little Mini Countryman and Russel would haul it up onto the flatbed. Then they'd deliver it to the old man, collect their bonus, and be out on the street again, onto the next job.

'Your Dad's taking it back,' he said to the girl. 'Reckon you got yourself in his bad books.'

Erin gaped at him. Blinked at the tow truck and back to the guy standing in front of her car like he had every right to be hitching a chain to it.

'My father?'

The guy shrugged, then bent down to the car, and a moment later her little Mini was on the back of the truck. Erin pressed a hand to her forehead, trying to process what was happening, and was still standing there in disbelief as the truck drove away, taking her only means of transport with it.

Burdock looked up at his person. He licked at her hand, wanting to tell her that everything was okay, and that the metal box on wheels had been way too small for them anyway. He'd had to tie himself in a giant knot every time they went anywhere.

He looked at his person and woofed, telling her the good news.

But she was just staring, mouth open.

Erin couldn't believe it. Her father had ordered her car to be repossessed? How was that even possible? They'd paid cash for it; she knew they had. There was no dealership to take it back to.

Which meant that her father was just getting it shipped back to him, to be put somewhere. Out of her reach.

But why?

Another thought tumbled on the heels of that one, and Erin spun around, running back to the cottage. She was gasping by the time she'd pounded up the stairs to the small room she'd set up as her office and lifted the screen on her laptop.

She had Internet service now, although she was trying to use it only for business purposes. For loading her art onto her Etsy store, for the website she was starting. She bit down on her lip as she waited for the browser to open and her banking page to load.

And then she sank into the seat. Downstairs, the front door slammed shut in the wind, but she barely heard it. Right now, there was only the page on the screen in front of her.

The one that showed her credit cards had been cancelled. All of them. Cancelled, closed, gone like the car.

Burdock pressed his cold nose into her palm, and she patted him, a lump in her throat, tears springing to her eyes as she checked the date against her bank balance. She should have got her allowance yesterday. It always went in the same day every week, a good, generous amount. Her parents had never begrudged it to her before. They'd insisted on it, even back when she'd talked about wanting to find a part time job. They had said it would continue no matter what until she was married.

Well, she was no longer getting married, and they'd stopped her allowance anyway.

Which would be okay, in the scheme of things, but now she had no money.

Erin closed her eyes and concentrated on the feeling of Burdock's warm head under her hand. It was bony, the top of his skull flat, the fur thick but coarse. She felt his head under her fingers and the seat under her legs, and listened to her breathing, trying to stay calm. Her phone was on the desk beside the computer and she opened her eyes and stared at it. Should she call her mother? She touched cold fingers to her throat which was tight and constricted. She swallowed. What would she say to her mother?

She already knew why they'd done it.

Hadn't they threatened to, sort of? They had, but Erin hadn't taken them seriously. She shook her head. The idea of Wilde Grove being a black magic cult? It was too ridiculous to entertain, and she'd told her parents that, over and over. Much as she hated to admit it, her birth mother had fed them a line of bullshit.

Erin let out a long, shaky breath.

Her parents didn't believe her, no matter what she said. It was a cult, they insisted. She was brainwashed already. Indoctrinated. Why else would she have decided to live in Wellsford? A small village in out-of-the-way nowhere?

And that was why she had no money anymore. So that she couldn't give it to the cult.

The knowledge made Erin tired, and she thought about getting up and walking out of the room and back to bed. It would still be warm in there, and she could pull the covers over her head, lie there in the dark and concentrate on not thinking about any of it. She could deal with it all another day. Or later. Or something.

Burdock looked at her and whined, his brow furrowing in a doggy frown. If they were up, could he please go back outside? In the excitement, he hadn't visited the apple tree, and now that he thought about it, he was hungry too. It was breakfast time; he was sure of it. She could have a cup of that tea stuff, or that bitter smelling coffee stuff, and he could crunch up some of his biscuits.

That was a fine idea. He went to the door and looked hopefully back at her.

Erin stared at the dog, then nodded her head. 'You're right, Burdock,' she said. 'I can't just go back to bed and hide from this.'

He woofed in agreement. He knew the word bed, and it had nothing whatsoever to do with breakfast, which was another word he knew.

'I don't know what I'm going to do though,' Erin added, looking at her bank account again. 'What with getting the Internet set up, and everything else, there's not much left.' Enough to buy groceries for two or three weeks. In other words, just a few hundred pounds. She was going to have to get a job if she wanted to stay here.

Which didn't sound easy in a place as tiny as Wellsford. And there were lockdowns happening again, so Banwell was out of the question too. She didn't have the slightest idea what to do. She needed some sort of income. That was the way the world was. She'd starve without money.

Burdock woofed again, but only quietly, and Erin sighed. 'You're right,' she said. 'Breakfast.'

Or breakfast for Burdock, at least, because now things

were done a little differently. It had been hard, at first, getting into the new habit, but Erin had discovered that if you simply made yourself do it, it got easier every day. Besides, it was interesting. Fascinating, even.

She shivered as she plucked her cloak from the peg at the back door and drew it around her shoulders. Now that Samhain was past, and the winter solstice – not Christmas, but the solstice – was coming up, the wind had developed an extra bite to it, a sharpness that nicked and cut and told of great adventures in the ice-bound north. Erin was glad of the thick wool as she left Burdock crunching into his biscuits and wove her way through the garden towards the well.

Pushing up the lid, she had to take a deep breath as she always did when she saw the fathomless cold water. Her throat tightened as some part of her suddenly stood ankle deep in Kria's loch, stuck there in the deepest mists of time.

She hadn't yet found the way out of the glen, hadn't yet discovered the key to the initiation, and often, when she closed her eyes, she was there beside the cold water, the bones of her long ago self bleached the colour of white shell on the shore with her.

Her breath was ragged but deep and she blew it out slowly between pursed lips, then took another, steadying herself where she was, and forced herself into awareness of her own body, of where she stood in the garden of Ash Cottage, of the wind blustering against her face, bringing with it the scent of winter, of the clacking of branches from the woods behind the wall of her garden. She lifted her head for a moment and gazed at the sky, thick and damp with clouds, the brightening etching of light from the far rising sun threading between them. Then she looked at the garden, dim in the heavy dawn, the soil dark and deep, the plants curled over themselves, fingers drawn in, tucked still away in their dreams.

She looked at herself, saw her hands, saw the rim of the well under them, and made herself aware of everything – of her breath, herself. Of the garden beyond her, of the world beyond the wall. It was a strange sensation, and one she couldn't yet hold for long, the sensation of being both inside herself and everywhere else. Of being calm inside herself and detached in observing what was around her. She looked down at her hands again and saw them, working her perspective so that she saw herself seeing them, and breathed in deeply, relaxed yet focused. It was in this state, Morghan had told her, that she could begin to truly *see*.

Morghan hadn't elaborated on what Erin would begin to see, but Erin was starting to understand anyway.

The answer was everything. Or almost everything, she supposed. Certainly, a lot more.

It was an odd sensation, but freeing. You didn't have to be stuck up in your head all the time, she'd discovered. You could be in your body, and in the room, or in the garden, in the world, all at the same time.

Morghan had called it flexing the spirit and insisted on it being the first thing Erin did each day. That and give thanks.

Erin looked down at the water, a deep black hole in the low light. She could smell it, the cold, metallic tang of it, and she could sense how deep it was, how it filled the well from far down in the darkness and mystery of the earth. She leaned a little closer over it and breathed deeply, letting herself feel the life of the water through her chest, with her heart rather than her head, as she was being taught. Then she straightened and looked around, holding stubbornly to the sensation of being inside herself, in her heart, and fully part of her surroundings as well.

'Blessed water,' she said. 'Blessed earth, air, and fire.' She thought of the rising sun, of the glowing embers in the firebox of her cooker.

'Spirits of the north, east, south, and west, I greet you, in peace and blessing.' She breathed in again, swallowed. Said the last line, the one that still made her shiver.

'I am called to weave the world with you. I am called to keep the weaving safe.' She remembered the shimmering threads she'd glimpsed crossing overhead the stone circle at the Samhain ritual and let out a breath between pursed lips.

She dipped her fingers into the water of the well, and the coldness was a shock that almost had her tumbling back to the valley where a long ago aspect of herself had lived and died, but she resisted, breathed through it, and continued with the now-familiar ritual, touching her wet fingers to her forehead, chest, shoulder to shoulder.

'May we be in peace,' she said, and sighed, closing the lid to the well and feeling the burn of cold water above her brow. She drew her cloak tighter around herself and headed for the warmth of the cottage and Burdock waiting for her in the kitchen.

Later, when the sun was higher in the sky and Morghan finished with her own morning devotions, Erin was due at Hawthorn House. She pulled open the door to Ash Cottage and stepped inside, hanging up her cloak and wondering what she would be learning today. Being still stuck in the long-ago initiation in the valley was complicating matters.

She filled the kettle and put it on the cooker to heat, looking around for Burdock. He grinned at her from his favourite chair, then went back to watching the morning lighten outside the window. Erin stood in the middle of the kitchen, fingers knotted together, thinking about her laptop upstairs, and the page that showed her almost empty bank account. She squeezed her eyes shut, realising again with a shock that went through her body like a wave that her car had been taken away that morning.

There was only one way she was going to get the car back, and the credit cards, and the allowance.

And that was by standing in front of Morghan Wilde today and telling her she'd changed her mind.

That she could no longer stay in Ash Cottage.

Could not continue with her training.

She'd had a month to decide. Now it was December, and she'd been reasonably sure she'd made the right decision. Until today.

How was she going to find work?

4

STEPHAN HEARD THE KNOCKING ON THE DOOR AT THE BACK OF the shop. 'I'll get it,' he yelled, wondering who it was this early in the morning with the sun just peeping over the trees. Or what there was of the sun. A bit of damp grey light might be a more apt description. He'd gone out earlier and greeted it anyway, him and Krista into their tiny backyard to pour offerings and give thanks, the same way they did every day.

The back door wasn't made of glass, and he tried to guess who was out there, then stopped two steps down and blinked. Why was he guessing, he wondered? He could try to do more than that.

So he did, standing still where he was, slowing his breathing and straightening. Weirdly, Morghan had told him – and Erin – that posture was an important part of walking between the worlds. He'd wanted to snort at that, because really, what did standing up straight have to do with anything much at all? Except maybe not having back problems when he was an old man?

But you didn't snort at the things Morghan told you, not when she had that clear grey gaze of hers on you, the expression that she'd learnt this nugget centuries ago. And so, he'd tried it.

And damned if it didn't make a difference. He felt stronger, more present, when he stood straight. Who'd have thought? Something so simple.

Now, he moved his awareness down into his heart. Imagined radiating outwards from there, imagined a cone – he always saw it a bit like a megaphone – in front of his chest, opening him up, letting him radiate outwards.

And drawing in energy and sensations too, a sort of deep breathing in. It worked both ways.

The person at the door knocked again, but Stephan stayed where he was a minute longer, determined to see if he could do this.

This was what Morghan had told them to do – to open themselves like this as often as possible. She said it was like stretching their muscles, the more they did it, the easier and more effective it would get.

This, she'd said, was the way they would bridge the worlds. Begin to move in flow with the universe. Do magic. Connect. Create.

He opened another cone from the top of his head, a third from the centre of his forehead. Two more from his ears. Listened and felt for who was behind the door at the bottom of the stairs.

The sudden burst of energy, of awareness, had him almost staggering. He could feel it like it was a thing he'd be able to reach out and touch. It came through the wood of the door, up the stairs towards him, a serpentine, sinuous cloud of blue energy – he felt like it was blue – and it reached for him, and he reached for it, feeling his own spirit jump at the touch, expanding outwards in a sudden leap.

He ran down the steps on rubbery legs and opened the door, grinning stupidly. 'Do you feel that?' he asked.

Erin stared at him, a slight frown between her eyes. 'Feel what?' she asked.

Stephan held up a hand as though expecting to see it glowing with blue light, then laughed. 'You have to, come on – touch my hand, it's you, after all.'

She looked at him in mystification for a moment, eyes going from his face to his hand, then lifted her own and touched her fingertips to his.

'You have to open yourself up, like Morghan taught us.'

Erin shook her head briefly, but Stephan saw her take a breath and do it anyway, and her eyes widened slightly. He looked at them, at the beautiful russet green of them, the colour of autumn, he thought, the colour of oak leaves and the wildwood. A man could get lost in those eyes, he thought, and the energy between them pulsed and grew, began a slow swirling.

Erin's eyes widened further, and she drew her hand away several centimetres, then closed the distance again, licking her lips and shaking her head.

'Do you feel that?' she asked, her voice hoarse. It was so real, the palm of her hand tingling. It swelled and slithered around them, between them, and Erin lifted her face to look at Stephan. She took in his unruly black curls, the dark stubble on his chin, the red of his mouth, and above his lips, the piercing blue of his eyes. 'It's the same colour as your eyes.'

She saw his throat convulse as he swallowed. The energy between them grew, coloured the air at the edges of their vision. Erin's heart skittered in her chest and her breath quickened.

'Wow,' Stephan breathed.

Erin was light-headed. 'Wow, yeah,' she echoed. 'Wha...' She was tongue-tied. Tried again. 'Wha...what is this?' She sucked in a breath and let it out in a shuddering whoosh.

'It's you and me,' Stephan said, and it felt like his heart was wide open. He remembered the first time he'd seen Erin, the way she'd stood, arms raised in the stone circle, not fully herself, but another, one he'd loved when he'd been another too. That was why this was happening. That was why there was this energy between them.

He stepped back suddenly, dropping his hand, snuffing out a breath, looking at Erin. She gazed back at him, lips parted slightly, eyes unfocused. Stephan shook his head. This wasn't the way he wanted it. He wanted to be with Erin because it was her, and him, together. Not because of some old bond that was dead but not, obviously, gone.

He cleared his throat, noticed Burdock finally, standing there with his head cocked quizzically, as though the dog could see the blue energy that rolled between them.

'Heyho boy,' Stephan said, bending to the dog and ruffling the big fella's ears. 'You're out and about early.'

Erin laughed a little, self-consciously, giving herself a surreptitious shake back to reality. 'Yeah. You busy?'

'Nah, of course not,' Stephan said. 'Come in – you want a coffee?'

She followed him up the stairs, Burdock pushing past them both and rushing up to the flat over Haven for Books. She heard Krista saying hello to him.

'Hi Krista,' Erin said, following Stephan into the kitchen where Burdock had already cornered Krista, wiggling in delight.

'Hi Erin. You're out and about early,' she said, echoing Stephan. She smacked a kiss onto the top of Burdock's head, then straightened to pass Stephan an extra coffee mug from the cupboard. 'What are the two of you busy at today?'

'Oh yeah,' Stephan said. 'You'll be seeing Morghan today, won't you, Erin?' He shook his head. 'I've got a pile of stuff to do with the gardens and getting ready for this next lockdown.' He grinned at Erin, still – weeks later – ecstatic over her decision to stay in Wellsford and in the Grove. It made his heart leap every time he thought about it, and he was already planning what he could give her for a Yule gift. Not that he'd had any brilliant ideas, yet. But he would.

Erin, however, was nodding glumly, remembering why she and Burdock had walked all this way. 'My car was repossessed this morning,' she blurted out, fiddling with the bowl of sugar on the table where she'd taken a seat. She turned and stared at Stephan and Krista, alarmed at the sudden tears threatening behind her lids.

'What?' Stephan asked. 'Repossessed?'

Erin turned back to the sugar bowl, blinked. 'My father got some men to come and tow it away.'

Krista walked over and sat down at the table, putting her hand absently on Burdock's head when he nosed against her. 'Your father?'

'That's really crap,' Stephan said, bringing over the mug

of coffee and sliding it in front of Erin. 'Why would he do that?'

Erin shook her head. 'Because he thinks Wilde Grove is a black magic cult.' She managed to roll her eyes. 'Still. Even though I've tried and tried to tell him and Mum that it isn't any sort of cult, let alone a black freaking magic one, whatever that is when it's at home.'

'They think that because of your birth mother, right?' Krista asked, and Erin nodded, dumping the spoon back into the sugar bowl.

'Yeah, and I'm so mad at the lot of them. Even my birth mother, even though she's dead. I don't know what to do about any of it.' She stared at the coffee in her cup. 'And they stopped my allowance.'

Krista and Stephan stared across the table at her, letting that one sink in. Stephan felt the pain come off Erin in waves. A side effect of playing with the energy between them before. He flinched like it was his own.

'What am I going to do for money?' Erin asked. 'I mean – I'm not making enough with my art yet. That's got a long way to go before it pays the bills. And I have Ash Cottage now, which means I do actually have bills.' She shook her head. 'They did it to make me go home.'

'But you can't go home,' Stephan blurted. 'I mean, this is where you belong, right? You've already decided and everything. It's a done deal, right?'

Erin nodded. 'Yes,' she said. 'I don't have any choice but to stay.' She didn't elaborate on her statement, but she didn't have to. The other two nodded. She'd told them both, haltingly, stumblingly, about the valley and Kria. They knew she had unfinished business there.

Krista sighed. 'You know what I think these days?' she asked. 'I think there's not one but two pandemics going around.'

'What do you mean?' Erin sipped at her drink, glad she'd walked into the village to come here. She still didn't know what she was going to do, but at least she wasn't alone. She thought of Kria. And of her own life before Ash Cottage, Wilde Grove, and Stephan, Morghan, Krista, and the rest of them. It had only been a few weeks – well, six or seven weeks, but already they meant so much to her. She'd been more alone before, even at home with her family and Jeremy.

This was better. No one should be alone like that.

Krista looked down at Burdock, smiling sadly into his big brown eyes. He licked her hand. 'I think the world has lost its collective mind, is what I mean.' She shook her head. 'No, let me get more specific with that – I think far too many humans are suffering a sickness of the soul.'

'You mean with all the guns and violence and stuff?' Stephan asked.

'Not just that,' Erin broke in. 'But I can't even fathom half the things people are saying on social media these days.'

'They've lost their minds,' Krista said, unable to stop herself from thinking about everything that had been going on in the world. The election back home in the U.S. for starters. It was over now, if you could even begin to say that, but she'd not slept properly for weeks beforehand. 'All over the world people are getting crazier.'

'Do you think so?' Stephan asked. 'Or have people always been crazy? I mean, think about it? Things are shit in the world right now – but haven't they always been? Right? I mean, somewhere along the line, humanity became inhumane. Hanging people, burning them, sticking their heads on spikes, homicide, genocide – it's like we evolved for violence.'

Erin shuddered. 'Surely not, though? I want to believe in us. Most of us are good people, just trying to get by. Just keeping our heads down and trying to feed our families and bring our kids up to be happy, well-balanced people.'

Krista ran her fingers through her hair. 'That's part of the problem, though, don't you think?'

'What is?' Stephan asked.

'That we're spending most of our time just trying to get by.' She gestured at Erin. 'Look at what's happened to you today, for example. I can see by your face, let alone your aura, that you're all scrunched up and worried suddenly. You weren't like that yesterday or the day before when I saw you. You weren't like that at Samhain. And what's the difference? What's made you afraid and small, all of a sudden?'

Erin shook her head and sighed. 'Money,' she said. 'Or more specifically, the fact that I no longer have any.'

'Maybe the bible was right,' Stephan said. 'Doesn't it say something about money being the root of all evil?'

'The love of money,' Krista said. 'And I think that there's truth in that, don't you? Further than that, I think lust for money and wealth and power have taken our civilisation far away from where it needs to be – where the truth about who and what we are lies.' She shook her head and subsided. 'I'm sorry,' she said. 'I didn't mean to give a lecture.'

Erin pressed her fingers to the mug of coffee. 'The trouble is – how can we live without money? We can't. If I don't get a job or something, the electricity in my house is going to get turned off. I'm not going to be able to run the Internet. I'm not going to be able to buy food. Money might be evil, but it's necessary.'

'The love of money,' Krista said, correcting it again. 'Money itself is at its base just a convenient way of swapping our time, energy, and service for the things we need.'

'Except that some hoard it and hold it over others. And for others – no matter how much time or energy or service they put into it – they will never have enough to meet their needs,' Stephan interjected.

'Which is where we've gone wrong,' Krista agreed on another sigh. 'And I've no real answer for it, except this – each of us as individuals must make the decision not to hoard or hold power over others.' She smiled sadly, because it seemed so little. 'We must share what we have with those who need it.'

'Which would be okay if everyone did it, but they don't.' Stephan shook his head and sank lower over the table.

'I wish there were a way to cure everyone with a wave of a wand, to make them connect with their kin, to know their own magic,' Krista said, getting up and going to the sink to wash her breakfast dishes. 'But there isn't. I can only make the right choices for myself and offer the world my compassion and generosity and example – weave the world with everyone else on the path towards the light.' She turned around and leaned against the counter for a moment. 'And remember, we are never alone. As Morghan would tell us – we must step into flow with our own purpose and have faith.'

Erin was gnawing at her lip. 'Faith in what?'

Stephan swallowed. 'Our spirit kin, ancestors, our soul family,' he said. 'The goddesses and gods. The truth.'

Taking a deep breath, Erin looked at Krista then Stephan. 'The truth?'

'That the world is more than we see. That it has meaning. That we have meaning,' Krista said. She straightened. 'I think a time of great change is upon us because things certainly cannot go on like this any further. Stephan, you're right that humans have been on the wrong path for an exceedingly long time, but even that time is coming to an end, because now the earth is under threat. We're destroying the very world we depend upon.'

They stared at each other, eyes wide, a sudden silence in the room. Burdock cocked his ears and looked from one to the other, wrinkling his brow in a frown.

'But what sort of change?' Erin asked at last, feeling suddenly like not having a car wasn't such a big deal, or even not having an income. She'd find some way around that. Somehow. There were larger, more important things at play.

Krista turned and gazed out the window. Then looked back at the two young people sitting at her table. 'I don't know,' she said. 'But dig deep, kids, and learn what you gotta learn real well because something has to give.'

And we're going to need all the magic we can have.'

5

MORGHAN WAS UPRIGHT, MORE OR LESS, BY THE TIME THE path crossed the border from her world to the Wildwood. She felt the air warm, for time in the Otherworld moved more slowly, the seasons taking longer breaths. It had always been this way, she knew, thinking of the old stories of men and women returning from a stay in the Fair Lands, dancing and feasting with the Fae, only to find themselves left behind by time, their loved ones either old beyond recognition or dead. If they managed to return at all, of course.

She reached a hand down, feeling instinctively for Wolf, for his steadiness and the reminder of her own powerful and wild nature, and he was there as he always was, and she took strength from his quiet assurance.

She remembered when he had first come to her. That journey to the Wildwood had been so long ago, now, but she remembered it as though it were yesterday. She remembered the shock and dazzle of it and found her lips quirking.

Clarice glanced at her. 'How can you smile?'

'I was remembering when Wolf first joined me as a companion,' Morghan replied, finding joy in the memory.

Clarice glanced down at the great black wolf glued to Morghan's side. Somewhere in the sky above them was probably also Morghan's Hawk. Snake would be lurking about too, somewhere.

Almost casually, Clarice held out a hand, and in a silent swoop of white feathers, Sigil came to land upon her arm, her great clawed feet circling Clarice's wrist. She blinked golden eyes at Clarice, then turned to look at the path. Clarice and Sigil had been together almost directly since Clarice had come, a bedraggled and serious little thing of two or three, to the Grove with her mother.

'That was also the first time you met Elen of the Ways, wasn't it?' Clarice asked.

'Yes,' Morghan agreed. 'And wasn't that a shock.'

They came across the tunnel that led down to the Fair Lands. It was little more than a sudden deep hole in the ground, steps spiralling around the edges down into the darkness.

'Are you steady enough?' Clarice asked, turning to look at Morghan.

Morghan stood staring down into the black depths, her expression unreadable. Clarice wondered what she was thinking, what she had seen, going so deep and far that she could barely keep her feet on coming back.

And the destruction of the veil? What would that bring them? What did it mean? Would hordes of humans be able to come back and forth between the worlds as she did? That would be intolerable. Clarice looked around at the woods, ancient and timeless, and imagined them cluttered with litter, fast food containers caught in the branches of the trees.

It could not happen like that, surely?

Not if it was the Othercrowd bringing the barrier down.

They would not do it if there was any chance of the pollution of their own lands.

She closed her eyes for a moment, then opened them to see Sigil gazing unblinkingly at her.

The Wildwood, she'd discovered as a child, was complicated. It was both here, linked to the same earth she walked upon in the Waking, and yet separate at the same time.

The fact that it was linked was important however, even if she didn't understand completely how. They overlapped, she thought, nodding slightly.

Which meant, of course, that if the Earth – if Gaia – was destroyed, then the Wildwood was also at risk. Was that not true?

She lifted a hand and stroked Sigil's dense feathers, aware that she was soothing herself with the gesture.

Morghan roused herself, the lightning-struck sky of her vision back to lurk behind her eyes. She knew the only separation between the worlds was a matter of seeing.

And humans had turned away from seeing, from knowledge of their souls a long time ago.

What would be the consequences of being forced to see the error of their ways? Of having to realise that there was much more to things than they'd ever believed? Wondering if ghosts were real would be the least of their problems.

'Shall you go first, or I?' Morghan asked Clarice, sighing, and straightening for the trek down the spiralling staircase.

'How likely are you to tumble down atop me?' Clarice asked.

'Perhaps I shall go first,' Morghan decided, and stepped down into the wide hole in the ground, clearing her mind to calmness, listening to her breathing, to the sound of her heels upon the steps, to Wolf's soft padding beside her.

She spiralled deep into the darkness, wending her way down and down and further down. It was a journey of trust and willingness into the dimness.

At the bottom, her feet on smooth stone, she looked back up the way they'd come, and saw the entrance to the hole so far above that it was like looking at the full moon in a dark night sky. Clarice stepped down beside her, a pale blur in the shrouding dimness. Sigil lifted her wings for a moment in a white fan, then tucked them back down at her sides.

Morghan drew a breath and touched her hands together and blew into the cupped space between them. It ignited into a dancing sphere of light and she spread her hands, letting the light bob off to illuminate the cave in front of them, a softly glowing orb.

'Are there always this many now?' she asked Clarice in a whisper, eying the ghostly, shuffling forms of spirits milling about, some on their own, more in silent clusters. They watched her as she stepped further into the cave following the light, but they did not come near, for which she was glad. Their number would be suffocating. 'There seem more than the last time I came this way.'

Clarice wrinkled her nose and held Sigil against her

chest. 'Their numbers change from day to day,' she said. 'If there are more or less, I can't tell.' She shuddered slightly. 'I prefer not to try counting them.'

They walked deeper into the cave system, the light leading them through a muffled, close series of tunnels, their breath and the dull thudding of their steps the only things to be heard. Morghan kept her chin tucked down, seeing again the writhing darkness threatening to blanket her world, and the expression on the face of the ancient one, the woman she herself had been so many, many years ago.

What had the vision she'd shown her meant?

Or rather, since Morghan was well enough aware of what it meant – what did the ancient one desire her to do about it? She stumbled and flung a hand against the cool stone wall of the cave, then stood a silent moment searching for her composure. Above her she thought she heard the sudden thick rumble of thunder.

The light bobbed by the ceiling of the tunnel, waiting.

Morghan felt Clarice's gaze upon her back, but the young woman was silent. After a moment, Morghan stood herself upright again and resumed the trek, one hand going to touch the crystal egg on the chain around her neck. It warmed under her touch.

They heard the rush of water before they saw it. It echoed along the tunnel, the sound bouncing off the stone walls so that they would have to yell to be heard over it. When they stepped out finally into the large cave through which the actual river ran, the rushing cacophony of it quietened in a trick of acoustics.

The river cut through the rock, wide and deep and dark.

In the small illumination of the light that Morghan had conjured, the water looked black. The scent of it filled her nose, throat, and lungs, so that she could almost taste its clear, dark chill.

'Where's the boat?' Clarice asked, stepping forward on the ledge beside the water and turning to Morghan, eyes wide in the reflected light. 'There's always a boat – a barge to cross upon.' She leaned out over the water to peer down the river in each direction, then straightened and looked at Morghan again. 'Where is the boat?' she repeated. 'We are in the same place as always, how can this be?' A nervousness near to fear crept into her voice.

Morghan looked at the black sweep of river and barked a laugh. 'Be calm,' she said. 'There is no room for fear here or you shall never get across.' She shook her head. 'They are testing me.'

Clarice stared at her, then narrowed her eyes and turned to the river. Its noise filled the cavern and she gazed across to the other side, able to see the ledge opposite them in the light of Morghan's orb, and the darkness of the tunnel that led away from the river and onwards to where they needed to go. She blinked.

'Well, go on then,' she said.

Morghan raised her eyebrows a moment, then gave a brief nod and took a couple steps further down the jutting path beside the river. She too looked across to the other side, listening to the deep-throated voice of the subterranean water. She thought about how it travelled so long and so far in darkness, gathered up in its own secrets and its own knowledge, singing songs of the hidden places of the worlds. If she were to step into its flow it would carry her away, drag her underneath the surface, caring not one whit for the fact that she did not sport gills. It would pull her along and she would be helpless against its strength. And although it would laugh and burble its stories, she would not have ears to listen for long.

Therefore, they would cross another way. It was a bridge that was needed since there was no boat. Raising her hands, Morghan breathed deeply, knowing this was the Other-world, and magic a far easier task than back in the Waking world. She sent forth her vision and spun a crystal bridge out over the water, steps that looked like they were made of glass, reflecting the flickering of her light, the river rushing underneath. She glanced back at Clarice who stood there staring at her then allowed herself a small smile of satisfaction.

'I guess I don't need to ask if they will hold,' Clarice said, refusing to be impressed.

'I guess you don't,' Morghan answered, putting her foot on the first step, and climbing upwards onto the bridge. She was over the river in moments.

'I didn't know you could do that,' Clarice said, giving up her feigned nonchalance. The truth was, she was impressed. She had become so used to being the one that came here so often that she had forgotten how well Morghan also knew her way around the ways of this world. But she would remember from now on. She walked after her stepmother with renewed respect.

There were more tunnels, but Clarice was familiar with the journey and paid almost no attention to them. She lifted a hand again to stroke Sigil's feathers.

'What will it mean that the veil is being brought down?' she asked.

Morghan shook her head in the dimness, unable to help her shiver, the vision from the clifftop rising before her eyes again.

'Once, of course,' she said. 'All worlds touched each other, and we were welcome to walk in all. Magic flowed between us. There was no true separation. This we know from the wisdom that has been passed down in the Grove for centuries.'

Clarice glanced back at her. 'I cannot imagine what that would have been like,' she admitted.

'You should ask your friends here,' Morghan answered. 'Their memories of it will also have been passed down. And their memories are far longer than ours. I'm surprised no one has spoken to you of it already.'

Clarice flushed, glad that Morghan could not see her blush in the dimness. She did not come to the Fair Lands for education. She came because she enjoyed being around beings who did not laugh at her for her differences, whose ease of manner suited her. These Neighbours were a people who enjoyed their connection to their land in a way that was intrinsic to who they were, and they treated each other with a deep respect and warmth. She knew they had their own politics, but she was not part of the circle of those concerned with that. Until recently, at least.

When she was here, she laughed and sang and feasted and on occasion danced in sacred union. She flushed in the dimness, thinking suddenly of Krista.

Clarice realised finally how much she had been using the Fair Lands as an escape and tucked this piece of information away in the back of her mind to bring out later when she had more time.

And perhaps she was being drawn into more important matters here, with her own summons from the Queen, who had been increasingly keeping her at court the last few months. She had vowed her service to the Queen many years ago, of course, if ever it should be needed, and she'd done so willingly, feeling more kinship with these faerie people than with those back in the Waking world. Since then, she'd been able to come and go as she pleased.

The thought that she should have been doing more made her nervous.

'Come on,' Clarice said. 'We're taking too long as it is. I spent way too much time finding you and the Queen has little patience.'

Morghan followed without a word, knowing that Clarice had little idea of Morghan's own relationship with the Queen of this Othercrowd. A relationship that had spanned lifetimes. She suspected that it was one of the reasons why Clarice had been welcome from the beginning to go back and forth.

They stepped finally into a cave so large that it opened out into a whole world, and Morghan's lungs filled with scented air. The top of the cave, so high it could not be seen, lifted upwards into sky and cloud. It was a sunlit land and Morghan blinked a moment in the soft light, lifting her head to breathe more deeply of the fragrant breeze. The light that had guided them bobbed in place for a moment then winked out of existence. Clarice smiled briefly at Morghan then took the lead again, down a grassy path to a pretty gate. She touched her hand to it, then turned to Morghan.

'Do you know, when I first came here,' she said, 'this gate confused me – because aren't the Fae supposed to be unable to bear the touch of iron?'

'And yet they can,' Morghan agreed.

Clarice pushed the scrolled wrought iron gate open and stepped under the lychgate laden with sweet roses, their green leaves glossy in the summer light. 'Yes,' she said.

'Because the iron that drove them away, that gave rise to the thickening veil between us, was not the metal, but the age,' Morghan said, walking out into the fair lands, the realm of her closest Fae neighbours and their Queen.

Two figures strode through the greenery towards her and Morghan immediately went down on one knee, lowering her face. 'Your Majesties,' she said, seeing the silver hem of the Queen's dress stop in front of her. She followed the folds of fabric upwards to risk gazing at the Shining One's face. And then stood, a smile blooming as the Queen reached out to take her hands, holding them for a moment in greeting.

'I see she has found you at last, Morghan of the Grove,' the Lady said.

'I apologise for not coming sooner,' Morghan replied. 'I've a feeling I ought to have.' She glanced over at the Queen's consort, whose blue eyes were arresting, drinking in the sight of her. Not for the first time, Morghan wondered exactly how close some of her ancestor's relationships with the Queen and her Consort had been.

'Indeed,' the Queen agreed, bringing Morghan back with the acerbity in her voice.

Morghan bowed her head in acquiescence, conceding the point. 'I am here to remedy that,' she said.

'Because I had the foresight to send for you,' the Queen answered, but she tucked her hand in the crook of Morghan's elbow and turned them down the path. 'Will you join us in our feasting?'

Although legend had always said that one ought not to eat with the faerie if one did not want to stay for ever and a day within their realm, Morghan knew that this was not necessarily always the case, depending on who you were. She smiled.

'It would be my pleasure,' she said. 'I would be honoured to sit and eat with you.'

The Queen's Consort led the way then broke off with a smile to take his place at the end of a heavily laden table, gesturing for the trailing Clarice to sit near him. Morghan watched for a moment as Clarice hesitated before taking the seat, as though unsure of the honour.

'Yes,' said the Queen, also watching. 'She makes a convenient, if somewhat slow, messenger. We shall be asking more and more of her, I think.' She sat and nodded as Morghan took the seat at her right hand, Wolf spreading himself out in the sun behind her chair. 'I required her to vow her service to me of course, when it became obvious she wanted to treat our land as her second home, and I have always been at ease with her presence here. This place has been known to soothe many wounds.'

She paused and blinked. 'For a time, anyway.'

'But things are changing,' Morghan said, and did not phrase it as a question.

'Yes,' the Queen agreed. 'They are changing.'

They stared at each other for a long moment, until the Queen inclined her head. 'Eat,' she commanded. 'Enjoy our bounty and entertainment. We shall deal with the serious matters afterward.'

Morghan nodded. 'Your hospitality is gracious and generous,' she said.

The table was laden with every manner of delicious morsel Morghan could have thought of. She smiled as she placed a small, fragrant pie on her plate. If only Mrs. Palmer could come here and experience this, she thought. The woman would be wide-eyed and rushing off to find the kitchens.

The pie was as marvellous as it looked, but still, Morghan thought it only equal to some of Mrs. Palmer's culinary delights. Perhaps the good woman did come here, after all. And why should she not? The way was hidden, but only if you did not know how to look.

Morghan listened to the chatter of those around her, enjoying the way their voices were like bells ringing in the soft air, somehow sonorous, fragrant, and colourful all at the same time. She tipped her head to listen to the Queen's occasional comments and forced herself to relax. They ate outside, within a curving arch of greenery, while peacocks strutted in and out of the trees, spreading fans of white and gold feathers. A large, golden-eyed leopard padded softly around the table, then stretched out at the Queen's side, his eyes staring a moment unblinkingly at Morghan before he closed them and slept in the dappled, soporific sunshine.

'You are not entirely at ease, Morghan of the Grove,' the Queen said at last.

'I beg your forgiveness, your Majesty,' Morghan

answered, wiping her lips on a snowy napkin. 'It has been a long morning.'

'You were shown what is happening,' the Queen said. It was not a question.

Morghan swallowed, nodded. 'The coming down of the veil,' she said.

'The revealing of the true nature of the worlds.'

'Is it the right answer?' Morghan ventured.

The Queen looked at her, gaze a light, chill blue. 'It is the only answer.'

Morghan closed her own eyes for a moment. 'I stood on a cliff above my world, above the Waking' she said. 'And the sky was torn open above me, and the sea raged below me.'

'Yes.'

She could hear the howling of the wind again, as it whipped the sea to a frenzy. She could feel the heavy sting of ozone in the air as lightning sliced the clouds apart. Morghan pressed her palms to the table in front of her and took a breath, looked across at the Queen.

The Queen returned her look, impassive. Then raised delicate eyebrows. 'We have run out of time for you all to come back to your senses,' she said. 'Do you not agree?'

Morghan bowed her head. 'The way was lost long ago,' she said. 'We tried to keep the connection.'

'And failed,' the Queen said. 'Things grow only worse, the imbalance greater, our very planet raped and wounded almost beyond saving.' She paused. 'There is no question anymore of what to do. There is no time left. There can be only action.'

She put down her napkin and stood. Immediately, everyone at the table stood also, their chatter silenced, eyes lowered. Morghan glanced down to the end of the table, where Clarice stood, white hair obscuring her face. She looked, Morghan thought, exactly like one of the Fae.

The Queen waved a hand, and everyone seated themselves again, resumed their feasting, their laughter spilling out into the air like gossamer threads.

'Not you,' she said to Morghan.

'You are to come with me.'

6

Mrs. Busby sidled up to Winsome after the service, rubbing at her arms. She felt pummelled, bruised, as though the currents she sensed in the air were capable of battering her about like the wind blowing and plucking at a plump ripe plum on a branch.

Even inside the church, during the service, it had been the same sensation, of unseen currents in the air, like wind, like electricity, like...

Rosalie Busby didn't know what it was like, how to describe it. She might even have thought it simply her imagination, her very overactive imagination, if it hadn't been that she'd felt this way before, a long time ago.

Thus, what she did know was that she didn't like any of it.

What she did know was that she was frightened.

'Vicar?' she asked, cursing the little voice that came trembling off her tongue. 'Can I have a minute of your time?' She blinked and gripped her handbag. 'If you've a moment, that is.'

She ducked her head down and looked at her best shoes, concentrated on sucking long slow breaths into her lungs. Her shoes were cracked and worn and if she'd had the money, she would have bought another pair to wear to the small church every Sunday.

'Vicar,' she repeated, her voice as thin as the wind as she wrapped her fingers around the strap of her old blue handbag in an effort not to reach out and tug on Winsome's cassock to get her attention. Her fingers clenched and unclenched around the strap.

'Mrs. Busby,' Winsome said, turning to smile at the elderly woman. 'You enjoyed the service, I hope?' she said, then raised her eyebrows humorously. 'Not too long-winded, I trust?'

'Not at all, Vicar,' Rosalie Busby replied, stretching a tight smile onto her face with an effort. She cleared her throat and glanced at the old graveyard beside the church. 'You're just as good as Reverend Robinson was,' she said, then added, hand tightening again around her handbag, 'God rest his soul.'

His soul did rest with God now, Winsome thought, and flicked her gaze up automatically to glance around the churchyard. Not a sign of the good Reverend, or his old parishioners. Nor anyone else not of the flesh and blood variety, fortunately.

'Thank you,' she said, coming back to look at little round Rosalie Busby, taking in automatically the worn handbag, the shoes and raincoat that looked like they had seen better days, the tired face, eyes large and faded amidst the wrinkled skin. Some of her parishioners struggled daily to make ends meet, she knew. Life could be a hard and cruel thing. She wished she could do more about that.

'How are you, Mrs. Busby?' Winsome asked. 'Do you have everything you need? – I know it's been particularly difficult for a wee while to get out and do the shopping. I can arrange for a box of groceries to be dropped right off to you, if you'd like, and we're having a clothing swap soon, so do come along to that.'

Rosalie frowned, finding herself side-tracked. She held her handbag close against her stomach. Then she straightened her spine and took a deep breath of the wind that flung itself about the churchyard.

'I...' She swallowed, tried again. 'I need your help, Vicar,' she said.

Winsome smiled. 'Of course, and it's no trouble, you know, to have some groceries and things dropped off to you.'

For a moment, Rosalie closed her eyes. She did need some extra things – it took a lot to feed five mouths – but her jaw was aching from tension and she had a headache blooming behind her temples, and she wasn't the sort to get headaches.

'Please,' she said. 'Please just listen a moment.' Her cheeks reddened, but she kept going. 'I need your help with something entirely different.'

'Different?' Winsome asked, turning properly and giving the older woman her entire attention. Something about Rosalie Busby's voice made the hair on Winsome's neck stand on end.

'It's my granddaughter,' Rosalie said.

'Your granddaughter?'

Rosalie nodded. Opened her mouth to speak. Closed it. Cleared her throat. 'She wants to be a witch, you see.'

There was a sudden buzzing in Winsome's ears. Whatever she'd been expecting, it surely hadn't been this. 'A witch?' she repeated stupidly.

'She's dyed her hair black, and found herself a cloak from somewhere, and well, I think she's been meddling.' Rosalie's voice trailed off, and she looked out over the damp graves parked in crooked rows to the side of the old church. The yew tree leaned over them as though trying to gather them in her gnarled old arms while the oaks stood about unconcerned.

Something flickered in the air and Rosalie blinked at it, taking a step back. 'Did you see that?' she asked before she could stop herself.

Winsome turned to look over at the small graveyard, unable to suppress a shiver at the sudden expectation that there would be a spirit standing amongst the gravestones, staring back at her. Rosalie had looked as though she'd seen a ghost.

But there was nothing there, and Winsome let out a low sigh of relief. 'See what?' she asked.

But Rosalie was staring with determination back down at her shoes. 'Nothing,' she shook her head. It had been nothing. It wasn't as though she could tell the vicar she was prone to seeing flashes of light on the wind, and sometimes feeling them too. It wasn't as though she could come out and say that, and also, while she was at it, that she'd begun seeing more of them, especially in her own home.

Especially in her own home. Where it was impossible to ignore them. And impossible not to be afraid.

Or to blame her granddaughter. Minnie had brought them into the house, she was positive of it. All this silly witch business. The dressing in black, the candle in the wardrobe, on one of her little tables, that a pot plant had sat on until recently. Minnie thought her old Gran didn't notice that she'd taken it, but Rosalie had. She'd looked through Minnie's things when the girl had been out.

She would have taken it back too, but the flashes of light were thick in Minnie's room. Thick, and dark.

'I need the house blessed, Vicar,' Rosalie said at last, launching herself right at her reason for being there. 'Right away. This week.'

'The house blessed?' Winsome repeated, speaking slowly. 'Because your granddaughter wants to be a witch?' She shook her head slightly. 'Mrs. Busby, that doesn't generally mean the Church needs to get involved. It's usually a phase girls go through anyway.'

There was an awkward silence and Winsome winced. A phase girls go through? Really? Had she really just said that?

Rosalie shook her head. Heaved a sigh from the pit of her stomach. 'It's not the wanting to be a witch so much as is the problem, Vicar,' she said, shoulders slumping. 'It's the magic she thinks she's doing. She's playing with the devil, she is.'

Winsome's mouth went dry. 'Erm, playing with the devil might be a little over the top, don't you think?' she asked. 'How old is your granddaughter?'

'Minnie's fifteen.' This wasn't going well, Rosalie

thought, gripping her handbag tightly again and keeping her eyes focused on her shoes, then on the vicar's poking out under her cassock. Winsome Clarke was wearing a pair of sheepskin boots.

'Mrs. Busby?' Winsome asked. 'Are you all right?' The woman's pained expression hadn't gone away, and Winsome had a sudden shivering premonition. She took a breath and blew it out discreetly but deliberately, widening her senses in the way Morghan had taught her, and she'd been practicing almost religiously for the last six weeks.

It was astonishing, she thought, and not for the first time, how many people's spirits – she preferred to think of it as a person's spirit rather than aura – were slack, tight, frightened things.

Last week, during the service, she thought she must have got the combination of songs and prayers just right, because she'd looked down from where she stood at the front of the old church and seen her parishioners expand and shine like rows of small shining angels. The building had been lit up from within with their glow.

The scene had not repeated itself this week. Everyone in their pews had stayed either droopy or tightly wrapped, even during prayers, when if she'd been asked, she would have said ought to be the proper time, surely, to expand and glow. It was the worry that was doing it, as most of the country around them reported growing cases of the virus. That and not knowing what the situation would be with the lockdowns over Christmas.

Winsome had been puzzling all month on how to get her parishioners to be able to expand and relax their spirits. She'd not had any real, practical ideas, yet, but wasn't prepared to let the matter drop in her mind. Perhaps, she thought, she could institute some of Morghan and Ambrose's practices and call them stress-relief exercises, or something. Maybe even set it up as a class. Like chair yoga, but better. Goodness knows they all needed it.

Rosalie Busby's spirit fluttered and twitched around her, ragged at the edges. Winsome frowned. It looked – Mrs. Busby's spirit looked – a little tortured, or at least upset. Winsome shook her head. A young girl enamoured with being a witch wasn't that serious, surely?

And yet, she was sure that Rosalie Busby was genuinely frightened. Of something. By something.

'Let's go inside,' she said. 'Have a cup of tea and warm up a little – and you can tell me everything that's going on.'

Rosalie looked at the young vicar, at her plump, smooth cheeks, and hair that didn't show any signs of grey yet. She gnawed on her bottom lip for a moment, then reminded herself that she didn't have anyone else to go to – Robinson, poor soul, was gone, and there was only this woman instead.

She shivered, as though a goose had walked over her grave.

Winsome stood watching, then dipped her head to look closer at the shorter woman's face. 'Would you come and have a cup of tea with me, Mrs. Busby?'

But Rosalie shook her head. She needed to get back home. There'd be lunch to make back at home. And she needed to see what was happening there. Hopefully nothing. Hopefully she was overreacting.

Another dark flash at the edge of her vision made her shiver. She didn't think she was imagining things.

'No,' she said with a shake of her soft halo of white curls. 'No, I'll not trouble you for that, Vicar.'

Winsome didn't know what to say next. She found that she was pulled in two directions. One part of her wanted to ask, probably in a whisper, if there was a *spirit problem* in Rosalie Busby's home.

The other part of her knew she couldn't, on account of being the vicar.

And wasn't that ironic?

'But I do need you to come bless the house,' Rosalie said at last. 'You can do that, right?'

Winsome nodded slowly. 'Yes,' she said. 'I can do that.' She wanted to ask more, but Dean Morton's voice suddenly piped up in her head, his falsely cheerful voice reminding her not to fall under the spell of superstition that abounded in Wellsford, reminding her that magic wasn't real.

'We need practical, hard-headed Christianity from you, Winsome,' he'd said at their little chat on Zoom. 'Don't go all woowoo on us, now will you? There's too much of that in Wellsford already.'

Rosalie Busby was looking straight at her now. 'When can you come, Vicar?' she asked. 'There's odd things been happening, things that distress me. We need it blessed. You can come by?'

She wasn't sure she understood all the regulations, but it was going to be reviewed again soon, and surely it could be done after that? And there weren't any virus cases in Wellsford, anyway.

'Vicar?' she said.

Quickly, Winsome nodded, swallowing down the sudden electric consternation inside her. 'Of course,' she said, totting up the days herself. 'How about Thursday? About 1.30?'

Rosalie nodded, and let herself sigh, feeling some of the weight lift from her already. 'Yes,' she said. 'And thank you, Vicar. Thank you from the bottom of my heart.' She turned and hurried down the path, clutching her blue handbag, determined to get home and see what there was to see.

She'd always been a bit on the sensitive side, ever since she was small, although she'd never have said so to anyone. But it was true, nonetheless. She could detect changes in atmosphere like she was a barometer. Except, it wasn't the air pressure she was noticing. She didn't have the words to explain it, didn't know any fancy terms, only that her mother had been the same way, and once, when her mother had been in her cups – a rare occasion – she'd called it being able to sense spirits.

Rosalie shook her head at the memory. She'd quite happily have only inherited her mother's, short legs and brown hair.

Especially now as she was sure those spirits were in her house, her refuge, modest as it was, from the world. Flickering around the edges of her mind, shadows in the dimmest corners. She shook her head as though she could dislodge them but knew there wasn't anything she could do on her own.

Winsome watched her go, eyebrows knotted in a frown, rerunning the conversation through her mind.

A house blessing? She'd not been called on to do one of those before, but of course that was no surprise, considering that this was her first real parish to look after. In the religious community where she'd lived for so long, there was little contact with people outside in the real world. It was what had prompted Winsome to finally leave.

She brooded upon it all the while she made her lunch, and when she looked down at the crumbs on her plate, she barely remembered making or eating the toasted sandwich. Should she call the Dean, she wondered? Ask him what to do?

But she could imagine his reply already. His voice would be bluff and hearty to begin with, then tinged with impatience once he realised she had nothing real to go on. Nothing but disturbed teenaged girls and more witches in Wellsford.

Dean Morton didn't believe in spirits, Winsome had discovered.

It wasn't as though she could explain to him the heavy feeling she'd gotten when Mrs. Busby had spoken of odd things happening.

Things that distressed her.

If only she'd come in for that cup of tea, said more about what was happening.

Winsome pushed her chair back and stood up, picking up her plate automatically and placing it in the sink. She'd wash it later. Right now, she needed to think, to deal with this dark sense of foreboding that had come over her like a cloud when Mrs. Busby had asked for her house to be blessed.

No, she decided, going to the kitchen door, and looking out through the glass at the church across the lawn, at the trees clustered about it. She couldn't go to the Dean, not with no information. She could imagine his response now.

You don't deal in feelings and premonitions, Winsome. You

are just a vicar, not part of the Deliverance ministry, and all you know is that the woman wants her house blessed.

Sometimes, she thought, for a man who claimed to deal with matters of the spirit, Dean Morton was terribly ill at ease with anything that actually, truly smacked of it.

Ambrose then. She glanced back at the door on the other side of the kitchen, thinking about the phone in her study. She had his number, since he'd come down and shown her how to clear and bless the vicarage. He would take her sudden, heavy feelings seriously.

A long, deep breath. Ambrose was the right person to talk to about it if there was anything to talk about at all. After all, he knew how to do house blessings.

Not Christian ones, though. Unfortunately.

She could hardly go to Mrs. Busby's house and waft smoke around into all the corners and ring the little bells on their silver branch that Ambrose had given her, could she?

Winsome leaned her forehead against the cold glass and closed her eyes. Of course she shouldn't call him. It wasn't even as if she knew anything yet. Mrs. Busby hadn't said much.

Just that odd things were happening.

Odd things that distressed her.

'Oh God,' Winsome groaned, touching the cross around her neck. 'None of this is at all what I expected, Lord,' she said. 'Am I going completely bonkers? Totally off-track?'

She shook her head, then rubbed her forehead. The skin was cold from the glass.

Winsome straightened. She wouldn't call the Dean. She wouldn't call Ambrose. Or Morghan. She would deal with this like it was her job to do so. Which it was. She didn't even know what she was dealing with yet, she reminded herself. She was getting all pre-emptive – and so what if she had a gnawing feeling of worry? She always had gnawing feelings of worry.

Prayer. That was what she needed. The calmness of prayer. The steadiness of touching, as much as she could, the divine. Winsome nodded to herself.

'No getting tied up in knots,' she said. 'Everything is all right.'

Abruptly, Winsome turned and pulled her coat from the peg by the door, stepping out into the blustery afternoon still trying to poke her hands through the sleeves.

IT WAS ONLY TEN MINUTES' WALK BEFORE SHE REACHED HER destination. Morghan had told her about this place, her lips half smiling, a twinkle in her eyes.

'It's somewhere I think you might quite enjoy,' Morghan had said.

Winsome had narrowed her gaze at her new friend. 'Why don't I trust you fully right this minute?' she said. 'I get the feeling you're teasing me.'

Morghan had laughed and held up her hand in a gesture of surrender. 'I am enjoying myself,' she said, 'but not at your expense, I promise you. I just think you might find a deep connection at this place, if you let yourself.' She'd leaned forward and the smile was still there on her face. 'It was built after all, for the private use of the clergy of Wellsford.' Morghan had sat back, waiting it seemed, for Winsome to take her bait.

And of course, Winsome had been unable to resist. 'All right,' she'd said. Explain yourself.'

It was a small building. Ostensibly, Winsome supposed, a summerhouse, built from the same fine stone that Winsome had noticed many of the houses in Wellsford, and the church itself, were built from. It was octagonal in shape and in each face of the building was an arched opening.

Carvings covered the outside of the small building above each window and Winsome stopped to look at them, as she did every time she came here. Gargoyles, she'd thought the first time she'd seen them but then she'd looked closer and discovered that they were carvings of the green man – and a green woman – their faces sprouting oak and ivy, their eyes staring ahead at the trees surrounding them. She'd seen similar carvings many times before on churches, although not on her little church back in the village.

There were also compass markings on each side of the tiny summer house and trailing around the outside that first time, Winsome had wondered if they were true – if they pointed in the correct directions and wondered also what they were for. Why would you need to know which direction you faced? She kept reminding herself to ask Morghan about them, their purpose, for it wasn't as though she could see any distance in any direction. Trees surrounded the building as though hiding it. Or guarding it.

Inside, the space was bare. There was room for her to stand and even to hold her arms outstretched. But there was nowhere to sit.

So she stood now, as she'd become accustomed to, visiting the small building several times in the few weeks since Morghan had told her about it. She placed her feet in the middle of the star pattern on the tiled floor.

Built for the clergy of Wellsford, Morghan had said. And when asked why, she had given her slow smile. 'As a proper place of prayer,' she said.

Winsome had laughed in shock and disbelief. 'We have a church for that.'

'Ah,' Morghan had replied. 'But churches, as beautiful as many of them are, are enclosed spaces. Whereas this particular place would be perfect if you wanted a sanctuary and a place of prayer a little closer to the world.'

Winsome had noticed that Morghan often used the term *world* in this sort of all-encompassing way that made it feel so much fuller and vaster than the world Winsome had ever known.

She stood inside the small building and took a deep breath, closing her eyes. Whatever this place might be or whoever had built it and whatever it had been built for, Winsome found that it was an excellent place to practice certain things she found herself too guilty to do in the church, or even, for that matter, in the rooms of the vicarage itself. Here though, in this strange pagan little building tucked safely within the forest, it felt appropriate. In fact, it felt as though the place had been purpose-built for it.

She slowed her breathing, breathed in. Counting as she did so.

One, two, three, four.

She held it for the same length of time.

Still counting. *One, two, three, four.*

Then let it slowly out. *One, two, three, four.*

She breathed in, she held her breath, and she breathed out, and as she did so, she reached out. She reached out the way that Morghan had shown her; she reached out the way she'd done in the church that morning to help Reverend Robinson and his flock pass over and into the next world. She stretched and she reached, breaking free of the confines of her flesh, seeking to fill the whole small room so that she could touch the cold stone above her, feel the small rustlings of the spider in the corner as it built its little web, feel the drift of leaves blown in by the wind like tokens, like offerings.

And here it was, this shining, gleaming feeling where everything about her hummed, where she could feel herself larger than her body, more than her body, where her spirit glowed and sang.

And as she stretched and reached and shimmered, Winsome prayed.

There were new words in her prayer now, but they seemed to belong there.

'Our Father, who art in heaven,' she said, her mouth tasting the words like they were alive, sweet and round upon her tongue.

'Our mother, whose body is the land.

'Hallowed be thy name, blessed it be thy flesh.'

She breathed in, deeply, gladly, hands reaching for the world outside the small building where she stood at the centre of it.

'Thy kingdom come, thy will be done, on earth as it is in heaven.'

She sighed softly, resumed the prayer. 'As above, so it is below. As it is without, so also it is within.'

Smiling now, she said the words, her heart lightening with gladness.

'Give us this day our daily bread and forgive us our trespasses as we forgive those who trespass against us.

'Your bounty is also our own. We are in service to your needs.

'Lead us not into temptation but deliver us from evil.

'For compassion lives in our hearts and kindness moves our hands.

'For thine is the kingdom, the power and the glory, for ever and ever.

'For we are eternal and connected and we grow in the spirit of love.'

Winsome open her eyes wider, holding onto the feeling of expansion. She was always surprised at this part of the proceedings that she was not surrounded by light, that there was not glitter at the tips of her fingers, for it felt as though surely there should be.

'Amen,' she whispered. And then, for the first time, she added more of Morghan's words.

'So it is,' she said, her voice low, full of passion. 'So it has always been, and so shall it remain, world beyond time, world without end.'

A sudden pang of guilt at the words made her blink, and her shimmering spirit collapsed around her and Winsome shrank back to size inside the flesh of her body and shuddered slightly.

What was she doing? Coming here to this tiny building like this? She should be kneeling before the altar at her own church. She should be begging Christ to guide her, not muttering pagan prayers. Did this, she wondered, happen to every vicar of the village of Wellsford? Is this what happened to Robinson? Had he come here too?

Why was she coming here to this small pagan temple – for that's what it was – to pray as she was now praying?

What was she now?

Who was she?

7

MORGHAN AND THE QUEEN OF THE FAE WALKED IN SILENCE, out in an open meadow sprinkled with white flowers like stars, leaving the sounds of feasting behind them. Wolf padded along at Morghan's side, and two lanky dogs trailed several steps behind them. They reminded Morghan of Burdock, but thinner. Deerhounds rather than wolfhounds, she thought. The light was soft and Morghan lifted her face to it, closing her eyes for a moment as she walked. When she opened them again, the Queen was watching her, and she flushed slightly under the assessing gaze of the faerie woman.

'Are you aware of what I saw today?' Morghan asked.

The Queen inclined her head. 'Yes,' she replied.

Morghan was unsurprised. 'You are working together? With the ancient one?'

'With Ravenna, yes.' A slight, significant pause. 'We are all aligned,' she said. 'She, I, you. Elen of the Ways.' She blinked her clear blue eyes. 'Others.'

Morghan ducked her chin down and looked at the grass. It was springy, healthy, wending its way up beside the path they were taking up a steepening hill.

'Ravenna,' she said, choosing not to comment on the Queen's pointed remark. She was not startled to have been included. This was the path she walked, the one she had long ago vowed to. The ancient way.

It was good to know the old one's name.

'Also Macha,' the Queen added, as if an afterthought. 'And Erin, as she is now, if she passes her testing.' She looked up the hill at their destination, eyes reflecting the blue of the sky.

'You are aware of Erin?' Morghan asked.

'Of course,' the Queen replied, then turned to look directly at Morghan. 'This has all been planned,' she said. 'We've been working towards this your whole lifetime.' She paused. 'My whole lifetime. Keeping the knowledge alive.' She swept her gaze towards the temple at the top of the hill, to what would come next. 'And once it became clear that the murderous, wasteful ways of your kind were putting the land itself at risk, and every species upon it, we began planning our move.'

Morghan followed the faerie Queen's gaze and looked at the building jutting from the side of the hill. Built of stone, it was a small temple, round, its walls open to the view.

'What is this place?' she asked.

But the Queen merely reached out and tucked a hand behind Morghan's elbow again and led her on until the ground flattened and the stone building rose to greet them.

It was small, a bare unmarked temple. A tree grew either side of the doorway and the Queen relinquished Morghan's arm and reached into the branches of one to pluck down a fruit.

It was a pear, golden and smooth, perfectly shaped. She handed it to Morghan with a slight smile. Morghan took it and held it, thrown instantly back in her memory to her first visits to the Otherworld.

'A golden pear,' she murmured, turning the fruit over in her hands. 'I've come across these before but have never been able to satisfy myself as to the significance.'

'Fortunately,' the Queen replied, watching her for a moment, 'the significance is not lost because you are too lazy to learn the meaning.'

Morghan laughed. 'I deserve that,' she admitted.

'Indeed,' the Queen said, and she turned to the second tree. 'However, the time for not bothering with such things is long past. What I do here is meaningful. Be mindful for you will need the knowledge.'

Morghan bowed her head. The Queen passed another fruit to her and Morghan took it, looking down at the silver apple in her hand, and knowing already that she would be enlisting Ambrose's help on this.

'I would have thought the apple should be the golden one,' she said, musing out loud.

'And yet that is not the case,' the Queen commented.

'No.' Morghan slipped the fruit into her pockets. 'Thank you,' she said simply.

The Queen smiled, but there was something remote in her expression and Morghan waited for what would come next. This was not the woman who had so familiarly folded her hand around Morghan's elbow as they walked.

This was the Queen of the Fae, and she was tall, magnificent, formidable. She shone.

'Come,' she said. 'We must do what I brought you here for.'

Morghan glanced into the temple building. It was small, plain, bare except for a stone altar.

'Which is?' Morghan asked.

Wolf went and sat under the apple tree, eyes unblinking as he watched.

But the Queen merely lifted the edges of her lips in a half smile and stepped into the temple. Her dogs ranged back and forth outside, looking in between the stone columns.

Morghan lifted her eyebrows, gave the tiniest of shrugs, and stepped in after her.

The Queen was swift, grasping Morghan's right hand above the wrist and laying it upon the bare stone altar. A moment later there was a knife in the Queen's hand, and a moment after that the blade had pierced Morghan's flesh, sliced between the bones, and Morghan's hand was severed.

Morghan, astonished to a gasping silence, gaped at her, then looked back at her arm, the hand lifeless on the stone, her own fingers still, already greying. There was no spill of blood. The wound was clean, magic.

Ignoring the shocked question in Morghan's eyes, the Queen lifted the stump of Morghan's arm, holding it up between them, her eyes pale and serious as she looked across at Morghan. Then, with a fluid movement, the Queen conjured a new hand from the air and set it upon Morghan's wrist where it gleamed in the dimness of the temple's light.

Morghan, shocked utterly into silence and stillness, tried to process what had happened. The words in her head stuttered, fell away. Instead, she smelt the sap of apple and pear trees.

The Queen picked up Morghan's old hand, the skin upon it dry and withering, and in another sudden movement, tossed it outside. Morghan followed the arc of its fall and flinched as one of the hounds caught it in mid-air and turned to run down the hill with it in its mouth, the other dog following, thin tails whipping in the sunlight.

Morghan closed her eyes for a moment, brain trying to catch up with what had just happened. When she opened them again, she was still standing there with her right arm in the air, and there was still a new hand attached to it.

A hand made of gold.

She flexed it, and it moved as usual, but gleamed as it caught the soft light. She turned her head to look at the Queen, to question her.

But the Queen was already leaving, stepping back out from the small temple, and walking away across the high meadow. Swallowing, Morghan walked after her, glancing at Wolf, who stood and regained his place at her side as though nothing had happened.

The Queen kept her face to the sky as Morghan caught up to her.

'You have the service of my people now,' the faerie Queen said, her gaze on the far clouds. 'If you should require it.'

Morghan shivered from this second shock. What sort of honour had just been bestowed upon her?

'This is an honour that comes with strings,' the Queen said as though in reply to Morghan's unspoken question.

Morghan took a deep breath. The air now was scented with honey, sat like light, sweet syrup in her lungs. She looked down again at her hand, that gleamed with a golden fire of its own.

'The veil,' she said. 'It is thinning.'

But the Queen turned to walk again, Morghan hurrying after her. She did not answer until they came to a standstill in front of a tunnel in the side of the hill. Morghan, dazed, looked into the dimness of the cave and saw Snake there, his great green-yellow body curled in the dirt, hooded, intelligent eyes staring. It was the way back to the Wildwood and the Waking world.

'Yes,' the Queen said, finally speaking again to agree with Morghan.

'Yes,' she repeated. 'And you must teach how to deal with the consequences of it.'

'This is your task.'

8

'What did Teresa do for transport?' Erin asked.

Stephan shook his head. 'She made me get everything, using Morghan's car or the van.'

'She didn't go anywhere?'

'I don't think she'd left Wellsford for like, a decade or something.' Stephan shoved his hands in his pockets as they walked. He wanted to hold Erin's hand, but she was busy thinking about stuff that wasn't him. Which was okay. Good even. To be expected, he thought. But his palms still itched to touch her skin.

Erin frowned over his answer. 'Didn't she go stir-crazy?' She shook her head. 'I was climbing the walls by the time the second week of lockdown was up. My mother was driving me barmy, and if I hadn't been able to get outside and draw, I don't know what I would have done.' She shrugged herself deeper into her green coat, looking down for a moment and forgetting to worry as she watched the blue of her dress against the green of her coat.

Beautiful, she thought. At least there's still this.

For now.

'She had everything she needed right here,' Stephan said. 'She seemed pretty content with that.'

'I used to want to travel, you know? See everything.' Erin watched Burdock lift his nose and scent the wind, wondering what he could smell.

'Where did you go?' Stephan asked.

Erin laughed. 'Nowhere. I never got to go anywhere, really – or at least not on my own, and travelling with my mother was not what I'd ever had in mind.'

'Why didn't you get to go anywhere?'

That made Erin lift her shoulders up to her ears. 'I couldn't be trusted not to have, you know, an episode.'

Stephan glanced over at her. She wore a hat made of green wool that matched her coat. It had a pompom on it. She looked really cute and he felt his spirit stretch towards her. He turned his gaze away, cleared his throat.

'Well, now you get to do a kind of travelling, right? Morghan's going to teach you how to journey to the Otherworld, and you kind of already pop back to the past, right?'

'Huh. Not to anywhere I'd choose. Back to that valley?' Erin shook her head and lapsed into a brooding silence.

'You have to find your way out of there,' Stephan said.

Erin rolled her eyes. 'You think?' She glanced across at Stephan, saw the sudden hurt on his face. 'I'm sorry,' she said. 'I'm out of sorts today. Thank you for your patience with me.' She took a calming breath, remembering Charlie telling her how important her words and thoughts were, telling her she was to make an effort to direct them in the way she wished to live – at all times.

She wanted to live here, in Wellsford. She wanted to take her place in Wilde Grove, learn the magic she knew was right within her grasp. She wanted to be a kind and decent person, the kind of person the world needed.

And she was, she was learning. Or at least, she was being taught. She'd just not expected it to begin so mundanely.

Learning gratitude. Ethics. Integrity.

Watching her thoughts. Her words.

Trying to let sink in what seemed to be Morghan's main message – that she wasn't alone.

'Learning from Morghan is weird,' she said, changing the subject.

'What sort of weird?' Stephan asked. They were out of the village now, on the road that wound through the woods to Ash Cottage, and farther on, Blackthorn and Hawthorn Houses. The narrow lane was white with ice in places, and thickets of frost lurked at the side of the road like a pale wash of snow. It was beautiful.

'Like, couldn't she just tell me things?'

'What do you mean?'

Erin resisted rolling her eyes again, even though this time it wouldn't have been at Stephan.

'She just takes me places and has me do things, as though I'm supposed to figure it out just by saying some prayers and doing some breathing exercises. Most of the time – hell, just about all of the time – I don't know what she's trying to make me experience and learn, I just know there's something I'm supposed to be getting.' Erin shook her head, looked at Stephan who had his chin tucked down, his dark eyelashes casting shadows on his cheeks. She swallowed and looked away, back at Burdock, whose tail swung straight out as he nosed under the frozen leaves at the side of the lane.

Stephan curled his fingers into his palms in his jacket pockets. He could feel the bear claw scrape against his chest. 'I reckon there's a reason it's taught that way,' he said.

'Well I'd love to know what it is,' Erin answered, and dug her fingernails into the soft flesh of her palms. She really was out of sorts today, and it wasn't just waking up to having her sweet little car taken away from her – and her allowance, she couldn't forget that.

It was the valley. Slipping back there in her dreams every night.

It was cold and damp and lonely there. So lonely it sank right down into her bones and made her feel hollowed out, mistrustful. It was a cruel place, she thought, and a cruel trick to make anyone stay there trying to find their way out.

For a moment, she felt Macha walking with them. Felt the fiery, spicy warmth of her.

'Not a trick,' Macha said. 'A lesson.'

Erin breathed out through pursed lips. Macha was gone again as silently as she'd appeared. Except Erin thought she was never really, properly gone. She was always there, waiting for the same thing.

For Erin to get out of the valley.

What would happen when she did? What would be in store for her then? She'd understand things then, wouldn't she? Could move on in some important way?

And she wouldn't be dreaming of that awful place every night, squatting beside the torn and broken body of someone she used to be.

She wondered what Kria's story was. What sort of person had she been? Why hadn't she managed to get out of the place? She must have had the knowledge in her somewhere as to how to do it – otherwise, well, she would never have been placed there, would she?

Erin blinked at the thought, turned to say something to Stephan about it, and realised he was talking.

Stephan rubbed a hand at the stubble on his chin then flapped his hand in the air. 'The reason we're not just straight up told this stuff, it's because, when you say something like the things we've been learning flat out – it sounds rubbish. That sceptical part of ourselves just kind of snorts and says *yeah, sure*. And also, the ancient way, it's experiential, right? We learn by doing it, by stepping out and being who we want to be, who we really are.'

Erin frowned at his words. 'I'd still like to flat out be told this stuff,' she said.

'Okay,' Stephan said, nodding. 'You're on.' He thought furiously. 'How's this – this is what I reckon Morghan is trying to teach you – the way out of the valley. It's probably the key to a whole lot more.'

'Yeah, and I know that. But can't she just tell me how to get out of there?'

Stephan turned around to look at Erin, walking backwards to do so. 'All right,' he said. 'So, here it is then – what you see isn't what's there. When you can see what is there, you can leave. Didn't Macha say they went there to learn to see?' He figured he couldn't be wrong saying that, since it held true with everything, and Morghan was teaching Erin the same things Teresa had done with him over the years.

And what working with Artois the Great Bear, was now showing him in technicolour.

Erin blinked at him. 'That doesn't help one bit.' She shook her head. 'That's just speaking in some sort of riddle. I've looked pretty bloody hard while I've been there. And still the only things there are the valley and the lake and a little stone building that gives me the major creeps.' She shuddered, thinking of the steel mist, the cold, brooding loch, Kria's bloodstained body. 'And besides,' she added. 'Morghan has said that already.' Erin reached up and tucked a long strand of hair back under her hat. 'I mean, she does say some things, right? But never the detailed explanations I need.'

'You gotta break open,' Stephan said, frowning.

'I'm not an egg,' Erin snorted, then laughed. 'You know what? I never in my entire life thought I'd be having conversations like this.'

'Yeah,' Stephan agreed, nodding and grinning. 'Isn't it awesome?'

They walked companionably together the rest of the way, Burdock zigzagging across the road in front of them, eyes peeled for movement in the trees whenever he caught a stray scent. He wrinkled his nose at the spirit fox that followed them on silent paws.

'The ravens love your place,' Stephan said as they rounded the long slow bend and reached Ash Cottage.

'Yes, they've moved in, for sure,' Erin said, fumbling with the house key. She hadn't yet been able to get over her city habits and leave the door unlocked. She glanced over at the ravens, still not really used to them, either, and thought again of Macha.

Another one waiting for her to make some progress. Erin pushed the door open, then turned, still holding the key in the lock, and looked at Stephan.

'What?' Stephan asked.

Erin thought of the strange, barren glen again, the fire pit next to where Kria lay, the lonely screaming of the gulls overhead. Her mouth was dry.

'What is it?' Stephan asked again. 'Are you okay?'

Erin nodded. 'I just had a thought, is all.'

'Ah,' Stephan said. 'I've had those before.' He wrinkled his nose at Erin's serious, pale face, trying to make her laugh. 'Not often, but still, I'm familiar enough with the concept.'

She croaked a laugh and shook her head, then pulled the key from the lock and let them into the warm cottage. It enveloped her like a hug, and she stood on the flagstone floor looking around in a sort of bemused satisfaction. How could she love a house this much?

Ash Cottage was now formally hers. She'd gone up to Hawthorn House the day her month was up, and Henry Block had been waiting there for her with a bunch of papers for her to sign. She'd been nervous but determined. She loved the cottage, loved the village, even. Her new friends.

And the magic she'd glimpsed at Samhain.

Now, with December wrapping itself around them in her wintry embrace, she watched Burdock run straight to his bed by the fire and flop down with a big sigh of contentment. Stephan closed the door behind them and moved into the kitchen, picking up the kettle.

Everything was perfect, except for one, big, enormous thing.

'How's your special elixir coming along?' Erin asked him.

He narrowed his eyes at her. 'Which one?' he asked. He had several he was playing with. It was absorbing, figuring out which plant energy went with which, for each desired purpose. He thought he could spend a lifetime doing it and not get bored.

'The one to help ground you after journeying, or travelling, or whatever Morghan calls it.'

'Ah, that one. Good, I think. Why?' The kettle dangled from his hand.

'Do you have any?' Erin rubbed at the sudden prickling on her arms.

'Yeah. Out in the potting shed, why?' Stephan had been using the potting shed for drying and blending his herbs, just like he'd done when Ash Cottage had been Teresa's. Well, not quite like that, he thought. Then, he'd worked to the sound of Teresa's tuneless humming, or good-natured grumbling. Now, more often than not, he worked to the sound of Erin's pencils scratching as she sat at the table in the glasshouse sketching.

He loved Teresa, but this was better.

He thought Teresa would understand.

Erin looked across at him. 'I want to try it,' she said.

Stephan had missed something. 'Try what?' he asked slowly.

'Try going back there,' Erin answered. 'To the valley.' She swallowed. 'The loch. See what there is to be seen. Do it consciously, you know?'

The kettle was still empty, but Stephan put it down without filling it. 'Are you sure?' he asked.

Erin nodded.

She wasn't sure, not really, but what else was there to do? 'I keep dreaming I'm there,' she said, and glanced over at Burdock, whose light snores rumbled through his chest. 'Every morning, I dream I'm there – my dream journal is just the glen and loch over and over. And every morning Burdock has to wake me up.'

At the sound of his name, Burdock's tail thumped once against his cushion.

9

MORGHAN COLLAPSED AGAINST THE CUSHIONS, STRETCHING her feet out towards the fire. The heat licked at her toes, crept up her legs to warm her. She closed her eyes.

'You're exhausted,' Ambrose said, bringing over a cup of herbal tea and putting it on the small table beside Morghan.

'It's been a busy day,' Morghan answered, eyes still closed. 'Thank you,' she added, smelling the sweet fragrance of the tea. Plain chamomile, she thought. 'You're trying to get me to take a nap?'

'Would that be so bad?'

She rolled her face closer to the heat of the fire and sighed, seeing behind her closed lids the view from the clifftop of the Isle of Healing. It made her take a slow, deep breath, then open her eyes. She sat up. Placed her hands over her face, then took them away and looked down at her right hand, turning it over in the light from the fire.

'What do you make of it?' she asked.

'Your new hand?' Ambrose said, and took the chair

opposite her. 'I'll have to do some research.' He sifted through the things he already knew. 'The only one I can think of off-hand,' he said, raising his eyebrows at the pun and smiling slightly, 'is the Slavic story of the Prince with the Golden Hand.'

Morghan looked at Ambrose, picking up her cup and sipping at the hot liquid. 'And what did this prince do with his golden hand?'

'Rescued a princess, of course – by using his golden hand to vanquish the living spirit of a hurricane.'

'Huh,' Morghan said, returning in her mind to the view out over the churning sea, to where she stood on the hill-top of her own world, the wind whipping at her hair, the sky rent open above her as the veil came down.

As the pressure of their mistakes altered the turn of the worlds.

What had the Queen said? That Morghan must teach the way to deal with the consequences of it.

She with the golden hand.

'I guess there could be parallels there,' she sighed. 'If you squint at it enough.'

'I'll refresh my memory of the tale,' Ambrose said. 'And tell you it when I have. And of course, see what else I can discover about a golden hand.'

Morghan nodded, gazing into the flames. 'It was extraordinary, Ambrose,' she said. 'The way she picked up my arm and calmly and swiftly sliced my hand from it.'

'And then threw it to the dog.'

'Yes.' Morghan barked a laugh. 'Who turned tail and scarpered with it.' She ran a finger idly around the rim of her cup. 'I wonder if he buried it or ate it?' Somehow, she hoped the dog had just buried it, but either way, it probably didn't matter. She had a feeling she'd never be seeing those familiar fingers again.

Ambrose leaned forward, his finely chiselled features shadowed in the lowering light of the afternoon. 'There's no going back from that,' he said, echoing Morghan's thoughts. 'There's no retrieving your hand – she made sure of that.'

'She did,' Morghan agreed, then turned her gaze upon Ambrose. 'But there's no going back for any of us, is there? We've simply run out of time. Humankind has come as far as it can like this. We must change. We must evolve.' She put her teacup down and sighed. 'We've destroyed almost everything right and precious about this place. We've taken up selfishness and greed instead, raped the earth herself, with whom we are supposed to be in loving relationship, and we've taken it so far that I have little hope for us.' Morghan sighed in frustration. 'It has to stop. Everyone has to stop. There is enough – there's no need any longer for anyone to be hungry or without shelter, or poor or scared. We have the resources and technology to take care of everyone.'

She stopped talking, lifted her hand – the one the Queen had given her, made of gold, her dominant hand – and rubbed at her eyes. 'I don't know how to do what she is asking of me, Ambrose. I am one person – what can I do?'

Ambrose blinked at her, taking in the tired pallor of Morghan's skin. The soft worry in her eyes.

'Tell me again,' he said. 'Tell me it baldly, the bare facts of it – what you saw on the clifftop.'

Morghan gave a small, thin shiver as she closed her eyes to see it again. She shook her head. 'I'm standing there,' she said. 'High above everything.' She lifted her hands, held them apart. 'Behind me, I know there are the Summerlands – the world we belong to as spirit. The place we go to when we die, if we're lucky enough, and don't simply spin back into existence, or join one of the flocks of those who seek to cause trouble.' She shook her head faintly.

'But that's not where I'm looking. I'm looking across at our world. The world we share with so many other peoples. The faerie, the spirits of the land, everyone, everything. And they glow and some of us – many, thank goodness – we glow too, and our light is growing, spreading, I can feel that.'

She paused. 'I believe that it must be.'

Morghan fell silent.

Ambrose let her look and think, while the fire crackled and rustled in the grate. He listened to it talking to itself and gave Morghan the space she needed.

She turned to look at him. 'I agree that the veil must fall from our eyes. We can no longer be separated.' She shook her head. 'Look how far from the truth this separation has taken us as a species. So much fear. We've forgotten why we're here. We've forgotten that we're not the only ones here.'

'But?' Ambrose could hear the hesitation in Morghan's voice.

'But,' Morghan said, 'I am afraid of the consequences. Already it is too easy for dark entities to latch onto us, create havoc, sow their seeds of discontent and fear. And there are so many of them. People need to be much more vigilant and realise how much influence these entities have. They will need to learn to guard their thoughts and hearts and to choose correctly with every decision and action.' She sighed. 'Things will get worse before they get better, and we have already waded out into the depths of how bad things can be. Otherwise, the Fae and the gods and ancestors would not have decided on this course of action.'

'Stepping back out into the open.'

'Restoring us to our correct relationship,' Morghan replied nodding. 'But my fear is that many humans won't make it.' She sighed and turned to look at the fire. 'They won't make it across the divide. They're too corrupted. It will drive them crazy with fear and they will see with twisted vision and then their fear will be fed upon and amplified.' She pressed a hand to her heart where it hurt for them.

'But they'll still have a chance,' Ambrose countered.

'Yes,' Morghan conceded. 'And here we are back at the beginning. 'How do we give them that chance? And two questions specifically for myself – how am I supposed to teach anyone anything? What does this mean for me – how am I supposed to do this? And the Queen - she said I had the service of her people, if needed. That seems...huge, don't you think? What do they want? How do I, just one person, make any difference?' She grinned suddenly. 'All right then, a lot more than just two questions.'

She shrugged. 'No. Back to two questions. One – what is my role in this to be, specifically? Two – how do we help as many people as possible survive the transition, to let go of their fear? Stepping from their material world back to one where spirits walk, and where the care of their soul and the experience of joy are the most important things?'

Ambrose sat back in his chair, nodding. This was, in fact, just the sort of knotty problem he relished. He pushed his hair back from his face.

'I think it's safe to say two things in answer to your questions,' he responded. 'Firstly, that you need to go back to the Otherworld – keep going back – and gain more guidance for the how of showing people that they must tend the seed and soul with the same care, that they can see the stars and know they shine just as brightly.'

Morghan nodded. 'I agree,' she said. 'And the second thing?'

'Perhaps the more difficult one,' Ambrose said. 'And that's to realise that you are not alone, that you are not just one person tasked to do this.'

Lips curling in a smile, Morghan laughed. 'Touché,' she said and laughed louder. 'You're absolutely right. And hasn't that always been the case, too?' She shook her head. 'We are not the only Grove to have survived.'

'And all over the world, outside of the Groves, there are those who are awake, who remember, who know.' Ambrose paused. 'I happen to think the numbers of us who live in true relationship – and those who want to, who recognise that there is something more that they need to be doing – are greater than we dare dream. It is all of us who will take the world to the next stage, if we realise we can, and have to.'

'Much like we always say, then,' Morghan mused. 'Begin where you are, do what you can, with what you have.'

Ambrose picked up his tea again. It was only lukewarm. 'I received a telephone call yesterday,' he said.

Morghan raised her eyebrows. 'And?'

'And, interestingly enough, in light of all of this,' Ambrose said, 'it was from a reporter.'

Now, her eyes narrowed and Morghan frowned. 'A reporter?'

'Yes. They want to interview us – which includes you – about how we're dealing with the pandemic here in Wellsford.'

'I don't understand,' Morghan said. 'Why? How is this news?'

'Well, for starters, we've not had many cases of the virus here. That makes it news indeed.'

'We've worked hard to make it so,' Morghan said.

'Exactly. The reporter – Molly Wainwright, I think she said her name was – wants to talk about how we are drawing together as a community and taking active responsibility for each and every individual who lives here.' Ambrose took a sip of the tea anyway. 'I'm excited about it, quite frankly.'

Morghan's grey gaze was on him. 'Because the way we're doing things might inspire others to try the same,' she said.

'Indeed.'

She sighed and leaned her head back against the chair, closing her eyes, immediately going back to the storm raging over the world. Lightly, she touched her fingers to her chest. Still solid and warm under her touch, from the inside she felt as though she'd been flayed open, broken apart, her heart beating in the cold air of the storm that swirled over the Earth.

'I suppose,' she said. 'I suppose it is a start.'

'A very good start,' Ambrose countered. He slid forward on his chair and leaned earnestly towards Morghan. 'Short of some sort of something we cannot predict, this is the way it's going to happen,' he said. 'On an individual and community basis, just as we teach our grove members here to strengthen their spirits, to weave themselves into the very warp and weft of the world. To properly and generously take care of themselves and their neighbours. We know that the stronger our light shines, the more people will be able to see their own paths.'

Morghan opened her eyes and looked at her closest friend. 'There's a lot of darkness in the world, Ambrose,' she said. 'A lot of broken soul aspects looking for whatever nourishment they can find, a lot more who delight in the havoc they're able to cause, and a lot of corruption in people's thinking, in the patterns of habit they've woven for themselves.'

'Yes,' Ambrose said simply. 'Yes, there is. But what of it?'

She blinked at him, then laughed. 'Indeed,' she said. 'Courage is necessary.' She mused upon it. 'The year of the Bear.'

They were both silent then, listening to the creaks and whispers of the old house that sat stolidly around them, and the wind that poked and teased at the rafters.

'And there is Erin,' Ambrose said, Morghan's comment about Bear making him think of Erin and Stephan. 'She has a role to play in this too, don't you think?'

'Yes,' Morghan said, nodding and gazing towards the ceiling with fatigue. 'I thought – and I keep making this mistake, don't I? That my role would be simply as teacher to Erin, to the two of them, Erin and Stephan. That they would carry the great task forward.' She sighed, looking over at Ambrose, taking heart from his calm, clear features, the charming mop of blond hair that kept falling over his eyes. 'And yet, apparently, I am not done with yet.'

'You have the benefit of years of experience and training, and the wisdom that comes with it, Morghan my love,'

Ambrose said. 'I never for a moment believed you would be taking a background part in all of this.' He gestured at the room, at the world outside the room.

'And you,' Morghan said. 'You have just as big a role when it comes down to it.'

Ambrose's smile was full of good nature and humour. 'Because I will follow you anywhere, and everyone knows it.'

Morghan stilled at the simple phrase. 'I said that to your sister, to Grainne, did you know that?'

Ambrose nodded. 'She told me.'

Morghan's throat worked as she swallowed. 'And yet, I did not follow her on that last journey. I did not follow her onto that boat, and under those waves.' She looked back at the fire, looking away from the image of Grainne taking her last breath, seawater filling her lungs instead of air.

'When I met her,' she continued, 'before I'd barely even spoken to Grainne, I dreamed of her.' She flicked a glance at Ambrose. 'I dreamed I was the Lady of the Forest, and she was walking through my woods, between the trees, magnificent in her spirit form, so full of energy, the colour of red-brown cinnamon, and so strong.' Morghan's lips quirked. 'So headstrong. And I thought, in the dream, *this one's a traveller, and I would that my forest be her true north.*

'You were that to her. You two achieved everything your souls demanded you do to heal the past rifts and misunderstandings between you, and reaffirm your strongest bond. That is more than many manage.' He raised his gaze from the fire to Morghan's face, then to the view outside the window where the light played in the bare limbs of the trees, creating shapes that flexed and changed in the breeze, playing with making the branches into bones. He looked back at Morghan's serious expression, her pupils wide in the dim light of the room.

He shook his head. 'Morghan,' he said. 'We've been through this and you know how I feel about it. Grainne needed to do the things she did. She needed to go out there on the water, feeling the wind in her hair, the salt on her tongue. It was where she was most truly alive, as you and I are when we walk through the trees of this Grove.' He leaned back, gave a little sigh then smiled. 'You achieved so much together, and you loved deeply and well. You have cared since for Clarice as a mother, and I want you to rest easy in your mind and your heart.' His smile widened.

'Now it seems, you must give your attention to a new task – not that I'm saying that my sister was merely a task, despite the job of mending the pain of old lifetimes being something along those lines. But you must open your heart with a clear conscience and turn your attention to what is at hand now, with no regrets for the past. Grainne's love is still with you, and you will see her again when this is done.' He narrowed his eyes, silent for a long moment.

'Or perhaps even before.'

Morghan stilled, then flattened a palm against her thigh. 'You think she may come back? Reincarnate here, while I am still here?'

Ambrose shrugged and relaxed. It had been a brief premonition, a small tinge in the air of his perception. 'I don't know,' he said. 'It was simply a sensation.' He shook his head. 'And not an issue for this day.'

Morghan stared grey eyes at him for a long moment and then turned her thoughts away from Grainne. She allowed her lips to curve into a smile. 'There is always another task,' she said. 'Isn't there? Always another job to do, always something else to strive for, always another need to be met.'

'Yes,' Ambrose agreed, then added, 'especially in our line of work.'

'Yes,' Morghan said, and she shook her head. 'Because we can always rest when we're dead, right?'

10

ERIN RUBBED HER PALMS ON HER THIGHS THEN SMOOTHED them over the fabric of her dress, looking around the room, feeling jumpy, as though electricity coursed through her skin, as though she were about to hatch from it. She huffed a little breath. What would she become – a butterfly or even some sort of exotic and beautiful night moth? Or would she come forth to burst open an anxious little monstrosity? These were questions to which she did not know the answers and she shook her head slightly. What was the point in even asking them? She was going to do this anyway, right? She looked across the room at Stephan whose blue eyes did not blink at her. She swallowed and heard her throat click dryly.

'Are you sure?' Stephan asked. 'I mean, it's not like you've really done this before – or at least like, not consciously, not with intention, you know what I mean?'

Erin cleared her throat. 'I know what you mean,' she said. 'And I'm nervous.' She laughed and held up her hands.

'My palms are sweating.' Her laughter became a croak as she looked at the lines and creases on her skin. 'But on the other hand,' she asked, 'what have I got to lose?' She shook her head and answered her own question. 'Nothing,' she said. 'I haven't anything to lose and I know for sure that I can't go on like this. At the very least, I need to do something so I can start sleeping properly.' She sat down on the small sofa that had been her grandmother's and patted a cushion before looking back at Stephan who stood gangly and uncertain in the middle of the room.

'You can't stand there looking like that,' she said. 'I need to be able to count on one of us at least seeming like we know what we're doing.' Her lips curved into a small smile at the sight of him, of his presence so warm and comforting even over his nervousness. 'I'm nominating you for that position.'

Stephan shook his head, but he knew he was going to go along with this anyway. 'We should get Morghan to be here for this, don't you think?'

'No.' Erin's voice was quiet but emphatic. 'I am going back and forth between here and Kria in that valley,' she said. 'I'm doing it almost every night and it's not getting any better.' She looked around at her grandmother's artwork on the walls, at the low shelves stuffed to bursting with books on magic, on plants, on herbalism, and she looked at the plants themselves growing green and vibrant and their pots, the life almost shimmering from them. She nodded and something welled up inside her, a sort of confidence, a knowledge that came from somewhere deep inside that she could do this.

'Macha will be with me,' she said. She believed it too,

except it wasn't just belief, was it? She could feel the connection there, a thread between them, thin and long and stretched but still strong. There was a thread like that between her and Kria too, she knew, looking at it in her mind where it was the colour red, red like the woollen threads that were being woven by Lindsay into a new dress for her. She looked at the thread and knew that it stretched back in time and place and through the mist all the way back to the glen and loch and Kria's bones, and the seagulls overhead that never stopped screaming. She reached out and touched it, felt it between her fingertips, and she followed it, the cosy sitting room in Ash Cottage slipping sideways as she shifted, then turned and tumbled, the red thread between her fingers.

IT WAS COLDER IN THE GLEN. THAT WAS THE FIRST THING KRIA noticed as she climbed down the steep sides of the valley and under the mists, disappearing from the view of the men on their horses above her. Not that she knew now whether they still stood there, with their expressionless faces as they looked down upon the desolate valley. She'd not asked the men whether they would, whether that was part of it all, to keep watch as she went to her doom, but maybe, maybe they were watching her still, she thought, twisting around on the dry and scrubby grass, raising her hand to shade her eyes, and peering back up the way she come. Could they see her? Were they watching her even now, full of their doubts about her abilities?

The thought was impossible. She hunched her shoulders and turned to keep moving, and the stone building grew gradually larger as she picked her way towards it.

The building grew larger and the reality of her situation bloomed into a fantastic explosion in her mind.

She was here. She'd come down the sides of the glen and now she was here.

She did not like the building, she decided, not at all. It was as bleak as a rest of the place, and when she finally came up to the open mouth that was its doorway and laid her hand upon the cold damp stone, a cry was rung from her throat.

'Why?' she asked her goddess. 'Why this forsaken place?' she cried out. 'You are not here – I can look around this place and see that you, my goddess, do not live here.' And so it was, for how could a goddess who had tended to her from the cradle live in such a place as this? Where the grass barely lifted its straw from the ground, where even bugs and slugs did not seem to care to go, where there was not the small, pleasant hum of insects upon the wing, where there was not the blossoming of a scented petal from a flower turning its head towards the sun. How could coming to this place – which the goddess did not bless with her gaze – keep the world from continuing to lose its magic?

It made no sense.

There was not even any sun here. How was she, Kria, to wake in this place every morning, turn towards the sun and greet the rising goddess with an open heart, connecting with the sun's power until it streamed through her, ground under her feet, light through her body?

How could you be who you were when everything was taken away from you?

Kria lifted her face to the sky again. She knew it was later in the morning from the weariness in her bones and the hunger in her stomach, a growling that would only grow louder as the day wore on. But the thought of having to tend to such needs in a place like this disheartened her. Nothing about it would be familiar; she would not tend the cooking fire in the warmth and chatter of her fellow priestess initiates. They would not be with her to sing the blessings over food and fire.

Here, she was alone, the only sound her breath rattling suddenly in her chest and the lapping behind her of water at stone. She brought her gaze to bear upon the loch and she shivered for in there surely, she thought, lurked something monstrous. Under the rippling surface the depths were untold, unknown and surely big enough, deep enough, to make home for all manner of beasts, and here in this forsaken place, she knew that they would be hungry, driven mad by the desolation as soon she was sure she also would be. She could not imagine bringing herself to brave these waters. Water was supposed to be life-giving; this was something she knew, that she had been taught, but the water back where she came from was not like this, did not have this hungry look. It had been a spring, fresh and bright, with flowers bent heavy over it to see their reflections.

Kria shook herself and lifted her voice to the air.

'You are being silly, she said around the lump in her throat. 'There is nothing in the water but, goddess bless me, fish to catch and eat.'

But the sound of her voice was thin against the weight of

the air, merely the mewling of a sickly baby unable to take its mother's milk.

She did not want to go into the stone building but there was nothing else for it. This was where she was to live, to learn the lesson that had been set. Turning again, she entered and found herself in a simple room with the cold remnants of a hearth and on the far side, a shelf for sleeping upon.

How many other women had slept there, she wondered? Was it they who had left the pile of blankets and skins? And had they left them for a return to the world above, or for death in this terrible place?

Had they felt here as she did? Alone and afraid?

Kria took a breath and laid down her bundle, hands shaking slightly as she plucked at the knot of her cloak, spreading it and her meagre possessions out on the bed. Twice, she looked behind herself at the brighter rectangle that was the doorway. It felt, she thought, as though something were watching her, pressing against the very air at her back. She shook her head and turned back to her possessions, picking up the knife and sliding it into her belt. When she stepped back outside the grey and shrouded sky crowded down upon her, glowering, and how small she felt under its heavy brow, all natural cockiness knocked out of her.

Erin struggled against the mist. She tried desperately to reach out a hand and touch Kria on her shoulder, to turn the young woman around. 'I am here,' she wanted to say. 'You are not alone.' She didn't know if this was what Morghan always meant when she told her that she was not alone, but Erin thought it was a good place to start, against the heavy solitude of this terrible place.

But her fingers did not touch the fabric on Kria's shoulder, did not even stir a breeze upon her skin and Kria did not turn her gaze towards Erin and did not hear her voice.

Erin withdrew her hand and the mist wrapped around her again, so that all she could do was watch her past self, hear her thoughts, feel her grief. It dug its fingers into the soft flesh of her belly, and she put her hand there, as though to stop the coming spill of blood.

There was no shelter in the building; Kria knew this from the beginning. She looked out over the water which stretched farther than she could swim, for she could not swim at all. The water in the blessing pool had not come higher than her breasts. She turned and looked back up the glen, whence she had come, but knowing that if she were to retrace her footsteps, there would be no way home in that direction either.

She was here to fulfil her destiny and she tried to draw strength from that, from the expectation of her people even though all she had seen in their eyes, as it was made clear to her that she was the one chosen for this, had been doubt.

Disappointment and doubt, she thought, and in more than one expression around her, there had been relief. Relief from the other girls who had not been chosen.

Doubt from the Priestess of the Grove, who had looked at Kria through her dark eyes and sighed, telling her that it would take more than Kria's copious skills with magic to find her way from the valley. It would take grace and humility and devotion, she added and they'd both fallen silent at that. Kria was talented, and prideful of the fact.

Kria barked out a laugh at the sudden memory and this time the sound matched her surroundings, dull and heavy and full of bitterness that the priestess had not believed her talent worthy.

Well, she did not want to be here, either. Had she not come here, she would have taken her vows, and along with them, the opportunity to take the magic among the people, show them what she could do, be the leader she was born to be.

But she was here, instead, and she did not believe, looking around, that it was any honour at all. It felt like a banishment. A denial. She could have been strong and celebrated without being sent here.

The initiation was famous, of course, although spoken of only in whispers. Those who came back from it were remembered in song and story. If it was even true that there had been some who passed the initiation in a single lifetime. Now she was here, Kria did not believe there were any. They were stories, nothing more.

About those who did not come back, nothing was sung except dirges.

Kria thought it all a barbaric tradition.

There were better ways to achieve whatever it was that this test was designed to do. This place was a cruelty. There was no way to survive here, and even though she could control the weather to some degree, the mists over this place were not simple clouds.

'They say it is haunted with all the souls who did not make it to the Isle of Healing and the Summerlands,' one girl had said with her voice full of excited terror now that she knew she was not the one chosen to go. Kria had lain there on her bed, on her back, staring at the roof watching in the dimness the last slow curls of smoke as they rose. She had not joined in the conversations, had tried not to listen to the rustling of excited and pitying speculation. It had been easy not to hear them for there was nothing but the rush of ice in her ears and her limbs were so heavy over the next days until she left that she could barely lift them.

Erin shook her head, listening to Kria's memories, but not understanding.

'What was the purpose of this?' she whispered. 'What did they say you are coming here to do?' She didn't understand how someone could be sent off for an initiation without being told how to get through it. She looked at Kria's slight body, her tight shoulders, her sharp elbows, and she shook her head, not understanding any of it.

How could something good and strong come from this place of lack and privation?

11

Ambrose tapped on the bedroom door, then opened it quietly and let himself in. Morghan turned around at his step and opened her mouth, searching for sounds that would make words, bending down into her mind to find them.

She had spent the night unrested. Whenever she closed her eyes, she was faced with the view from the hilltop once more. She could feel the storm buffeting against her.

'She has arrived?' Her words were slightly slurred with the effort of speaking.

Erin, of course. She was preparing her to *see*, to be her true self. To pass the ancient initiation. Erin, whom Morghan had thought would take over her own part in the Grove, her only task left to teach her the way.

Morghan shook her head at her own foolishness. She held her right hand up in front of her face, seeing the golden one the Queen had placed there upon her wrist. Responsibility could not be given up, no matter how important, how capable were those you were giving it up to. She felt the sting of her own short-sightedness. Of course the Lady of the Ways would not simply be done with her, content to watch her teach what she already knew.

No, she acknowledged; when one thinks they have absorbed the important lessons, learned what there is to know, that is when they must be broken open, shown more, required to be more.

There would be no graceful slide into retirement such as Selena had achieved when she'd taught Morghan the ancient ways. Not for Morghan herself. Not in this time and place. She closed her eyes.

Ambrose looked over at Morghan, at the tears streaming from her eyes. He wished he could take some of this burden from her, carry it himself, the weight a stone on his back, a deep pain in his heart as it was in hers. But he had not been the one with whom the ancient one shared her vision, and so, although he understood it intellectually, seeing it, being there, was completely different.

'She will be here shortly, I expect,' he said.

Morghan turned back to the window, searching for her beloved trees outside. And she saw them, she did, but she could not reach them. The sky overhead was the wretched, tortured sky over the chasm, and although she could feel her feet flat upon the floorboards of her own bedroom, she felt too, the crumbling perch on the hill where the wind buffeted her and below, so far below, churned the ocean between Earth and the Isle of Healing. She pressed a hand to her heart and wanted to open her mouth in a scream of pain.

Instead, she managed a smile. 'My apologies, my dearest

friend. Yesterday morning's vision has overcome me.' She pulled in a deep breath. 'The depth of the pain in this world, Ambrose.' She shook her head. 'The lack of true connection. It hurts me to see it.'

Morghan looked around at Ambrose, gathered herself, concentrated.

'There is much work for Erin to do,' she said, and it was as though she spoke to Ambrose from a great distance. She blinked slowly, feeling her wet lashes, her damp cheeks. There was no point wiping the tears away, for right now they would not stop flowing. 'But I shall struggle to come down today.' She blinked, heard the storm's thunder. 'Please give her my apologies when she arrives.'

Ambrose looked at her. 'She will understand,' he said. 'I will explain.'

Morghan nodded, held up her hand. 'Two things, for her,' she said, drawing her fragile thoughts together.

'Yes?'

A nod, and Morghan closed her eyes, to the wind swirling around her, the great bowl of sky above her split by lightning. She forced herself to concentrate.

'She must find her way back from the initiation of her old lifetime.' Morghan sank into silence. 'To be caught in two places is intolerable.'

Ambrose watched his closest friend struggle. 'I agree,' he said softly.

Morghan's lips curved into an acknowledging smile and she breathed in deeply. 'I have begun to show her the way back, but we must accelerate that.' Her head dipped and she closed her eyes again, listened to the howl of the wind, turned her face away from the intolerable pain of her world.

She searched for the thread of her thoughts. 'I must teach her to sing the way,' she said. She reached further.

'I will tell her,' Ambrose said, nodding. He waited for Morghan to be able to tell him the second thing.

She looked down from the hilltop, searching for the shreds of her normal life, peering through the clouds, past the waves that thrashed in fury out on the ocean. She fought the vision in her head, the view that persisted behind her eyes, and focused on the second task for Erin.

What had it been?

'Wayne Moffat,' she said at last, finding the name deep in her mind.

'What about him?' Ambrose asked slowly. The man presented them with a difficult situation.

Morghan nodded, her plan for him coming back to her. She wiped a wet cheek. 'We cannot ignore him. His connection to Erin means something here and now, or he would not have come into our orbit.

Ambrose shook his head. 'It is not a comfortable connection.' A sigh. 'But I am in agreement with you.'

'I would like it if you could check up on him, keep ahead on his care.' Morghan glanced out the bedroom window again, relieved to see the trees more clearly now. The sky above them, however, was still the sky of the storm, the clouds dark and roiling, split with the jagged edges of lightning. 'Winsome and I have broached with him the subject of his future needs, and I have offered him a place in our small care home whenever he requires it, as you know. But I would be grateful if you could take the lead on all arrangements from here, or delegate the task as you see fit.' Something else occurred to her, and she narrowed her eyes. 'Do you require an assistant, Ambrose?' she asked. A slight smile creased her lips. 'An apprentice, perhaps?'

Ambrose stared at her, turning her words over in his mind. 'I had not thought of it,' he said. 'Why have you?'

'I keep you very busy,' Morghan replied. 'And we have Stephan to consider in all of this.'

'You have been including him alongside Erin in some of your lessons.' Ambrose shook his head. 'And I am no herbalist.'

'No, but he is far enough along that path to continue it under his own steam. What he needs to learn is what the Great Bear wishes from him.'

Ambrose thought about it. Nodded. 'I can do that,' he said.

'Good,' Morghan said. Then, 'back to Erin. I want her to work in our care home.'

For a moment, Ambrose was silent. 'You are sure?' he asked. 'Moffat will likely be taking a bed early next year.' He shook his head slightly. 'You want her still there, then? You want Erin to nurse him, the man responsible for her mother's death?' He frowned. 'Does she even know exactly how Becca died yet?'

'Only the bare bones of the story as Henry has told her. I've not spoken about it to her yet, although Charlie has had conversations with her about Teresa and Becca.' Morghan glanced back out the window, but the sky was unchanged. She shivered slightly, her senses high, alert.

'Are you sure?' Ambrose asked at last.

Morghan turned her gaze on him, and her eyes were full of storms and tears. She closed them. 'There isn't time anymore,' she said. 'It will be expedient.'

'But she is so young.'

'It is the quickest way to bring her to understanding.'

'She will be hurt,' Ambrose said.

Morghan raised her hands to her face and wiped her wet cheeks. 'She will learn, and she will not be alone. We will be there to guide her.'

Ambrose shifted where he stood, pushed back the flop of fair hair over his forehead, then nodded. 'Very well.'

'Our spirit kin – ancestors and animal guides – and our gods do not pamper or coddle us,' Morghan said, turning again to the window and placing her hands on the glass. It was cold against her skin, cold like the spume from ocean waves. 'We will have faith in their purpose.'

'And bringing Erin face to face with the man who killed – accidentally or otherwise – her mother, is the will of her kin?'

Morghan turned back and leaned against the windowsill.

Ambrose continued, concerned. 'Do we presume that, or do we know?'

'Ambrose,' Morghan said softly. 'You and I both know that at some point we must trust that the weaving of circumstances in their particular patterns is not without meaning.'

Looking down at his shoes, Ambrose shook his head. But it was not in disagreement. 'You are right,' he said. 'She is in the flow of her own life now, and we must let her go with the current.' He cleared his throat. 'But you are not being gentle.'

'They are not being gentle,' Morghan corrected. 'This is the lesson she must learn, one way or another. And Moffat has six months at most left to him.' She waved a hand and looked away from the way it stirred the clouds around her. 'How slowly do you think she is meant to take it? It is not I who has brought this about.'

'But will you be there to show her the way through it?' He gestured at her wet cheeks.

It was an unfair question and Ambrose regretted it the moment it was out of his mouth.

'No,' Morghan said, reading the look on his face. 'You are entitled to ask that.' She tipped her head back, closing her eyes and sighing. 'I will find my way,' she said.

But the tears were back, and the pain in her heart clouded her mind. She lapsed into silence, listening only to the screaming of the wind.

Ambrose stared at her for a moment and clenched his fists in his helplessness. He considered – was there a way for him to join Morghan where she was? To bolster her.

Grainne would have been able to, if she were still here, still alive. Perhaps. Grainne had touched the web in ways none of them had managed. And she had touched parts of Morghan that Morghan held close and did not allow another near.

But his sister Grainne was not here. Had not been with them for five years. And he, despite his many talents, could not do the things she had done, and could not now reach Morghan where she was. He turned slowly for the door and let himself out.

In the bedroom, Morghan heard the door click shut over the sound of the wind and knew she was alone again. Alone in her bedroom, and alone on the hilltop trying to straddle the two worlds. She looked out over the Earth, unable to stop herself from feeling the seething chaos and pain of its people's disconnection. She sank to her knees on the floor of her room and covered her eyes.

She did not know how to live with what she was seeing. She did not know how to come down from the hilltop nor what to do when she did.

She was one person, one person against this tidal swell of pain.

Why had her ancient self showed her this vision?

What did the Queen of the Fae suppose her to do with her golden hand?

12

ERIN PULLED ON THE BOOTS SHE'D BOUGHT FOR TRAMPING about the woods in and stood up. There was a lump in her throat, and she spoke around it. She'd dreamed again of Kria – her travelling back to her yesterday had done no good, made no difference. Still in her dream she had stood ankle-deep and shaking in the cold water of the loch beside Kria's bones.

'Ready, Burdock?' Today, she needed to ask Morghan directly – how to get out of that terrible place? How to get Kria out of there?

No more pussyfooting around. No more roundabout answers that were not really answers at all.

Burdock looked back solemnly at her, picking up on her mood. She'd been behaving strangely all morning, he thought, pacing the room like she needed to go for a good run outside. But they were only going outside for a romp in the wind now.

'Okay,' Erin answered. 'Let's go, then.' Her fingers were

white against the wool of the cloak and she drew up the hood, then bent her head against the icy teeth of the wind as they crossed the lawn to the path leading into the woods.

She was nervous, she realised, turning her mind away from Kria and the valley towards what was ahead of her. Nervous, because she also needed to broach the subject of money with Morghan. Ask if there was some job she could do. Confess that her parents had cut her off.

Because they thought Morghan Wilde and the Grove were evil.

She could barely swallow around the lump in her throat.

The path in the woods forked in front of her, one direction looping back around to Wellsford and the other going deeper into the Grove, to the stone circle and Hawthorn House, and Erin stood a moment at the crossroads, considering it, holding her cloak tightly around her neck, remembering how she'd felt the day she'd come this way to tell Morghan and Ambrose that she would be staying in Wellsford.

Taking her place in the Grove.

It had been as though there had been a path forking in her mind as well, and once she made her choice, she'd known there would be no back-tracking. If she left Wilde Grove, she could never come back – or certainly not to Ash Cottage. And it wouldn't be the same without the cottage her grandmother had lived in all her life, would it?

And if she stayed, then there was no going back to her old life. It had already felt a thousand miles away, and even though Morghan had said she would always be free to come and go, and that no one would ever want her to stop visiting her family, she had also warned that Erin would feel increasingly different to them, and that difference might come at a cost to the relationship.

Well, the cost was already being paid, Erin thought, ducking under a branch. They had already been at a stand-off with each other for weeks, and now her parents had finally made their move.

Without even warning her. Except, she thought, they kind of had, hadn't they? When she'd last spoken to her father on the phone, he'd yelled that he'd be damned if she was going to give all his money away to some bloody cult. Hadn't they already paid enough to get her out of there?

She'd puzzled over that for quite some time. What had he meant? Stephan thought it could only mean one thing, and she knew he was probably right – her parents had paid her birth mother for her. They'd bought her. She was a thing they'd bought, like they'd gone out one day and come back with a new couch. Except the couch was a baby.

Charlie had known her mother. Becca. They'd gone to school together. And when she'd asked her, Charlie had told her what her real mother had been like.

It had been hard hearing it. Erin wanted her birth mother to be someone she could look up to. She wanted there to be a compelling, and hopefully comfortingly tragic reason she hadn't been able to keep her.

Not money. Not for that.

Charlie had shaken her head over it. No, she'd told Erin. Becca knew she would be no fit mother. She'd done the best thing by Erin, giving her to a loving family.

But Erin had asked why, if that was the case, hadn't

Becca let Teresa take her? Everyone said Teresa had wanted her.

Charlie had shaken her head again, but sadly this time.

So it did come down to money, Erin said then, and thought again now. She'd been sold to the highest bidder, effectively. Becca hadn't been thinking about the welfare of her baby at all, or she would have let Teresa bring her up.

Charlie had demurred again, at that. Becca had a difficult relationship with Teresa. With Wilde Grove. With Wellsford. She'd felt suffocated in the small community and had left at the first opportunity. Charlie had reached out and touched Erin's clenched hands gently.

'There's always more than one side to a story,' she'd said.

But even now, Erin's blood boiled over the whole fiasco. To think she could have been part of Wilde Grove from the very beginning. She felt like Becca had taken her heritage from her, had torn her from her rightful life. And Veronica and Vincent had paid for her. Cold, hard cash for a pretty little baby to give them the perfect little family. She was furious about all of it.

All of which meant, she knew, as she called Burdock to her side and scratched the damp fur between his ears, that there was no reversal of her decision to be made, despite the repossession of her car, the terrible state of her bank accounts. Even though the thought of being without money scared her.

Despite Stephan trying to soothe her fears over it. They'd figure something out, he'd said.

She hoped so, because now she was too far along this journey, and she needed to stay. Not just wanted to but needed to.

Because there was Kria.

She'd come so close to reaching out and touching her. Erin shook her head, watching her feet on the path that was more familiar than not now. She'd been right there, right there in the glen with Kria, hearing her thoughts, however that was possible, feeling the abandonment, the desperate fight not to be afraid in that terrible place.

Erin had to help her. She just had to – and there would be a way, surely? She'd try to do something during her dreaming. She took a breath and reached out to feel for Macha's presence there amongst the trees. A raven called out, but that was all.

It was enough. Macha had been adamant that Erin could find the way out of the glen. In fact, hadn't she said that if Erin did so, she took all of them with her? Erin's memory conjured up the image of Kria's dead body there on the shore and she shuddered. She'd do anything to stop that from happening, to rescue Kria from dying there like that.

She stopped on the edge of the woods to look at Hawthorn House, remembering then the first time she'd come here. It seemed already like that had been so long ago, and yet, it was only close to two months.

This time, when she approached the sacred well, she didn't drop to her knees and tumble down into its mysterious depths. This time, she stood in front of it and breathed in its cold tang, standing there relaxed and straight as Morghan had been teaching her. Then she opened Teresa's old bag and took from it one of the late roses from her garden, lightly caressing its silky petals before dropping it onto the water.

'Blessed be the water of life,' she said and tried to leave

her brooding thoughts behind for a moment to expand herself in gratitude. Because really, wasn't there so much to be grateful for?

Water rippled and something touched a bare ankle in the dark depths of her mind, but she ignored it, lifting her face to the wind instead, feeling its sharp breath slicing against her skin, reminding her that she was alive and breathing, here and present. Her heart lifted, and she sighed, from pleasure this time.

A glance at the pale, fading pink rose floating on the dark water of the well, a moment's brief but fervent appreciation for the simple, stunning beauty of it, and Erin moved off to the house, turning her mind to what was to come.

What would Morghan want to do today? More of the grounding and centring? Practicing the expansion of spirit, walking through the trees, touching their spirits, learning their songs?

Learning, as Morghan put it, to weave the web?

Which was confusing, because wasn't the web already there, stitching everything together? Erin shook her head at how complicated it all was.

Stephan would not be with them today in their lesson, and her heart fell slightly at that. She would miss his sparkling eyes, the warmth of his body that she could feel even standing apart from him. She shivered at the memory of their energy twining together. The vibrant blue beauty of it.

They were still only friends, had not even repeated their unexpected kiss, but that was all right. When he was around, she felt both electrically alive and completely, paradoxically comfortable. She knew already that she trusted him with her life.

Ambrose answered her knock at the door, a smile of welcome on his face. 'Erin,' he said. 'How are you this vigorous and chilly afternoon?'

She pushed the hood of her cloak back and fumbled with the catch at her throat. 'I'm very well, thank you,' she said, then smiled guiltily, remembering the stack of books Ambrose had delivered to Ash Cottage for her to read. She'd only picked at them so far. There'd been too much else on her mind. She grimaced. 'I haven't read the books yet.'

Ambrose let himself laugh. 'I brought you enough for a year, I think. Make your way through them at your own place. I realise history, archaeology, and anthropology books aren't for everyone, but you will find enmeshed in there your own past – the history of the Great Turning.'

Erin cleared her throat and nodded. 'Thank you,' she said. 'Your notes in them are interesting. I'll study more, I promise.'

'Please don't hesitate to come to me with any questions you might have about any of it, either,' Ambrose said, standing back so that Burdock could make a happy dash to the kitchen. He took Erin's cloak and hung it up before leading the way into the main sitting room, where the big fire was roaring as usual. 'Are you feeling well?' He took in the pale face and wide eyes.

She turned her large eyes on him and put on a smile. 'Family trouble, I'm afraid,' she said. Then frowned. 'And the usual, I guess. With Kria.'

'Ah,' Ambrose said, nodding. 'You're still dreaming of her, then?' The story of this ancient initiation was one that fascinated him. He'd instructed Erin to keep a detailed journal of all her dreams – every detail she could remember. He did hope she was doing it, not only for her own benefit, but because it was only through the details she could give him that he would be able – possibly, hopefully – to find out when it was carried out, and by whom, and where.

Erin looked down at her feet in her grandmother's colourfully knitted socks. She'd taken her boots off before stepping inside. After a moment, she nodded. 'Yes,' she said. 'Still dreaming of her every night.' The lump was back in her throat. She looked around for Morghan.

Ambrose noticed it.

'I'm afraid Morghan is unable to join you today as usual,' he said, making sure he didn't let his gaze stray to the ceiling, as though to look through it at the upstairs rooms where Morghan was. He forced a smile to his face and gestured for Erin to sit.

'I want you to know that your staying on at the Grove is very important to Morghan,' he said. 'It's very important to all of us, and we are glad beyond measure that you have decided to continue the work your grandmother began, and that you are also continuing the work that you yourself began long ago in the past.'

The room seemed a little empty without Morghan's presence, and Erin realised how much already she'd come to depend on the older woman, and how much she trusted her. Morghan's enduring calmness soothed her, made her want to be like her. She frowned at Ambrose's words. He was trying to say something, but she didn't understand what.

'Staying on here at the Grove means a great deal, and we are aware that you are making sacrifices to do so.' Ambrose sat down too, finally, opposite Morghan's young apprentice. 'I'm aware that your family does not approve. Have they come around any since we last spoke?'

Here was her opportunity, Erin realised. And she guessed it was okay that she was telling Ambrose, rather than Morghan. Telling one was much like telling the other, she'd realised some time ago. They were a team. Unassailable, aligned. She nipped a tooth at her lip.

'Is Morghan all right?' she asked. Then shook her head. 'Actually, my father had my car repossessed yesterday morning.' Her voice cracked as she spoke, and she winced. 'Two men came and loaded it on a truck and drove away with it. They said my father had paid them to do it.' She pressed her lips together and looked down at her hands lying limp in her lap. 'He has stopped my allowance as well. Which means I have nothing to live on. I'm not making enough money from my art, yet.'

There was a heavy silence in the room apart from the rustle of the fire as Ambrose digested this news.

Morghan was right, he thought. Erin's spirit kin – her guides and ancestors – were deft, if ruthless, in their arrangements. He cleared his throat.

'Perhaps then,' he said, 'Morghan's request of you will not be an unwelcome one, in light of this news.'

Erin looked up. Frowned. 'Her request?'

Ambrose made himself smile at the young woman. It felt tight on his face. Although obviously the wish of Erin's kin, these next few months would not be easy on her. She would be required to learn what was probably the biggest lesson in life, and learn it thrown in the deep end. But how often did it happen that way?

Most of the time, he thought.

'She wishes you to work several hours a week in the new Wellsford Care Home.'

Erin blinked at him. Whatever she'd expected, it hadn't been that. 'What?' she said.

'You'll be paid, of course,' Ambrose said.

'A job?'

'Yes.'

A frown creased itself between Erin's brows. 'But I was under the impression, that well...' Her voice trailed off.

'That Morghan would be teaching you each day,' Ambrose finished for her, and this time he did flick a quick glance up at the ceiling, thinking of Morghan still in her room, struggling back from the horror of what she'd seen. He looked across at Erin and nodded. 'This is part of it, please know that.'

'Working in the Care Home?' Erin flushed with confusion. A job would be welcome – more than welcome, but this was a bolt from the blue and she struggled to understand.

'Yes.' Ambrose leaned forward in his chair, his face earnest. 'Compassion is the foundation of our Grove,' he said. 'And there is no better place to learn it than in the service of those who cannot care for themselves.'

'But they're dying!' Erin gasped before she could stop herself.

Ambrose looked steadily at her, his expression kindly.

'I'm sorry,' Erin said. 'Of course I'll take the job.' She blinked. 'Only, I've never been around anyone sick before.'

She winced. 'Or dying. Or even old, really.' Her grand-mother was old, she supposed, but Botox was holding her together and every infusion of the stuff seemed to give her a new lease on life.

'You will find it a valuable experience, if not an easy one,' Ambrose said.

'And this is part of being Morghan's apprentice?' Erin asked. 'Of learning the lessons of the Grove?' She nipped at her lip again, harder. It seemed a long way from the magic she'd felt at Samhain. That was the magic she wanted to learn – continue to learn.

How could feeding old people and making beds compare to that?

Erin wanted to kick herself as soon as the thought had crossed her mind. Compassion, she reminded herself.

And a job. Wasn't she in desperate need of a job? And here, one had just landed in her lap. It was amazing timing. She ought to be grateful.

She was grateful, she decided.

Turning her head, Erin gazed out the window, across the lawn to the trees. Somewhere in there was the way to the Wildwood. In there somewhere, a spirit fox was waiting for her. Macha was there, with her ravens. Their ravens, Erin corrected herself, thinking of the bird that kept hopping into the house to look at her. Kria was missing, but Erin was determined to do something about that. What, she didn't know yet, but Morghan would teach her.

The way out of the glen for both she and Kria was there. Freedom from the vision of Kria's bloodied body lying by the green and deep water of the loch as Erin stood in the shallows unable to tear her gaze away. All the answers were there in the Wildwood, waiting for her to be brave enough to go looking for them, to learn their ways, to become what she needed to be, what she was.

She thought of Macha, of the fire in her past self's eyes, the intractable demand that was her presence.

Welcome to the ancient path, Macha had said.

She would walk that path, even if it meant doing things she didn't understand.

'I'll do it,' she said. 'Thank you.'

Ambrose took a deep breath, feeling a shiver of apprehension through his body. He dismissed it and sank back into the worn groove of his faith in the ancient ways instead.

'I am pleased to hear that,' he said. 'And so shall Morghan be when I let her know.'

Erin frowned slightly. 'Where is she?' she asked and looked around the room as though to suddenly see her there.

'Morghan meant to be here, but she is dealing with something and had to leave it to me, I'm afraid.'

There was something, something small, about the way Ambrose shifted in his seat almost imperceptibly, that had Erin sitting straighter. 'But she's all right?' she asked. 'Is there anything I can do? May I help in some way?'

'Thank you,' Ambrose said, meaning it. 'Your concern is appreciated deeply.' It didn't seem the right moment to begin sharing the ancient one's message, or to tell what the Fae Queen had done. Morghan would decide with him how and when would be the right time for that. 'I will let you know if you can help. And it may be that you can – Morghan will let me know, when or if she needs to.'

Erin frowned. There was something Ambrose was

holding back. She'd thought perhaps Morghan had been called away to the hospice or something – something normal, but now, she wasn't sure. And the hospice in Banwell was in lockdown already, so it couldn't be that, when it came to it. No one in Wellsford was travelling anywhere except out for the absolute necessities. It was winter and virus cases were back on the rise.

She wanted to demand that Ambrose tell her what was wrong, what Morghan was doing, or if she was sick or something. Was she sick?

'Is she sick?' she asked. Had she caught the virus, somehow? Everyone who left Wellsford had to take all the precautions, but the virus was so contagious, it was possible, of course.

But Ambrose was shaking his head. 'No,' he said. 'Morghan isn't sick.' He decided to elaborate a little. It was a pity Erin wasn't further down the path of her training so as to be of real assistance, but that was as it was. 'She travels to the Otherworld frequently, as you know,' he said.

Erin nodded. Not that she and Morghan had really discussed that yet, but it was kind of obvious.

'And sometimes the things she sees and experiences there must take some time to be...assimilated into understanding and action here.' Ambrose smiled. 'It is not always an easy path she treads.'

Erin stood up suddenly. 'May I see her?' she asked. 'I would like to see her. Perhaps I can help.'

Ambrose stood up and looked kindly at her. 'Morghan is in no danger. She is perfectly well, and I will let you know if there is anything she needs you to do. Right now, she wishes not to be disturbed.'

Erin backed down at once. What had she been thinking anyway? She didn't know anything about anything.

Yet.

Taking a deep breath, she nodded. 'Okay,' she said. 'Okay.'

She let Ambrose lead her to the door and hand her cloak to her. As though he'd been listening for her, Burdock came ambling out of the kitchen, looking pleased with himself. He always enjoyed visiting Mrs. Palmer. Especially when she was doing her cooking and baking. He licked his chops.

Erin said goodbye to Ambrose and stepped away from Hawthorn House, Burdock at her side. The wind whistled up and tugged at her clothes as she skirted around the sacred pool, seeing her offering of the rose still there on the surface of the water.

She thought of Morghan as she walked. Dealing with whatever it was she'd seen deep in the Otherworld.

'Burdock,' she said. 'I want to help,' she said. 'I want to be able to help, if necessary.'

Burdock looked at her, then down at the ground. He smelled snow on the wind. Far off yet but coming closer.

Erin walked in between the trees, her heart lightening. She had a job; she'd be able to meet her bills, buy food. She'd be able to stay in Wellsford, in the Grove. And somehow, she'd unlock the secret of that centuries-ago initiation and learn its lesson.

Then she too would walk the ancient path that led through the Wildwood.

Because deep down, she felt it.

Wasn't it the path everyone was supposed to walk?

13

'YOU'RE GONNA BURN THE HOUSE DOWN WITH THAT.'

Minnie scowled. 'No I'm not. Go away.'

Tiny shook her head and crossed her arms over her narrow chest. 'I can't,' she said. 'Mum told me to play in here and this is my room too, and if you don't stop messing around with that candle, I'm gonna tell on you.' She paused, small eyebrows knotted. 'Whaddya doing, anyway?'

'Magic,' Minnie said. 'You wouldn't understand. I'm a witch.'

'Are not,' Tiny said, but she crept closer to where her big sister stood at the dressing table, staring at the candle without blinking. 'How do you do magic with a candle? And does Gramma know you pinched one of her candles?'

'She never uses them.'

'They're for when the electric goes out.'

'The electric's still on, so everything's all right, then, isn't it?' Minnie stared at the flame, willing it to move like it had been doing since Samhain. She was proud of herself – she could go a whole couple minutes now staring at it without blinking. A small smile curved her lips as the flame wavered. It was doing it again and she shivered in delight. She really was a witch. This wasn't her imagination. A burst of satisfaction flared through her at the same time as the candle flame brightened in the small, dim bedroom.

There. It was working. Now she just had to figure out what she wanted to know.

There were so many things. And her Dad was smarter now that he was dead.

'So?' Tiny demanded.

'So, what?' Minnie had forgotten about her sister. She wished – not for the first time – that she had her own room. Staying here in Wellsford still sucked in quite a few ways.

Except of course, for the Grove or whatever. She hadn't got brave enough to ask to join yet. She wasn't ready. There was stuff she needed first.

She glanced down at the black hoodie and jeans she was wearing, wishing she had more money to spend on clothes. There were some places online selling stuff real cheap, but it was from China and she didn't know if it was legit or not.

Her Gran's church was having some sort of rummage sale. She supposed she could go along to that, see if there was anything there that might do. She just needed a black skirt and some boots, really.

'Sooo, how do you do magic with just a dumb old candle?'

Minnie startled. She'd forgotten about her sister again. But Tiny always was like an itch that just had to be scratched. The kid never knew how to mind her own business. And she obviously hadn't seen the candle flame just shoot up a whole, like, two inches. Minnie thought about yelling at her sister to scat, but then the little bitch would just go tearing down the stairs yelling for their mum. And she was right – there'd be trouble if her Mum or Gran knew she was messing around with a candle. Except of course, it wasn't just messing around, was it?

'I'm talking to Dad,' she said.

Tiny's eyes widened, and she stepped back a bit. 'But you can't,' she said, her voice low, almost a croak. 'Dad's dead.'

Minnie rolled her eyes, which was almost as good as blinking, so she did it again. 'I know that, stupid,' she said. 'Which is why I have to do magic to talk to him. I'm a witch – didn't you hear me say so? That means I talk to my ancestors, and Dad's our ancestor now, isn't he?'

But Tiny didn't know what an ancestor was. She did know their father had died two years ago though, and how would he talk to Minnie through a candle anyway? But the thought of it made her scared, uncomfortable. Minnie had been talking a lot of weird, scary stuff lately. Tiny swallowed.

'How do you talk to Dad when he's dead?'

'I talk to his ghost, okay? Now go away and leave me alone so I can concentrate.'

Tiny backed towards the door, then turned around and ran, mouth open, screaming. 'Mum!'

'Fuck,' Minnie said and blew out the candle, waving an arm to clear the smoke. It had stopped moving anyway. And how could it do what it was supposed to when Tiny was running her mouth off, and Mum and Gran were downstairs arguing like usual? Minnie wished she were old enough to get her own place. Then she could do whatever she wanted, whenever she wanted.

There were heavy steps on the stairs, and Minnie whipped up the candle and put it in the wardrobe on her little, hidden altar, then closed the door and flopped down on her bed, picking up her phone. She was pretending to look through it when her mother appeared in the doorway.

'What's Tiny saying about you talking to your father's ghost?' Her mother leaned in the doorway, folding her arms, face paler than usual, huge shadows under her eyes.

'I only said that to make her go away,' Minnie lied, staring at her phone.

'You scared her.'

'She's a baby. Why do I have to share a room with her anyway?'

Natasha Abbott rubbed a hand over her face. 'You want to share a room with Robin, instead?'

Minnie rolled her eyes again. Robin was one and a half and an even bigger pain in her rear end than Tiny. 'No,' she said. 'Tiny is welcome to, though.'

'Which would mean you bunking in with me. That work for you?'

Minnie looked at her mother. 'Why can't we get our own place?' she asked.

Natasha's mouth grew pinched and she wished for the twenty millionth time that Rog hadn't died. Hadn't died and left her trying to bring these three up on her own. She didn't know how much bad luck one woman was supposed to bear in one life, but she figured she'd crossed the line some time ago.

'You know exactly why,' she told her 15-year-old daughter. 'Because I don't have a job anymore, and I can't get one because there's a pandemic going on out there.' Forcing herself to move, to do the right thing, she went and sat on the edge of her oldest daughter's narrow bed. 'I know it's not ideal,' she said.

'Like a million miles from it,' Minnie said.

'And I know you miss your school and your friends.'

Minnie didn't say anything. Even if they'd stayed in their old house, school was closed. She'd hardly have got to see anyone anyway. 2020 had turned out to be the worst year ever.

Natasha reached out and lifted up a long strand of Minnie's hair. 'I wish you hadn't dyed it,' she said. 'Most girls want to be blonde.'

Minnie scowled and shrugged her mother's hand away. 'I'm not most girls,' she said.

Her mother barked a quick laugh. 'That you are not, for sure. But listen, your Dad's dead and gone and we're getting along as best we can, all right? Don't go scaring your sister like that. I need you to be nice.'

That was too much, coming from her mother. Minnie shot up in her bed and raised her eyebrows, which she'd also had to darken with the dye because her real ones were so fair. She had her father's colouring. Maybe she should have gone with something like pink or blue. Except she'd wanted black. Black was powerful and dark and well, powerful. She needed to feel powerful, because the fact was, she wasn't. She was stuck here in this house, with her mother and grandmother and brother and sister, and it was pretty shitty all round.

'You need to be nice!' she exploded. 'You and Gran are always fighting.'

'We are not!'

Minnie rolled her eyes. 'Okay, you don't yell at each other, but you'd need a carving knife to cut the air around you two most of the time.' She picked up her phone again and looked at the blank screen, mortified to feel tears threatening.

Natasha was silent for a moment. 'Yeah, okay,' she said. 'Fair enough. It's not easy being here. But we've got nowhere else to go, you hear me? Nowhere. If Gran hadn't let us stay, we'd be on the streets, all four of us.' She sighed. 'I guess we all need to try a bit harder to be grateful we're not.' But it was hard, what with her mother's constant martyred expression, which made it perfectly obvious that she missed her peace and quiet. Well, there was a lot that Natasha missed too.

Her job, for starters. It hadn't been much, just working behind the counter in a betting shop, but it had been a good job and she'd had some good mates.

And she definitely missed the girls being at school. And Robin at day-care.

And then there was the other stuff that had been happening around the house. The weird stuff. She rubbed her hands together, suddenly cold, the skin paper on her palms paper-dry and rasping because she couldn't afford to buy moisturizer anymore.

Weird stuff. Like things always going missing. She'd spent a good hour looking for her keys, sure she'd set them down in the usual place.

She finally found them under her pillow.

And her mother, going on about shadows moving about in the house, her eyes all wide and jumpy in her face when she talked about it – whispered about it. Natasha hadn't seen any of that, thank goodness, but just the thought of it made her skin crawl.

Neither of them had let on to the kids about it, though.

Natasha swallowed. So, the last thing she needed on top of everything was Minnie deciding to talk to her dead father.

That was the very last thing she needed.

Natasha hadn't asked for any of this, had she? A goddamned pandemic, for crying out loud. And she for sure hadn't asked for Rog to keel over from a heart attack while going for a run to the local chippie at the ripe old age of thirty-eight. She hadn't asked to be left with three demanding kids, one who never seemed to sleep for more than five minutes, and another who had gone and dyed her hair jet black and decided to be a goth or a witch or some such useless rubbish.

She hadn't asked for any damned bit of it.

She got up from the bed, tired and fed up. 'Don't scare your sister again,' she said, her voice rough with how hard things were, and she went downstairs thinking about sneaking outside for a ciggie while Robin was still napping.

Minnie turned over on her bed, punched the pillow, and stared miserably at the wall. What was she supposed to do if she wasn't allowed to do anything? How was she supposed to work on her magic if she couldn't even light a candle?

Tiny crept into the room. 'Sorry,' she whispered.

But Minnie shook her head. 'Go away.'

'But you said you were talking to Dad.'

That had been the thing though, hadn't it? She was talking to her Dad and had been since Samhain. Tiny was usually asleep when she tried it, along with everyone else in the house, and no one noticed the candle glowing bright and yellow in the middle of the night. She'd got the idea from the book at Haven. It was for beginner witches like her – she had trouble understanding what some of the others were on about, and couldn't afford all the candles and essential oils for the spells anyway – and it said right there on the page that a seance was a good idea on Samhain. It didn't say how to go about it or anything, but Minnie had decided that wasn't going to stop her. She had to work with what she had.

And what she'd had was a candle, and the idea to talk to her dad. It was Samhain, after all, the time of ancestors, like she'd said. And her dad was dead, just fell down on his way to fetch them fish and chips one night.

She was still furious with him for doing that. How dare he just keel over and leave them like that? And now look at them, stuck here in this tiny house, nothing to do.

Which was why she'd risked getting the candle out during the daytime. She was bored. She didn't even want to contact her father this time – she'd had a better idea. There were more powerful spirits out there than her father who had been stupid enough to die of a heart attack when he wasn't even forty years old.

That was what she needed – someone powerful on her side. Someone who could get them out of this stupid house with not enough bedrooms for them all. Minnie lay on the bed and looked around at the room. It had been her Gran's bedroom until they'd come, but she'd given it to them because it still had the two single beds in it from when Minnie's Granddad had been alive.

It was weird, Minnie thought, how they'd slept in single beds. Hadn't they liked each other?

Her Gran slept in the boxroom now, and if it had been even a little bit bigger, Minnie would have wanted it for herself. But it wasn't. There was only room for the camp bed and a box for a bedside table that Gran kept a lamp on and whatever magazine she was doing the crossword in. It was a horrible room.

Minnie scowled and sighed. She plucked at the pillow and pressed her lips together. She wanted to do it again. The thing with the candle. All she wanted to do was light a stupid candle! But no. She wasn't even allowed to do that. Being a witch – being powerful – was finished before she'd even properly begun.

Then she had a thought that had her sitting up, staring at her phone.

'What's the matter?' Tiny asked, on the floor with her colouring books. She was mad about colouring and always had a pocket full of crayons.

'Nothing,' Minnie said, and a slow smile dawned on her face. 'Everything's brilliant, in fact.'

Tiny looked at her through narrowed eyes, then shrugged and returned to her colouring. This page was an underwater scene, and she was colouring the whale carefully, thinking how much she'd like to swim with a whale one day. It would be scary, but amazing.

Minnie swiped through to the app store and typed carefully into the search box, biting down on her lip as she did so. *Ouija boards,* she typed, then watched in satisfaction as app after app appeared on the small screen.

Twenty minutes later though, and the dissatisfaction was back. They were all rubbish – just silly games. She'd tried one, and the only thing the planchette would spell out was *help me escape.* It was a total con, and she leaned back against her pillow grunting in frustration. She didn't want a dumb game – she wanted something real. She'd make a proper Ouija board, and pinch one of her Gran's crystal wedding glasses from the china cabinet, but that would be awful hard to hide from everyone. There wasn't an ounce of privacy in her Gran's house.

At least they had the Internet now though. When they'd first moved to Wellsford to live with Gran, she hadn't even had the Internet connected. Minnie hadn't been able to fathom how her grandmother lived through the day without it, but her Gran had told her she didn't need it to run the radio or the telly. At least Minnie had managed to convince her mother to get it hooked up or whatever, because Gran might be content with watching Britain's Numbnut Baker or whatever the show was, but Minnie needed more from life than that.

One of the recommended apps made her pause as she scrolled. It was called *Ghost Radio* and she got a weird shivery feeling when she opened it up and read what it did.

Yeah, Minnie thought. This was what she needed. This was how she could talk to spirits – and it would be much better than a candle where all that happened was the flame wobbled this way or that.

Ghost Radio was a spirit box.

A spirit box.

Her skin tingled with goose bumps, but in a good way – as though she'd stumbled onto just the right thing, and that witchy part of her knew it. The app was £3.99 but the reviews were great. Everyone said it was the real deal. One woman said she'd used it twice and was never using it again after it said the word Satan. Minnie snickered at that. She didn't believe in Satan, or Jesus, or God. Gran had tried dragging her along to church on Sunday mornings, but Minnie had refused out of principle. She'd told her Gran she wasn't going to have anything to do with an institution that had burnt witches.

Her Gran had given her a strange look, and oddly, told her to learn her history, and that witches had been hung, not burnt, in England.

Her grandmother was weird. Wellsford was weird.

Even with Wilde Grove, or whatever it was called. She felt a familiar sensation when she thought of Wilde Grove. A sort of itchy shiver up her spine. She wanted to join the Grove. She wanted to be one of them. From the snatches of conversations she'd eavesdropped on in the streets, people seemed to think Morghan Wilde was pretty special. And the conversations about her were always whispered, which Minnie thought meant even more.

She sat up straighter. If she managed to talk to spirits – showed an aptitude, so to speak – then no one could say she couldn't join the Grove. They'd recognise straight away that she was important.

She clicked buy and thought regretfully for a moment of her dwindling bank account. Her mother only gave her twenty pounds a month, and that was supposed to cover everything she needed, including her own clothes. It was quite a while until her Mum was due to give her more as well, and Minnie had a sneaking suspicion that it would be late arriving in her bank account this month, if it came at all. Which would suck doubly, since it was Christmas in a couple weeks.

Yule, she corrected herself. Winter Solstice.

Minnie tucked a long strand of black hair behind her ear and bent over the screen of her phone, waiting for the app to install.

She scrabbled for her earphones and plugged them in. Tiny was folded over her colouring book still, the tip of her tongue poking out like it always did when the kid was concentrating. Minnie didn't bother teasing her about it, and went to the bathroom instead, locking herself in and sitting on the closed lid of the toilet. She opened the app, scanned the instructions, then clicked it on.

Her ears filled with static, and she swooped the phone around in a figure eight just like she was supposed to, so the app could calibrate itself. Apparently, it doubled as an EMF meter as well as a spirit box, and she watched the numbers down on the bottom of the screen as they hovered around the two hundred mark. She didn't know what that meant, and decided she'd have to do some research on it. Did two hundred mean there was a ghost present?

Suddenly, the number dropped to one-thirty-five and Minnie gave an involuntary shiver.

Two words flashed up on the screen over the picture of static. *Entity present.*

'Hello?' she said, excitement rising. 'Dad, is that you?' She'd forgotten she was going to try reaching out to someone better.

The line in the audio box blipped a bit, then sank down back to level. Minnie cleared her throat and realised that torch on her phone had turned on too and guessed that it did that when an entity was present.

It would be pretty spooky at night, she decided.

But in the bathroom in the middle of the afternoon, it was just exciting. 'Hello?' she said again. 'Are you there?'

The ghost radio was still calibrating. One of the reviews said it took ages, so she tried to be patient.

Then the audio blipped again and this time someone said something. She couldn't make it out, but the app had a record function, so she turned that on, which meant she'd be able to listen to it over and over if necessary.

Another word in her earphones and she leaned forward, holding her phone up to the room, straining to make out the sound. It spoke again.

'Are you there?' she asked. 'What's your name?'

Another word, deep, electronic-sounding, but this time she was pretty sure she made it out.

Daughter. She was sure it had said daughter. Her eyes widened.

'Dad?' she asked and chewed on her lip. 'Dad, are you okay?'

Here, the disembodied voice said, and this time it was clear as day.

'You're here? To see me?' Minnie asked.

There was a long pause, and she kept her gaze riveted on the screen waiting for the blip in the audio display. It came again finally.

Be with you, it said, and the hair on the back of her neck stood on end. Be with you. That's what it sounded like it had said. She was sure of it. She swallowed, her anger at her father turning to sudden, sharp grief. This was better than the candle by miles. She was having an actual conversation with him now.

'Do you miss me?' she asked. Tears stung her eyes.

This time the words were unmistakable. *Miss you.*

Now it was impossible to hold the tears back and Minnie sat on the toilet, face wet, eyes streaming.

'Why did you have to die?' she asked at last. 'Why did you have to go and leave us? We need you.'

The ghost radio was still calibrating. Minnie watched it. 97% now. More words flashed onto the screen.

Entity present.

And finally, the odd, strangled electronic voice again, sifting through the word bank in the app, choosing the right ones.

Not dead, it said.

Here with you.

14

'YOU CAN SEE INTO THE PAST, RIGHT?' ERIN SAT DOWN AT ONE of the tables in The Copper Kettle and stared apprehensively at Lucy. 'I mean – that's your gift, right? To see things that happened, even way back?'

Lucy narrowed her eyes and slid into the chair opposite the girl. They weren't supposed to be meeting in the cafe, not really, and it was closed to the public, in that no one was supposed to come in and sit down to have a coffee or piece of Simon's cake. Lucy would be fretting more about this, if it weren't for the fact that Simon seemed even more busy taking phone orders for his soup, crusty bread, and cakes. She would be playing delivery woman in a little while, but right now, there was Erin.

'Only in glimpses,' Lucy hedged. Then asked the big question. 'Why?' She drew the word out, suspicious of the expression on Erin's face. It was grasping somehow.

Erin shook her head and blew out a puff of air. 'You saw something – when we first met – do you remember?'

It wasn't possible for Lucy to forget. That had been one of her bigger seeings. She nodded but lifted her coffee to her lips so that she didn't have to answer.

'Can you tell me about it again?' Erin asked, looking across the table at Lucy and widening her eyes in a plea.

Lucy put her cup down and tucked her hands into her lap. 'All right,' she agreed slowly. 'And then you can tell me what you're up to, okay?'

Erin opened her mouth to say she wasn't up to anything, but she closed it again. Lucy belonged to the Grove. She could trust the woman.

'And why aren't you with Morghan, talking to her about whatever it is?' Lucy asked.

That had Erin shaking her head. 'Morghan is…indisposed, I guess.'

'What?' Lucy hadn't heard that Morghan was sick. 'What do you mean, indisposed?'

'I don't know, really. 'I went to Hawthorn House like normal the day before yesterday, and Ambrose told me Morghan couldn't do our usual thing together. When I went there this morning, Mrs. Palmer told me the same thing.'

Lucy wanted to get up from the table and call Hawthorn House. 'Is that all they said?'

'No,' Erin confessed. 'Ambrose said something I didn't really understand – that sometimes what Morghan has to see and do in the Otherworld takes time to assimilate.' She frowned. 'Should we be worried? About Morghan, I mean?'

Lucy shook her head automatically. 'No,' she said. 'I'm sure not. Ambrose will have everything in hand.' She took a breath. 'And it is true. When you can see and do things otherworldly, sometimes it can be hard to deal with.'

Didn't Morghan always have it under control, though? That was how it always seemed. A frown creased itself across Lucy's forehead. What had Morghan seen or done that would cause her to be unavailable for two days?

She focused across the table again. 'So,' she said. 'What can I help you with?'

Erin wrapped her hands around her own coffee cup, feeling the heat burn into her fingers. 'Can you please tell me again what you saw when we met? The day I came in here when I first got to Wellsford?' It seemed so long ago now that it felt like a different lifetime.

Lucy had told Erin before, of course, what she'd seen that day. Just briefly, as a way of encouraging the girl to make the hard choice to stay in the Grove. She'd said she'd been able to tell at her touch that Erin belonged here in a way few others did – that she'd been part of the Grove in the past.

The very distant past.

Lucy cleared her throat now and toyed with her cup, part of her mind still on Morghan, wondering what was going on there. Perhaps she would pop around to Hawthorn House later. See if there was anything that Morghan needed. She knew, really, that Ambrose would call if that were the case, but still, perhaps she would go over and check. 'Well,' she said at last. 'I saw two things.'

Erin leaned over the table. This was news to her. 'Two?'

A nod. 'I saw you as you were many, many moons ago – thousands of years, would be my guess.' A slight smile curved her lips. 'You looked an awfully feisty thing, quite formidable, I would say.' She nodded towards Erin. 'Your

KATHERINE GENET

hair was a brighter red, and you had feathers and beads and wotnot twined in it.'

'Bones,' Erin said and cleared her own throat. 'Bone beads.'

Lucy's eyes widened. 'Really? Huh. They had some quite macabre practices back then, didn't they? I wonder what sort of bones they were?' Then she shook her head. 'So you recognise this woman?'

Erin nodded. 'She's made her presence felt,' she said. Which was a gross understatement. 'She has tattoos on her face, and ravens fly with her.'

Picking up her cup, Lucy looked at Erin over the rim. 'You have met her.' Her smile matched the curve of the cup. 'I knew you were going to be talented. She had a fox with her – has Fox come to be with you yet?'

Erin shook her head. She'd caught glimpses of a spirit fox, but for some reason, they stayed just that – glimpses.

'Oh well. He'll come to you when he's ready. Or, more likely, when he thinks you're ready.'

'Do you have a spirit animal?' Erin asked, letting her curiosity get her side-tracked. This, she'd discovered, was par for the course in the Grove.

'Everyone does,' Lucy said. 'Whether they're aware of it or not.'

'What's yours?' Erin blinked. 'Or is it rude to ask?' Stephan's was a hare; he'd told her that. And Krista had a coyote.

'No, it's okay,' Lucy replied. 'My kin is the dragonfly.'

Erin's eyes widened. 'The dragonfly? I didn't realise they could be insects.'

Lucy shrugged and smiled. 'And birds, and reptiles.' She

pursed her lips, thinking again of Morghan. 'Perhaps even trees.'

Erin nodded. Trees were very special, she thought. 'Morghan has several animal kin that work with her.'

'When you do what she does, I'm sure you would too,' Lucy said. 'My own experience says we often have a bird as well as an animal or insect. And often particular kin will come to work with us for a while before leaving again. And those are just our animal kin, of course. We also have our ancestors and guides. By guides I mean the spirits who have agreed with us to be our trusted helpers while we are on Earth. They can also be ancestors, whether blood ancestors or soul aspects, or they can be other members of the soul family we are part of when we are between lives.' Lucy took a sip of her coffee. 'Terminology is difficult, I'm afraid.'

Erin nodded. This was all new to her, but she liked it. It felt right. It felt...connected. And wasn't Morghan always going on about connection?

Our lives are short but wide, she would say. *And they all touch. We all touch.*

'The other vision I had was simply of you,' Lucy said, picking up her coffee again and glancing out the window. The street outside was empty. These awful lockdowns, she thought.

'Me?' Erin twisted around to follow Lucy's gaze out through the window, but there was nothing there – that she could see anyway.

Lucy nodded, giving the girl her attention again. 'Yes,' she said with a smile. 'Simply you, slipping through the woods with a fox by your side and a sprite on your heels.'

Silent for a moment, Erin considered that, letting a

small smile curve her lips. 'A sprite? I often draw small folk. Perhaps you were picking up on that.'

'Perhaps,' Lucy agreed.

'Are they real, do you think? Sprites and the like, I mean? Fairies and elves and goblins and things?'

Lucy inclined her head. 'All manner of things are real, Erin. The world is much more than you can ordinarily see, you must be learning that.'

That made Erin nod. 'Boy, am I learning that, all right.' She sighed and stared down into her cup.

'Is there something specific you wanted to talk about, Erin?' Lucy asked.

Erin hunched her shoulders in tight to her neck then shook them out, made an effort to relax. 'I've been slipping back in time,' she said, the words simply streaming from her lips in a relieved gush.

Lucy was silent.

'To a past life,' Erin said. 'Where I – Kria, as I was then – was undergoing some sort of initiation.' She swallowed, the loneliness of the glen suddenly swamping her.

Lucy's eyebrows lifted in surprise. 'What sort of initiation?'

But Erin shook her head. 'That's the problem. I don't know.' She drew in a deep breath, let it out slowly. 'Kria's only a kid, really. Fourteen, maybe?' She pressed her fingers against the cup. 'No older than fifteen, I'm sure. And they took her to this place – this terrible barren, lonely place, and they left her there.'

Erin's voice had risen to almost a wail.

'And what was she supposed to do there?' Lucy asked, keeping her own voice calm, soothing.

For a moment, Erin just shook her head, dark red hair hanging over her eyes. Then, she pushed it back and took another deep breath. 'I don't know,' she said. 'That's the problem. I keep slipping back there – I can't stop myself, and I can't get out either. She and I are both stuck there.'

Lucy's eyebrows raised. This sounded more like a problem for Morghan.

Except apparently, Morghan was having problems of her own.

She tapped a fingernail on the table. 'All right,' she said finally. 'Tell me from the beginning.'

And Erin did, coming to a halt only after reciting what she'd learnt the other day when she'd gone deliberately to the valley for the first time.

'So, you see, I just don't know what they're asking of her, of Kria,' she said.

'Her task is to achieve something particular and so be able to leave this place?'

Erin nodded. 'Right now she can't get through the mists.' A tight shrug. 'I guess they're magic, or something.'

'That's some magic,' Lucy commented, impressed. She shook her head. 'And Morghan knows about this?'

Erin nodded again.

Lucy gazed back out the window, but this time she wasn't seeing Wellsford's main street, or the girl dressed in black scuttling along in the wind.

'What has Morghan been teaching you?' she asked, giving her attention back to Erin.

Erin's brow wrinkled. 'Prayers,' she said. 'How to open up my senses to what's really around me.' She blinked. 'Connection, she calls it, flexing the spirit.' Grimaced.

'Grounding. Singing and dancing.' A pause. 'That's kind of been it, to tell you the truth. I keep asking her to tell me how to get out of the valley, but she just ignores it and takes me down to the stream and makes me listen to it sing, or something.'

Lucy laughed – she couldn't help it. She shook her head. 'I'm sorry, Erin. I'm not making light of your plight, I promise. But there will be a method behind everything that Morghan is showing you. She'll be teaching you the way out of the valley, I'm positive of it.'

'Then I must be stupid, or something,' Erin said. 'Because I just don't understand.' She lifted her gaze to meet Lucy's. 'I'd hoped that you could go back there with me, somehow, and see if you can find the answer.' Now she was gnawing on her bottom lip.

Lucy's first instinct was to shake her head and say no, she couldn't do that, of course she couldn't. But was that true? She flattened her palms against the wood of the table and frowned, looking down at her fingers.

'I don't know,' she said. 'I was going to say no straight away – but I'll tell you what – let me think about it, okay?'

It was as much as Erin could have hoped for, really. She straightened in her chair, giving Lucy a brilliant smile, her heart lightening already.

'Thank you!' she said and pressed a hand to her chest, still grinning. 'I feel so much better already, just knowing you'll think about it.'

Lucy held up her own hands, gesturing for Erin to slow down. 'Whoa,' she said. 'I haven't made any promises; make sure you're clear on that. I've only said I'll think about it.'

But Erin was glowing anyway. She bounced a little in

her seat. 'I know,' she said. 'But even that feels like you're helping, you know?' She grinned again, then glanced at the clock on the wall. 'Wow, I didn't know it had gotten so late – I have to go to work!'

Lucy's eyes widened. 'You've got a job?'

'Yup. It's at the new care home.' Erin frowned slightly. 'Morghan wants me to work there, apparently. Ambrose told me it was part of my training, but I'm not sure what it's all about, really.' She smiled again anyway. 'But considering that I really need a job at the moment, it's come along just at the right time.'

'I see,' Lucy said. 'Well, that's good then, and I'm sure you'll do really well there.'

A shadow passed over Erin's face. 'I hope so,' she said. 'I've never been around sick or old people, though. I don't really know what to expect.'

'You'll be fine,' Lucy said. 'Just remember to be kind, always, and be there with an open heart.' She looked at Erin's hand on the table and wanted to reach across and give it a reassuring pat but made herself keep her own hands to herself. When it came to Erin, she suspected, physical distancing was a good and necessary thing.

Erin let herself out into the blustering wind, and tucked her woolly hat back on her head, pulling it down over her ears. She glanced around at the empty street and shivered. It was unnatural, she thought, seeing nobody about.

It made her want to think of Kria in the glen, but she pulled her mind away from there, giving herself a little shake.

Unlike Kria's goddess-forsaken valley, Wellsford wasn't empty. Behind the windows of the houses, there were people. Erin stood a moment on the footpath, gazing around. Behind the windows of the upstairs flats, behind the doors of the neat little terrace houses, people were busying themselves with their lives. Listening to the radio, watching television, reading whatever. They were living and breathing, thinking thoughts, and dreaming their little daydreams.

The town might look empty, but it really wasn't.

Erin turned and walked towards Wellsford's care home, thinking about the valley.

There, there really wasn't any life. Only Kria living and breathing.

Right?

15

STEPHAN ANGLED HIMSELF NEXT TO THE BACK DOOR TO THE care home at just the right time to bump into Erin there. He grinned at her, a big box of groceries in his arms.

'Fancy meeting you here,' he said, and then widened his big blue eyes in a parody of innocence.

Erin looked at him and her body flooded with warmth. She sucked in a breath of cold air to stop herself from flushing. 'Yeah,' she said. 'You'd almost think you'd arranged it like that.'

Stephan was still grinning. 'I did,' he said, unembarrassed, and shouldered the door open. 'Thought I'd wish you good luck as you started your new job.' It was warm in the kitchen and he put the groceries down on the big table, then looked over at Erin. They were the only ones in the kitchen of the farmhouse which Morghan and Ambrose had converted into a care home and hospice. It had only five beds, but it was already an essential resource for the small town.

'Thanks,' said Erin, rubbing her hands against the rough fabric of her coat before shrugging it off and looking around for a place to hang it.

'There's a cloakroom through there,' Stephan said, pointing to another doorway.

Erin nodded and hung her coat up, sticking her hat with its cheerful pompom on a hook too. And her little backpack, in which she'd packed a lunch for herself, unsure of whether she needed it or not. She returned to the kitchen and grimaced.

'I'm so nervous,' she said.

Stephan was unpacking the box and putting things away. 'Nah,' he said. 'You'll be brilliant. Old Mrs. Ruston is great, a real sweetie, and Mrs. Sharp – you gotta look out for her, she'll demand you sit down and play cards with her, and then she'll fleece you for all you've got. She lives up to her name.' He grinned, a giant tin of peaches in his hand. 'Mr. Roberts, he used to be a policeman and wow does he have some stories. I never thought it would be much of a job, policing a tiny place like this, but...' Stephen made his eyes comically wide and laughed.

'Do you know everyone here?' Erin asked. 'In fact, do you know everyone everywhere?' Stephan was constantly surprising her.

He shrugged. 'Well, yeah. I grew up here, remember. There's what, fewer than four hundred people in the whole village? You kind of get to know everyone – and they certainly get to know you.'

Erin shook her head. 'Sure, okay, but you sound like you've spent time here at the home. Recently.'

Stephan, having stuck the peaches in the pantry was digging into his box again. He pulled out packages of wine biscuits. 'I have, I guess. I come here in the evenings sometimes when I don't have anything else to do. Play cards with Mrs. Sharp – I owe her two pounds now, would you believe? And we watch movies together. Last week we watched some old Alfred Hitchcock movie. A black and white thing.' He shook his head and put the biscuits into a tin. 'It was awesome, actually. We're going to make a regular night of it.' He smiled at Erin. 'You should join us. We're gonna watch another Hitchcock film. Say you'll come?'

He stopped jabbering away and looked over at Erin, who stood in the middle of the old kitchen, an odd look on her face. 'What?' he asked. 'What's wrong?'

She shook her head. 'Nothing,' she said. 'You're just a wonder, you are, Stephan Reed. An absolute marvel.' She stepped across the floor and kissed him on the cheek. He smelled of wind and trees, and something underlying, musky and secretive. She thought of the Bear dance he'd done and swallowed.

Wilde Grove was an amazing place. Wellsford was an amazing place.

Stephan looked down at Erin, her russet eyes glowing, her hair pulled back in a long plait down her back. He tried to speak, but she was too close, he could still feel the softness of her lips against his cheek.

He wanted to put down the tins of baked beans and sausages and wrap his hands around her slim waist, feel the heat of her body through the dress she wore. He groaned aloud at the thought, couldn't help it.

Erin stepped back, her eyes wide, pupils dilated. She gave a self-conscious laugh. Rubbed her hands against her hips again. Her palms itched with the longing to reach for him.

'Well,' she said. 'Um.'

Stephan cleared his throat. 'Yeah. I guess you better go find Mary, tell her you're here.' He blinked, looked at the tins of beans and sausages in a daze.

Erin nodded, but couldn't move. She felt as though she'd stuck her fingers in an electrical socket and was now barely more than a humming live wire. 'Wow,' she breathed. 'Gosh.'

Then she made herself close her eyes for a long moment and turn for the door. Find Mary White, she told herself. Start your new job.

Stephan watched her go, a lump in his throat roughly the size of Australia. He put the tins of food down and sucked in a deep breath, feeling like he was going to explode right out of his skin. The kitchen counter was cold stainless steel, and he flattened his hands on it, using the sudden chill to bring him back to his senses, zip himself back into his body. He reeled himself in, his energy in, like he was winding twine. When he figured he had himself under control enough not to leave half of himself behind trailing after Erin – was that possible? He didn't know, but it felt like it – he put the rest of the groceries quickly away into the cupboards and slipped out the back door.

Stephan tilted his face to the sky and closed his eyes against the stone-coloured clouds. He could feel the hard, cold rain held in them and breathed in the scent of it. It smelled like water, soil, and dark, deep secrets. He filled himself with the scent, feeling his boots planted hard against the earth, his face turned toward the sky, and for a long pausing moment, he was still, gathering himself, placing himself back in the world where he stood, letting it pivot around him.

Being around Erin could leave him feeling a little ragged. A lot all over the place.

He set off through the village, heading to the edge of it where the trees waited to usher him between them, scooping him up into their hushed and dreaming world. Their limbs were free of fringing, all their leaves mulching the ground now, preparing it for new life in the summer. The wind rustled about in it, poking its fingers here and there before swooping away to clatter about in the branches. Stephan walked and listened, enjoying the flex of his muscles as he made his way up the sloping path toward Blackthorn House.

For a moment, he thought he felt Erin walking with him, the spicy energy of her swirling in a sudden breeze by his side, but then the sensation floated away, and he shook his head.

Ambrose was in the garden – not that it was a garden at all. Just a small damp lawn between the house and trees. He was moving slowly, deliberately, his body lean and graceful as he did the qi gong exercises. His eyes opened and he smiled quietly at Stephan, nodding just a little.

Stephan fell into place beside him without a word, and took the same position, breathing deeply so that his lungs filled with the damp air the trees breathed upon them. He centred and steadied himself, then began the slow, controlled and yet relaxed movements, joining in Ambrose's rhythm with only a little effort. According to Ambrose's instructions from the day before, he fashioned a ball of energy between his hands, gratified to feel it there so real, so present. He moved it around, and made his mind clear, serene, going through the sequence of exercises Ambrose had begun teaching him. They felt right on him, despite being so new.

When they'd gone through the whole sequence, Stephan turned and bowed to Ambrose, as Ambrose did the same to him. It was only then that they spoke, Ambrose's clear, calm face breaking into a smile.

'That was well done, my friend,' he said. 'You are a fast learner.'

Stephan blushed under the praise. 'I like it,' he said. 'What's it called again?'

'Eight Brocade Exercise,' Ambrose replied, moving over to the front step of the house and picking his things up.

'It's good,' Stephan said. 'Makes me feel strong and centred.'

'Which is exactly what it's supposed to do.' Ambrose had his drum in one hand, and a satchel over his shoulder, its leather worn soft from long use. He nodded for Stephan to retrieve the rucksack ready packed with bear mask and pelt.

Stephan picked it up, and his own Druid's bag and nodded. A little wiggle of nervousness threaded back through him, but he turned his face away from it and drew himself up on a breath. 'I'm ready,' he said. Then swallowed.

Ambrose's smile was amused and understanding at the same time. He said nothing, however, simply turned to walk along the strip of lawn and slip into the trees behind the house. Stephan walked after him, listening to the sudden pounding of his heart that shattered the calm he'd managed with the qi gong. For a moment, he beat himself up over it, then stopped and let it go.

His nervousness was natural. What he was setting off to do was new to him. This humming anxiety in his blood was only to be expected.

So long as he went ahead anyway, it was okay to feel like this.

The pep talk helped. His limbs grew looser again, just a little, and when he glanced up at Ambrose's sturdy back in front of him, he had a sudden glimpse of himself walking these deep tracks, a bow in his hand, his muscles warm from exertion.

Stephan stopped moving and frowned, reaching for the sensation of being someone else. He strained towards it, hunting for it between the trees, looking down at his legs, his hands that were empty in this time, but had held a supple and well-worn bow at one time deep in the past.

Ambrose turned and looked at him. 'What is it?' he asked, seeing the expression on Stephan's face, which was at once perplexed and fascinated.

Stephan swallowed, held up his hands. 'I used to walk this way, once, long ago. With a bow in my hand.'

For a moment, Ambrose was simply quiet, then he nodded. 'And you had a glimpse of yourself as this man?'

'Just then,' Stephan said, and his voice was wondering. 'It was so real.'

'It was real.'

'How long ago?' Stephan asked, still looking down at his

hands. He glanced up at Ambrose. 'How long ago, do you think?'

Ambrose had already given this question a lot of thought. 'Thousands of years ago. During the Great Turning. When this Grove was established to keep the magic.'

'The Great Turning?' Stephan was unfamiliar with the phrase.

Ambrose nodded. 'It's what I've come to call the period of time when humans began seeking power for their own hands – when they began using the axe to stop others from sharing in the wealth. No longer were we in equal and reverent relationship with the land and all peoples upon it; instead there was a shift to ownership and dominance and the warrior took the place of the hunter.' He paused and looked around them. 'It was a change that took many generations, but it was relentless.' He gestured at the woods, the hill, everything and everyone in it. 'From my understanding, Groves such as this one were established to hold and keep the knowledge of the old ways, to pass them down through time.'

'We're not the only one?' Stephan asked. 'Wilde Grove isn't the only one?' He frowned. 'I mean, I know we're not the only Grove, but there are others that go way back like you're saying?'

Ambrose lifted his shoulders and sighed. 'Yes,' he said. 'But they vary in their success. And they are few.' He tipped his head to the side. 'On the other hand, Druid Groves and Witch's Covens grow more numerous, and they touch the same truth, so there is hope for us all yet. And many of course, are choosing to walk the old path on their own.' He breathed deeply of leaf mould and cold wind. 'What you are learning, Stephan, is important. We have another Time of Turning coming upon us, and we must make the right choices this time.'

Ambrose nodded down at the young man then and turned to resume their trek up the steep hill, thinking now of Morghan. She hadn't yet come back to herself. Not properly. When he'd met her in the woods – deliberately – this morning as she performed her prayers, he'd seen the haunted look in her eyes. He'd seen that part of her still stood on that clifftop, staring over at a churning sea and a shroud of moving darkness. His heart had clenched itself in his chest.

Morghan had to find the way to live with what she was seeing.

He blew out a strained breath. Until then, he thought, he would do what he could, and that was to take over training Stephan. The time was urgent.

They reached the cave and its small, rocky clearing after another twenty minutes of walking, and Ambrose's muscles burned. He was getting too soft, he thought, sitting at his desk poring over his volumes of fairy tales and myths. This training would do him good, as well as Stephan.

But he would fashion a sling for his drum. It was too awkward to carry it up this steep path.

Looking over at Stephan, Ambrose took a deep breath. He wasn't used to this task of teacher. His skills were in organisation, research, experiments. And yet, here he was with this young man looking to him to teach him what came next.

Times, he said in his head to Morghan, are asking the unexpected of both of us.

But he wasn't going to think about Morghan. She would be fine. She was the strongest woman he'd ever met. And she was not alone. None of them were alone.

And right now, his task was Stephan.

Stephan and this cave, and the Great Bear.

He took another deep breath.

16

THE DRUM BEGAN ITS HEART BEAT QUIETLY, WINDING ITS WAY around the scented smoke Stephan wafted up into the sky. He held the bowl aloft, as if showing it to the sky, and used the fan he'd recently made from feathers – black and white, discarded from Clarice's owl Sigil and some of Erin's ravens – to send it the smoke in upward spirals to the sky. The bear mask was on the top of his head. In a moment, once the offerings were made, and a sacred space carved into the world, he would pull it down over his face again.

'For you, Great Bear,' he said, and his voice wobbled in the smoke. He cleared his throat and resisted glancing over at Ambrose. He tried again. 'For you, Great Bear,' he said, and now his words were stronger on the breeze. 'This breath of life, the sacred smoke of my heart.' He wafted the smoke towards himself for a moment and breathed deeply of it, letting it stream out again through parted lips. 'Breath of my life,' he said. 'Breath of my heart. I honour you.' He fanned the burning herbs in the bowl again, watching the cloud of fragrant smoke billow forth.

'I am grateful,' he said, closing his eyes. 'Great Bear, may I embody your virtues today and going forward. Great Bear, I am honoured to be called by you.' He took a breath, said the words that had come to him before Samhain.

'Your strength is mine. I will protect that which needs protecting.'

Giddy from the lungful of smoke, Stephan put the bowl down, tucking the feathered fan beside it. Now, he glanced at Ambrose, whose eyes, the colour of green moss, gazed steadily back at him.

Ambrose gave a small nod, and Stephan turned to look at the cave, his mouth drying, heart pounding with the beat of the drum that was louder now, insistent.

A light sheen of sweat beaded his skin.

Stephan took one more look at the sky, then ducked his head and entered the cave.

The wind was muffled from inside the cave, but somehow the drumbeat was just as strong. It vibrated around the stone walls of the cave like a living heartbeat.

The heartbeat of a bear.

Stephan stood stooped slightly in the centre of the cave for a moment – it was wide and deep, large enough for several people to gather, and light from the outside world seeped in through the entrance. He was glad for it, his own heart pounding as he swallowed convulsively.

Was he going to be able to do this? Go back to the Wildwood – not slipping and tumbling accidentally there, but deliberately, actively?

Meaningfully.

Stephan rubbed his hands on his jeans, drawing in a breath. He stood in the pose Ambrose had taught him – used, he'd said, by Bear shamans all over the world. Knees slightly bent, feet planted solidly on the floor of the cave. He curled his fingers loosely and held his hands over his solar plexus so that his index finger knuckles were just touching. This was the bear stance, Ambrose had told him, and the energy point over the solar plexus would be the one through which he would open himself, and draw energy inwards.

Stephan tried not to think about the weight of earth and stone above him and sucked in a deep breath instead, forcing himself to focus on the sound of Ambrose's drumming. He drew it to himself, let it sink in through his skin, into his solar plexus and through his body, down into his bones where it reverberated, until he could feel its pulse in every limb.

The bear mask fit snugly over his face, and he felt the snout – his snout now – sniffing around the cave, breathing in the heavy, quiet air. Reaching up, Stephan drew the bear claw on its cord from around his neck and held the long sharp curve of it in his hand, closing his eyes, taking the pose again. He was ready.

There was the drumming. There was his breath, deep and slow, deep and slow. In, held, out, slow, a pause and a sinking, in again. Slow, deliberate, the drum keeping time.

From somewhere deep in the hill behind him, Stephan thought he heard singing, the words muffled, just a rhythmic sound, a humming. It wound in and out of the drumbeat and the claw in his hand bit into the flesh of his palm. He breathed, deep and long, holding it, letting it go.

Letting himself go. Sinking into the ground under him, into the roof of the cave above him, into the stone and soil behind him, spreading out into the dimness of the cave, his small bear ears twitching, his bear nose sniffing, his bear shoulders rounding, thighs thickening, glossy pelt warming, covering, and still he breathed, deeper, deeper, longer, in and out down and through, apart and between, sliding, letting go, moving.

From one world to the other.

Hare sat outside the entrance to the cave, whiskers quivering, long ears listening. The drumbeat quickened from far off. Stephan watched him with lazy bear eyes, smiling a wide bear smile. Hare entered the cave, leaping past him, down into the shadows at the back of the cave. Turning, Stephan followed him, muscles thick with bear strength, the pelt heavy across his shoulders.

There was an opening at the back of the cave that Stephan knew hadn't been there before. He'd crossed the boundary, was in the Wildwood now. For a moment, his heart skittered against his chest, but he gripped the claw tighter and straightened his shoulders. This was what he'd come here for, after all.

To learn to walk here. To do as Morghan did and walk in both worlds.

And he was doing it. He was walking in his spirit now, his body back there in the cave, curled in its bear fur, but he was following Hare, stepping further and deeper into the tunnels at the rear of the cave. Tunnels that hadn't been there before.

Hare didn't stop to listen to Stephan's pounding thoughts. He simply led the way, his white fur glowing dimly in the almost-dark. Stephan blinked and wished for more light, looked around for the source of what little there was, but could see nothing. They were far from the entrance of the cave now, wending deep into whatever Otherworld landscape this was, and the light seemed to come from the very rock itself. He gripped his bear claw with one hand, and the long staff he found he was holding with the other. The wood it was made from was light, but he could feel the sinewy strength of it, the sweet silk of the grain under his skin, as though worn smooth with age and use.

Then, the tunnel ended, and Stephen stepped out into the sparling darkness of night, into a clearing that was scented with the warm touch of a summer. He looked up and saw stars wheeling overhead, a great swirl of them, and there, brightest among them the Pole Star.

The chanted song was louder here, and Stephan saw that he was not alone. A man danced in the flickering light of a fire, twirling and spinning, feet stamping, burnished skin glowing. Something bounced on the old bear fellow's sinewy chest and Stephan recognised a claw, just as he had back around his own neck. He glanced off into the shadows, feeling another gaze upon him, and saw there the hunter he had once been, standing with his muscular body at ease, skin gleaming as though he'd just stepped from the dance. His dark eyes stared at Stephan.

But the old bear fellow grinned, raised a hand and beckoned Stephen to come closer, to dance. The drum beat louder, and Stephan swallowed, propped his staff against the side of the cave and stepped out into the clearing and into the dance.

'*Sing our spirits home, Bear*

Sing our spirits back to the womb of your cave
Weave our spirits home, Bear
Weave our spirits back to the womb of your care,' they chanted, Stephan's feet pounding up and down on the dirt in time to the drum. He sang and he danced and under his feet there glowed a great wheel, its golden outline fading and sharpening as they danced.

The fire drew sweat from his chest and still Stephan and the bear fellow danced, chanting their song, telling of the great gifts of bear, of the way bear knew the plants and the hills, the caves and the way to birthing.

And as they sang, Bear joined them, her fur glowing in the firelight, and her feet stomped up and down and she danced the wheel with them, face lifted to the stars, around and around, spiralling around the glowing wheel that pointed in each direction and turned, turned, turned as it always did, as it always had.

17

Morghan walked out of Hawthorn House, stepping over the wet grass, her feet bare, the skirts of her tunic flapping around her ankles. She stilled her breath at the afternoon chill and straightened her spine into the breeze before stepping into the woods. There, it was hushed, with only the thoughtful dreams of the trees, and the small rustlings of animals seeking through the mulch underfoot. Morghan walked silently, staff in hand, her fringed headdress in the other.

She sought the stone circle, the consecration of its ancient sentinels and next to them, her roots pushing deep in the dirt, twining themselves around the stones where they were set deep in their earthy sockets, Grandmother Oak, her skin wrinkled and venerable with age.

She stepped lightly to the centre of the circle, glancing upwards at the ribbons of energy they had danced there into being, seeing that it was still strong, humming with the power of centuries of singing.

The wind soughed and sighed in the trees. Grandmother bowed her branches low and reached to touch Morghan, a twiggy and gnarled benediction. Morghan slipped her headdress on, so that its fringing covered her eyes.

She was on the hilltop, and she swayed slightly from the height, from the noise of the thunder in the sky over the Earth, flinching as the lightning tore strips from the sky. She wanted to bend her head from the racket, the stippled sky, but she forced herself to stand straight, made herself loosen the tension from her shoulders, to stand there looking at the black and bruised sky and breathing in the singed ozone. She planted her staff in front of herself and held it with both hands. It was made from a thick and strong branch given her long ago by Grandmother Oak, and it would keep her steady. Against her hand fluttered feathers given her by Hawk, their soft fringing a reminder of the heights to which they soared together.

Wolf was not with her here, nor Snake, and she tightened her fingers around the wood of her staff and called to them. Come to me, she sang on the stiff breath of the wind. Come to my side if you will.

Wolf's paws were on her back, the claws needle points against her skin for a moment, before he leapt into her, curled up around her heart.

Snake came noiselessly across the grass of the hill-top and slithered across her feet, letting a portion of his weight rest on her.

Morghan stood on the clifftop forcing herself to look. Made herself open her eyes to the chaos of her world.

She saw the swath of moving, flocking darkness.

The restless and trapped soul aspects of humanity's dead. Those who had not died well. Those who had not been sung on their way. Those who did not believe in the singing.

There was more than one plague coming, she thought, making herself look down on the vision, on the blanket of chaotic, hungry darkness.

Snake moved on her feet, restless suddenly, and she acknowledged him.

'You are right,' she said, the wind tearing the whisper from her mouth. 'The plague is already here.'

Wolf turned around inside her chest, settled back down, his great sweep of tail curling around her heart.

She sighed, and the wind whipped off with the sound, turned it into a keening.

'We are not supposed to suffer this way,' she said, leaning forward to look down at the churn of the waves far below her.

The light from the Shining Ones flared behind the darkness, with them the golden flickers of souls moving in their light. There was hope in the sight.

There was always hope. Truth. The light.

But it was the flocking darkness that bothered Morghan, that made her stomach queasy, her mind stutter with the sight of its ravenous swarming.

'What was once ours will be so again,' she said, pushing her words out against the storm.

'The Shining Ones are with us and we shall walk with them in our rightful place, for we shine also.' Her fingers tightened around her staff. The Hawk feathers lifted in a sudden gust.

'But before us darkness swarms, and seeks to sap our strength, to further sow its seeds of chaos and lies.'

She tipped her head back to the torn and seething sky of her vision. 'How to dispute them?' she asked, and her voice cracked on the question.

'How to shine brightly in this darkness? To weave the web ever stronger for all to see?'

WINSOME FROZE ON THE PATH, RECOGNISING MORGHAN'S voice on the cool air of the day. She'd come for a walk, slipping into the treeline behind the vicarage, trying not to feel guilty for doing so. Just a stroll, she'd told herself. Goodness knows, she needed exercise, correct?

And privacy. Sometimes a woman needed privacy, the sort she wouldn't get were she to go for a perambulation down the public street.

So, she'd come walking on what she knew full well was Wilde Grove land, tripping in between the trees, part of her trying to reach and see even a fraction of what Morghan did. The other part of her yelling in her head to stop these pernicious pagan ways before they overtook her love for Christ.

But they couldn't do that, could they? She'd been working with Morghan for weeks now, visiting Wayne Moffat and soothing his traumatised heart, and her love for her living God had only strengthened.

It was simply that her eyes were opened to a whole raft of other things too. The world was neither as narrow nor as simple as she'd known it previously.

And she'd never thought it was all that simple then.

Her throat was dry as she listened to Morghan, and the touch of the tree under her fingertips rasped against the sensitive skin there.

There was something about Morghan's voice. It was little more than a harsh whisper, but still, Winsome touched her throat with her other hand and felt like she was hearing a prophecy.

A prophecy and a question. She quaked where she stood, trying not to believe it.

It was nonsense. It was just Morghan speaking, doing her priestess thing. Winsome made herself swallow and step forward on the path where she lurked.

She wanted to know who Morghan was speaking to.

The stone circle loomed up ahead of her, and there was Morghan, standing in the middle of it, hands clasped white around a tall staff from which feathers fluttered on beaded cords.

Winsome's breath caught in her throat. Morghan, a fringed headdress over her eyes, spoke to no one.

No one visible, anyway.

Winsome tripped over a small log, falling to her knee then scrabbling quickly to stand back up. In the circle, Morghan stilled, her face turning in Winsome's direction. Winsome wiped the leaves from her hands, from her knees, stood awkwardly. Cleared her throat.

'I'm sorry,' she whispered. 'I didn't mean to disturb you.'

Down below Morghan on the hilltop, a woman stood, glowing warm and golden. Morghan wanted to shout at her not to come closer, to stay where she was, to protect her from this view. She lifted a hand, held it out to ward Winsome off, then let it drop, realising that she stood in the middle of the stone circle, and Winsome was on the path outside it. She put her hand to the eye covering and took it off, blinking in the sudden bright grey light of the day.

She glanced up at the sky, leaden with clouds between the stark branches of the trees. In the far corner of her vision, lightning forked the sky. Morghan wondered shakily if she would always see that now. She could almost feel the push and shove of the flocking darkness.

'Morghan?' Winsome said. 'Are you all right?' Morghan was shivering, although Winsome wasn't sure if the woman was aware of that. And no surprise, really, that she was. Morghan was barefoot. Barefoot in December. And without a jacket. Not even the wool cloak she sometimes wore. Winsome shrugged out of her own jacket and stepped forward, holding it out.

'Here,' she said. 'You're shaking. Cold. Let's get you warm, okay?' She stepped into the stone circle and put the down jacket around Morghan's shoulders before the woman could object. Morghan gazed at her with eyes that seemed very far away.

Whatever Morghan had been doing, Winsome had broken the spell now anyway with her stupid stumbling. 'Come and have a cup of tea with me,' Winsome said. 'You can warm yourself up.'

Morghan continued to look at her, and Winsome was shocked to see tears streaming down Morghan's cheeks.

'What is it?' she asked, alarmed. 'Where have you been? What on earth have you seen?'

Morghan shook her head, tucked her chin down and closed her eyes.

'I'm sorry,' she said after a moment. 'I cannot seem to stop the tears.'

Disquiet prickled at Winsome's skin, chilling her better than the cold air could without her jacket to warm her. She took a breath, became determined.

'Come with me,' she said. 'We're going to sit down at mine and have tea and chocolate biscuits together.'

'Hawthorn House is closer,' Morghan said, letting Winsome lead her from the circle as though she were a blind woman. She was not blind, but she was seeing too much. In every direction she saw lightning and swarming darkness like wasps. The pain of it cut into her like knives to flesh.

Winsome merely nodded, folding her hand around Morghan's waist and leading her back into the woods, stepping carefully on the narrow path.

'Where's Ambrose?' she asked after a while, making the turn onto the trail that led to Morghan's home.

'He is with Stephan,' Morghan said, the words like cold round pebbles in her mouth. She let Winsome lead her, grateful for the hand under her elbow. 'There is no time anymore, you see,' she said, thinking of not just Stephan, or Erin, but everyone.

Winsome was desperate to ask what there was no time for, but she made herself wait. Morghan was cold, almost insubstantial under her hands.

Which was very un-Morghan-like. And extremely worrying.

She glanced away from the round pool in the garden of Hawthorn House. It made her feel...odd...whenever she looked into its multi-hued depths. Almost as if it called to her, beckoned her to take a tumble down under its surface. She didn't like to think what would happen if she did that. What was down there that called to her?

The door was unlocked, and Winsome pushed it open, waited while Morghan stepped inside after her and leaned her staff carefully against the wall. For some reason, the calm carefulness with which Morghan did this made Winsome feel even more worried about her friend. Morghan looked as though she was walking on glass.

Her face lacked its usual confident serenity. Instead the cheeks were wet, her expression brittle.

Winsome looked up the stairs, turned to Morghan. 'Which room is yours?' she asked. 'We have to get these damp clothes off you, put some thick socks on your feet.' She wanted to scold the woman – what did Morghan think she was doing, traipsing about barefoot at this time of the year? But she stopped herself. Morghan was far from a child, and Winsome had quickly learnt that everything the priestess did had a reason behind it.

Morghan gazed up the staircase as though it was a mountain. And for a moment, it was. Stone steps cut into a steep hill from which she could gaze down and weep at what she saw.

Winsome took her hand and they climbed them together. She could feel the bones of Morghan's hand under its thin sheath of skin.

Morghan opened the door to her bedroom and Winsome stepped in with her, casting a glance around at the large room. There were two plump chairs by one of the windows and she led Morghan to one of them, sitting her down.

'Where are your socks?'

Morghan gazed up at her for a moment, her tear-stained cheeks luminous in the light from outside. She pointed to the chest of drawers.

Winsome went to them with a nod and rummaged in them until she'd found what she wanted. A good thick pair of woollen socks. She took them back to Morghan, handed them over, then went to the bed and pulled off a soft blanket, taking it back to Morghan and tucking it around her.

'Put the socks on,' she said. 'I'll go and make us tea.'

Downstairs, she greeted a surprised Mrs. Palmer.

'Hello, Vicar,' Mrs. Palmer said. 'Is all alright?'

'Has Morghan been unwell?' Winsome asked. 'I found her in the woods, barefoot, and somewhat dazed.'

Mrs. Palmer's brows beetled above her eyes and she turned to put the kettle on straight away. 'Our Morghan often goes about barefoot,' she said. 'No matter the season.' She fetched cups and put them on a tray. 'As for unwell and dazed, she's not been unwell, so far as I know, but neither has she been quite herself the last few days.'

Mrs. Palmer had been at Hawthorn House for all her sixty-seven years, however, and had seen a great deal and understood almost as much. She reached for the box of tea. 'Sometimes there are things that simply aren't easily reckoned with,' she told the new vicar.

'What sort of things?' Winsome demanded, then flushed. 'I'm sorry,' she said. 'I'm just worried for her, that's all. She's crying.' This last was said in an almost appalled whisper. Morghan, so calm and collected. Crying. It was almost more than Winsome could bear.

Mrs. Palmer nodded as she spooned the tea leaves into

the pot. 'She's seen something, and it's hurt her,' she said. 'You'd need to ask herself, or Ambrose, as to exactly what.' She paused, the spoon in mid-air and glanced over at Winsome. 'Sometimes, it's hard to come back, you know? To stop seeing whatever it is.'

Winsome nodded slowly, thinking she might understand what the older woman was saying. 'You can't unsee something once it's been seen,' she said in a low voice, remembering the way Reverend Robinson had followed her around trying to get her attention. He hadn't gone away no matter how many times she'd squeezed her eyes shut and told him he wasn't real.

'Exactly,' Mrs. Palmer said, pouring water into the pot and setting everything onto a tray. 'Morghan's strong – stronger even than Selena, I reckon – Selena was her aunt, and Lady of the Grove before her, but these are bad times, and Morghan does push herself. Always has.' The housekeeper pressed the tray into Winsome's hands.

'Feels a bit odd to be saying this, what with you being a vicar and all, but I've a feeling you're just what Morghan needs right now,' Mrs. Palmer added, then nodded towards the door. 'Go on, now. Warm her up with this.'

Winsome took the tray with a word of grateful thanks, touched that the woman had such faith in her. It was odd, she knew, that she was here, taking this role. Almost as if she were part of the Grove as well.

But she couldn't be part of the Grove, could she? She belonged to Christ and the Church of England.

'Love the sinner, not the sin,' she muttered, taking the tray carefully up the stairs. She shook her head. *Love the sinner not the sin* had never been a sentiment she could abide. Because of the condescension she always heard behind it. And the excuse to judge.

She would not judge Morghan. She would refuse to judge anyone. At the door to Morghan's bedroom, Winsome paused.

'Blessed are we all in the light of love,' she whispered. 'God, guide my hand and my heart.'

Morghan was not in the chair when Winsome entered the room, and Winsome shook her head slightly, wondering why she was surprised. This was Morghan Wilde she was dealing with. The woman with a spine of steel and a heart that was both wide and deep.

'Mrs. Palmer made us some hot tea,' she said, placing the tray on the table and glancing over at Morghan, who stood looking out the window. At least, however, she'd put the socks on and was holding the blanket around her shoulders. What sort of physical and mental fortitude did it take to go walking barefoot at this time of year? Winsome couldn't imagine it, herself. Her feet were baby-soft from years of sticking them in shoes.

Morghan drew her gaze from the window and turned to Winsome. 'Thank you,' she said. 'Tea will be welcome.' She was pale but composed. Or, at least, the tears had stopped their dreadful flowing.

Behind her, on the other side of the glass, lightning speared the sky.

18

THE FRONT GARDEN WAS FULL OF RAVENS, TURNING THEIR heads to stare at Erin as she stepped at last onto the driveway, the stones crunching under her feet, the raven's glassy black eyes looking impassively at her.

She swallowed, her skin prickling. There was an electricity to the air she was coming to recognise even while it made her nervous.

Erin licked her lips. 'Hello Macha,' she said.

Her voice was the only sound in the sudden stillness.

Macha's voice was amused as she spoke from behind Erin's shoulder, her presence filling a fold in the space. 'You are getting good at this.'

Sudden warmth flooded Erin's body at the unexpected praise but she shrugged. 'You're rather hard to miss.'

'Yes.'

Erin looked towards the front door of Ash Cottage. Burdock was barking, his voice high and excited. She'd missed him too.

'Kria needs you,' Macha said.

Spinning around, Erin looked for Macha, felt as much as saw her, the ancient woman's presence filling her mind. The red hair, the tattoos, they swirled around inside her.

'What?' she asked. 'Needs me? How?'

But Macha was fading away again. 'Go to her,' she said, withdrawing into the shadows of Erin's consciousness, leaving her only with the command ringing in her ears.

'Go to her,' Erin repeated, reaching up to pull the elastic from her plait so that she could tug her fingers through her hair. 'Go to her.' She lifted her head. 'And do what?'

But there was no reply. Macha had come and gone on a sweep of energy.

She dropped the key and had to scrabble around for it before finally getting it slotted into the lock. Burdock stuck his nose in the gap before she even had the door properly open, and then his great front paws were on her shoulders and her face was wet from his tongue.

'Burdock!' she spluttered, but he was heavy, and she couldn't push him off. Finally, she just laughed and hugged him. 'I missed you too, you great goof.'

That seemed to satisfy him, and he gave her one last lick for good measure, then went outside. The ravens were back – he'd been watching them from his favourite chair – and he lifted his head to sniff at them, then wrinkled his nose. They smelled of magic and he ducked his head again, deciding to give them a wide berth. Better to visit his apple tree.

Erin left the door open and dropped her bag on a chair. She looked longingly at the kettle – surely there was enough time for a sit down and a cup of tea? Her legs ached from all the walking, and she was tired from her first day at a new job.

The largest raven – the one with the grey feathers on his back – swooped in through the open door and landed agile and sure on the back of a dining chair. Erin stared at him, eyes wide.

'No cup of tea then?' she asked, backing up a step.

The bird regarded her with its unblinking gaze.

Erin took another step away, towards the stairs. She nodded. 'Okay. I get it, all right? Just a visit to the loo, first, how's that?'

The bird lifted his wings, then tucked them back at his side again. He looked away, as though settling to wait for her and Erin nodded, then turned and scrambled up the stairs.

In the bathroom, she used the toilet, then washed her hands, staring at her reflection in the mirror. Her hair hung about her face, making her wide-eyed expression all the wilder. She swallowed and watched her throat convulse. Took a deep breath and closed her eyes. When she opened them, she was as pale and uncertain as she'd been the moment before.

Burdock pushed his way into the room and joined her reflection in the mirror, his ears perked, eyes curious. Erin looked at his liquid brown eyes.

'You'll stay with me, right?' she whispered. 'Since Stephan isn't here?'

Or was there time to call him? She scrabbled in her pocket for her phone, pulling it out with shaking hands. Stephan's number was the first in her call history and she listened to it connect.

Then go straight to voicemail.

She disconnected without leaving a message. Burdock stared up at her.

'Guess it's just you and me, then,' she said and glanced towards the door. 'And our feathered friend downstairs.'

Burdock didn't know exactly what she was talking about, but he gave a soft woof and pushed his nose into her cupped palm. There was always him, he tried to tell her. He was her very good dog.

'You're such a good guy, Burdock,' Erin whispered, and dropped a kiss on the top of his whiskery head. 'Let's do this, then.'

The raven gazed at her as she came back down the stairs. It was in the same place, on the back of the chair, and she marvelled once more at the size and weight of the bird. She wished she could draw it, every little detail as it perched there in her kitchen, but she knew that would be stalling.

And the raven wouldn't let her, anyway. It was all business, the way he looked at her.

She cleared her throat. 'I need to close the door,' she said, talking to the bird as if it could understand her. For all she knew, it could. She walked around it to the front door, which was wide open, the rest of the birds resting easily on the hedge around the garden, regarding her with bright interest.

'You ought to join your friends, don't you think?' she asked, hating how uncertain her voice sounded. She drew herself up to her full height, remembering Morghan telling her how important posture was. And a deep breath for composure. 'Out,' she said.

The bird regarded her without moving.

Erin opened her mouth. 'Or not,' she said. And waited a

beat longer, then closed the door with a quiet snick. Burdock stared at her.

It was quiet in the cottage, the thick stone walls insulation from the creaking and sighing of the trees in the wind. She looked once more at the bird, then went into the sitting room, opened the stove and stirred the fire to flames.

Morghan had taught her to speak to the flames as well. To water, to wind, to flame and stone.

All of them, she'd said, were alive with spirit.

As was everything in the world.

Erin was still adjusting to that idea, still trying to even figure it out, but she said the brief words of greeting and honour anyway, liking how they made her feel – a part of things. A part of all the important things.

'Friend of flame,' she said. 'Burn bright and beautiful. Your warmth wraps around me.'

She nodded her head, then fed a pair of neatly cut logs to the small tongues of flame that leapt from the embers of the fire that never really went out anymore. She kept it going night and day, looking after it like it really was alive. Putting it to bed at night, stirring it awake come the dawn.

Erin shut the door of the stove and went to the kitchen. The fire in the cooker could wait, she thought, aware that her thoughts were like feathers loose in a wind, fluttering here and there. She gathered them in with an effort, filled a glass with cold water from the tap, then, without glancing at the bird watching her every move, she went to the small sofa in the sitting room, put her glass down on a table and sat.

Burdock walked over and sat too, looking at her. Erin looked back at him.

'I have to go see Kria,' she said, as though the dog would understand her. 'I have to go back there. Macha said she needed help.'

And as if the words had conjured it, there was a sudden crackle of urgency in the air and Erin's hands tightened on the cushions. She wished Stephan were with her.

She lay back on the sofa, folding her hands across her chest, listening to the great thumping behind her ribs. How had she gone back last time? She tried to find the certainty and conviction she'd felt that time, that this was necessary, that she could do some good, that she was needed.

She was needed this time – Macha had come to tell her so, hadn't she?

Kria needed her.

And that was because there was a thread between them. Tying them to each other. Erin remembered this and reached for it. The red thread binding them together through time, through the mist – the only thing that could get through that mist, all the way down into the glen where the cold waters of the loch bit down on the stony shore, grinding its teeth on the gritted ground.

There it was. The thread, then the mist, the wash and slip of water on the shore. Erin stood there, hands clenched in the fabric of her dress, gazing around.

It was cold, and she shivered, hunching lower into her dress, wishing she hadn't taken her coat off. If she hadn't removed it and left it on the bannister, would she be wearing it now, too? Was that how it worked?

She didn't know because she'd taken it off. The air bit into the tender skin at her neck, wrapped itself around her wrists, and pressed against her cheeks, clammy, cold.

Kria was not there on the shore. Erin looked down at the stones at her feet, saw the ring of a cooking fire, the bits of wood in it burnt and black, crumbling. She reached down and put a hand over it. Cold. There had been no fire in there recently.

For a moment, Erin thought she could see Kria lying on the stones next to the fire, her spilled blood scarlet against the greyness, but the image shivered and faded. Erin swallowed, heart still pounding, in her ears as well as her chest.

The gravel of the loch shore crunched under her feet as she stepped away from the water, then turned to look out over the expanse of the lake. It was tight and deep between the steep hills of the valley, a huge crevasse filled with water the colour of milky emerald. It would have been beautiful, Erin thought, if it weren't quite so overwhelming. If the sun shone on it, turning the surface to dancing light.

But it was opaque, brooding under the sky of mist, under the weight of the land rising steeply from it, and the weight and bulk of it made her shiver harder.

Perhaps Kria was in the small stone building. Perhaps, Erin thought, Kria was ill, alone and suffering from fever in this terrible place where there was no one to help, no one to call to, no one to hear her cry out.

Except Erin was there. She was there to hear Kria's calling.

But the tiny building was empty. Erin stood in the middle of it, looking at the hearth, which was also dry and cold, and the bed, on which was a lumpen pile of furs and blankets. Erin reached for one, touching her fingertips to the thick pelt of an animal she didn't recognise, and stared at it for a long moment. Then she snatched it up, wrapping it tightly around her shoulders. The fur warmed her at once, and she stood looser, straighter, peering around the hut to see what else was there.

Some tools on one side, a couple earthenware pots. Erin wondered what year it was here in Kria's loch. She wished she'd paid more attention to history, but they'd never taught much of it at school anyway.

She wished she'd read the books Ambrose had left her with. Several of those had been history books, plotting their way through the palaeolithic to Neolithic to whatever came after that. All Erin knew about any of it was that the paleo diet was named after one of the eras. Or she guessed it was anyway.

Pulling the fur tighter around her shoulders, her fingers fumbled with a fastener she found on it, and then it was wrapped securely around her, hanging down to her knees.

'I'm sorry,' she whispered to whichever animal had given its skin to warm her now, then drew breath. 'I honour your life and sacrifice.'

The words were little enough, but she meant them with the whole of her heart. She no longer felt like a walking stalagmite. And perhaps – surely, considering the circumstances – the hunter of this beautiful animal had admired and appreciated them and been grateful? She tucked her hair behind her ears and ducked through the low doorway back out into the glen.

It was impossible to tell what time of day it was. The sky, when she gazed up at it, was a thick soup of cloud, an ashen helping of mashed potato piled up over the rim of the valley. Erin gazed about, scanning the length of scrubby land, as brown and barren as Kria had feared it would be.

The knowledge of how Kria had anticipated this initiation would go startled Erin. She looked inward at the knowledge that lay in her mind, certain and sure. Then nodded to herself, a thick, wet, and sluggish breeze flapping her hair damply against her cheeks.

Kria had felt nothing but fear and horror at this initiation. For her, there had been no honour in being chosen. Erin blinked.

Kria had been frightened and bitter about it before even stumbling down the sides of the glen. Erin closed her eyes. Caught a flash of something, chased it around her mind, lost it, shook her head.

If she wanted to know more, she'd have to find Kria herself, and perhaps this time, the girl would be able to see her, speak to her.

A gull pierced the cloud overhead, skimming its wings along the mist, and Erin lifted her chin to watch it, admiring the sleek stretch of it, committing the image of it to memory. When she woke, when she left this place, Burdock's tongue wet against her cheek, she would pick up pencil and paper and draw it.

It was the only living thing about and a moment later, it vanished back into the mist. Erin stood outside the house and looked at the point where it had disappeared, high above the steep sides of land. When she looked back down at the glen, she shivered, not from the cold this time, but from the heavy solitude of the place.

Everything was damp, cold, grey, and lonely. She needed to find Kria. To see another living person. To hear someone's else's voice, and then, perhaps, this place would seem more alive.

The grass under her feet crackled as if filled with frost as she stepped over it, not knowing where she was going, only heading away from the body of water at her back. There weren't many options of directions in which she could search for Kria. The glen was a narrow, steep-sided gash in the land. Kria would be somewhere in its barrenness.

Erin thought while she walked, scanning the side of the valley. She thought she could make out tracks through the scrub, and scrambled onto one of them, heading upwards to walk along halfway up the side of the valley.

A loch, she thought. A glen, she thought, repeating in her mind the words that came without prompting when she considered this place. Did that mean she was somewhere in Scotland? How many lochs were there in the country? She had no idea.

She had no idea of anything much. Erin stopped walking and gazed out over the barren valley. Already, the stone hut looked smaller, forlorn and dismal in the dim light. The water beside it was green-black from this height. Something made wide ripples across its surface and she shuddered, thoughts of loch monsters rearing up in her mind.

'I want to go home,' she said, her mouth dry, lips chapping in the cold. 'I want to wake up now.'

Because what good was she here, in this place?

The mist weighed down on her.

She knew nothing, she thought.

Nothing that could help anyone get out of this place.

19

Erin squeezed her eyes shut, willing herself to wake up. She cast around for the red thread, opening her palms hoping to find it twisted around her fingers.

But it was not there, and when she opened her eyes again, she stood where she'd been when she closed them. On the straggling path along the side of Kria's valley.

She felt like Alice in Wonderland. Well and truly down the rabbit hole. She looked up at the bowl of grey mist that was the sky, feeling the weight of it bearing down on her shoulders.

'Macha?' she said, her voice flat in the still air. 'Macha? Where are you?'

But there was no tingling in the air over her shoulder, no sizzling energy with which Macha introduced her presence. She was not there.

Erin gazed around the valley and shivered under her fur cloak. No one was here. Just her.

She took a gulping breath of the damp air. What had

she just told herself? That she was the only one here? That wasn't true – somewhere in this valley was Kria. Erin looked down at herself, checking that she was still herself and not Kria. The boots on her feet belonged in the twenty-first century. There was even dog hair on the skirt of her dress, Burdock's wiry brown hair. Erin rubbed her hands over the wool of the tunic she wore over thick leggings. It was as though this place sucked the life and hope from you.

Was that part of the spell, she wondered?

Another glance up at the sky. Undoubtedly, this place had some sort of magic spell over it. For a moment, she marvelled at the skill and knowledge it must have taken to make this valley like this in the first place. Skill and knowledge that had been lost in time since then.

The thought made her shiver and get moving again, balancing on the steep path along the side of the glen, following the bare trace of it, lips pressed together, determination grim inside her.

And in the back of her mind, the thought: how was this magic done? Why had it been forgotten?

She had so many questions.

She needed Macha – except she already knew Macha would tell her nothing, would simply stand there, lips twisted in amusement, waiting for her to figure it out all for herself.

She needed Morghan. Except, Morghan was almost exactly the same as Macha, despite one being spirit and one being flesh. Neither would tell her the answer. Morghan seemed determined not to teach her magic at all, only that everything was alive and beautiful, and everything in all worlds was connected.

This place was not beautiful, and it seemed barely alive, or if it was alive, then it was infected, a place of deep loneliness and despair.

Erin hushed her thoughts, finally, dizzy at their looping round and round. Instead, she focused on Kria. Where was she? Macha had said she needed help – but where was she?

Standing still again, leaning into the stiff grass on the hillside, Erin looked around her. She had a good vantage point, could see almost the whole length of the glen, shuddering away from the claustrophobia of the steep hills pressing in on her. She relaxed her clenched fists, forcing herself to relax, to seek Kria.

Because weren't they the same person, sort of? And didn't Morghan say there was always a thread of connection between soul aspects? That they could reach out and touch each other if they knew how. And even if they didn't know how to do that, the deep wounds and joys of one lifetime often echoed through to others.

Erin hadn't even believed in reincarnation before she'd come to Wilde Grove. She blinked into the chill breeze, letting her breathing slow. She hadn't ever really thought of it though – reincarnation. She'd been too busy trying to live the life she'd been saddled with.

There was a thread between her and Kria, though, and she found it, pinched it delicately in her mind between her fingers and held onto it.

She found Kria squatted on her haunches in a cave in the side of the hill. Mouth tugged downwards, Erin balked at edging into the tight space where there was every possibility that the earth would decide to close itself up around them. She squeezed her eyes tightly shut and telling herself there was no choice, she ducked her head and clambered into the cave, directing her mind away from the thought of spiders and long slithering beasties, walls and ceilings that pressed against the crown of her head, and she tucked herself beside the girl she'd once been several thousand years ago.

Kria had her hands in tight knots, the fingers white with pressure in the dim light from the mouth of the cave. Erin reached out and brushed her fingers against tensed shoulders, but Kria did not feel the touch, did not move or flinch. For all she knew, Erin was not there at all.

Erin, bent over, folded herself to her knees, fingering the fur she'd tugged around her shoulders. How could she have picked that up and be wearing it, yet not be real enough to touch Kria?

Her mind hurt with the puzzle of it and Erin touched the side of her head, wincing.

'Get away spirit,' Kria croaked suddenly, twisting her head slightly in Erin's direction. 'This is no place even for thee.'

For one long moment, Erin's head was blank, the screen of her mind white with static. She had seen what Kria was hunched over.

Bones.

A skeleton.

'If ye be this one,' Kria said, 'you're forsaken in this place, and I cannot help ye.' A choked laugh. 'I haven't the magic to do for either one of us.'

Who did the bones belong to? Erin blinked, pressed her fingertips to her eyes now, then looked again, shaking her head.

'How many have died here?' she asked out loud, her voice cracking in the dimness of the cave.

Kria's shoulders raised and fell. 'More than have left this goddess-forsaken place.' She reached out and touched the foot bones, lying like pebbles on the dirt floor. 'Mine will join them soon enough, I'll warrant.'

Erin shook her head, knowing even as she did so that it was true. Kria's body would lie on the shore of the loch, flesh rotting away until her bones were all that were left, like bleached driftwood.

'You must not do it,' Erin said, desperate. 'Please, don't do it.'

Kria's laugh was harsh like the cry of the gulls she so despised. 'You're a likely one to tell me so,' she said. 'Seeing as how we are squatting over your own bones.'

'They are not mine,' Erin said.

Kria's head dropped to her chest. 'That is sad news for me then,' she said. 'For I thought I'd found a soul to talk to, and now I learn 'tis only my desperate need speaking to me as though from another's lips.'

Erin shook her head, hair flying around her face. 'No,' she said. 'I mean, I am you, but...' She wound down to silence, tongue-tied at the complicated tangle that she herself did not understand.

Perhaps she was dreaming this? Simply one of her episodes? And she was only making up meaning where there was none, just because it was better than wandering lost in the mists as she'd used to do.

Kria had turned to gaze at Erin beside her in the cave, narrowing her eyes at the form of a woman in fur. 'Aye,' she said. 'You're a spirit for certain, but you're not myself.

I've not a face like yours.' She touched her own skin, running her fingers over the spiral tattoo on her cheek. 'Your skin is as smooth and clear as an infant's.' She turned back to the bones. 'Which do you belong to, then?' she asked. 'If not this one, is there then another I've yet to come across?'

'No,' Erin answered. 'I mean, I don't know. But I'm not one of them.'

Kria's eyes were dark, shadowed in the dimness. 'Do ye ken anything, then?' she asked, and turned away again, shifting on her feet. ''Tis what I'd expect of me,' she said idly, staring at the bones. 'To conjure a spirit as empty-headed as this one is now.' She stared at the skull that looked sightlessly at the roof of the cave.

She spat on the ground at the foot of the skeleton. 'Bah,' she said.

Her scramble backwards from the cave into the open air was ungainly, but she was long past caring about such things. For starters, who was there to watch her do anything here? Kria turned and eyed the spirit emerging from the cave, taking in the long red hair, the fur tucked around her shoulders. The spirit shimmered in the grey light, a bright flame in the dullness that was Kria's valley.

The spirit was wringing her hands. 'Aren't you going to do something?' it asked.

Kria raised an eyebrow. 'Do something like what?'

It glanced towards the mouth of the miserable cave, the hands still knotting themselves around each other, as pale as pearls. 'With...that?'

'With that?' Kria shook her head. 'And tell me for a moment why I should? When my bones will lie here in this valley too before long, and no one to say the prayers over them? Why should I do for her what no one will do for me?'

The spirit turned and blinked at her with eyes as deeply shadowed as the loch below them.

'Macha said you needed help,' it whispered.

Macha?

Kria snorted. Now she knew she was merely dreaming awake. The solitude had finally eaten through her mind. She had conjured a shade of her own guilty conscience. Well, that as may be, but she'd have none of it all the same.

'The goddess no longer cares what happens to me,' she said, and turning, she picked her way down the steep slope. The sun was already waning, and her stomach groaned with a sudden, sharp hunger.

'The goddess?' Erin repeated, following Kria down the slope, stumbling where the other woman leapt as fleet footed as a goat. 'How long have you been here?' she asked.

'You're still here?' Kria shook her head, long hair snarled with braids and twigs. 'You've no need to keep me company if you've only absurdities to utter.'

Erin frowned and fell silent. This wasn't what she'd expected. For all the loneliness that Kria must suffer in this dreadful place – here she was pushing her away. It made no sense.

Of course, Erin thought, Kria did not believe she was talking to a real person. She licked her lips and tasted the wetness of the mist upon them. Bending her head, she followed Kria in silence.

In the growing huddle of twilight, Erin watched as Kria built a fire in the hearth between stone hut and loch. Her face was shadowed, but the skin was still smooth with youth under the grime. The tattoo on her cheek glowed in the lingering light. Erin raised her hand and touched her own cheek, as though to find the same symbol there. She'd seen it on Macha's skin, and now Kria's. When had they stopped etching it in ink on themselves?

The answer came to her with a sudden certainty. With the coming of the Christians. When such pagan practices became evil, had to be stamped out.

'How will you light it?' Erin asked, looking at the carefully positioned pile of twigs in the hearth.

Kria looked up at her with a frown. 'Why are ye still here?' she said, then shook her head. 'Stay if ye wish, if ye have never seen magic done.' Everyone knew this could be done, even if most no longer had the skill. This shade was even stupider than she looked.

But for a moment, Kria forgot about the spirit watching her. She had to concentrate. It had been long enough she'd spent here that her magic, without praise and reward, grew dimmer. Less important. It was just a tool now.

There was nothing to delight in here in this place.

She cupped her filthy hands together and breathed deeply, reaching out to seek the spark of fire in the damp air. Then, as every time she did this, she had to remind herself that there was no spark of anything in this heavy, dead place.

And so she pulled the spark of fire from herself, knowing as she did so that she pulled from a lessening pyre. How could she replenish her own vitality, her own spark, when she was in this glen where nothing but stiff, tasteless grasses and roots grew, where even the fish tasted of nothing but green water?

Erin gasped as light flared within the cupped container of Kria's hands. She pressed her own hand to her chest when Kria dropped the tiny flame she'd magicked from nowhere and it bit into the dried grasses and twigs that lay there waiting for it. Her head spun as she watched Kria lean forward and blow on the fire until the tiny spark was hissing flame.

'How did you do that?' she said, shaking her head slowly from side to side.

'What?' Kria asked. 'Do ye not have the ability from wherever it is I've conjured your likeness?'

Erin shook her head harder and dropped to her knees beside the fire, wanting to feel the heat from it, reassure herself that what she'd seen was real.

Kria's dark eyes took her in. She shifted uncertainly on the stony shore. 'Tell me where I've conjured ye from.'

Mouth dry, Erin swallowed. 'I am you,' she said. 'Sent to help.'

'Nay, but ye are not me, nor any resemblance.' She looked down at her fire and shook her head. 'And the goddess would not send me anyone – not here. That is not how this place works.' She heaved herself to her feet and made for the stone hut. 'We are left here to rot, that is how this place works.'

Erin stared after her, mind whirling. Kria thought she was talking to a figment of her imagination – and Erin didn't think she could blame her.

But when Kria returned, a dead fish in her hands, Erin looked away from the scales that silvered Kria's hands and tried again.

'How can that be?' she asked. 'Has no one ever gotten out of here?'

Kria's shoulders hunched as she bent over a stone and worked her knife into the fish's belly. 'They have,' she answered.

'Then do you know how?'

The tip of the knife bit into the flesh and sliced a line, Kria's hand only trembling slightly. 'I do not,' she said. 'That part of the story is never told.'

Erin closed her eyes as Kria scraped the guts onto the stones. She swallowed and looked out over the brooding rippling water of the loch.

'What part is?'

The knife stilled a moment in Kria's hand. 'What part of which?' she asked, looking at last over at her visiting spirit. 'Ye have an enormous number of questions for a piece of my own mind.'

'Well, perhaps that is what you need,' Erin retorted. She spread a hand. 'To be asking more questions. From what I see, you're not doing anything to find the way out.' Huh. Maybe she had a bit of Macha in her after all.

Kria left the fish splayed open on the stone and stood slowly, her knife hand falling by her side, its blade red with blood.

Erin dragged her gaze from the knife, knowing it was the same one she'd seen beside Kria's dead body. She swallowed down the sudden lump in her throat.

'What did ye say?' Kria demanded.

'I think you heard me,' Erin said faintly.

'I heard ye say I was doing nothing to get myself out of this miserable and forsaken hole in the earth.'

Straightening, Erin looked over at Kria from the opposite side of the fire. 'If you can make fire out of thin air,' she said. 'I'm sure you can find the way past those mists.' She shrugged a shoulder at the sky.

Kria stared at her a long moment, then shook her head and dropped to her knees, turning her attention back to the fish and her dinner. 'Bringing forth fire is child's play,' she said. 'I have no problem working the elements.'

'The mist – isn't that water, or air, or something?' Erin heard the rising desperation in her voice and drew the fur tighter around her neck as if to stop the noise of it reaching her lips.

'They are a different level of magic,' Kria answered. 'Do ye not think I've been up there and tried?'

Of course she had. It would have been the first thing Erin would have done, in her shoes.

But Kria hadn't finished. 'I've many skills, or so I was led to believe, but none come close to what is needed to part those mists. They are woven tight over this damned place and will not budge.'

'Then how are you supposed to get out of here?' Erin cried.

Kria chopped the head off the fish. 'Aye, well, if we knew that, we wouldn't be here now, would we?'

Erin sat down on the stones and held her hands out to the fire. Despite its mysterious beginnings, it warmed her skin like any other flame.

'What did they tell you, then?' she asked. 'When you were brought here?'

'Only that I must see my own way out,' Kria replied. She glanced over at the spirit, sitting for all the world like a real person warming its hands at the fire. 'Ye are a real spirit, are ye not?' she asked suddenly, knife blade paused over the fish's tail.

Erin thought about it for a moment. 'I guess so,' she said. 'I mean – that's probably what it looks like, since this isn't my own time or life.'

'Time or life?'

Plucking up a water-smoothed stone, Erin weighed it in her hand before answering. 'I'm who you will be – or rather,' she corrected herself, thinking of Morghan's lessons, 'I'm an aspect of who you are.' God but it was complicated. 'I mean, we are aspects of the same soul.' She huffed out a breath.

'Ye are a shard of my own soul?' Kria asked, the fish forgotten. Perhaps this was a spirit worth the energy of conversing with.

'Yes, or at least, I guess so.'

'Ye don't seem to know an awful lot.'

'You got that right,' Erin muttered. 'I know barely anything, except that if you don't get out of here, you're going to die.' She blinked. 'Right here, on the shore of this loch.'

Kria's laugh was as loud as any gull cry. 'Aye, well, you've got that one right. And there'll be no one to sing over my bones, just like that poor thing in the cave we saw.'

For a moment, Erin felt the stirring of Macha's presence behind her, and then the air stilled, and she was gone. 'You could sing over them,' she said. 'The bones in the cave.'

Kria picked up the fish and flung it carelessly onto one of the stones in the hearth. 'She is long gone without me, and her failure is no antidote to my own.' She rocked back on her heels and for a moment, her face softened in sadness and grief. 'I've no songs left, you see.' She touched her chest. 'This great aloneness, it takes all softness from your heart. Leaves you like stone.' She turned to stare out over the water that ate constantly at her mind. 'No songs, and the goddess has not listened to a single prayer since my arrival in this place.' She shook her head and her braids slapped against her cheeks.

'I do not think the good lady lives here.' The water darkened towards black as the sun sank from the reach of the glen. 'Nothing lives here except horror and myself.'

Kria's mouth twisted. 'And soon, shard of my soul, I'll not be here but for my lifeless corpse either.'

The image of Kria's bleeding body rose in Erin's mind and she stuffed her knuckles in her mouth to stifle her scream.

20

'Who are the Shining Ones?' Winsome asked, pouring the tea and feigning nonchalance. She put a cup in front of the other chair and sat down, hoping Morghan would come away from the window, out of which she kept staring as though seeing something there that Winsome could not.

'The Fae,' Morghan answered. 'The ancestors. Us.' She came away from the window and sat down, frowned at the tea steaming pale amber in the cup. She could smell the herbs Stephan had used to make it, and knew it was one of his special blends, with chamomile, lavender, holy basil, and lemon balm in it. She could recite every ingredient because Mrs. Palmer had been very excited about it when Stephan had first given the calming blend to them.

'Us?' Winsome asked, glad Morghan was answering her questions.

Morghan took a long, slow breath, trying to place herself in the room with Winsome. She glanced up at the ceiling of her bedroom, half expecting to see the sky above the hilltop.

And it was there, off-centre, in the very edges of her gaze. Barely a shadow. She looked about the rest of the room, and over at Winsome, blinked a few times, but what she was seeing now did not go away. Leaning forward, she looked in her cup at the tea. It glowed with the vitality of the herbs Stephan had put into it. She shook her head slightly and transferred her attention to Winsome, looking with her new gaze.

'You've been doing a lot of work,' she said after a moment of seeing.

Winsome flushed. 'Work?' she said, nonplussed. Whatever she'd expected Morghan to say, it hadn't been that. 'What do you mean?'

'Exercising your spirit,' Morghan said, seeing the delicate golden light threading through Winsome's aura. It was beautiful and her own spirit lifted to see it, floated a little on the warmth of the sight.

Winsome cleared her throat. 'Well, erm, yes, I suppose so. I've been doing the exercises you and Ambrose taught me.' She paused for a moment. 'And prayer, of course.' She couldn't help it – she had to ask. 'That little...summerhouse in the trees behind the church..?'

A smile lifted Morghan's lips. 'The temple. What of it?'

'Never mind,' Winsome said. 'Never mind at all.'

'It's a lovely spot. Have you been making use of it?'

She shouldn't have mentioned it, Winsome thought. 'Once or twice,' she admitted. Then decided to turn the conversation back to what should be the matter in hand.

'I heard what you said,' she continued. 'In the stone circle, I mean.' Winsome picked up her cup and looked in it for a moment. Morghan had stared so strangely into hers.

'But I don't know what you were talking about – or to whom.'

Morghan gazed about the room. She wanted suddenly to go outside, see what it looked like out there. To see if this new effect would stop by the time she got down the stairs and out the door into the garden. How much more astonishing would it be to see the trees in all this glory? She was used to sensing the general energy of the web, but this was far more, this was seeing the warp and the weft of the world as the web wove through everything.

This was like stepping again into the ancient one – Ravenna, the Faerie Queen had called her – and seeing the world through her eyes. Morghan looked down at her hand, the one she knew gleamed gold in another reality. She caught a glimpse of it and sucked in a breath, blinking.

'Morghan?' Winsome said. 'Are you all right?'

Morghan shifted her gaze to Winsome sitting across from her. 'I have split open,' she said and touched her head, then moved her hand to hold the egg she wore against her breast. 'Everything is alive, connected by a living web of energy – information.' She squinted a moment, but the vision didn't change. She could see the web. 'Love.'

Winsome gazed around the room as though looking for it, then zeroed back in on Morghan. 'And you can see this?'

A nod. 'At the moment I can, yes,' Morghan said, and if she'd had any tears left, she'd have wept again. 'And it's such a relief, after the things I've been seeing the last few days.' She breathed slowly and deeply, steadying herself.

Aware that Winsome was looking at her, she put on a smile. 'What did I say in the stone circle? Do you remember?'

'Do you?' Winsome asked suspiciously.

But Morghan shook her head. 'Not entirely, no.'

'It sounded...like some sort of prophecy or something.'

Morghan laughed and the sound danced out into the air, a series of small golden bells. She had many gifts, but none had ever been the gift – or curse – of prophecy.

She sobered. Until now, perhaps. With all Ravenna had been showing her.

'Help me remember.'

Winsome licked her lips. She was slightly dazed. One minute Morghan had been bawling her eyes out and shaking like a leaf in a storm, and now she was gazing around the room like a child seeing butterflies for the first time. Winsome couldn't keep up.

But then, this was Morghan Wilde, and Winsome seldom felt as though she could keep up.

'Erm. Something like this, I think,' Winsome said, and brought the words to her mind again, where they'd been lurking since she'd heard Morghan utter them.

'What was once ours will be so again. The Shining Ones are with us and we shall walk with them in our rightful place, for we shine also.'

Winsome's voice faltered for a moment, but she cleared her throat and recited the rest of it. 'But before us darkness swarms and seeks to sap our strength, to sow its seeds of chaos and lies.' She stared down into her teacup. 'And then you asked: How to dispute them? How to shine brightly in this darkness? To weave the web ever stronger?'

Morghan nodded as her own words were said back to her. She sat in the chair for a long moment, still, considering, then sighed. 'I've had a very eventful few days,' she said.

Winsome shifted in her seat. 'Mrs. Palmer said that sometimes things can be seen that are...difficult,' she said and lifted her eyes to Morghan's. 'Is that what has happened?' She paused only a second before asking her next question. 'And what is this swarm of darkness?' Just saying the words made her shiver and for a moment, she was back in the churchyard for some reason, listening to poor Rosalie Busby's quavering voice saying *There's odd things been happening, Vicar. Things that distress me. We need it blessed.*

And Winsome remembered the feeling that had crept over her then, like a premonition.

Morghan sighed where she sat, her cup held loosely in her hands. She set it on the table and pressed her palms to her head instead, holding it for a moment and closing her eyes. Inside her skull everything felt expanded, wide open.

'I've seen things I can't unsee,' she said, eyes still closed, looking inside at her own mind instead. Seeing the clifftop, the view of the churning sky and ocean, the black swarm shadowing the Earth. The refugees landing upon the shore of the Isle of Healing, bruised and shaken.

And yet.

And yet, over it all, hung the threads of the web, knitting everything together the way it always had, the way it always would.

She dropped her hands back to her lap and opened her eyes to look across at Winsome, who still shone, whose aura wavered back and forth in some unseen draft, shot through with threads of gold.

'I've not told you, I think,' Morghan said. 'Of the way things used to be.'

Winsome didn't know. Morghan had told her so many things over the last month. Too many to be taken in. Winsome found she had to sit with them, digesting them one at a time, seeing where they fit in with what she knew of the truth. It had been a greatly disconcerting time.

She shook her head a little.

Morghan smiled, little more than a twitch of the lips. 'I've told this more than once recently, so it is hard to remember.' She breathed in, picking out the fragrance of the tea again, bright clear notes in the air, and underneath it, the keen scent of the wind on the other side of the glass, carrying with it the dark undertones of soil and tree.

'But I have been shown it over and over lately,' she continued, and went on to speak as though telling a story.

'Once,' she said. 'A long time ago, many thousands of years ago, we were a people who lived in knowledge of our souls, in relationship to the land, moving across it in time with the seasons, honouring the gifts it gave us to sustain us, acknowledging the goddesses and gods, honouring their kin – our kin – and living, if not in step, then in respect with our faerie neighbours. No life was more or less than another, whether man or woman or wolf.' Morghan looked down at her hands as she spoke, turning them one way then the other, watching the way her right hand gleamed in the light from window and lamp.

'But,' she sighed. 'Flesh has weight to it, and while it brings experiences we cannot help but value, it also eventually chafed and bruised the soul that was unused to the limitations of flesh while at the same time enamoured with it. Eventually, after a very long time, we became forgetful and entangled. Our minds grew concerned with our hungry bellies, with the strength of our own arms and legs, and the apparent weakness of other's. We grew greedy alongside our forgetfulness, for land, resources, food, sex. We spent less and less time between incarnations, our focus grew narrower, towards physical gratification. We forgot that our bodies were meant to be only vehicles of experience for our souls, a dance and a joy.'

Morghan paused, picked up her tea and took a sip. 'We forgot that everything we do has consequences, until the point we're at now, when we look away from our deaths because we believe nothing comes after them, and so life is cheap and sharp and there is only the fleeting pleasures we can wrangle for ourselves.'

She looked out the window, seeing again the swarming darkness, the hungry ocean, the Shining Ones. She saw it, but was not cowed by it, because she could see too the web that knit together the world. All worlds.

'There are many spirits out there,' she said, watching the seething darkness and feeling the dribble of tears upon her cheeks once more as her heart hurt for them. 'Many who find themselves lost, either trapped not knowing they've passed, or tumbling back into life after life, not awake enough to make choices, too materialistic during their incarnations to find their way to their true soul's purpose.' She sighed. 'So too are there as many more who enjoy the chaos, the meanness, the tricks and games, who come back deliberately over and over to see how much damage they can do. Their experience of flesh, their delight in the power of it, has maimed them.' She winced at the pain of it. 'They flock together between lives, like schoolyard bullies, and are hungry for whatever power and sensation they can wrest for themselves, attaching to those of us who are vulnerable, depressed, angry, desperate.'

Morghan wound down a little, looked across at Winsome, wiped her cheeks with her golden hand. 'We have forgotten so much about death, you see,' she said. 'We've forgotten how important it is. How it is the doorway back to our souls, to wholeness, to more and continued life. We do not face our own deaths, and we do not take care of those around us who are ready to depart this world for the next.' She shook her head. 'We've forgotten too, how important life is, how valuable this experience can be for our souls, and how it is supposed to be joy-filled. We have made it instead filled with pain and suffering and constant want. We have become filled with fear, of living, of others.'

'And it's worse than ever,' Winsome said in barely more than a whisper. 'Now we are killing the very planet we live on, with our selfishness and hunger for money.'

'Yes,' Morghan agreed. 'We've been corrupted in this way for a great long time. The faerie separated themselves from us as we turned from them, from reciprocity towards dominance, and our violence and rot became too much, but now, this is the first time we have put the very ground at our feet in danger. And while the faerie have been living just out of the seeing of most of us for thousands of years now, our worlds are still joined. What we do affects them.' She drew in a deep breath and looked Winsome in the eye.

'And they will act,' she said. 'Are acting. They will confront us, claim sovereignty over the land, and their faces are many and fearsome and we will find them terrifying.' She shook her head. 'Unless we all wake up to the reality of the world, I fear for so many of us.'

Winsome's mouth was dry. Her tongue lay in her mouth, thick and ungainly. She licked her lips and her tongue rasped against them. 'What will happen to us?' she asked.

'I don't know,' Morghan replied. 'We must wake up, to have any hope. We must evolve.' She swept a hand around at the room. 'This collective losing of our minds that we see everywhere must be brought to a halt. Our world is clotted with spirits who have lost the ability to remember themselves and something needs to be done about that.'

Winsome was shaking her head, although not in disagreement. 'And the, erm, Shining Ones, the faerie, they will do what?' She coughed slightly. 'Is there, erm, going to be some sort of war?'

'They have other means than war,' Morghan said, and she looked down at her golden hand again. What was the story Ambrose had said referenced a golden hand? She needed to hear the story properly, learn just what the Queen's gift meant. Learn just what she was supposed to do – how she was supposed to teach enough so that it made any sort of difference. 'They will pry minds and spirits open, even of those not ready.'

'What are we supposed to do, then? How do we be ready for that?' Winsome asked, in an echo of Morghan's own thoughts, part of her appalled at the fact that she found herself believing every word of what her friend had said. She plucked from her mind the questions Morghan had asked in the stone circle.

'How to shine brightly in the darkness?' she asked. 'How to weave the web ever stronger?'

Morghan put her hands on her knees. 'There are only a few things that allow us to shine brightly and strengthen the web.' She smiled slightly. 'Right thought and right action. Compassion. Remembering and stepping into our soul's true journey.'

'Oh,' Winsome said. 'That will be a piece of cake, then.' She made a show of glancing at her wrist to check the time. 'We should be able to round up all seven point six billion of us to start doing that by, well, Thursday at the latest.'

21

WINSOME TUCKED HER HANDS UNDER HER ARMPITS AND pressed her lips together. Her hands wouldn't stop shaking and they had to. She couldn't go visit one of her parishioners doing a good impersonation of a jellyfish now, could she? No, she couldn't.

The trouble was that ever since her chat with Morghan the day before, she'd been nervous, peering around corners as though she was going to see one of Morghan's Shining Ones pouncing on her.

She swallowed, her mouth dry as the Gobi desert. Or worse, she thought, would to be see one of those marauding dark entities. It was one of those she really wasn't prepared to meet.

'Why, God,' she croaked, 'is there so much to be afraid of in this world?'

She closed her eyes and held that question in her mind, seeking the answer for it. When it came to her in the form of another question, she was surprised.

Why are you afraid?

The answer to that one was obvious, wasn't it? The swarming dark entities. The ones Morghan said went searching for mischief and mayhem, thriving on chaos and pain.

Yeah, those ones. Winsome held her hands out in front of her. They still shook.

That's why she was afraid, and wasn't that a good enough reason? She rubbed her face, standing in front of the table where she put her handbag and keys. She was only going to talk to Rosalie Busby and her family, she reminded herself. She wasn't toddling off to perform an exorcism.

Now she'd scared herself worse. The trouble, she thought, with acknowledging that there was a whole unseen – usually unseen – world alongside the one you so blithely walked about in, ate, slept, and laughed in, was that you couldn't make the awareness of it go away. It lurked there at the edge of consciousness ever after, and everything you did or thought had to take it into consideration.

And yet, she considered, Morghan hadn't been afraid. The tears that had streamed down her cheeks had not come from fear. When she'd spoken of the dark entities, she'd been crying for their pain, not from fear of them.

Winsome took a deep breath then barked a laugh. Instead of *what would Jesus do*, she kept finding herself asking what Morghan Wilde would do.

'Right,' she said out loud. 'I'm going.' It was only for a sit down and a chat, she reminded herself. Even though Mrs. Busby had asked for a blessing, Winsome wanted to get the lie of the land before she did one. Not that she had anything against doing blessings of any sort – quite the opposite, in fact – but families were complicated things, and she wanted to get a better idea of what might, or might not, be going on inside Mrs. Busby's tiny terrace house.

MINNIE HAD HER EARPHONES IN. NOW, ALL SHE COULD HEAR was static, but she didn't care. Every now and then a word or phrase would come through, and her dad would be talking to her again. She'd been wearing her earphones practically since she'd downloaded the Ghost Radio app.

'What do you want?' she asked, ready to come up with some reason why she couldn't do whatever it was her mother was leaning in the doorway to ask her to do. 'I'm busy.'

'What are you doing?' Natasha asked.

'Nothing.'

They stared at each other for a moment, then Natasha sighed and dropped her eyes. She just didn't have the energy to deal with Minnie and her horrible black hair and the silly cloak she'd taken to wearing all the time. Robin had a cold, and even though Natasha knew it was just a cold – he got one every time the seasons changed, and it was full-on winter now – she couldn't help the niggling thought that it wasn't just a simple innocent cold, but the virus. Even telling herself that was nonsense, that no one in Wellsford had the virus, she couldn't stop waiting for him to have convulsions, or stop being able to breathe normally, or whatever it was the virus did to little kids. Didn't it do extra special things when the person with it was just a little kid?

She rubbed her hands together, a compulsive gesture. She'd been washing them a lot, recently. Not wanting to get the virus from Robin, even though she knew he didn't have it. She didn't seem to be able to stop washing them anyway, and they were red and getting raw. She yanked down the sleeves of her jumper over her knuckles. Cleared her throat.

'Gran is having the vicar around and would like all of us to come down and have a cup of tea with her.'

Minnie looked across at her mother from where she was sitting on her bed. Her eyes were wide, incredulous. 'You're kidding me, right?' she said.

Natasha rubbed at a knuckle. 'I think we need to remember whose house we're living in.'

'I didn't ask to come live here,' Minnie said, and she looked back down at her phone. The torch had just come on and the words she'd really come to like flashed across the screen.

Entity present.

She closed her eyes and felt herself swell inside with importance. Her Dad was here. He hated her being at her grandmother's place too. He was doing his best to comfort her, even from the afterlife.

There was a loud crash in the room across the hall, and Natasha turned, startled, eyes widening. 'What was that?'

Minnie shrugged. 'Dunno,' she said.

In her ears, the Ghost Radio crackled, hissed. *Me,* it said. *I'm here.*

Minnie giggled. Got up from the bed and pushed past her mother. 'Guess we'd better see what it was,' she said, curious herself now.

The crash had come from her Grandmother's tiny room and Minnie pushed the door open. She didn't need to step into the room to see what had made the noise. 'It's the lamp,' she said.

Natasha squeezed into the doorway beside her, then stepped into the room, bending to pick up the lamp. 'Ugh,' she said. 'What's this water on the floor?' Confused, she looked at the lamp she was holding, but it was a lamp, not a vase, and the water couldn't have come from it. The lamp wasn't even broken, even though from the noise of the crash, by all rights it should have been.

'Gran must have knocked over some water,' Minnie said, turning away before her mother could see the smirk on her face. 'Well done,' she whispered.

Her father knew she hated being here, stuck in this tiny house with her Grandmother who walked around all day with her mouth all pinched together and disapproving. He'd said he'd help Minnie convince her mother to get them their own place.

She didn't believe Natasha when she said they couldn't afford to move out. Even if she didn't have a job, she still got the dole or whatever, right? And there were places around town to rent, Minnie knew there were. She'd been on a scouting mission, looking for empty houses they could move into.

The only thing her Dad hadn't been enthusiastic about since she'd got the Ghost Radio was her joining Wilde Grove.

His electronic voice had called them losers and boring. He said she was made for better things. That together they could do more than she'd ever be able to do if she joined them.

Minnie had been kind of disappointed about that, but

then she'd realised that of course her father was in a better position than she was to know what was what.

And it meant that she wouldn't have to worry about nicking a pack of tarot cards from Haven. She was planning to do just that as soon as the shop opened up again after this latest boring lockdown.

Natasha came out of her mother's room and looked at her daughter. Minnie had flopped back down on the bed again, her phone gripped tight in her hand, the white wire going from phone to her ears like some new sort of umbilical cord.

Tiny had said that she kept hearing Minnie talking in the middle of the night, but when she'd asked Minnie about it, her daughter had just rolled her eyes and said Tiny was dreaming.

'So,' Natasha tried again. 'Will you come down and at least say hello?'

Minnie blinked at her. 'Hello to who?'

The voice in her ear spoke. *Prunish bitch,* it said. Or it might have been prudish, Minnie didn't know. She got the idea anyway. 'Mum or the vicar?' she asked.

Natasha frowned at her. 'What? I'm right here. The vicar when she gets here, of course.'

Basher.

Basher? Minnie puzzled over it for a moment before understanding dawned. Bible basher, he meant. She shook her head.

'No way,' she said.

'What about if I asked you to,' Natasha said. 'As a favour to me?' She cleared her throat and wrung her hands. Her mother had insisted she get Minnie down to see the church woman. They'd had an argument about it. Ever since Tiny had gone racing downstairs saying that Minnie was talking to her dead father, Rosalie had decided the shadows she'd been seeing were because of that.

Personally, Natasha hadn't seen any shadows, but there were a few odd things happening. Clunks and thunks in the pipes, and the electric seemed screwed up. Sometimes things worked and sometimes they didn't. And the light bulbs kept blowing. They were spending a fortune on new bulbs.

She waited for Minnie to answer her.

Minnie opened her mouth to repeat herself. No way. But then, she had a thought. Wouldn't it be fun to play with the vicar a little? She could have her on about being part of an institution that was single-handedly responsible for the destruction of thousands of innocent women.

'Okay,' she said.

Natasha stared at Minnie, then narrowed her eyes. 'Okay?' she repeated.

'Yeah,' Minnie answered. 'Sure. Why not.'

Natasha regarded her daughter for a moment, but Minnie had turned her face away towards the wall, hand going to her ear to push the earphones in tighter. Natasha backed away and went down the stairs to get a tea towel to wipe up the spill of water in her mother's bedroom. Her mother wasn't getting Alzheimer's, was she, she wondered? That would be all she needed on top of everything else. A dead bloody husband, a baby who was sick with what might be the virus, two daughters, one of whom had decided she was a militant witch feminist whatever, and now a mother turning doddering in her old age and all the care homes closed with the lockdown. Not that they'd ever be able to afford a care home anyway.

She sighed and went into the kitchen, snatching up a towel. How her mother hadn't noticed the bloody great puddle in the middle of the floor, she didn't know.

When she got back upstairs, she sniffed at it, just to make sure it was water. And not something worse, since there was no water glass on the box her mother was using as a bedside table.

But it smelt just like water, and it wasn't yellow at all, so Natasha mopped it up, and carried the dripping tea towel back downstairs, then forgot about it.

'VICAR,' ROSALIE BUSBY SAID, HOLDING THE DOOR OPEN JUST wide enough for Winsome to squeeze through. 'I'm so glad you could make it.' She ushered Winsome through to the tiny front room, where the two bars of the electric heater were glowing hot.

Winsome nodded, glancing surreptitiously around the room. The wallpaper was old, faded, unchanged, she thought, from the sixties or seventies. There were no family photos on the mantlepiece, just a couple faded prints on the walls, and a biggish television taking up one corner opposite the sagging sofa and armchair. A pile of crossword magazines sat on a table beside the couch.

'Please,' Rosalie said. 'Make yourself comfy, Vicar, and I'll get us some tea and tell Natasha that you're here.'

Winsome smiled her thanks, and took her coat off, tucking it on the armchair behind her. There was a damp spot on one of the walls, and she winced, wishing people weren't forced to live like this.

But the room was tidy enough, a young child's toys tucked away into a box in the corner. And someone had vacuumed recently, she guessed.

The door opened again, and Rosalie came in, carrying a tray with cups and a teapot on it. Trailing behind her was a tall thin woman with hair that needed a good cut. And a wash.

'This is my daughter Natasha,' Rosalie said, setting the tray down on the table and awkwardly sweeping the magazines onto the floor. 'She's been staying at mine for a couple months now, her and her kiddies.'

Winsome smiled. 'I won't get up and shake your hand,' she said. 'I'm not entirely sure we're even supposed to be meeting like this, but to my mind it's essential work, so there it is, and I'm pleased to meet you.'

Natasha moved her lips in what Winsome guessed could pass for a smile, but was really more of a grimace, and sat down on the couch, tucking her hands between her knees, the fingers twined together as she hunched over herself.

Rosalie was fussing with the tea things.

Winsome accepted a cup from her and murmured her thanks. When Rosalie sat down next to her daughter, her brow wrinkled in a worried frown, Winsome gave them both her most sympathetic smile.

'This year has been such a tough one,' she said, her voice smooth and warm. 'You've had an especially difficult couple years, I understand, Natasha?'

She got a nod in response to the question, but that was all. Natasha looked down at her hands, rubbing her thumb across her knuckles. Robin would be awake in a few minutes, and she wanted to pop outside into the narrow backyard, where she had a plastic outdoor chair set up, and have a ciggie before he started up his yowling.

'Natasha's husband died two years ago, didn't he, love?' Rosalie said, looking at the thin twig of her daughter. 'Left her with three kids to bring up.'

Natasha cleared her throat. 'I was pregnant with Robin when Rog died. Heart attack,' she said, looking away from her hands finally and shaking her head. 'We did alright for a while though, mostly.' Her voice trailed off for a moment, then started up again. 'I had a job, and they kept it open for me after Robin was born.' She shrugged, worried at a hangnail. 'It wasn't much, but it kept me sane, you know?'

Winsome nodded. She could well imagine.

'And then the virus came along, right? And I lost the job, because my neighbour wouldn't look after Robin anymore, and I wasn't making enough for regular childcare, and the place where I worked closed down, and the kids were home all day.' The words came out of her mouth in a rush. Her voice was thin, aggrieved. She hunched tighter into herself. 'Then I couldn't pay the rent, and we were on the street.'

'So you came home to Wellsford,' Winsome said, wondering how often the same story had played out all over the country.

Natasha stuck her thumb nail in her mouth and bit down on it, then realised what she was doing and looked at her hands in horror. She needed to go wash them – what was she thinking, sticking them into her goddamned mouth?

'Didn't want to come here,' she said suddenly, harshly.

'Mum and I haven't been close in forever, you know? And it's tiny here, and there's nothing in Wellsford. No work.' She got up, rubbing her hands against the blue denim of her jeans. 'Robin's gonna wake up,' she said. 'I gotta go get him. He's sick.'

Rosalie watched in dismay as Natasha scuttled from the room, head down, teeth biting down on the knuckle of her thumb, gnawing at it where it was already raw. She looked back at Winsome.

'I'm sorry,' she said. 'She's not doing very well.' Rosalie picked up her cup and saucer and they clattered against each other.

'It's completely understandable,' Winsome said. 'Why don't you tell me how you're getting on.' She smiled gently. 'You said things were happening in the house that were causing you distress? It must be very difficult for you all, to share such a small space.' Winsome leaned forward a little. 'And for you – when you were used to your own space and routine. I imagine it's been quite an adjustment.' She blinked, trying to see Rosalie Busby's spirit to take the temperature of it, so to speak. It was mottled and faded looking when she saw it and tucked in tight around the small woman.

Rosalie cleared her throat and looked down into her cup of tea. She'd not tasted it yet. Instead, she sighed, risked a glance over at the vicar. She wished it helped, Winsome being a woman, but it wasn't like going to the doctor for a problem down below; it didn't really help at all.

'Well,' she started. 'It's not so much that, although it is a strain. Natasha isn't feeling herself, really, and the children are a trial. Little Robin is constantly ill and fretting, and then there's Minnie.' Rosalie tucked her elbows in and grimaced.

'Did someone say my name?' The door pushed open and Minnie came in, chin in the air, ready to do battle. Her Gran and the silly vicar wouldn't know what had hit them by the time she was done.

She'd dressed for the confrontation too. Her black cloak, of course. It was too good not to wear. And she didn't have the boots or anything yet, but her black jeans and hoodie were okay under the cloak. It was her hair and makeup that really did it if she did say so herself. She'd ringed her eyes in black and put about fifty layers of mascara on her lashes to turn them dark. Her lips were bright red.

She felt fantastic.

Her phone was in her pocket, and it was still tuned to the Ghost Radio.

It had been since her father had started talking to her.

The torchlight on the phone was on now, she knew. He was there with her.

Rosalie looked at her oldest granddaughter in dismay. She'd had such pretty blonde hair before. And the makeup – she looked like a raccoon. Rosalie cast an embarrassed glance at the vicar and realised suddenly that this had been a terrible idea.

For starters, she thought, the vicar wouldn't believe in ghosts. They never did, in her experience. Not that she'd ever broached the subject with them, not really, but one could tell. She'd thought that perhaps old Robinson might have come around to something resembling belief in the spirit world, but he'd also been awfully careful to toe the company line. She sighed again and stood up.

'I'm sorry, Vicar,' she said. 'Thank you for coming, but I think this was a bad idea.'

Winsome's brows shot up. 'A bad idea?'

Rosalie nodded, glancing at her granddaughter standing in the doorway in the silly fleece cloak she'd bought. The girl wanted to be a witch, she'd said. Well, that was all very well and good, except Rosalie wasn't happy with it coming to roost in her house.

She was aware that there was a large and active group of pagans in Wellsford. There always had been, but for the most part they were discreet and kept their business to themselves. Morghan Wilde had been more open and visible than her aunt before her, but Rosalie had had to concede some time ago that Morghan had been good for the village as a whole. She'd put money into it, got it thriving again – Rosalie had hoped that Minnie would show some interest in the new art and dance classes that were starting up, run by the woman at Haven for Books.

Rosalie preferred the church than gathering under the full moon or whatever it was Morghan's lot got up to. There was something solid and comforting about sitting in the pew with the light streaming in through the stained-glass windows. You knew where you were in the church, even if you found it a bit hard to believe in everything they taught, and if you wished they believed in a bit more.

'Of course it isn't a bad idea, Gran,' Minnie said. 'We should all be able to sit down and have a cup of tea together, don't you think?' She turned her dark blue eyes to Winsome. 'Unless you've something against breaking bread with a witch?' She blinked, enjoying herself. She'd threaded one of the earphones under her hoodie and it was plugged into her left ear. She could hear the Ghost Radio hissing and cackling like it was laughing. 'I expect you do, of course, being from an institution with a long history of persecution against witches.'

'Minnie,' Rosalie said. 'That's quite enough of that.'

Minnie turned her gaze on her grandmother. 'I don't think it is, actually,' she said. 'This is a subject that feels very real and personal to me. I would like to see how your vicar justifies it.'

She looked back at Winsome, her mouth a wide slash of red.

22

'MORNING LOVE, YOU'RE UP EARLY,' SIMON SAID, WIPING HIS hands on the towel hooked in his apron and moving straight away to the coffee machine. 'Want one?' he asked.

Lucy looked longingly at the cup he held up then shook her head. 'Later,' she decided. 'I'm popping up the hill to see Morghan first.'

Simon's brows rose. 'Is there a problem?' he asked. Lucy usually stayed in bed until the last possible moment in the mornings.

'I don't know,' Lucy answered, brushing her hair back with her fingers and reaching to pop her hat on top of the unruly mop. 'Erin was here the other day and mentioned that Morghan was under the weather, or something.'

'Chicken soup under the weather, or...something else?'

'Something else would be my guess.' Lucy disappeared from the kitchen for a moment and reappeared with her jacket in her hand. 'I know I probably don't need to go trooping up there to see her,' she said. 'I know Ambrose will have everything under control...' She trailed off, frowned at her jacket, then stuck an arm in the armhole, wrestled with it for a moment, got it on and sighed.

'But?' Simon put the cup down and watched his wife.

Lucy gave a one-shouldered shrug. 'I don't know. We all tend to think Morghan is invincible, you know? And she's not. She's just as vulnerable as the rest of us, and this has been a hard year, especially with the passing of Teresa. Morghan and Teresa were close – who does she have now? And it wasn't so long ago that Grainne died.' She fiddled with the zipper for a moment. 'That's a lot of loss, even for Morghan.'

'Well,' Simon pointed out. 'There's still Ambrose.'

Lucy nodded. 'But a woman needs female friends to count on.' She got her jacket zipped up and promptly started sweltering in it. 'But that's not even the point. I'm not angling to become Morghan Wilde's next bosom buddy or anything. She's the leader of the Grove. If I can help, if there's anything at all I can do for her, then it's my duty and pleasure to do so.' She took a deep breath. 'So I'm off, then. I'll have that coffee when I get back, my love.' Leaning over the counter, she kissed her husband on his prickly cheek, smiled at him, and headed for the door.

Mrs Palmer answered her knocking at Hawthorn House. 'She's out doing her morning prayers, Lucy,' she said.

Lucy chewed her lip for a moment. 'She's feeling better, then?'

That got a nod in reply. 'Morghan is well,' Mrs. Palmer said. 'Would you like to come in and wait?'

Lucy turned and gazed out at the rising dawn. 'I think

I'll go find Morghan, actually,' she decided. 'She goes to the stream, doesn't she?'

'Yes, I believe so.' Mrs Palmer smiled at Lucy. 'Pop down to the kitchen when you get back, will you? Simon was asking about a recipe and I've managed to dig it up for him. He says he can put a flourless spin on it, and I've got to say I'm all agog to see that done.'

'I will do exactly that, Mrs. Palmer,' Lucy said. 'Simon will be excited to know you've found it.' She nodded then turned to pick her way over the wet lawn towards the silent trees. The wind hadn't got up yet, and there was a stillness in the air that had Lucy lifting her face to the canopy and breathing deeply.

She should probably do this sort of thing, she thought. Get up early and get outside, do her devotions. In fact, there was no question of it – she absolutely should.

But it was so hard to get out of bed in the mornings. And so cold outside at this time of year, even when the sun was out. All she wanted first thing, was to have a piping hot cup of coffee and check the news headlines as she came around to the idea of being awake. Doom scrolling, Simon called it, but then, he hardly paid attention to the news at all.

'Lucy, good morning.'

The voice, low and pleasant, made Lucy jump. 'Morghan,' she said. 'I didn't see you.'

'You were lost in thought.' Morghan stood with a hand against a tree, her expression clear, eyes calm.

Lucy searched Morghan's face for any sign of distress and found none. Morghan looked the way she always did. 'I was thinking I ought to get out every morning and do something like this,' she said.

'Like this?'

Lucy took a deep breath and felt her shoulders loosen. 'Starting the day with a grounding ritual, I suppose. Being outside does wonders, doesn't it?' She tipped her head to the side. 'It's a bit harder in town, and we've not much of a garden.'

Morghan bent her head in acknowledgement. 'A morning ritual is important,' she said. 'What do you do?'

Lucy flushed. 'I have coffee,' she said and laughed at herself. 'Although after breakfast, I do like to spend half an hour with my cards and journal.' She gazed around at the trees spreading out bare branches around them both. 'Simon's good – he gets up early and has a whole ritual of thanks and meditation.'

'It's important,' Morghan said. 'Morning is usually a difficult time for people, since they've much to prepare for to meet the coming day, but still. Even a short prayer or grounding ritual is beneficial.' She stepped onto the path. 'Would you like to join me in mine?'

This wasn't what Lucy had come for, but she nodded. 'Thank you,' she said. 'I think I'd like that.' Risking a sideways glance at Morghan as they walked together along the path through the winter trees, Lucy decided to broach the subject of why she'd come.

'I spoke to Erin the other day,' she began. 'She was worried about you.' Another glance at Morghan's calm, clear face. 'You weren't feeling well?'

Morghan turned to smile at Lucy. 'I had come back from a difficult travelling,' she said, perfectly willing to explain in the face of Lucy's gentle concern. She looked off through the trees, seeing the dreaming of the trees, breathing in the crisp coolness of the morning. Soon, probably, it would snow. Perhaps in time for Yule.

'I was given a vision,' she said. 'Of the state of the world.'

Lucy's eyes widened. 'Bet that didn't look too healthy.'

'No,' Morghan agreed. 'It was alarming to see.' She touched her cheek, remembering the tears she hadn't been able to control. 'There are so many lost souls about, Lucy, I found it hard to bear seeing them.' She blinked, remembering the view from the hilltop, the screaming sky, churning ocean, crowd of seething, dark spirits. 'The veil is being brought down,' she added.

Lucy looked sharply at Morghan. 'What?' She stopped walking. 'What consequences will that have?'

'In the end?' Morghan asked. 'A return to true balance.' She drew breath. 'In the meantime? A time of turmoil.' She gazed at Lucy tucked warmly into her coat. 'And an even greater need for us all to strengthen our spirits and walk the soul's purpose.'

Swallowing, Lucy looked around the dim forest about them, feeling the damp chill of winter among the trees, the sense of secret places, secret truths just unseen. She nodded. 'No time to be complacent, then,' she said, her voice low, matter of fact. She looked at Morghan.

'No,' Morghan agreed. 'It is time for all to develop their gifts, and to practice walking in both worlds. There is much to evade and avoid in the world, and we can only do that by walking in the strength of our relationship to spirit. To being strong and joyous and full of integrity.'

Lucy nodded. 'News like that would have thrown me too, for longer than a few days, probably.'

Morghan inclined her head, nodded. 'But I was also

given the gift of seeing the web, the binding of the world in an energy of pure love.' She smiled. 'So, there's that.'

Morghan's words startled a laugh from Lucy. She shook her head, sucked in a breath of damp air, looked over at Morghan again. 'Erin,' she said. 'She asked me for help in bringing her back from this...what is it?'

'An ancient initiation,' Morghan said, turning to walk towards the stream again. 'Her situation there has become urgent.' She sighed. 'I will take care of it, I promise you.'

'Is there...is there anything I can do to help?' Lucy asked. 'It sounded a rather dire place.' A frown puckered between her brows. 'I can see things, from the past, I mean, but I don't know that I can go there, actually interact, or anything.' She rubbed her hands on her jeans. 'But I'll try if it would help her.'

Morghan thought about it. 'I don't know,' she said. 'Likely it will not be necessary. Between Macha and I, she does not have to be there alone if it comes to it. Although being there alone is part of the test.' She stopped walking suddenly and turned to Lucy. 'May I ask your opinion on something?'

Lucy nodded immediately. 'Of course. Please.'

Morghan looked down at her right hand. Now, in the dim light of the early morning and to Lucy, she knew it looked merely flesh and blood, the skin pale, freckled with age spots, but to her new vision, it glowed golden and extraordinary.

'I've just told you about the falling of the veil,' she said, picking and choosing the right words, a light frown on her face. She looked up at Lucy. 'People must learn who they are, and how to navigate the real world – the world that is spirit as much as flesh.'

Lucy nodded.

'But how do we teach them this?' Morghan asked, shaking her head. 'Lucy,' she said. 'How do we teach them this?'

Caught off guard by the anguish in Morghan's voice, she shook her head. 'I don't know,' she said.

'I am tasked with this,' Morghan said, tipping her head back and breathing in the scent of the forest, the mystery and steadiness of it. 'Our Grove is tasked with this.' She opened her eyes to the tangle of bare branches overhead and saw their gossamer dreams spreading like threads between one tree and the next and the next. 'How?' she asked. 'How do we do this?'

'Us?' Lucy asked. 'Just us?'

'No,' Morghan replied. 'Many of us with the same job.'

'We're not proselytizers,' Lucy said, shaking her head. 'We don't do missionary work, forcing our beliefs on others.'

'No,' Morghan agreed. 'We are not. And each individual must experience the life of their spirit for themselves. That is how it works.'

Lucy was silent. 'I don't know,' she said at last. 'I need time to think about it.'

Morghan smiled. 'Of course. But I would value any ideas you or anyone else in the Grove might have.'

'I can tell the others?'

'Yes. Please. Perhaps we will discuss before the New Moon ritual on Monday.' Morghan nodded. 'And with that, let us proceed in greeting the day.'

Morghan stepped out of her boots and into the icy rush

of the stream as Lucy watched in consternation. She saw Morghan close her eyes, breathing into the shock of the freezing clamp of water around her ankles and shook her head. A moment later, Morghan opened her eyes and smiled back at Lucy.

'You need not,' she said.

'Why do you?' Lucy asked.

Morghan's eyes closed again. 'I step into the world and the world steps into me. The stream sings in my blood. It is an exercise in relaxing into the world, breathing into it.'

She paused. 'I do not expect others to go to these lengths – this is, after all, my entire calling.'

There was no challenge in her voice whatsoever, but Lucy slipped her feet out of her Wellington boots anyway and bent awkwardly to remove her socks. Her jeans would get wet, but there was nothing for that. Morghan had rolled up her trousers and hitched the skirt of her tunic into her belt.

'You must breathe into the shock of it,' Morghan warned. Then she turned back to the tumbling water, reaching out with her spirit to greet it.

'Spirit of this river, I greet you in honour and pleasure,' she said, spinning her voice out in a stream of sparkling sound over the water. 'We move in and out of the worlds together and it is a joy to be here with you on this day.'

Lucy closed her eyes and stepped into the shallows, breathing in the shock of the cold water, swallowing her gasp. She reached out, eyes still closed, to see the water, and found it laughing as it burbled about her ankles.

'Spirit of water,' she said, breathing deeply. 'I touch you with my spirit and find we are kin.'

'We bring our thanks to you,' Morghan continued. She leaned over, and touched the water with her fingertips, listening to the song of the stream as it swirled around her, to its tales of its journey from deep within the earth to here, to its anticipation of the ocean and all that it would find there. It spun secrets and fancies and told of the animals that had come to sip at it, at the fish who flashed silver-tailed through its depths, at the rocks who held themselves steady as it poured over and around them, and the jokes they told each other, the songs they sang together that shouted out their joy to be alive, to exist, to be spirit and stone and fish and water, to be life.

'Carry our song with your own,' Morghan said. 'Carry the song we sing of being spirit and flesh, two legs, thick heads, in awe of your beauty and in gratitude for you, for without you we would not walk this earth as we do.'

Lucy felt the water about her legs, and its touch was not of sharp glass anymore, but the caress of silk. A feeling of incredible well-being overwhelmed her, and tears sprang to her eyes. This was life, she thought.

'You are life,' she said, and hummed a little, a song to the stream, and then she let herself sing to the water as she felt it was singing to her, filling her with a gratitude that was as simple as it was profound.

'Water our friend,' she sang. 'From deep in the earth to the sea in the end. Water our friend, from world to world without end.'

'Carry our blessings with you on your travels,' Morghan said. 'Take with you our love of the world and the promise of our service to it.' She watched as her blessing spread out over the water, silvery and delicate, to sink into the current and be carried with it. She stood up, stretched.

And reached her hands up to the sky, breathing in the scent of the water, of the land behind her, of the roots under the soil, of the trees reaching for the sky, of the dark, rich dirt at their roots, of their secret buds biding their time until spring.

From root to sky, she thought, seeking the light of the sun, tipping her head back and closing her eyes in search of it, drawing it down into her body to fill her like golden sap.

Lucy dug her toes into the mud of the stream bed, imagining that she had a root system so deep and sure that it went almost to the centre of the earth, anchoring her in place, so that she could not fall, could not falter, so that she was part of the earth, strong, glorious.

From root to sky, they bridged them both, sun at fingers, earth at feet, water in flow around them, hearts ignited in love.

'We hold ourselves in honour to you, earth, sky, water,' Morghan said. 'We walk in balance between you, world to world to world.' She touched a finger, still wet from the stream's water, to her temple, then her breastbone.

'By sky and stream and root, through all worlds,' she said, then touched her right shoulder, then her left.

'From each birth to each death, my life dedicated.' She bowed her head, hearing the spirits of stream and earth and forest whispering to her.

Lucy breathed in deeply, split open through the heart to the beauty and knowledge of the world. When she opened her eyes, she saw stars, and trees, and over on the far side of the stream bank, a shimmering form watching her. She blinked at it, wondering if this were just her imagination.

'Do you see her?' she whispered to Morghan, reluctant to interrupt but unable to hold her wonder. She pointed across the water. Then turned her head slightly and saw another. Faerie come to watch. She'd never seen them so clearly before. This must also be the falling of the veil.

'I do,' Morghan said, her voice was low. She bowed her head to the Fae spirits. 'Our greetings to you,' she said. 'May you be honoured and blessed this day.'

Lucy dipped her head in greeting too, and something sang in her heart. It sat lightly in her chest, full of glory in everything.

Morghan smiled at her as she climbed from the stream bed, dripping glittering droplets of water. She reached for her boots and Lucy, with one last glance at the figures across the stream, clambered after her. She reached for her own boots in astonished, awed silence, feeling her heart vibrate in her chest.

When she could think again, she decided to leave the news headlines to later in the morning.

It was time to come up with a way to greet the day, the world.

And all the spirits living in it.

23

'WHERE ARE WE GOING?' ERIN ASKED, FOLLOWING CLOSE behind Morghan as they climbed up into the hills behind Wellsford. Erin's words were breathless, huffing out into the chill air on puffs of mist that Erin turned her mind away from. Burdock, who had been invited along, was well ahead of them both, turning every now and then to check they were following.

Morghan bounded up the rocky slope like a mountain goat, following a path so faint that Erin wasn't sure it was even there. They'd wound their way out of the trees and were now, it seemed, making their way right around the side of the steep hills and far away.

'Not far now,' Morghan said, her voice almost cheerful against the early morning haze.

This was another thing Erin wasn't sure she understood. 'Can I ask something?' she huffed.

'Always,' Morghan said, glancing at Erin behind her and smiling.

'Yeah,' Erin said, scrabbling at the ground and heaving herself over a rock. 'But will you actually answer it?'

Morghan laughed. 'You've changed so very little.'

Over the rock, Erin paused, hands on knees, to catch her breath. Morghan didn't look winded at all. In fact, she looked suspiciously radiant, with her long hair flowing out behind her, silvering the breeze. Erin narrowed her eyes at her.

'Do you remember me that well?' she asked. 'And how is that?'

Morghan closed her eyes for a moment and breathed in the sharp chill of the air. When she opened them again, Erin was staring up at her, with her hands on her hips and a frown between her fine brows. Morghan laughed again.

'It is more a knowing than a remembering,' she said. 'A recognition.'

Erin shook her head. 'I don't know,' she said. 'Macha appears to me, but it feels very separate.'

'It is. You two are different people. You share many traits however, and as you walk together, you will feel this kinship more, to the point where you may be able to remember things she has lived through.'

It was so strange, Erin thought. So different, to be having conversations of this sort. She scuffed a foot at the ground, thinking.

'Does it work the other way around?' she asked. 'Can she see as much of me as I can of her?'

'More,' Morghan replied.

Erin shook her head. 'How's that?'

'She was trained to be able to do so,' Morghan said with a widening smile. 'By me.'

Erin stared at her with round eyes for a moment, then flung her hands into the air. 'How do I believe any of this?' she asked in exasperation.

Morghan sobered straight away, bending down slightly to look Erin in the eyes. 'Because you are experiencing it.'

'What if it's all just my imagination?'

'Then what a marvellous way to live,' Morghan said, smiling again. 'Now, any other questions? We are almost there.'

Erin was silent a moment, digesting Morghan's words. It was a rather marvellous way to live, she decided. Even Kria and the trial she was going through, the pain and horror of the place she was trapped in – it was consuming and yet fascinating too. She touched her hair with an absent hand. More interesting than a life of shopping and getting her hair done.

Better than being married to Jeremy.

She flashed on Stephan, the scent of him, the way he hummed as he tended his herbs with deft fingers. Her hand moved from her hair to her heart, pressed there.

She swallowed. 'What did you say?' she asked at last.

'I wanted to know if you had another question. You stopped us to ask one.'

'Oh. Er, yes.' Erin cast around trying to remember what it had been. Everything with Morghan moved at such a pace, and there were so many questions. What had that one been?

'I wanted to ask why we have to do so many things so early in the morning?' She cleared her throat. 'I'm sorry; that sounds so whiny.'

Burdock slithered back down the slope and cocked his

ears, wondering what was keeping his two-legged people. Didn't they know this was the best day ever?

Morghan smiled again and shook her head. 'Because,' she said, 'dawn and dusk are liminal times. We see more easily at such hours.'

'See?' Morghan used this term so often, and Erin was only slowly learning what she meant by it.

'Yes. The worlds are more accessible during liminal times, and in liminal places.'

'Liminal places?' Erin winced. She sounded like such a dunce.

But if Morghan thought so, she gave no sign of it. 'Where one thing crosses another, that is a liminal area. The veil is always a little thinner in these places and at these times.'

Of course, Morghan thought, that would soon not be such an issue. The veil was tissue thin as it was. She did not know how long it would take for it to come down completely and thought it unlikely to be an overnight thing – but on the other hand, did she know that for sure? She did not. She knew little of anything for sure.

That was the way of being an embodied spirit.

'And we're going to one of these places?' Erin asked.

'We are,' Morghan said.

'Is this a special one?'

'It is,' Morghan agreed, turning back to the path. 'And we'd best be moving. The sun is rising ever higher.'

Burdock gave a woof of delight and raced ahead, tail splicing the air behind him. This was the life, he thought in his good-natured doggy mind. The rising sun, a good run, an excellent number of wonderful scents.

'Oh my goodness,' Erin said, when Morghan finally stopped and declared them where they needed to be. 'Oh wow.'

Wow indeed, thought Morghan, looking out over the view. From here, the vista spread out over the coastline to the ocean that shimmered in the low-slung dawnlight as though the water was white and glittering like diamonds. She breathed in long and slow, filling her lungs with the distant scent of salt.

It was a challenge for herself too, coming here. To stand and look out over the ocean in the waking world, to stand planted upon the ground and live with whatever vision came to her – that was a necessary task.

And she could see, in the overlap of her vision, the slice of lightning in the far-off sky. Could see the overlay of turbulence upon the bright sea.

But she could also see the web, could see the vitality in everything. Could feel the deep humming contentment of the hillside beneath her feet, the ribbons of light and life that streamed through the air connecting everything.

Everything.

She turned and looked at Erin, examining the healthy glow of the young woman, seeing the places where uncertainty and old wounds pinched at her, watched as wonder and joy spread through Erin as she took in the view.

Erin raised shining eyes to Morghan's. 'It's amazing,' she said. 'I had no idea we could round these hills and see this.' She shook her head, looking back at the land and sea spread out far beneath them. 'We can see so far. It's like being in an aeroplane.'

Morghan nodded. 'A bird's eye view, for sure,' she said.

'And a perfect place to learn the gift of true sight, among other things.'

'True sight?' Erin asked, frowning.

'Everything I've been teaching you so far has been leading to what I hope we begin to achieve today.'

Erin's eyes widened. 'That sounds...' She searched around in her mind for the right words. 'Intimidating.'

Looking out over the land and sea, Morghan shook her head. 'It's not, I promise,' she said. 'It's simply an extension of what you've been doing already when you begin to flex your spirit.'

'Like what I do when I go through my morning prayers? What we do when we're together greeting the day?'

'Yes, exactly like that, only hopefully a little more.' She blinked at the clearing sky, glad to see the sun rising into a blueing bowl. 'We're going to try a little shape-shifting too, I think.'

'What?' Erin gaped at her, mouth suddenly dry. 'What?' Her voice was little more than a squeak.

'We have to get you out of that valley somehow,' Morghan replied, 'and there's no time to take things slowly.' She'd been musing upon this for the last few days. Considering, mulling over what first Elen of the Ways, then Ravenna, and the Queen of the Fae asked of her. To teach. They wanted her to teach.

How that would make a great difference, Morghan did not know. Her reach was only within Wilde Grove. At least as far as she could see.

And since that was, at the moment, as far as she could see, she would start there.

Turning her grey gaze on Erin, she smiled gently.

241

'Shapeshifting will come easily to you, Erin with Fox,' she said, bowing her head slightly in acknowledgement.

Startled again, Erin looked around. But although she knew that a spirit fox waited somewhere for her, she did not see him or her here. 'I will be shape-shifting to fox?' she asked.

'Perhaps,' Morghan said. 'But I mentioned her mostly because those with Fox as their kin generally show a great aptitude for shape-shifting.'

'They do?'

Morghan nodded. 'Fox is a liminal animal, seen most often at dawn and dusk. She also makes a good guide into the Wildwood. She crosses naturally back and forth into the faerie realm, which means in turn that those to whom she is kin will find it easier to travel there too.'

Erin's head was spinning, flabbergasted into silence.

Grinning suddenly, Morghan nodded. 'Fox too, will help you with putting on glamour – with blending into your surroundings and moving unnoticed through situations which may require it.' She smiled wider. 'Something you will likely find useful as time goes by.'

'What do you mean by that?' Erin asked.

'It is an extremely valuable skill,' Morghan said. 'For all of us. To move without causing ripples – there will always be times when that is necessary or wise. Especially when travelling in the Otherworld.' She nodded, gazing now back out over the far stretch of sea. 'There are places in the Otherworld where one must tread quietly, without drawing attention.'

Erin's curiosity was piqued. 'Why is that?' she asked. 'What sort of places?'

'I believe everyone sees the Otherworld slightly differently when they travel there, but there are certain places there which stay essentially the same, to my knowledge.' Morghan thought quietly upon it. 'There is one such place that requires a stealthy approach. I often need to go there when doing soul retrievals for healing,' she said.

'Wait,' Erin interrupted. 'What?'

Morghan breathed in. The air was fresh, damp, flavoured with sunshine and salt. It was like breathing nourishment into her lungs and spirit.

'When we suffer extensive trauma,' she explained, 'we lose aspects of our spirits – they break from us and leave.' She paused only a moment. 'For the purpose of true healing, these shards of ourselves need to be considered, sought, and brought back to reintegrate, most preferably,' Morghan tipped her head to the side.

Erin listened to the explanation with growing consternation. 'Will I have suffered this? she asked, shaking her head ready to refute it even while she voiced the question.

Morghan glanced over at her, eyes kind. 'Most likely,' she said. 'Really, it is hard to avoid.' She lifted her hands in a gesture of acceptance. 'Your adoption may have caused one, being taken from your mother and given to another.'

It was difficult to think about. Erin was silent, looking out over the vast and beautiful view, astonished at how big and wide the world really was. 'Why don't people know this stuff?' she asked.

'We used to,' Morghan said. 'We all used to. Many of us still do. People who still live close to earth and spirit.'

That made Erin shake her head. 'What do the rest of us do about it, then?'

'We learn it all again,' Morghan told her. 'Starting with you here, today.'

'My head is spinning.'

Morghan laughed. 'Then let us begin with grounding and reaching for a simple connection between earth and the rising sun.'

Burdock had flopped down on the edge of the clearing, next to a bowl of water his people had set there for him and watched with interest as two of the people he admired and loved greatly in the world reached out and touched the light, held it in them.

Erin was confident with this exercise. It was almost the first that Morghan had taught her. She stood in the clearing on the side of the hill, shaking the tension out of her hands and arms, loosening her shoulders, standing straight but not rigid. Then she concentrated on her breathing, slowing it until it was deep and unhurried, breathing in and holding the scent of the soil under her feet, the rising dew, the sweet musk of growing sunlight. She let it out in the same, considered measure, using her imagination to clear her spirit and body of the sludge she'd gathered since doing this same exercise the day before. It was like housekeeping, she thought – except she was the house being cleaned and cleared.

'Stretch your arms up,' Morghan said, following her own instructions and reaching upwards to the sky. 'Breathe. In and out. Nice and slow. Long and deep. In and out. Relaxed and focused. Here where you are.'

Being there where you were was important. Always the thing. The present moment was always far more expansive than people thought.

Her voice was low on the light of the morning. 'Your heart has many threads. We connect to the world through our hearts.'

Not the head, she knew, one of the first lessons she herself had been taught at seventeen, standing in the grounds of Hawthorn House, Selena at her side, her voice like a song, telling her to get out of her head. Thinking was all well and good, Selena said, but if you wanted to know, to connect, to burn with passion for the world, you had to lead with the heart.

'Send one of these threads deep down into the earth,' Morghan continued, sending a slender, tender root down into the soil, down through the rock. 'Let it slip into the dirt under your feet and into the secret darkness of stone and soil. Deep. Go deep.

'Seek the central fire and heart of the Earth.'

Erin, eyes closed, dug deep into the ground under her feet, feeling the burrowing bugs in the soil as she passed them, then the slow humming of stone and she sought the heart of the world, feeling its heat, its enveloping fire.

'Let the heart of the Earth touch your thread with a spark,' Morghan's voice said to Erin, who listened and found the spark alive and vibrant with a light and heat that burned brightly but did not singe.

'Draw that spark, that gift, up your thread and into your heart,' Morghan said. 'And then on up your spine and out through the top of your head.'

Erin's mind filled with brilliance.

'Let this glorious spark of fire, of life, travel upwards to the sun, right into the heart of the sun, where there is a sun spark to meet it, and to join together with it. Earth and sun sparks. Let them travel together back down your glorious thread, down through the top of your head and into your heart.' Morghan paused for a moment, letting her chest fill with light and power from earth and sun. She breathed and the spark burned inside her until she felt weightless with light.

'Hold it there,' she said, almost in a whisper. 'Hold the light inside you, knowing you are a bridge between the two, connecting them, being the connection.'

Erin held it, and every speck of her was bright with the two sparks. All she could see behind her closed eyelids was white light. It ate through her skin so that she became the light herself, not just Erin anymore, but Erin of sun and earth spark. Erin bright and on fire, pure, clean.

'Let the spark move back down into the heart of the earth now,' Morghan said. 'Back up to the heart of the sun, leaving your heart full of the knowledge of them. Gently, slowly, reel your threads back in and return to yourself, standing where you are, between sun and earth.'

She paused only a moment. 'This is your life,' she said, to herself and to Erin. 'This is where you are.

'This is the way you sing your connection with the world.'

24

'WHAT'S WRONG WITH YOU?'

Minnie turned away from her little sister, scowling. 'Nothing's wrong with me,' she said. 'Everything is brilliant with me, actually.'

But Tiny shook her head. 'No, it's not. You used to be okay, now you're weird.'

'Weird is good,' Minnie said, sitting down on her bed and hunching over her phone.

'Mean isn't.' Tiny looked at her sister, a frown creasing her young forehead. Something was different about Minnie, but she didn't know what it was. Only that she didn't like it. She picked up her colouring book and went downstairs, her pockets stuffed with her crayons.

Gran was in the sitting room, her pencil making scratching noises against the paper as she filled in one of the crossword puzzles in her magazine. Ordinarily, Tiny would have sat on the sofa next to her and asked what she was going to win, since each puzzle her Gran filled in could win something if she sent away her answers in a neatly stamped envelope.

This time though, Tiny slumped down on the floor and opened her colouring book. She looked half-heartedly at the picture she'd been working on. She had thought it was her best yet, but now it was hard to bring herself to care. In fact, she wasn't sure she even liked it anymore.

She stared at the picture of a group of tiny fairies with summer organza wings flitting like dragonflies around a ring of mushrooms and puckered her lips.

'Gran,' she asked. 'Are fairies real?'

Rosalie shivered and stopped filling in the answers to the crosswords. She only liked doing the ones in her magazines. They were easy enough and she didn't have to worry over the words. Not like the ones in the newspapers. They were too hard.

'Are what real?' she asked, even though she'd heard the question perfectly well. It was the sort of question she didn't like however, because the answer frightened her. That sort of thing had ever since a long-ago day in the woods when she'd fallen asleep and dreamed of dancing with a group of people who shined and laughed and wanted her to stay with them, perhaps forever. She'd cursed her sensitivity every day since until it had begun finally to fade away.

'Fairies,' Tiny repeated. She crossed her legs on the floor and regarded the colouring book unhappily. 'Are they real? There are an awful lot of stories about them, I just thought they must be real. Or something.'

Rosalie shook her head. Honestly, she thought Tiny was probably smarter than all of them put together. The poor kid.

'I don't know,' she hedged.

Tiny's eyebrows shot up. 'You don't know? Does that mean they might be? Mum says they're not. She says they're just baby stuff. Just fairy tales.' Tiny had frowned over that one, because of course they were fairy tales if they were about fairies. 'Do you believe in fairies?' she asked.

Rosalie decided to head the question off. 'I believe in Jesus and the Holy Spirit,' she said. It was safer that way. She wasn't due to feast with Jesus until after she was dead.

But Tiny was frowning up at her from her seat on the floor. 'But what about fairies?' she asked, impatient for her grandmother to give her a straight answer. 'Have you ever seen one?'

'I can't have seen one if they're not real,' Rosalie answered, staring grimly down at her magazine. What was a seven-letter word for courage? Not Rosalie, that was for sure.

'But someone else might have seen one,' Tiny said, putting her hand in her pocket to curl around the crayons there. 'And they must have, right? Or there wouldn't be so many stories about them, right?'

'There are lots of stories about things that aren't true,' Rosalie said. 'That's what writers do – they make stories up.'

Tiny's mouth puckered in dissatisfaction. 'I don't know,' she said. 'I think they make stuff up around things that are true. Otherwise, it wouldn't feel like they were real, and the best stories always feel like they're real.' She paused. 'I think fairies might be true.'

There was something in the child's voice that had Rosalie looking sharply at her, mouth suddenly dry. 'Have you seen something?' she asked.

Tiny's eyes widened at the tone of her grandmother's voice. Then she swallowed and looked down at her colouring book again. 'They don't look like the picture,' she said.

The pencil dropped from Rosalie's frozen fingers and her hands tightened instead around the magazine. She tried to speak normally.

'What do they look like?' she asked.

Little shoulders shrugging, Tiny frowned. 'I was just dreaming, I think,' she said, her voice wavering with uncertainty. 'But I thought there was something in the corner of the room last night. I thought it might be a fairy.' She looked over at her Gran, eyes wide with fear, glistening with held-back tears. 'Are fairies good?' she asked, because she'd rather it be a fairy than a ghost.

She didn't want it to be a ghost.

'Minnie is still talking to Dad's ghost,' she whispered, staring at her grandmother.

'What?' Rosalie's eyebrows reached her hairline. 'She's doing what?'

Tiny looked miserably down at her crayons. She picked up the one that was green-blue, her favourite, and held it gripped tight in her palm. 'She's been talking to Daddy since the bonfires at Halloween.'

Rosalie's fingers were numb. She could no longer feel the paper under them.

Something scratched inside the wall behind her. Her neck creaked as she turned slowly to look at the faded wallpaper.

The scratching came again.

'What's that?' Tiny asked, picking up her colouring book and holding it tight against her narrow chest.

'Just mice,' Rosalie said automatically.

The scratching came again, this time from the ceiling above them. Rosalie looked up at the ceiling then over at Tiny. 'Come here, love,' she said.

Tiny didn't need telling twice. She scooped her crayons up and crammed them into her pockets then climbed up onto the sofa where she tucked herself against Rosalie's soft body, trembling.

'Is it really mice, Grandma?' she asked.

'Of course it is, sweetheart,' Rosalie said, but she knew she was lying. Mice always had a go at coming into the house during winter, but she was assiduous at putting down traps and usually caught them on their very first explorations. Her vision was streaked with colours. Dark, smudged colours.

It could be mice, she thought. It could be.

The scratching came again, from the floor this time. Rosalie scooted her feet back without thinking.

'It's loud,' Tiny said, pressed against her side.

Rosalie cleared her throat. 'Maybe it's rats,' she said. 'I don't have traps down for rats.'

Tiny nodded, looking down at the floor. 'But what if it's a ghost?' she said. 'What if it's Daddy?'

'Of course it's not your father,' Rosalie snapped. What had that girl Minnie been up to?

'Minnie says she talks to him every day.'

'How?' Rosalie asked. The scratching stopped, as though pausing to listen to the answer too.

'On her phone, I think,' Tiny said. 'She was doing it with

a candle, but I told Mummy and she told her she wasn't allowed to do that anymore.'

Rosalie patted her granddaughter then shook her head. 'Your sister's going to get us in deep trouble,' she muttered.

Tiny heard her and widened her eyes. 'In trouble with who?' she asked. Then she swallowed, her throat dry with fright. 'Daddy wouldn't hurt us.' But even as the words were out of her mouth, she wasn't sure. Her father had been scary sometimes when he was in a grumpy mood. Maybe he didn't like being dead. Maybe it was making him mad.

'Was it Daddy I saw last night?' she asked, shrinking closer to Rosalie.

'What did it look like?'

Tiny was only eight, but even she realised that her grandmother was taking her question seriously, that she hadn't scoffed and said Tiny hadn't seen anything at all. That was what her mother had said when she'd told her about it. Her mother had just looked at her blankly for a moment, then told her stop being silly, that she hadn't seen anything at all.

But she had. She had too seen something.

'It was just a shadow,' Tiny told Rosalie. 'On the wall.'

'Which wall?' Rosalie asked, moving her gaze from the floor to the ceiling. The two girls were in her old room, at the front of the house. Right overhead, then.

Tiny hunched in on herself. 'It was by the door,' she whispered. 'Just standing there.'

Rosalie nodded. 'What happened then?' she asked. 'What did it do then?'

'I don't know,' Tiny said, looking at the crayon still

tightly in her fist. 'I pulled the covers up over my head so I couldn't see it.'

'Good girl,' Rosalie said. 'If you don't see them, then they have to go away.' She'd spent years not looking at spirits and it had worked. Now she barely ever saw them. It had been so long, in fact, that she'd managed to convince herself that they weren't real after all, and she'd just suffered from too much imagination when she was young.

It seemed less scary that way.

She wanted to ignore the shadows right now.

Tiny looked up at her grandmother. 'Was it real?' she asked, voice quavering a little. 'Was it Daddy?'

To that question, Rosalie shook her head. 'I don't think so,' she said. 'Your daddy is long gone on his way, I would think.'

'But maybe Minnie brought him back?'

It was a valid question, Rosalie thought. Maybe the dratted girl had, for all that.

There was a sudden, loud bang from somewhere upstairs, then a moment of absolute, vibrating silence, and Robin started howling. Rosalie looked down at her wrist where it poked out of her threadbare old cardy and saw that all the hairs on her arm were standing on end.

Robin cried louder.

'Where's your mother?' Rosalie asked, knowing she was going to have to haul herself out of the couch and go upstairs.

Not to tend to Robin, but to see what the noise had been. The loud bang.

It had cracked through the house like nothing she'd ever

heard before. Not the crash of something falling, not the smack of something being dropped, or even thrown.

No. It had sounded...like a loud crack in thin air.

Robin's howls turned to screams.

'Let me up,' Rosalie said, pulling Tiny's panicked hands from her clothes. 'I've got to get Robin. Where's your mother?'

Tiny snatched up a cushion and held it across her stomach. 'I don't know,' she said.

And Minnie, Rosalie thought – where was she? Surely she could hear her brother's screams?

Minnie had heard the cracking bang – of course she had, it had been loud enough. She could hear Robin screaming from the other room as well, but so what? The kid was always screaming. Sometimes Minnie thought he must have been born screaming, because he'd done it every day since her mother had brought him home. She wished she felt like going out. It was shit, being stuck here all day with nothing to do.

There wasn't any school, or at least, there wasn't for her. She didn't think Natasha had enrolled her in one when they moved to Wellsford, and she sure wasn't going to remind her to do so. Besides, with so many lockdowns, no one was going.

The Ghost Radio whispered in her ears. She couldn't make out any words, just the whispering static. It sounded like a conversation someone was having just out of hearing distance.

She kind of liked it. It sent shivers up and down her spine and made her feel special.

She knew what sort of witch she was now, you see. Her

father had told her and now, every day a bit more, she was seeing it for herself.

She was a spirit witch. She could communicate with the dead.

She could summon them.

Reaching under her pillow, Minnie touched the notebook she was using for a grimoire. A grimoire. She rolled the word around in her mouth, loving the way it felt there, the way it sounded. So dark and exciting. Powerful.

The Ghost Radio hissed in her ear and she sat up, on alert.

The bedroom door opened, and Rosalie appeared in the doorway, Robin on her hip, his lower lip pouting, cheeks stained from crying.

'What are you doing?' Rosalie demanded.

Minnie stared at her grandmother for a moment, wanting to yell at her for speaking to her that way.

'Nothing,' she said instead. 'There's nothing to do in this place.'

Rosalie blinked at her granddaughter. 'How did you make that noise?' she asked at last.

Minnie's forehead creased in a frown. 'What noise?' She'd forgotten about it already.

'That loud bang,' Rosalie said. 'It was very loud. It woke up Robin.'

'Everything wakes up Robin,' Minnie said, turning her head to look out the window. She didn't want to talk to her grandmother. In her ears, the Ghost Radio hissed and laughed. She glanced down at her phone. The torch light was on at the back of it. It held steady for a moment, then flashed off, then on again. It did it twice more.

Minnie looked around at the room, ignoring the fact that her grandmother still stood in the doorway staring at her like she'd grown an extra head. How many spirits were in the room, she wondered? More than one? More than just her father?

The thought excited her, and she felt her skin tighten, her hair stand on end. This was the life, she thought. She could make anything happen, feeling like this.

She cast around for something to do.

'Where's your mother?' Rosalie asked from the doorway, where she'd been standing very still, holding the snuffling child in her arms, and watching her oldest granddaughter.

Minnie shrugged carelessly. 'How should I know?'

Rosalie bit down on the soft flesh of her inner lip and backed out of the bedroom. She didn't want to admit it to herself, but Minnie, with her dyed black hair and her stupid cloak and her phone always attached by earphones to her, made her feel angry. And helpless.

And scared.

All at the same time.

If only the idiot girl hadn't chased off the vicar with her hectoring about the inquisition.

The house, Rosalie thought, still needed to be blessed.

More than ever, perhaps.

She drew herself up to her full height, glanced at Robin in her arms, his fingers stuck in his mouth, nose all snotty, and grimaced.

Well, if she couldn't get the vicar around to do the blessing, then she'd have to do it herself.

After all, God listened to the prayers of any poor soul, didn't he? Wasn't that what they taught you?

Ask and you shall receive?

That was easy. Rosalie would ask for her life to go back to the peace and quiet it used to be.

When the spirits knew better than to come around bothering her.

She sighed, and something scratched up in the corner of the hallway ceiling. She refused to look at it, simply aimed for the stairs. Natasha would be outside in the garden, freezing while she smoked and paced. It was all her daughter did these days.

Life was rubbish, Rosalie thought. Life was hard, then shit came along and made it harder.

She opened the back door and stepped into the wind, Robin ducking his head down and getting snot all over her shoulder.

And don't ever say things couldn't get any worse, Rosalie said to herself.

Because they always could.

You could always get a lot more scared.

25

ERIN STOOD WHERE SHE WAS, LISTENING TO MORGHAN'S voice.

'The world is more than we've been brought up to see,' Morghan said.

'We walk in the waking world, but we may also walk lesser-seen paths.'

The Wildwood, Erin thought.

'We stand blind where we are, eyes not open to seeing what is really there.'

Erin looked around, taking in the view without moving her head. Beneath her, the hill tumbled, trying to catch itself on its own stones, downwards to the coast where the ocean threw itself at the rocky shore. Above her, the clouds were thinning, and a weak, welcome stream of sunlight pierced the lid of the world.

What was she missing, she wondered? What was she not seeing?

She remembered dancing at the Samhain ritual, seeing

those who danced with her, and those who had gathered to watch.

Not all of them had been human.

And above her as she wove in and out in the dance, bending and ducking between the other dancers, hadn't she seen something glimmering between the stones, between the trees?

'The Wildwood is all around us. The ancient land of our ancestors, the land of the faerie. Everything has spirit, and with our eyes and our hearts open, we may see it still.

Erin swallowed. Her eyes were open, but was her heart? How did you have an open heart? The world she was used to was a difficult place – and she hadn't even had it hard. She'd not struggled for anything except to be seen and heard and taken seriously. She'd not ever had to choose between paying the electric bill or buying food.

But the world was a difficult place. Even now, she carried wounds from it. From her mother giving her away when she was a helpless baby, from her times spent later in hospital, wandering grey pathways, lost.

And Kria. She carried Kria's pain inside her like a thorn.

Erin swayed slightly, hands gripped on the slender, fallen branch Morghan had found for her to use as a staff to steady her.

'We may use our own strong centre to stand in both worlds. We may move through our lives knowing we tread on more than the ground we see with our eyes.'

Morghan's voice was like the breeze, winding around her, inviting her to see more, feel more, be more.

'Come to me, my friends,' Morghan called suddenly and Erin turned her head slightly, catching movement out of the corner of her eye. There was the beat of wings in the sky, and at first, she thought it was the wind, and then it was more than the wind.

A hawk circled in the sky overhead and Erin stared wide-eyed at it, not knowing if it was really there or not. She felt both inside herself and outside herself; she overflowed her skin, her senses reaching out and up and out and out. Morghan's voice had moved her out from her own skin.

'Call for your kin, Erin,' Morghan's voice said to her. 'Call for your kin to come to you on feathered wing. Sing her to your side.'

Sing to her? Erin did not know how to sing her kin to her. She opened her mouth, not knowing what she was going to say.

'Come,' she croaked. Then tried again, touching her heart as she did so. A heart-song, she thought. Her kin asked for heart-songs.

The world asks for heart-songs.

'Come to me, my friend,' she said, and the words streamed in golden feathered trails from her lips. 'Come to me on the wind, come to me on the beating of your wings.'

A second bird circled in the sky above her, and Erin realised she had her eyes closed but was seeing the sky anyway. She kept them closed, for she could see perfectly well.

'Come to me, my kin,' she whispered.

For a moment, the wings beat black against the sky and she smiled, for it was Raven – Macha's raven, and she welcomed him an old friend. Her raven.

He flew up to her and his beaked face filled her vision, the dark eyes, the black feathers, the wings outstretched, and then he was gone, and there was another bird instead and Erin cried out.

This one stared at her from eyes rimmed in yellow, feathers white on the head, wings a soft grey, flight feathers tipped with black. She recoiled slightly, recognising it at once.

This was a gull. She'd seen them, flying over the loch where Kria was. She'd seen them on just about every holiday she'd taken as well.

The raven she'd expected, if she'd known to expect anyone at all.

But the gull?

It beat its wings in front of her and she stared back at it, wanting to deny it, to turn away, search for a different bird, look for her raven. But the gull was right in front of her – she could see nothing past the white feathers on the top of its head, the grasping yellow beak with its red spot.

And then it wheeled around, wings outstretched, and she felt its feathers brush her face, smelt the salt-soaked scent of them, felt the wind under them, and the gull was nipping her shoulder with its beak, snatching hold of her clothes, and lifting her.

And she was in the sky, the thick beating of wings above her.

And then they were her wings, and she flexed her feathers, admiring her black wing tips and the graceful way they lifted her higher and higher into the wind.

She screamed as they swooped down off the hillside, skimming over the water, her voice harsh as a sea gull's as the waves sprayed spume in her face.

She screamed with the glorious freedom of flight, crying

out in her new seagull voice. Morghan, she cried out. I am a bird. Kria, she called. Fly on the wings of the gull!

She flew out far over the water in her new feathered body, listening to the steady beat of her wings against the wind. She turned her head and looked at them, one at a time, stunned at their simple flex and beat, at the feel of the air under her feathers, and then she looked down and screamed once more for the water was under her, if she turned slightly, her wing feathers would clip the tops of the waves, so she kept them straight, gliding on the current of the wind, over the water, looking down with eyes sharp enough to spot the movement of fish under the deep green sea and then there was a shadow down there, a great moving, swimming shadow keeping pace with her and when it rolled slightly, it looked up at her with one great large eye and she stared down at the whale, and it gazed back at her as though seeing her – a woman flying in bird feathers – was nothing out of the ordinary for it, as if for whales this sort of sight was quite usual, and she grinned at it with her yellow beak with the red dot on it because perhaps it was, perhaps whales saw such marvels all the time. She dipped her wing in greeting, then pushed herself higher into the sky around and around in a great spiralling climb higher and higher into the air so that the shadow of the great whale beneath her grew smaller and smaller until she could taste the clouds, damp against her feathered face, full of the scent of elsewhere, and she flew through them in a wide circle crying out again at the fierce freedom of flight, of the wild beauty of the world, at her own fast-beating bird heart.

Oh, to be a seagull was glorious.

Land loomed again, and the small clearing on the hillside where Morghan stood, an enormous black wolf at her side, a hawk on her shoulder, beak curved and wicked, while across her feet was draped a green and yellow snake. Erin marvelled at the sight, then opened her beak and called out to them.

Look, she cried out in her seagull voice. Look! I am flying!

Then the land was under her feet and she put them out, slowing her wings, pushing down on the air to bring herself to land and as her webbed gull feet touched the grass they were her own feet again and after a moment longer, her fingers were no longer feathers and her lips no longer a beak. She was herself again, but forever changed, for she had flown as a bird, out over the ocean, and she had looked into the great gaze of a whale and dipped a wing in greeting to it.

Collapsing to her knees, Erin knelt there, palms in the grass, shaking her head side to side in disbelief. When she looked up at Morghan, she knew her eyes shone with her adventure.

'Was it real?' she asked.

Morghan looked at her, lifted an eyebrow.

Erin swallowed, squeezed her eyes shut for a moment. Took a deep breath. 'It felt so real,' she said in wonderment. 'I wasn't here anymore, on this hill with you. I really was flying out there as a seagull.' She turned over and sat a moment looking out to sea. 'My body was still here, right?' she asked. 'I mean, I didn't physically turn into a seagull?'

Morghan was standing where she'd been when Erin had come into land, and when Erin glanced at her, she wondered if the animals she'd seen with Morghan were still there.

'You did not today physically turn into a seagull,' Morghan said. 'Your spirit left your body and took on the form of your kin, at their invitation.'

'I saw a whale,' Erin said, pressing her palms again into the dirt, bringing herself back to ground. She felt light as a...feather.

Morghan was gazing out over the ocean. 'Whales are blessed creatures,' she said. 'They live such long and complex lives.'

Erin nodded, although she'd already moved on to the next thought. Or back to a previous one. 'When I came back,' she said, 'I saw you had some animals with you.'

'My spirit kin,' Morghan said.

'Your spirit kin,' Erin agreed, taking the correction in stride. 'Does everyone have as many as you?'

Morghan shook her head. 'No, although it is entirely possible to have as many or more. Each of us has animal and ancestor kin who stay with us for the course of our lives here, and others also who come and go according to need.'

Erin looked up into the sky. High up she thought she saw white and grey wings with black tips outlined against the blue sky of the morning. Was it a real gull, she wondered, or was it the one that had come to her?

'Is the seagull kin who will stay with me, or kin who will go when I have learnt...whatever?'

'I do not know,' Morghan replied.

'I thought it would be a raven who came to me,' Erin continued. 'And he did, for a moment, and then there was the gull.' She paused and nipped down on her lip for a moment. 'The only living things, aside from bugs and fish, I guess, that Kria sees are gulls.' She shaded her eyes and looked over at Morghan. 'Do you think that's why a gull came to me?'

'Yes,' Morghan said.

Erin waited for her to elaborate but Morghan said nothing more, standing there in the cool breeze and watery sunlight.

At last, Erin nodded. 'I think so too,' she said. 'Why, though?'

Morghan tipped her head to one side. 'Why do you think?'

The question made Erin laugh. 'Talking to you is like talking to a shrink. They never answer questions either.'

'I cannot answer all your questions, Erin,' Morghan said gently.

'I don't expect you to know all the answers,' Erin broke in. 'But you know, a little more would be nice.'

Morghan smiled and looked out over the ocean again. 'It's not that I don't know the answers. It's that a lesson is learned best when effort is put into the knowing of it and the experiencing.' She paused, feeling herself standing calm and strong where she was while overhead the web tied the worlds together, and below her, the blades of grass glowed in their chlorophyll splendour.

'So you could tell me how to get out of Kria's valley?' Erin looked over at Morghan, watching her turn her gaze on the ground at her feet, then up at the sky.

'Yes.' But Morghan touched her heart. 'You must, however, know how to do so here,' she said. 'I have been showing you how, since the first morning we said our prayers, stepping into the stream in the grove.' She nodded towards the gull flying over the beach below them. 'Your kin is showing you also. The lessons are everywhere around you, all you have to do is see and learn and let your heart lead you to the answer.'

Erin turned away to look out at the water. 'Aren't there magic words?' she asked. 'Or spells, or something.'

'Of course.' Morghan shifted easily on her feet, weighing up how much to say. 'There are words and prayers, which are spells. There is the flight of the gull, the gaze of the whale. There is the rustle of the grass, the tiny sawing song of the beetle. There is the water that floats in the mists, the fire that springs from between fingertips, the wind that whispers in your ear, the soil that hold your roots. There is all of it, waiting for you to see it. To sing it.'

'To sing it,' Erin said, but she was talking mostly to herself. 'How do you sing the world?'

The question spread a smile over Morghan's face.

'Indeed,' she said. 'How do you sing the world?'

26

Morghan watched Erin walk down the path back to Ash Cottage, feeling hopeful that the young woman was learning what she needed to. There was a lightness to Erin's steps, as though she was still buoyed by wings upon her back. Erin turned at the last bend before going out of sight and looked back at Morghan, lifting her hand in a wave.

Morghan nodded, seeing with her second sight Erin shimmer between herself and Macha for a moment. For a breath, it was Macha there, stepping between the trees, the bright red of her hair glowing in the dimness, her body strong and supple, brimming with magic.

Turning, Morghan looked away. Macha reminded her too much of Grainne. They both had magic that was wild and fierce, hard to hold, almost impossible to temper.

They did their magic by throwing themselves against reality, always pushing at it. They moved with a challenge in their eyes through the worlds, and Morghan smiled a little at the thought. A challenge they were always determined to win.

And Grainne had won. She had come to the lifetime she had shared briefly with Morghan to work a miracle of healing, undoing the knots of several lifetimes that had caught and entangled her. And she had won. Against expectation.

Morghan looked forward to the day they would be reunited.

She stepped back along the path, lost in her memories. Once, she had walked this path and fallen into a lifetime she and Grainne had shared, and she had been a young man then, and they had been on the run – she did not know from whom – and he had been careless, and Grainne, the young woman she had been then, had been caught, taken from him, hung from a tree for him to find, the rope tight around her neck, and he had cut her down, lowering her to the ground and screaming for her.

Morghan stopped walking and pulled herself back from that short and violent lifetime. It was done, that one. The woundings she and Grainne had suffered were healed. She waited for her heart to steady then drew in a deep breath, held it, let it slowly out, looking around with her open eyes, her grateful heart, seeing the shadows and gleamings of the forest surrounding her. The trees were shrouded in the mists of their dreamings, their branches still reaching out to touch the web that surrounded them. Morghan placed her hand upon the trunk of one, and her hand was made of gold, resting upon the slow-moving sap of the dreaming tree.

She smiled at the sensation, the feeling and the knowing of the tree's vitality, the awareness of the living, breathing forest all around her, all of it held in the intricate beauty of the web.

'Blessed creature,' she whispered to the tree and stepped along the path again, touching her heart with her hand, wide open to the world. To the dreaming of the winter forest, to the scurrying of its animals and insects. To the spirits that walked this way too. The ones that shuffled among the shadows, and those that stepped out along with her. She walked with them all in her vision.

And she ended up in a place she did not know, with Snake by her side, and knew she had wandered into the Wildwood again, deep into the forests of the Otherworld. She wound through the undergrowth after Snake, following his sinuous twining along a narrow path.

Wolf walked at her side and she reached down her golden hand to touch him. Felt his thick fur under her fingers and thanked him for his constant protection. For the constant reminder that was his presence.

Wolf reminded her to take care of what was precious in her life.

Her work. Her own wild nature.

Snake slithered behind a mossy boulder and Morghan followed him, into a cave – always so many caves – and through the cave into a tunnel. She thought they were going to the Faerie Queen's realm, but it was not this way, the tunnel did not lead to the ones she knew went there.

Snake did not turn to see if she followed.

She followed, her steps quiet on the red dirt of the tunnel floors. She followed with Wolf at her side, and her questions quiet inside her. Snake would not answer them, she knew. It was her job simply to trust him, and to follow.

She was well used to it.

The tunnel widened finally into a cave and Morghan looked around at the rough-hewn walls. They were black and she recognised the volcanic rock. Obsidian.

Immediately, she remembered the way to the Isle of Healing. The steps of obsidian. What were the attributes of obsidian, she wondered? For she was experienced enough to know that nothing was by chance. Everything in the Wildwood, in the Otherworld, had meaning. The language of the Otherworld was symbolism, as if it were half dreamworld.

Obsidian was a powerful stone, Morghan knew. With no crystalline structure, it was not a stone of boundaries or limitations. And it was at home deep in the shadows and craters of the worlds. She did not work with crystals, however, and determined that once back in the waking, she would ask Charlie's daughter-in-law Rima about it. Rima knew crystals as Morghan herself knew forests.

There had been a crowd of people in this cavern just a moment ago, Morghan was sure of it. A figure moved in the shadows and she caught a glimpse of an elderly wizard slipping from the cave, a wide grin on his face as he looked back towards Morghan. She blinked at him, then smiled and lowered her head in silent greeting.

Then, there was no ignoring the other person in the room. Morghan sank slowly to a knee in front of the goddess, looking away from her shining form and down at the dirt of the cavern floor.

'You are well again, Morghan of the Grove?' the Lady asked.

'I am, my Lady Elen, although the last days have been full of surprises.'

'Which shall pale against those of the years yet to come,' the goddess said and there was a vibration of emotion in her voice that Morghan could not place. 'Come,' Elen said, without elaborating.

Morghan stood and walked closer to the goddess. Elen stood in the chamber, of ordinary height, her skin and dress glowing softly. The first time they had met, Elen had been blinding in her shining aspect, and almost as tall as the trees she had stood in front of.

'Drink this,' the goddess commanded.

Morghan took the bowl without question and put it to her lips. One did not question those to whom you had long ago sworn service. She had already made all her promises to follow the will of the goddess.

The red syrup was fruity, spicy, delicious.

There was movement in the cavern and the Queen of the Fae stepped up beside Elen of the Ways. Morghan looked with curiosity at her.

'My Lady,' she said, dipping her head at the faerie Queen. She felt only the smallest measure of surprise to find these two in the same place for the same purpose and realised she was now bound to both, in deed and word. Her right hand, holding the bowl, glowed golden in the light from the firepit next to her.

The Queen gestured towards the large cauldron that stood over the fire. Morghan turned to look at it, the bowl in her hands empty, her stomach warm from the spice of the syrup. The bowl dangled from her fingers.

Suspended in the air above the cauldron glowed a large

KATHERINE GENET

white egg. Morghan blinked at it, then squinted and blinked again. She glanced at the two women standing on the other side of the fire and then looked down at the bowl in her hands.

'What did you give me?' she asked.

Neither of them answered and Morghan realised they'd given her some sort of drug, some sort of hallucinogen.

How odd, she thought, to be travelling in spirit, and while so, be given hallucinogens. Her gaze went back to the egg.

She wore an egg around her neck. It was there because of Grainne, because of things that had happened to them. And because the egg was a potent symbol of the soul. Others in the Grove had taken to wearing it too. Erin, that very day, had worn Teresa's egg on its leather thong.

Elen stepped over to the egg and lifted her hand to it. A small egg detached itself from the larger and she plucked it from the air and walked over to Morghan, the white egg gleaming in her palm. She held it out.

'Take it,' she said.

Morghan took it. She put the bowl down at her feet and looked at the egg. It was smooth and warm. A reminder that soul work was the most important work of her world. She closed her fingers around it, and it sat in her palm as in a nest.

'Tell us the gifts we have given you,' the Queen said.

'The golden pear and silver apple,' Morghan said, keeping her voice steady, not knowing where this was going. She raised her gaze to meet the Queen's. 'The golden hand.'

She thought she saw the Queen tip her head slightly in acknowledgment and let herself think back to previous journeys. There had been so many over the years. Ambrose's notebooks were thick with her accounts of them. And there were more she hadn't had the patience or inclination to share with him.

'The ruby heart,' she said, remembering the day, many years ago, that the faerie Queen had summoned her and given her a handful of treasures.

That had been before Grainne had died.

'Two wedding rings.' She looked away for a moment, then continued. 'The splinter of wood.' That was all that one had been, a thin needle of wood the length of her finger and yet holding it had made her woozy. Morghan looked over at Elen, thinking of their first meeting and what the goddess had placed in her palm that day. 'The handful of diamonds,' she finished.

Then added – 'And now, the egg.'

Morghan struggled to keep her eyes open. The drug – whatever it was – made her stagger slightly and she flung a hand out to steady herself. Then there were cool fingers holding hers, and the Queen led her to a seat. Morghan sank down gratefully.

'What have you given me?' she asked.

'Something to aid your seeing,' one of the women answered.

'So that your questions may be answered,' said the other.

Morghan managed a brief laugh. 'You've drugged me.'

'You travelled here,' the Queen told her in a mild voice. 'But now you must go farther, see what we need you to see.'

Morghan let her eyes close. That was a reasonable

answer, she supposed. A journey within a travelling. What did they want her to see?

She had so many questions. Were they all about to be answered?

Her last coherent thought was that it would never be that simple.

The horse under her tossed his head, snorting, nostrils wide in the cool air. His hooves thudded against the ground as he ran across the wide, grassy plain. Morghan looked to her side, saw a hundred or more other riders keeping pace, spread out over the green.

The air smelt of horse and hot sweat in chill air. Above the sound of hooves, birds circled in the air above them, crying out into the streaming wind.

Morghan looked ahead, eyes wide in the wind. They were making for a great dark forest and she bent forward in the saddle, low over the horse's neck, urging him on.

The Forest of Lost Souls was dark, thick trees close together, their branches holding trailing vines like thick cobwebs. Morghan's horse slowed to a walk, picking his way between the trees, deeper into the silent darkness. Around them rose the trees, a thousand trees, tall and straight, and Morghan ducked and brushed away their branches, aware that the other riders were also making their hushed way into the depths of this ancient wood.

Spirits flitted wraith-like between the trees and Morghan touched her heart, gazing upon these souls, knowing each belonged to a person who walked the earth and had become lost along the way.

Ahead, a small child burrowed in the pine needles and Morghan's horse stepped lightly up to her on his big hooves.

She turned as he came nearer with Morghan on his back and held up something that gleamed in the dimness. Morghan leaned over and took it from her, feeling the egg cool and perfectly smooth in her palm. The child smiled then stood up, and a moment later she leapt up behind Morghan's seat on the horse, threading her small arms around Morghan's waist.

The horse turned his head, eyes soft in the dimness, and they rode on through the forest, and as they did so, spirits turned and looked at Morghan, holding up their eggs in upturned palms, a pale congregation among the trees. Morghan let the horse take her where he wanted to go, knowing that he knew their purpose as well, if not better, than she did. The spirit child was light behind her, swaying with her in time to the horse's quickening gait.

The forest thinned and they were on a small hilltop, trees spreading out below them in all directions, and more hills in the distance.

Something about it was familiar, Morghan thought, eyes flicking to look here then there, taking in the sight as she tried to figure out what was happening, what she was being shown.

And then, someone lit a fire, smoke and flame curling around a huge pile of tinder, and she knew at last what she was seeing and lifted her head to look towards a far hillside.

Another beacon was lit, and Morghan shifted slightly in the saddle to turn, looking for the next and the next.

Across the land, beacons were lit. The child's egg warmed in her hand.

All around her, riders watched the fires, souls no longer lost riding behind them, each holding an egg. The precious egg of the soul, from which anything can be born.

Morghan lowered her head and closed her eyes in a whispered prayer of gratitude.

When she opened her eyes, she was back in the cave, slumped sideways on the bench she'd been put upon. Groggy, she sat up, rubbing a hand over her face, looking about and seeing the giant cauldron, the egg still hanging suspended above it.

'You will understand now,' the Queen said.

Morghan blinked at her.

'What is necessary,' Elen added.

Morghan shook her head. 'I do not know how to go about rescuing so many souls,' she said. 'Even if I am not the only one doing so.' She thought for a moment upon the beacons, so similar to what they'd done in Wellsford for Samhain.

'When one fire is lit, the light spreads,' the Queen said, then looked towards the entrance to the cavern. 'It is time for you to continue on. They are waiting for you.'

Morghan gained her feet, drawing in a deep breath as she steadied herself. She expected to feel the effects of whatever she'd been drugged with, but it had passed already. She felt fine. Bowing to the Queen and the goddess, she stepped back into the tunnel, taking all her questions with her.

Wolf padded up to her side, took his place there and she could feel his warmth even through the skirts of her tunic. Hawk dipped down from a tree, landing on her shoulder, his taloned feet gripping her. She searched for Snake and sure enough, he was there, waiting to lead her back to the path that led into the Wildwood. She walked with her kin and her questions through the forest, listening to the dreaming trees, to her own swirling thoughts.

At the path where usually she would leave the Wildwood for the Waking, Morghan came up short. A horse stood there on the path, the same horse she'd just been riding in her travelling. Shaking her head, she stepped up to him, grinning at the child sitting in the saddle waiting for her with her egg tucked safely under her arm.

Nimbly, Morghan mounted the horse, and the child passed the egg to her then wrapped her spindly arms once more around Morghan's waist.

There was a fork in the path, and the horse took it, walking out of the Wildwood and up against the Waking. The Otherworld lay, Morghan knew, upon the Waking like an extra dimension, sharing space in places. Always, she'd found it complicated to wrap her mind around.

Now they walked a path that was both Otherworld and Waking, an intersection point. These were the places the falling veil would most reveal. The Middle world, some called it.

She rode onwards, waiting to see where she would end up.

For this was the way with travelling, she'd long since discovered. There were forces at work that knew more than she did, and she must go with them, do what was necessary. Her own will was not to be imposed in her travellings, for her spirit led the way.

They came at last upon a village, and the horse's hooves clopped through the streets as he took them unerringly towards a boxy Victorian church. Morghan looked at its brickwork, gazed up at the square belltower, and ducked her head when the horse led them straight inside the church. Moments later, still on her horse's back, she was making her way up the stairway into the bell tower, then leaning over, she took the child's soul egg and hung it under the bell, where it floated suspended in the air.

She looked at it in satisfaction, knowing this was right. This was why she'd come here.

The horse turned and they made their way back down the steps and out of the church building. Morghan turned to look back up at the tower and there was the egg, glowing there under the bell.

The light from it brightened as she watched, and as she sat on the back of the horse, people crowded out of the buildings of the village, drawn by the light of the egg in the bell tower. Hushed, in awe, they stood staring up at it, bathed in the light that streamed down on them from it. Morghan looked at all their shining faces and felt hope flare into her heart.

There were so many people in the world, she thought, people with good hearts trying to make their way in a difficult world. People holding their souls, knowing they were precious.

With the reins in her hands, Morghan turned the horse away, back the way she'd come.

Back towards home, to the Waking world, where she had much to do.

Much to teach. Even if it was just to one person at a time.

Because light spread.

27

Stephan tucked himself next to Erin as they walked the path back from the stone circle to Hawthorn House.

'I've hardly seen you the last couple of days,' he said.

'I know,' Erin replied, reaching a hand from under her cloak and sneaking it around Stephan's elbow. She'd missed him, missed the clear joy she felt whenever they spent time together even while it made part of her afraid. 'When I haven't been at the Care Home, I've been working with Morghan. It's exhausting, on top of everything.'

'And I've been with Ambrose,' Stephan said, putting his hand over Erin's, his heart singing at her closeness. 'He's been teaching me to walk between the worlds.' He shook his head. 'I never imagined I'd be doing any of that; it's amazing, you know?'

Erin did know. 'Morghan's been teaching me to shape-shift,' she said. 'I wonder why she's not doing it for both of us like she was for a little while?'

'Probably easier to do it like this. Shapeshifting – that's pretty radical stuff!'

'I suppose so. I miss you there with me, though.'

Warmth surged up through Stephan's chest and he hugged Erin tighter to his side. They were just about at the house. 'What did you shapeshift to?' he asked before there wasn't time. His body quivered at the memory of his own adventures with Bear.

'A seagull,' Erin said.

'A seagull?'

She nodded. 'It was so unexpected. But Stephan – flying!'

The fire burned brightly in the hearth as they spread out through the room. Ambrose had asked them to come back to Hawthorn House after their new moon ritual.

He looked around at their shining faces as they each found seats in the room lit simply by the fire and the low afternoon light. The new moon ritual had gone well, bringing them together in a dance that concentrated on weaving the web, drawing together, drawing apart, remaining connected, drawing on the knowledge that even though she couldn't be seen – like so much in the world – the face of the moon looked down on each of them. Each of them had been aware that they were dancing under the dark face of the moon, part of the mystery of the world, even though it was daylight. Not everyone could attend for the new moon rituals, since they held them during the day when the moon was actually in the sky, although her face wasn't seen. But enough of them were here.

'I'm going to tell you a story,' he said, then grinned. 'In true bardic style – and a Slavic fairy tale, none the less.' He glanced over at Morghan and saw her raise her eyebrows. 'This is particularly for Morghan,' he continued, 'who likely thought I'd forgotten all about it.' He made a sweeping, laughing bow towards her.

Morghan smiled, knowing full well that Ambrose rarely forgot anything.

'Because as you all know,' Ambrose said, straightening again, 'the Fae Queen has given Morghan a golden hand – and left the purpose of such a gift for us to decipher. This story is one of the few references I've been able to find for such a thing.' He paused, looking around his audience, then nodded slightly. 'I've taken out the obvious Christian overlay to the story, not because that offends me in any way, but because I think it clarifies the message the better.'

With that stipulation out of the way, Ambrose cleared his throat and began.

'This is how the story starts,' he said, standing beside the fire, 'and most stories worth the telling do: once, long, long ago and far, far away, there lived a king and Queen who had been blessed with only a single daughter, a princess of such beauty that none compared. Her forehead was brilliant as the moon. Her lips were like the rose, her complexion as soft and delicate as the lily, and her breath held the sweetness of jessamine. Her hair was a bright gold, and she was so enchanting that none could help listening to her or looking at her.'

Ambrose smiled at his audience, and the fire crackled in the hearth, as though agreeing with his story so far.

'The princess lived for seventeen years in her own rooms, gladdening the heart of her parents, teachers, and servants, although no one else ever saw her. The sons of the king and all other princes were forbidden to enter her rooms. She was kept from their sight. She never went anywhere, never looked upon the outside world, and never breathed the air of the wind, nor felt its breath upon her face.'

Erin squirmed slightly at this. Never allowed outside? Why, she wondered?

'She was, however, perfectly happy, until one day, by chance or by the will of fate, she heard the cry of the cuckoo. This sound made her uneasy and she dropped her beautiful head into her hands, falling into thought so deep that she didn't not hear her mother enter the chamber. The Queen looked anxiously upon her only daughter and went to tell the King of what had happened.'

Ambrose nodded, noting again the many peculiar aspects of this story. He listened to the rising wind for a moment, glanced at the gathering dusk of late afternoon, and resumed his tale.

'For many years, kings and princes had been asking for the princess's hand in marriage, but always her father had put them off. Now, after a long debate with the Queen, he sent messengers to all the foreign courts to proclaim that the princess was now ready to choose her husband, who would also gain the right of succession to the king's throne.

'The princess, upon hearing of this decision, was over-joyed, and looking out through the golden lattice of her window, desired suddenly to walk upon the smooth lawns outside, and to wander through the gardens below. With great difficulty she persuaded her governesses to allow her to do so, on the condition that she would stay near them. '

Drawing breath, Ambrose continued.

'So, the crystal doors were thrown open, the oaken gates that shut in the orchard turned on their hinges, and the princess breathed of the fresh air, and sighed over the flowers, and marvelled over the brightly-coloured butterflies.' Ambrose shook his head and raised his brows. 'But, to quote the version of the story I have – 'she could not have been a very prudent maiden, for she wandered away from her governesses, with her face uncovered.'

'And at that moment, a hurricane, fast and furious, passed by and happened upon the garden, there to roar and rage and it snatched up the princess and carried her far away. The governesses were speechless with grief at the loss of their charge and could not think what to do for a time. Finally, they ran back to the palace and threw themselves on their knees before the king and Queen, telling them in sobbing voices that the princess had been carried away.

'The king and Queen, overcome with grief, didn't know what to do. Faced with the crowd of princes newly arrived to vie for the hand of the princess, the king told them that sorrow had touched his white hairs since the hurricane had carried off his beloved child, the Princess with the Golden Hair, and he shook his head. 'I do not know where she has been taken,' he said. 'Whoever finds this out and brings her back to me, shall have the right to take her as his wife, and half my kingdom as a wedding gift, and the remainder of my wealth and titles upon my death.''

Ambrose rolled his head on his shoulders for a moment, then set back about his story. It was full of symbolism, and, he thought, fit amazingly neatly into present circumstances.

'After hearing the words of the king, all the princes and knights set off on their horses to search throughout the world for the Princess with the Golden Hair, who had been snatched from her garden by Vikher, the hurricane. Two of these princes were brothers, and they travelled many miles asking for news of the princess, but no one had anything to tell them. They continued across country after country, and at the end of two years, arrived in a country that lies in the centre of the earth, and that has summer and winter at the same time.'

An Otherworld country, Ambrose thought, with a glance over at Morghan, who stared at him, rapt. What other sort of land lies at the centre of the earth? What other place has summer and winter at the same time?

The story was magical indeed.

'The princes thought it likely that this world was the place where the hurricane had hidden the Princess with the Golden Hair. So, leaving their horses, they climbed one of the mountains. At the top, they stopped short at the sight of a silver palace supported on a cock's foot, while at one of the windows the sun's rays shone upon a head of beautiful golden hair. Surely, this was the princess they had sought so long?

'Suddenly, from the north, a chill wind blew, and it was so violent and cold, that the leaves of the trees crackled and withered on the branches, and the very breath of the princes froze. They tried to keep their footing and battled with all their strength against the sudden storm, but at last they were overcome by its fierceness and fell together back down the mountain, frozen to death.'

Listening, Erin frowned at the story. What did it all mean, she wondered? She knew Ambrose wouldn't be telling them the story unless he thought it meant something. It reminded her of dreaming, she decided. Perhaps fairy stories used the same sort of symbolism as dreams did.

'The parents of the dead princes waited for them to return, but they never did. They made offerings to their gods, and spread goodwill and alms to all around, but their sorrow was not lifted. One day, when the princes' mother was helping a poor old man, she begged him to add his prayers and blessings to hers for her missing sons to be returned to her in good health. But the old man shook his head. 'That prayer would not be worth anything,' he said, 'for the dead have their own business. But in return for the love you have shown to the poor and needy, I am charged with this message – that the gods have taken pity on your sorrow, and that soon you will find yourself the mother of another son, the like of whom has never yet been seen.' And with that, the old man vanished, leaving the Queen in tears, a strange joy entering her heart. She went to the king her husband and repeated the old man's words to him.

'And so it came to pass – in only a week, she gave birth to a son, and he was not in any way an ordinary child.'

Ambrose paused, smiling slightly, then continued. 'His eyes were those of a falcon's, and his eyebrows were a sable's fur.' Ambrose turned and bowed slightly to Morghan. 'His right hand was of pure gold, and his manner and appearance were so full of an indescribable majesty, that he was looked upon by everyone with a feeling of awe.' Ambrose smiled at her.

'This young prince's growth too, was not that of an ordinary child. By three days, he climbed from his cradle, too large for his swaddling clothes, and when his parents saw him, he ran towards them, asking why were they so sad, why were they not happy at the sight of him?

'They replied, of course, that they felt blessed indeed to have him, but that they could not forget his brothers, who had been so handsome and brave, and worthy of the greatest destiny. And they told him that their sadness was even greater that his brothers were not resting in their own country but were lost somewhere far from their home in an unknown land. 'Alas!' they cried. 'It is two years since we had news of them!'

'The youngest prince wept for his parent's sorrow and he gathered them in his arms. 'Do not be sad,' he told them. 'Next spring, I shall be a strong young man and I will go to look for my brothers and I will bring them back to you whether alive or dead, and though I will have to seek them in the very centre of the earth.' The strange prince then, as if guided by an unseen hand, rushed into the garden, and bathed in the dew while the sun rose. Then he threw himself down near a little wood on the fine sand, rubbed and rolled himself in it, and returned home no longer a child, but a youth.

'The young prince grew from hour to hour. At the end of two months he rode on horseback. In three months he had grown a beautiful moustache of pure gold. Then he presented himself before the king and Queen. 'My honoured parents,' he said. 'No longer a child, I ask your blessing to go now to seek my brothers. To seek them, I will if necessary, go to the furthest ends of the world.'

'But his parents shook their heads. 'You are too young,' they told him, and they wished for him to stay safely with them. But their youngest son shook his head. 'I have no terror,' he told them. 'Our destinies find us whatever we may try to do to prevent them.'

Morghan looked down at her hands in her lap, the right one glowing golden in the light from the fire. It was true, she thought, what the young prince said about destiny. One could walk in the flow of their purpose or fight against the current. But their purpose still waited for them, to be achieved in this life or the next.

She clasped her fingers together.

28

Ambrose paused, took a sip of tea to wet his throat. 'So,' he continued. 'Weeping, the king and Queen bade their son goodbye and blessed him and the road he was to travel.

'The young prince rode his horse through deep rivers and climbed high mountains across many countries. At last, he came to a dark forest and in the middle of the forest he saw a cottage supported on a cock's foot and standing in the middle of a great garden of poppies. He made his way towards the cottage and was seized suddenly by the urgent need to sleep, but resisting the longing, he urged his horse on, breaking off the poppy heads as he galloped through the flowers to come up close to the house. Then he reined in and called out:

'Little cot, turn around, on thy foot turn thou free.

To the forest set thy back, let thy door be wide to me.'

'The cottage turned around with a great creaking noise and presented the prince with its door. He left his horse and entered the cottage, finding within an old woman sitting at a table, head resting on her hands as she stared at the ceiling lost in thought. She was an awful hag, with long white hair and a face covered in wrinkles.'

Erin couldn't help it; she rolled her eyes. Why were old women always thought of as hags? Age looked just as bad on men.

'Near the old witch were two beautiful girls,' Ambrose continued. 'Their complexions were clear, like lilies and roses, and they were sweet to see.

'Old Baba Yaga spoke to the young prince. 'How do you do, Prince with Moustache of Gold, Hero with the Golden Fist?' she said. 'What brings you to my cottage in the woods?'

'And she listened as he recited the reason for his journey. Afterwards, she shook her head. 'Your brothers perished,' she told him, her voice crackling with age and knowledge. 'They died on the mountain that touches the clouds, while in search of the Princess with the Golden Hair, who was carried off by Vikher, the hurricane.'

'The prince shook his head. 'And how may I get at this thief Vikher?' he asked.

'Baba Yaga rolled her eyes towards the ceiling. 'My dear child,' she grimaced. 'He would swallow you like a fly. It is now a hundred years since I went outside this cottage, for fear Vikher should seize me and carry me off to his palace near the sky.'

'But the prince shook his head. 'I am not afraid of him carrying me off, for I am not handsome enough for that,' he said. 'And he will not swallow me either, for my golden hand can smash anything.'

'Baba Yaga considered this momentarily. 'Then, my

dove,' she said. 'If you are not afraid, I will help you as best as I may.' She looked at him. 'But you must give me your word of honour that you will bring me some of the Water of Youth, for it restores even to the most aged the beauty and freshness of youth.' She touched a gnarled hand to her face.'

Ambrose nodded. 'The prince gave his word to Baba Yaga, and she believed him, for it was obvious to her that his word was his honour and his bond. And so, she told him what he must do.

'She told him: 'I will give you a pin cushion to guide you. This you must throw in front of you and follow whithersoever it goes. It will lead you to the mountain that touches the clouds, and which is guarded in Vikher's absence by his father and mother, the Northern Blast and the Southern Wind.' She shook her head. 'Do not lose sight of the pin cushion for then you shall be utterly lost. If attacked by the father, the Northern Blast, and suddenly freezing with cold, put on this heat-giving hood. It overpowered by burning heat from the South Wind, then drink from this cooling flagon.' She handed the items over. 'Thus you will reach the top of the mountain where the Princess with the Golden Hair is imprisoned. Deal with Vikher as you will, only remember to bring me some of the Water of Youth.'

Ambrose glanced out the window, where the first flakes of snow were falling. He stopped for a moment to look, and his glance was followed by everyone else in the room, and for a long moment they were mesmerised by the silent swirling of snow.

Then they turned back expectantly to Ambrose and the fire crackling in the grate.

'The young prince took the pin cushion, the heat-giving hood, and the cooling flagon and bid farewell to old Yaga and her two lovely daughters and got back on his horse, riding off, following at a good clip the pin cushion rolling at speed in front of him. Through two kingdoms he rode, until he came to a land in which lay a beautiful valley stretching to the horizon where a mountain reached so high above the earth that it touched the clouds.

'At the foot of the mountain, the prince left his horse to graze, and with a quick prayer, he followed the pin cushion up the steep and rocky paths towards the summit. Halfway there, the Northern Blast blew upon him and its breath was so cold that the wood of the trees split, and his breath froze. He was chilled right to the heart.

'Quickly then, he put on the heat-giving hood and cried out:

'O Heat-Giving Hood, see I fly not to thee,

Lend me quickly thine aid;

O hasten to warm ere the cold has killed me,

With thee I'm not afraid.'

'The Northern Blast doubled its efforts, but the prince was now so hot that he steamed with sweat and had to unbutton his coat to fan himself as he continued his climb.

'The pin cushion rolled to a stop at a snow-covered mound. The prince cleared away the snow and discovered the frozen bodies of two young men. He knew them immediately to be his lost brothers and he knelt beside them to offer prayers over their bodies. Then, he turned to follow the pin cushion again, which was already rolling higher and higher up the mountain.

'At the top of the mountain, the young prince saw a

silver palace supported on a cock's foot, and at one of the windows, shining in the sun's rays, a head of golden hair which could belong only to the princess. But suddenly, a hot wind blew from the south and the heat was so intense that the leaves withered and dropped from the branches of the trees and the grass dried up where the prince stood, and great thirsty cracks opened in the earth's surface. Thirst, heat, and weariness began to tell upon the young prince, so he took the cooling flagon from his pocket and cried:

'Flagon, bring me quick relief

From this parching heat;

In thy draught I have belief,

Coolness it will mete.'

Morghan looked around the room and found several people nodding. Charlie, her husband Martin, and their son and daughter-in-law. They knew too, that words – spells – were important. You could be given the most marvellous gifts, Morghan thought, but without the correct action, or words, or intent, they were dormant in your grasp.

'After drinking, the prince was cooled and refreshed, and buttoned his coat again to warm himself. Still, he had a way to go, following the pin cushion as it rolled higher and higher. They crossed a place of heavy clouds and came at last to the topmost peak of the mountain. Here was the palace, a dream of perfect beauty in every aspect. It was supported on a cock's foot, and was built entirely out of silver, except for its roof of solid gold.

'Before the entrance was a deep precipice over which none but birds could pass. The prince gazed upon the marvellous building and while he was doing so, the princess leaned out of one of the windows, and seeing him there, light shone from her sparkling eyes, her lovely hair floated in the wind, and the scent of her sweet breath filled the air. The prince leapt forward and cried out:

'Silver Palace, oh turn, on thy foot turn thou free,
To the steep rocks thy back, but thy doors wide to me.'

'At these words, the palace revolved, creaking and groaning, until the doorway faced our intrepid prince, its drawbridge down over the great chasm. He entered with ease and as he did so, the palace returned to its original position. Going through the palace, the prince came at last upon a room as bright as the sun itself, in which the walls, ceiling, and floor were mirrors. He stood looking, marvelling, for he saw not one, but twelve beautiful princesses, all with golden hair and graceful movements.

'But of course, eleven of them were only reflections of the one real princess who ran crying to him. 'From which family, city, or country have you come all this way?' she asked him. 'Perhaps you have been sent by my beloved mother and father?'

'The prince shook his head. 'No one has sent me,' he told the beautiful princess. 'I have come of my own free will to rescue you and restore you to your parents.' Her eyes widened at this news and she shook her head, her joy fleeing. 'Vikher the hurricane is invincible,' she said. 'And so, if you value your life, then hurry back the way you have come for I expect his return every minute and he will kill you with one glance from his eyes.'

'But our prince would not leave,' Ambrose said. "My purpose is to save you,' he told the princess. 'If I cannot do so, then life means nothing to me.' He was, however, full of confidence and asked the princess to give him some of the

Strength-Giving Water from the Heroic Well, which he knew was drunk by the hurricane.

'The princess drew him a bucketful of the water and the young prince emptied it in one draught and asked for another. Astonished, the princess refilled the bucket, and he drank again. And when he had, he shook his head and asked for a chair. 'Allow me to sit for a moment to regain my breath,' he said.

'The princess led him to sit in an iron chair, but directly he sat down, it broke under him into a thousand pieces. She then brought him the chair used by Vikher himself, made of the strongest stone, and it groaned as he sat upon it but did not break. 'Now, here I am,' said the prince, 'grown heavier than your unconquerable hurricane, so be sure that with your blessings and the god's I shall overpower him.'

Ambrose took another sip of tea, wondering as he had the first time he'd read the old fairy tale, why there was a mirrored room that showed twelve golden princesses. Surely something to do with the sun? He cleared his throat and continued his story.

'The prince asked the princess to tell him about her life here in the silver palace on the top of the mountain. She shook her head in distress. 'I have cried many bitter tears here,' she told him. 'But I am glad to have been able to keep Vikher at a distance, for all that he implores me to marry him. Two years I have been here, but he has not won my consent yet.' She shivered. 'On his return from this last trip, however, he has said that he will marry me despite my objections and even if he has not guessed the answers to the riddles I have set as a condition to marrying him.' Her beautiful face fell in sadness.

'But the prince was jovial. 'I have come just in time,' he pronounced. 'I will be priest on this occasion then, and he shall have death for his bride.' At this moment, a terrible whistling was heard, and the princess was terrified for the hurricane was returning to his silver palace.

'The palace spun round fast on its leg, and fearful sounds were heard all through the rooms. Thousands of ravens croaked loudly and flapped their wings, and all the doors opened with a cacophonous noise. Vikher, who was indeed the hurricane, with the body of a giant and the head of a dragon, leapt into the mirrored room on his winged horse that breathed fire, then stopped amazed at the sight of the prince before him. 'What is your business here?' he roared and the sound of it was like a lion.

'The prince was calm and answered conversationally. 'I am your enemy,' he said. 'And I am here for your blood.' The hurricane, hearing this, roared again, but with laughter this time, then told the prince he would take him in his left hand and crush every bone in his body with his right.

'Our Prince with the Golden Moustache was unbothered. 'Try, if you dare,' he challenged, and called the hurricane a woman-stealer.

'Now was Vikher enraged, and with his mouth wide open breathing fire, he threw himself upon the prince, thinking to swallow him. But the prince stepped neatly aside, and putting his golden hand down the hurricane's throat, he seized him by the tongue and dashed him against the wall with such force that the monster bounced upon it like a ball and died within a few moments.'

Ambrose looked down at his feet where he stood, then

gave Morghan a quick smile. 'Our tale is almost told,' he said, 'but we are not quite done yet.'

'The prince then drew water from the Spring that Restores, from the Spring that Revives, and lastly from the Spring that Makes Young, and taking the princess who had swooned from fright during the battle, he led the winged horse to the door and said:

'Silver Palace, oh turn, on thy foot turn thou free,

To the steep rocks thy back, the courtyard may I see.'

'And so, the palace creaked and groaned as it turned around on its foot and the courtyard now faced our victorious prince. Leaping upon the horse, he placed the recovered princess before him, and cried:

'Fiery Horse, with strength of wing,

I am now your lord;

Do my will in everything,

Be your law my word.

Where I point there you must go

At once, at once. The way you know.'

'He pointed to the place where his brothers lay frozen under the snow, their bodies cold and dead. The horse rose, beating the air with his wings, then flew down the mountain and landed gently on the ground beside the two princes. The Prince with the Golden Hand sprinkled their bodies with the Life-Restoring Water, and instantly their faces regained their colour and breath filled their lungs once more. He sprinkled them next with the Water that Revives, and they got up, looking around. 'How well we have slept,' they exclaimed. 'But what has happened, and how is it that the beautiful princess we have been seeking is here in the company of a stranger?'

'The Prince with the Golden Hand explained everything and embraced his brothers tenderly, then took them with him on his horse, showing the horse that he wished to go in the direction of Baba Yaga's cottage. The horse took heed and flew them with beating wings over the high forests and to the cottage. The prince said:

'Little cot, turn around, on thy foot turn thou free,

To the forest thy back, but thy door wide to me.'

'Immediately,' Ambrose said, 'the cottage turned to face the brothers and the princess. Baba Yaga, who had been looking out, came to meet them. The prince gave her the Water of Youth and she sprinkled herself immediately with it. Instantly, she was young and charming and so pleased was she to have her youth restored that she kissed the prince's hands and said, 'Ask of me anything you like, I will refuse you nothing.'

'At that moment, her two daughters looked out of the window and were seen by the two elder princes, who admired them greatly. 'Will you give us your daughters for our wives?' they asked the Yaga. She agreed with pleasure and beckoned her daughters forward. With a curtsey to her future sons-in-law, she laughed and vanished.

'The new brides were placed on the horse with them and the Prince with the Golden Hand, pointing where he wished to go, said:

'Fiery Horse with strength of wing,

I am now your lord;

Do my will in everything,

Be your law my word.

Where I point there you must go

At once, at once. The way you know.'

'The horse rose immediately and with a flapping of his wings, he flew them far above the forest. After an hour or two, he descended into the garden of the palace of the Golden-Haired Princess's parents. When her mother and father saw their only daughter, so long lost to them, they ran to meet her with joy and gratitude in their hearts and kissed her lovingly while they thanked the prince who had returned her to them after all this time. When they heard of his great adventure, they gave him the hand of the Golden-Haired Princess in marriage and with it, half of the king's lands and the right to the rest when he died. 'Let us celebrate this day too with the weddings of your two brothers.'

'The princess was much pleased by all of this, but she turned to her father. 'My much-honoured prince and bridegroom knows of the vow I made when carried off by the hurricane, that I would only give my hand to him who could answer correctly my six riddles.' She shook her head. 'It would be impossible for the Princess with the Golden Hair to break her word.'

'The king stayed silent, but the prince stepped forward and bade her to ask him her enigmas. 'This is my first,' she said. 'Two of my extremities form a sharp point, the two others a ring, in my centre is a screw.'

'The prince knew the answer straight away. 'A pair of scissors,' answered he. And so the princess smiled upon him and told him her second riddle. 'I make the round of the table on only one foot, but if I am wounded the evil is beyond repair.'

'Again, the prince had the answer. 'A glass of wine,' he said. 'That is right,' the Princess with the Golden Hair told him. 'This is the third, then. I have no tongue and yet I answer faithfully; I am not seen, yet everyone hears me.'

'The prince had the answer. 'An echo,' he said. 'True,' the princess replied. 'This is the fourth: fire cannot light me, brush cannot sweep me, no painter can paint me, no hiding-place secure me.'

'Again the prince knew straight away the answer, for it was sunshine. The princess recited her fifth riddle: 'I existed before any person. I am always changing in succession the two colours of my dress. Thousands of years have gone by, but I have remained unaltered both in colour and form.' The prince did not even have to think upon the answer, for he said it must be time, including day and night, and he was correct. The princess was gratified that he had answered so easily her five most difficult riddles, and told him the last, the easiest of them all. 'By day a ring,' she said, 'by night a serpent; he who guesses this shall be my bridegroom.'

'The prince knew the answer. 'A girdle,' he said, and the princess replied to him, 'now they are all guessed,' and she gave him her hand. They knelt before the king and Queen to receive their blessing. The three weddings were to be celebrated that same evening, and a messenger mounted the winged horse to carry the good news to the parents of the young princes and to bring them back as guests.'

Ambrose swept his gaze around the room. 'Meanwhile,' he said. 'A magnificent feast was prepared, and invitations sent to all friends and acquaintances. From that evening until the next morning, they ceased not to feast and drink and dance in celebration.' He paused. 'And so is my tale finally told. I too was a guest and feasted with the rest; but though I ate and drank, the wine only ran down my beard, and my throat remained dry.'

It was an odd conceit on which to end the story, but that was how it went, and so Ambrose also finished with it. He gave a short flourish of a bow and fell quiet, into the woven spell of the story.

Because fairy tales were like travels into the Otherworld.

Full of symbolism and mystery.

29

'YOU MUST COME,' ROSALIE SAID, HUNCHING DOWN DEEPER into her new coat from the clothes swap. 'Now,' she added. 'Nothing I've done has worked and now it's much worse, see? God's not listening to me.'

Winsome blinked at Rosalie where the old woman stood outside her kitchen door, fluffy hair dishevelled where it poked out under her woolly hat.

'Come inside and wait while I get my coat on,' Winsome said.

Rosalie looked for a moment like she didn't want to wait even that long, but she gave a short nod and stepped inside. The vicarage kitchen was blessedly warm, and she looked around for a moment, marvelling over how big the old building was compared to her tiny terrace.

'Get your holy water and whatever else you need to bless a place,' she called to Winsome's disappearing back.

Winsome turned for a moment and looked at Rosalie. 'Things are that much worse?' she asked.

'Yes,' came the short answer.

With a nod, Winsome turned back to go into her study, a great lump in her throat. Unsure of what much worse might look like, she hesitated for a moment on the threshold, looking wildly around, wondering what she needed.

A deep breath, she told herself. That's what you need. A few of them, perhaps. She reached for the wardrobe and drew her cassock out, slipping it on over her jersey and jeans. Unsure of what she was going to see at Rosalie's house, she knew she needed the authority of her position behind her.

'I'm ready,' she said, going back to Rosalie in the kitchen and taking another of those deep breaths.

Rosalie looked her over. Then nodded. 'Good,' she said. 'You got changed.'

'Are you able to tell me what exactly is happening in your home, Rosalie?' Winsome asked. She'd feel much better, she thought, if she had even an inkling of what she'd be walking into.

But Rosalie shook her head. 'Best if you just see for yourself, I reckon, Vicar,' she said, then scrunched her face into an anguished frown. 'I walked here, but we could take your car, couldn't we?'

'Yes.' At least Winsome could be emphatic about that.

At the door to the small terrace house, Rosalie turned back to Winsome and grimaced. 'It's a mess,' she said. 'I hope you can help, Vicar. I tried to bless the house myself, but it seemed to just make everything worse!'

Winsome watched the door being opened with her heart in her throat. What was she about to see? 'You weren't at service this morning, Rosalie,' she said while she waited for the old woman to step inside.

'I was too busy, you see,' Rosalie said, and made room for Winsome to come up next to her in the small hallway in front of the stairs. 'Dealing with this.' She pointed up the stairs.

'What?'

Winsome gazed up the stairs, unsure what she was seeing. It made no sense. She shook her head. 'Who did this?' she asked.

The door to the sitting room opened and a young girl dashed out and wrapped her arms around Rosalie's waist, burying her face in the thick coat Rosalie still had on.

'This is my granddaughter,' Rosalie said. 'My other granddaughter.'

'Where is Natasha?' Winsome asked.

Rosalie nodded her head toward the kitchen. 'In there,' she said. 'With the baby.'

She didn't mention Minnie.

Winsome noticed. 'And your other granddaughter?'

A jerk of the head. 'Up there. Behind that lot.'

Winsome gazed up the stairs, disquiet shivering through her body. 'But how did it all get there?' she asked.

'It was the bad fairies,' Tiny said. 'Are you here to tell them to go away?'

The bad fairies? Winsome creaked down onto her knees and looked at Tiny. 'Did you see who did it?' she asked.

Tiny shook her head. 'No,' she said. 'Not this time.' She squeezed her eyes shut so that she wouldn't start crying again.

'It's true, Vicar,' Rosalie said, and her voice cracked and

quavered. 'Odd things been happening, just like I told you last time, only it's gotten worse, you see.'

Winsome did indeed see. The top of the stairs was impassable. A wardrobe lay on its side, blocking the steps, and behind that, she counted two beds jammed into the tiny space that was the landing. A dressing table was legs-up on top of them, and incongruously, a lamp, its bulb burning, sat on top as though there was nothing wrong with the scene at all. The doors to the boxroom and the bedroom were barely visible.

She licked her lips, but her tongue was as dry as her throat. 'And your granddaughter - Minnie, isn't it? She's in one of the rooms behind all this?'

Rosalie nodded.

'Is she okay? She's not hurt?'

'She's not hurt. Not physically.'

Tiny piped up. 'She thinks it's funny.'

Winsome raised her eyebrows at the child. 'Funny?'

Tiny shrank back and looked up the stairs with her face creased in unhappiness. 'I think I heard her laughing. There's something wrong with her.'

Good God, Winsome thought. What has been going on in this house?

Rosalie was looking at her. 'Can you do something, Vicar?' she asked.

Could she? 'I've never come across anything like this,' Winsome said, staring up at the tangle of furniture. She spotted a teddy bear staring down at her from between the legs of the dressing table and pressed a hand to her heart.

'It's spirits,' Rosalie said darkly. 'It's evil spirits doing this.'

'The bad fairy,' Tiny said, nodding her head. 'I saw it. Minnie thinks it's Daddy, but it's not.'

Winsome looked at her. 'What did you say?'

It was Rosalie who answered. 'Minnie's been talking to a spirit,' she said, spitting the words out. 'She thinks it's her father.'

Tiny stuck a hand in her pocket and clutched a crayon. 'It's not Daddy. He got angry sometimes, but he wouldn't do this. And besides,' she added. 'He's dead and Gran says he would be gone to heaven by now.'

Winsome could feel her circuits blowing. Inside her, fuses were shorting out and she shook her head, dazed. This was Wellsford, not The Exorcist. The Exorcist was a movie. This was real life. Things like this didn't happen in real life.

Did they?

Except of course they did. Ghosts, hauntings, poltergeists. She'd heard stories of them – hadn't everyone?

She'd not heard stories of what to do about it, though.

A loud thump from upstairs startled her and she jumped. 'What was that?' she gasped.

It was followed by a flurry of bumping sounds.

Everyone gazed up the stairs.

Winsome cleared her throat. 'Minnie?' she called. 'Minnie are you all right?'

There was no answer. Just more bumping sounds. Winsome huffed a breath out through her mouth and rubbed her sweating palms on her cassock.

'We have to get those things moved,' she said.

'I tried,' Rosalie said. 'I'm not strong enough to get past the wardrobe, and everything is jammed so close behind it.'

Rosalie was right of course, Winsome knew. And she wouldn't be able to do any better.

'We need help,' she said. 'To get it cleared.'

They looked at each other.

Rosalie wrung her hands. 'I don't want anyone at the church to know,' she said. 'Please.'

Most of the congregation was elderly anyway, Winsome thought. Besides, she already knew that if she wanted to get something done quickly – and from the looks of the situation, quickly done was needed – then she already knew who she had to call on.

'I'll be right back,' she said. 'I know who to get to help.'

Rosalie looked at her, apprehension making her sweat lightly. 'It's not someone from the church, please promise me, Vicar?'

Winsome swallowed. 'No,' she said, then closed her eyes and said a small prayer.

Please God, smooth the way.

'No,' she said again. 'I don't believe the Church is the best one to deal with this particular situation.'

Rosalie squinted at her, running her words through her tired mind again. She put her hand on top of Tiny's head as another smatter of bumps and thumps sounded from the bedroom upstairs.

She cleared her throat. 'So, the rumours are true then, Vicar,' she said.

'What rumours?'

'About you being friendly with the Grove. With Morghan Wilde and Ambrose.'

Winsome felt faint. Of course there would be rumours –

hadn't she been working alongside Morghan with the Care Home? And visiting Wayne Moffat with her.

She groaned. 'Julia Thorpe,' she said.

Rosalie just shrugged. 'Can't stop gossip in a village this size, love,' she said. 'Unfortunately.' She took a deep breath and glanced up the stairs at the monstrous tangle of furniture blocking the way. 'I say perhaps this is more up their alley anyway.'

'Right,' Winsome said after an awkward moment. 'I'm going to pop along the road and get young Stephan to help clear this lot. That seems a good place to start.'

'We'll be in the kitchen, praying,' Rosalie answered.

STEPHAN GAPED AT THE MOUND OF FURNITURE AT THE TOP OF the stairs. 'How did this get there?' he asked, exchanging a glance with Erin and Krista.

Rosalie stood at the door to the sitting room, arms folded tightly across her chest. 'They moved on their own,' she said.

'You saw it?' Krista asked.

But Rosalie shook her head. 'Heard it. We were in the kitchen, making a late breakfast.' She coloured slightly. 'I haven't been feeling well.' She let out a long slow breath. 'Anyway, we heard an awful racket, and when we came out to see what was going on...' She gestured helplessly at the stairs. 'We found it like this.'

'Minnie, Rosalie's oldest granddaughter is up there in one of the bedrooms,' Winsome said.

'Right then,' Stephan answered. 'Let's get it cleared away.'

He'd never seen anything like it. It was something out of a movie, not real life. 'I think I'll have to climb over the top of it all,' he called down.

'I'll give you a hand,' Erin said and joined him at the top of the stairs.

'If we can squeeze over and get that door open there, we ought to have enough room to start clearing everything away,' Stephan pointed.

'I tried to get Natasha to do that, but she wouldn't leave the kitchen. Natasha's not been coping.' Rosalie swatted away a tear and sniffed. 'And the kids are hurting, and everything's been so very terrible.' She snuffled a hand into her pocket and dragged out a hanky. 'It's just all been so hard.'

'I understand,' Winsome said. 'It's going to be okay. You're not on your own with any of this now, and we'll get to the bottom of it, I promise.'

And once they'd dealt with this poltergeist or whatever it was, she'd do something to make life easier for Rosalie and her family in whatever way she could. She couldn't make everything better for everyone in the world, but she would do what she could in her little piece of it.

Erin winced as something sharp poked her in the stomach, but she squeezed herself over the top of the beds and wardrobe anyway. 'I can touch the door,' she said.

'Great,' Stephan answered. 'Can you get it open?'

She could, and a moment later, she'd slithered off the pile of furniture and into the tiny room behind it. She wrinkled her nose at the size of it – little more than a cupboard, really, and yet there was a cardboard box of clothes and another box that was obviously being used as a bedside table beside a rickety camp bed. An electrical cord trailed out the door to the lamp.

'The floor in here is all wet,' she said, her feet squelching on the sodden carpet. She switched the lamp off at the wall, not trusting the wiring with the water.

Krista tried to peer over the mound of furniture and into the room. 'Water puddles are common in poltergeist hauntings,' she said.

Erin plucked up the lamp and gingerly replaced it on the box in the corner of the room. 'How do you know so much about poltergeists?' she asked.

'I run a bookstore, remember?' Krista said, then blinked as Stephan dived into the room where Erin was. 'With a big occult section.' She pushed experimentally at the wardrobe but the beds behind it would need to be moved before she could get it to budge. 'Poltergeist phenomena is more common than you'd think, actually,' she said. 'Like, really common. All over the world.'

She leaned over as far as she could. 'Can you open that other door?' She thought they ought to find Minnie sooner rather than later. 'Teenagers are usually the focus for it,' she added.

Erin's face was pale as she tried to squeeze past the furniture. 'Can't,' she said.

'We'll have to move some more of this stuff first,' Stephan added, reaching for the dressing table. 'Can you grab the other end of this, Erin?'

Winsome joined Krista on the stairs. She spoke in a low voice. 'Why teenagers?' she asked.

'All that insecurity coupled with hormones, I suppose,' Krista said. 'The entities feed off it.'

'Entities?' Winsome listened to the word come out on a squeak. She cleared her throat.

'Yeah. There's been a lot of speculation for the cause of it over the years, but I'm willing to bet the farm that it's lowlife entities. There are a lot of those about, just waiting for someone to start leaking energy all over the place from stress or whatever, that they can play with.'

Winsome shivered, remembering what Morghan had seen. The dark flock of entities.

'I never thought I'd see one, though,' she muttered.

'I'd say you're about to do a lot more than see one,' Krista said as Stephan and Erin got the dressing table out of the way and started tugging at one of the beds.

'But I don't know anything about them,' Winsome whispered.

Krista nodded. 'Then we'll need someone who does.'

30

THERE WAS ONLY ONE PERSON WHO KNEW EVERYTHING
necessary about spirits, Winsome thought, drawing out her
phone. And she wasn't too proud to ask that person for help,
either.

Gossips be damned, she decided.

'The doorway's clear,' Stephan said as Winsome finished
her conversation and put her phone back in her pocket.

'It's closed?' she asked.

He nodded. 'Can't hear anything from in there.' Erin
appeared at his side and he reached out to her, holding her
hand like it was the most natural thing in the world. 'I guess
this part is yours,' he said to Winsome. 'We'll wait out here
in case you need us.' He shrugged.

Winsome drew in a deep breath and climbed back up
the stairs. Minnie was in the front bedroom, according to
Rosalie. She tapped on the door.

'Minnie? It's Winsome,' she said. 'We met the other day
– your Gran introduced us; do you remember?'

There was no answer. She knocked louder, cast a glance back at Stephan, Erin, and Krista who stood poised still on the landing watching. Then Winsome turned back to the door, leaning her forehead against it. The wood was cold against her skin. Behind it, the room was silent.

Was the girl all right?

'I'm too frightened,' she said.

There was a light touch on her shoulder. 'Too frightened for what?' Krista asked.

'To, you know – open up my senses.' Winsome looked over at Krista. 'I don't know what I'll find.'

Krista's face blossomed in a soft smile. 'Nothing that will be able to harm you,' she said. 'Only a hurt child being taken advantage of.'

Winsome straightened, nodded. 'Of course.' For a moment she felt foolish – she should have been thinking of it like that all along. If she held herself in the light of her love for God, for the world, as Morghan would say, then no, she needn't be afraid.

'Deep breaths,' Krista said.

Winsome nodded. 'I'm going to open the door. We have to make sure she is okay.'

The door creaked slightly as Winsome eased it open, taking deep slow breaths, letting her spirit unfurl, spreading out about her so that her awareness prickled around her and she was bigger than her skin, and remembering too, everything that Morghan had taught her about protecting and shielding her energy.

'Hello Minnie,' she said.

Minnie turned her head and looked at Winsome. 'I don't feel well,' she said. Her phone lay in her lap where she sat on the floor beside the bed, the wall at her back. 'I couldn't open the door.' She grinned suddenly, but there was no humour in it, only pain that radiated out to touch Winsome's senses. 'Dad said the others needed to be shut out.' She closed her eyes. 'He tells me all sorts of things.' She held up her phone and Winsome saw that the light on the back of it was on for some reason, even though it wasn't dark in the room.

She could feel Minnie, curled up in on herself, and she frowned, sensing a great bloating darkness in the middle of the girl, that she was curled around.

'And he shows me things too,' Minnie said, her eyes opening to look over at Winsome. 'Awful things. I've been having terrible dreams. Why would my Dad make me have terrible dreams?'

Winsome lowered herself to the floor. Minnie's skin was pale, a light sheen of sweat covering it.

'Because it's not your Dad,' she said.

'Of course it's my Dad,' Minnie told her. 'He said he misses me.'

'I'm sorry sweetheart,' Winsome said, feeling her heart twinge with pain. 'It's not your Dad. The spirit's tricking you.'

'Don't be silly,' Minnie said. 'I made sure it was him. I'm not stupid, you know.'

'Of course you're not stupid,' Winsome answered. 'I've a feeling you're a very smart girl who has also been missing her father.'

Minnie shook her head. 'He shouldn't have died. It was too stupid for words. Dropping dead at the chip shop – who does that?' She grabbed a strand of hair and wound it around her finger, flicking the end over her thumb. Flick, flick, flick.

There was a light scratching from the wall behind Minnie.

'He wants to stop being dead,' she said after a minute.

'The spirit?'

Minnie nodded. 'He wants to come and live with me.' She put her phone down carefully on the floor and wrapped her arm around her middle, drawing her knees up further.

'What does that mean?' Winsome asked. 'Come and live with you?'

Minnie tucked herself tighter into a ball, letting her hair go. She shrugged.

Winsome tried a different tack. 'Do you want him to?'

Minnie didn't answer. 'I don't want to talk to you,' she said. She really did feel sick. 'I'm a witch. I don't like the church. Only idiots go to church.'

'You're a witch?'

'I want to be.'

'I know some wonderful people who might be called witches,' Winsome said, prodding around the edges of the darkness Minnie was hunched over.

'You can't know any,' Minnie said. 'You're a vicar.'

Winsome shrugged. 'Vicars can have friends on different paths,' she said.

'The church burnt witches,' Minnie said.

'In some places, yes,' Winsome agreed. 'And I think we can all agree that is a terrible thing.'

There was a soft knock at the door. Winsome looked up in relief at Morghan, who exchanged a glance with her.

'May I come in?' Morghan asked. 'I think you know who

I am, don't you, Minnie?' She smiled gently and sat on the edge of the bed. 'You've followed me a few times through the woods.'

Minnie lifted dull eyes to look at Morghan. 'How do you know that?' she asked.

'I felt you there.'

'You felt me?' Minnie frowned. 'What do you mean? What did I feel like?'

Morghan thought about that for a moment. 'Better than you do right now,' she answered. 'You're not very well at the moment, are you?'

'My stomach is sore.' Minnie said. 'Did you come here to see me?' she asked.

'I did,' Morghan said. 'The vicar here asked me to come.'

Minnie turned her frown on Winsome.

'We are friends,' Morghan said.

'You can't be friends,' Minnie told her.

'But we are,' Morghan said. 'And you know what else? We work together too.'

Minnie wished they'd go away, even if it was Morghan Wilde sitting in her bedroom. She felt sick. Too sick to ask if she could join the Grove.

There was a crackling from her phone, and an electronic voice said a couple garbled words.

'That's Dad,' Minnie said and put out a hand to grope for the phone. 'I've got to hear what he's saying.'

'That's not your father,' Morghan said. 'I can guarantee it.'

'What would you know about my Dad?' Minnie hissed between clenched teeth. A door slammed outside the room.

'I know this isn't him,' Morghan said soothingly. 'You're being tricked.'

'And made sick,' Winsome added. 'Your dad wouldn't hurt you now, would he?'

Minnie didn't answer for a moment. 'No,' she said eventually. 'My dad loved me.' She squeezed her eyes shut. 'He was the only one who did. Mum's useless.' She sniffed, mortified to find she was crying. 'I hate my life,' she whispered. 'I hate it.'

'It's been so hard, hasn't it?' Winsome said. 'But it's going to get better, I promise.' She glanced at Morghan. 'First though, we have to get rid of this spirit who has been pretending to be your father. Who has been hurting you and scaring everyone.'

Minnie looked down at her knees. It felt like someone had punched her in the stomach. And when she'd tried to get out of her room before, the door wouldn't open. Not even when she needed to go to the toilet. She swallowed, her dry throat clicking. Her dad had kept badgering her.

Be with you, he'd said, as though he'd wanted to climb inside her.

Now she was confused. Had it been her Dad at all? She looked up at Morghan.

'What were you doing in that cave that day?' she asked.

Morghan knew immediately the day Minnie was talking about. 'Travelling to the Otherworld,' she said.

Minnie blinked at her for a moment. 'What sort of witch does that?' she asked.

A smile. 'A hedge witch,' Morghan replied.

There was another pause, longer this time. 'Will you teach me how to do that?' Minnie asked.

'Certainly,' Morghan said. 'One day, when you're a little older.'

'Can I do stuff with you guys before that?'

Morghan laughed. 'Would you like to be part of the Grove, Minnie?'

A sharp pain sliced through her stomach and Minnie groaned. Then nodded. 'I want to be a witch,' she said. 'I'm sick of not being able to do anything.'

'Well then,' Morghan said. 'Let's deal with your entity problem, and we'll see about it, shall we?'

Minnie was suddenly frightened. 'How?' she asked. 'How do we get rid of it? It keeps saying it wants to be with me.' She blinked. 'Like, be with me all the time.'

Morghan nodded. 'You are young and vital, and it's feeding off your energy. All your unhappiness and fear and anger – it's like food to these things.'

'I didn't mean to do anything like that,' Minnie said, head hanging, greasy hair over her eyes.

Winsome reached out and touched her shoulder gently. 'It's all right,' she said. 'It's been a difficult few years for you.'

'And your whole family will have to work at restoring harmony to your lives,' Morghan said. 'But we're all here to help now.'

Minnie raised her eyes and looked at them, the witch and the vicar. It was weird, them working together. How did that go? How did it even happen? She looked over at Winsome with new respect. Maybe she wasn't such a bad sort after all. Maybe she wasn't as close-minded as most vicars and the like.

Her phone hissed again, spat out some more static.

Morghan reached over and picked it up, closing the app and then deleting it.

Wincing, Minnie shook her head. 'Are you sure it's not my Dad?'

'Very sure,' Morghan replied, getting up from the bed and going to the door.

Stephan and Erin were putting the furniture back to rights in the other room. Morghan gestured to them.

'Would you two be kind enough to go find the necessary items and cleanse and clear this house, please?' she asked.

'Of course,' Stephan said promptly. I have a bunch of mullein made into smoke bundles already. They're at home, so it won't take a minute to get them.

'Excellent,' Morghan replied.

'You want us to do the clearing?' Erin asked, wide-eyed with doubt. So many things she'd never thought she'd be doing.

Morghan smiled gently at her. 'Yes, I do,' she said. 'Winsome and I cannot do everything ourselves.'

'But...'

'Follow the lead of Stephan and Krista,' Morghan interrupted. 'And I think it will come naturally to you anyway.' She touched Erin's chest lightly, at the base of her throat. 'Things out of balance must be brought back into balance. Beauty flourishes everywhere, even in a mean little house such as this, even in those who are full of pain, if it is given a chance.' She raised her eyebrows and tilted her head with a smile at Erin, then turned around and went back into the bedroom.

For a moment, Erin was silent. 'I think I want to be just

like Morghan when I grow up,' she said. 'She's not afraid of anything.'

'When you know what happens after you die,' Stephan said, 'I guess there's not much to be afraid of.' He made for the stairs and Erin trailed after him.

'That's bollocks,' she said, stepping out the front door and into a cold wind that blasted down the hills into the village.

'Why?' Stephan asked. 'What's the worst that can ever happen? You die? If it's only your body that dies – which it is – then what's to be afraid of?'

'Pain. Suffering.' Erin pulled a face. 'All that stuff, you know?'

Stephan frowned, zipping up his jacket. 'Yeah,' he said. 'And there's way too much of that – look at this family, right? They're suffering, and it hurts to see them like that.'

'That's not really what I meant.' Erin shoved her hands in her pockets. 'Suffering hurts. It hurts when you're going through it, when you're lost inside it.' She grimaced. 'People in this world hurt, Stephan. Some of them hurt so bad they can't take it anymore. And almost everything in this world hurts. Even love – being in love hurts.'

Stephan stopped walking and turned to her. 'It does?'

Erin took her hands out of her pockets and wrapped her arms around herself. She nodded. 'Yeah,' she said. 'It does.' Her eyes were wide, round, the skin under them dark, shadowed. 'Because what if something happens and the person you love leaves or dies or something, and you're alone?' She shivered, shook her head. 'There's nothing worse than being alone, Stephan.' She paused. 'I've seen it. Felt it.' Thinking of Kria.

But Stephan was already shaking his head. He reached out and put his hands on Erin's shoulders. 'But Erin, that's the thing, isn't it? You're never alone.'

'If you died, I would be.'

'It would be hard,' Stephan admitted. 'Living without your soulmate.' He blinked suddenly watery eyes. 'But that doesn't mean you're alone. Or that you'll never be with them again.' He grew suddenly brave. 'Look at us, Erin. How many lifetimes have we come together?' He shrugged. 'Who knows?' A smile. 'At least one other. And between lives? I'm pretty sure we've hung out together then as well.'

Erin looked down at Stephan's hands on her shoulders. He had such fine, strong hands, she thought.

But she shook her head. 'That doesn't matter,' she said. 'I'm alive here and now. What I feel is here and now. And I don't want to be hurt or alone. I don't want to go through that.'

Stephan shook his head as well. 'But Erin,' he said. 'Right here and now, you aren't alone. We're here, together. If you're thinking about you and me. That's exactly right here and now.' He paused a moment. 'And yes, it might not always be like that, which is why also knowing the bigger picture is important. We live so many lives, Erin. We're never truly alone or truly apart and our lives have purpose, even when we can't see that purpose clearly. And like Morghan just said – beauty is everywhere all the time, if we just look for it.'

Erin closed her eyes. She knew what Stephan said was true, but it didn't touch her heart. She didn't feel it.

What she felt was Kria's pain and anger at being alone, abandoned in that goddess-forsaken valley.

31

'Is this going to hurt?' Minnie asked.

It was Winsome who answered, glancing at Morghan, who seemed different than the last time they'd seen each other. Morghan's usual calmness was back, but there was something else in her eyes too and Winsome tripped over the words trying to think of it.

Serenity, maybe. An even greater depth.

Whatever, Morghan radiated it.

'No, Minnie,' she said gently. 'It's not going to hurt at all.'

There was a voice at the door. 'I can sit with you,' Rosalie said.

Minnie looked at her grandmother, then nodded. Maybe it would be nice to have her there. Better than no one, perhaps.

'You might be more comfortable on your bed, Minnie,' Rosalie said, coming into the room, gathering up the skirts of her courage to be with her granddaughter. Minnie was difficult and hard to get along with, but the child was hurting, she thought. At root of it all – all her acting out – was that one thing. She patted the bed and when Minnie lay down on her side upon it, knees tucked up to her stomach, her head on Rosalie's lap, she stroked the side of Minnie's face gently.

She nodded at the two women. Morghan sat down on Tiny's bed, and Winsome dragged over a small chair.

Morghan looked over at Winsome. 'Do you need some help?' she asked.

But Winsome shook her head. 'I don't think so.' Already, she could feel herself humming and there was that expansive sensation coming over her, that slightly woozy, tipping sideways, double-vision, floating, letting-go feeling, and she went with it, swaying slightly where she sat, ready to follow Morghan's lead.

Morghan touched Winsome's hand, held her fingers lightly, and turned to her own breathing, closing her eyes.

The shadows in the house were hiding now, knowing they were there, knowing they were going to be turned out. They were hiding, hoping they couldn't be weeded out, made to leave. She could feel them there.

She stepped lightly into the space in the world where she straddled spirit and the material, and she brought Winsome with her. It was only a short step to the side, just a small wiggle through the veil, the thinning, parting veil that had never really been there for Morghan anyway.

Winsome looked around, sucking in a breath before turning startled eyes to Morghan, who simply nodded. Winsome shook her head, looked back at the room, and at the girl on the bed.

Morghan turned her gaze to her as well, then back to Winsome. 'It will be easier if we go deeper,' she said.

'Deeper?' Winsome answered.

'To the Wildwood.' Morghan breathed in. Out. 'To the healing clearing.'

Winsome nodded. She had been to the place Morghan spoke of, a fact she still could barely fathom. It was in another world, and yet when she was there, it was as real as any dream during the dreaming, and as real as any memory afterwards.

'How will Minnie come?' she asked.

'We have her agreement,' Morghan answered. 'Her spirit agrees, and that is all we require.'

Winsome nodded, and then she was no longer in the bedroom in Rosalie Busby's small terrace house in Wellsford, but deep in a forest where she could not tell the year or the season, except that this place seemed eternal and ancient at the same time.

She walked beside Morghan, resisting the urge to reach out and catch hold of Morghan's skirt like a small child trailing after their mother. She stood straighter.

A long, large snake slithered out from the undergrowth and cast a glance at Winsome before falling in beside them. Winsome closed her eyes for a moment. The snake she could not get used to. It was so large.

But then, so was the wolf that walked at Morghan's side, thick black fur bristling over it.

Morghan glanced over her shoulder at Winsome. 'You should call your own kin to you,' she said.

'What?'

Morghan tipped her head to the side. 'Your animal kin. It is past time you called them to you.'

Winsome couldn't stop herself looking at the snake, who stared back at her with unblinking eyes. She licked her lips.

'How?' she asked.

'Simply call,' Morghan replied. 'Ask for them to come to you. They will be waiting for you to do so.'

Winsome stopped walking and looked around. In every direction, there were trees. She wondered how far this forest stretched. She wondered if she was somehow walking around inside Morghan's head. Or if this place was real. The Otherworld. Morghan called this forest the Wildwood.

The Otherworld was part of the knowledge of so many cultures. Those that hadn't forgotten. Ambrose had told her that. Had spoken of it with passion before remembering himself and breaking off.

Impulsively, Winsome reached out and touched the trunk of a tree. She felt its bark under her fingers. More than that, she felt its life in its wood. Its consciousness. It was alive in ways she'd never stopped to consider that a tree might be.

She wanted to know which animal would come to her. Who would her kin be? She looked around while Morghan stood watching her, one hand on the neck of her wolf.

Winsome took a deep breath. 'I'm ready,' she said, not knowing that was what she'd been going to say. 'Come to me, my kin. I want to know you, to walk with you through these woods.'

She glanced at Morghan, who smiled gently at her.

There was a rustling in the undergrowth and Winsome

turned, fingers curled nervously into her palms, the nails digging into the soft flesh there.

Who would it be?'

She started in surprise at the shaggy face looking up at her own. 'You're a dog,' she said, then glanced again over at Morghan. 'It's a dog. He looks like Burdock.'

Well, somewhat. This dog was about the same size and build, but the colour of his coat was much lighter. Sort of wheaten, Winsome decided. Very handsome, anyway. She looked at the dog, and the dog looked back at her, and she swore she saw his eyes twinkling at her, but she didn't know what to say.

'Lovely,' Morghan said. 'You are well met, I think. Dog is a protector of that which you value and hold sacred.' She smiled slightly. 'He also leads you, if you will go, to the very heart of mystery.' She turned. 'We must get on.'

Winsome fell in beside her again, but this time, the dog walked at her side as if he'd always been accompanying her like this. She wondered if she could reach out and touch him, and as if he could read her mind, his head swung around, and he looked at her with his amber brown eyes.

Well, she thought. Morghan touched her hand to her wolf's fur often.

The dog's hair was thick, warm. He peeled his lips soundlessly back from his teeth as she touched him, and she realised with a start that he was smiling at her.

A dog, she thought, bemused. What did it mean that a dog could lead her to the hearty of mystery? She knew, from talking to Morghan about it, and Ambrose, that each animal kin had their own attributes they brought to the relation-ship. She walked more lightly along the path, determined to ask more about the dog's when she returned to the waking world.

There was a small figure curled up on the soft forest floor of the clearing when they stepped into it. Winsome's chest hurt when she realised how slight and vulnerable Minnie looked there, and she fell to her knees in front of the girl, shaking her head. She'd never had children, but the sight of Minnie tugged at her heartstrings.

There was a snuffling from the low bushes at the edge of the clearing, and a white sow, heavy with piglets came forward to lie down behind Minnie's back.

Morghan contemplated the scene for a moment, then knelt beside Winsome, and reached for the entity that had attached itself to the teenager. There was a bright wound in Minnie's abdomen, and the dark mass of the entity was suckled to it, attached like a jellyfish. Morghan grasped it, recoiling at the liquid-filled, leathery feel of it, knowing that back in the bedroom, her body would be twitching and jerking uncontrollably while she did this part of the job.

It came free with a hiss and Morghan held it in her hands for a moment, before tossing it gently away into the trees, where it floated like a misshapen balloon for a few long seconds, then disappeared.

'This child is not yours,' she whispered. 'This child's kin protects her now, and you will leave her be.'

Morghan turned back to the weeping wound in Minnie's side.

A shining figure stepped out from between the trees and Winsome looked up at its arrival, then stumbled back in shock, heart pounding at the sight of the great white wings growing out of the figure's back. The angel – for what else could it be? – smiled down at Winsome splayed out in shock on the ground, then turned their attention to Morghan and Minnie. The angel held something in their hands, a glass bottle with a blue liquid in it. Bending down, the bottle was handed to Morghan.

She took it, pulled the stopper from it, and tipped the contents gently and slowly over the wound in Minnie's lower torso. For a moment, Minnie's skin gleamed blue, and then the liquid seeped into the skin, and the wound closed around it, clear and unblemished.

Morghan tucked the bottle absently against a tree root and turned to examine the rest of the child. She was covered in what Morghan always thought of as barnacles, hard extrusions attached to the tender skin of Minnie's back and shoulders. How often had she seen these things? So often, she thought.

They were the crusting and scarring of wounds, of hurts borne and given. Morghan closed her eyes for a moment, for the sight of them distressed her on the deepest level.

And then, she set to work, loosening and removing them, one at a time. Many of them had long strands to them that had worked deep under Minnie's skin, twisting and twining around her organs, threading their way along her veins. Morghan drew them out, careful not to break them, careful to remove them all. It was slow, painstaking work, but she did not turn once from it.

Only when Minnie's skin was red, raw, but clear, did Morghan lean back from her task. She drew from the pocket of her tunic a vial of silver liquid and poured it in a thin stream over Minnie's ravaged skin, so that it could heal clear, without infection, so that the barnacles would not easily regrow.

She stood up, looking down at the flowers that had grown up where she had thrown the barnacles upon the ground, then again at Minnie. The girl was unconscious still. Morghan took a breath.

'Gather the child up,' she said to Winsome. 'I must find the shard of her spirit that is missing.'

Winsome looked at Morghan wide-eyed, then glanced at the angel who still stood there, watching. 'Gather her up?'

'As a mother would,' Morghan said with a smile. 'Hold her the way your heart tells you to. I shall be back shortly.'

Winsome could only nod as Morghan left the clearing. She looked at the angel, but the shining figure only smiled slightly at her, and transferred their gaze back to Minnie. Winsome looked at the sleeping teenager too, lying now in a sweep of white flowers. She reached out to smooth a strand of hair from Minnie's forehead and was overcome with compassion for the girl, and did as Morghan had said, gathering Minnie into her arms, and rocking her like she was a baby.

'We all need to be held sometimes,' she whispered. 'We all need to be loved as a mother should love us.'

From somewhere, she found a lullaby to sing, as the angel looked on, and the white sow lay beside them, snout and ears twitching.

Morghan followed the flick of Snake's tail through the trees, searching for the lost part of Minnie. It would have happened when Minnie's father died, she knew, for a wounding of that sort often caused a soul aspect to fracture.

But where that part would have run to, she would have to find out.

The undergrowth rustled with Snake's movement and Morghan picked up her pace, stepping out after him into a narrow city street, where an unseen wind caught up a drift of discarded fast-food wrappers in the gutter. Grimy houses lined the street with windows that looked blankly back at her. Morghan's heels rang out on the road.

She heard nothing else but the wind. No one looked out from the houses; no one lived in them.

Snake pushed open a front door, its paint bright, cheerful in the dank street, except when Morghan stepped through it after him, she saw that the paint was bubbled, peeling. The floorboards sagged slightly under her feet, and when she reached out a hand to touch the wall, her fingers came away damp with water.

Somewhere in the house a tap dripped.

Snake's tail flashed away through another doorway.

Morghan followed.

Minnie sat at the dining table, an empty plate in front of her. She fiddled with a fork.

Morghan sat down at the table and looked at her. 'Hello Minnie,' she said softly.

Minnie turned her face away, blonde hair falling over her eyes.

'What are you doing?' Morghan asked.

That got her a tight shrug. Minnie's throat worked. 'I thought it would be better if I just stayed here and waited.'

Morghan nodded. 'Waited for what?' she asked.

Minnie put the fork down beside a bottle of tomato sauce and hugged herself. 'No one wants me there,' she said.

'No,' Morghan replied. 'That's not true. Minnie needs you. Without you, she's not whole.'

Another shake of the head. 'No. I can't just keep going on. It's not right.'

'You're alone here,' Morghan said, her voice low, gentle. 'It's time to go back to her.'

Minnie looked around. 'I've tried to keep the place nice.' She blinked, lashes fair against the bruises under her eyes.

'Yes,' Morghan said.

Minnie splayed her fingers out on the table. Then wrapped her arms around herself. 'Does she remember at all? Does she care?'

'She suffers all the more because you are not there with her.'

There was silence at the table. The tap dripped steadily from somewhere else in the house. Plink, plink, plink.

'It's time,' Morghan said at last. 'It's time to go back.'

For a moment, the shard of Minnie sat stubbornly at the table. Then she pushed herself back and stood up.

'Okay, then,' she said.

Morghan smiled at her and retraced her steps through the house. 'She will take good care of you,' she said. 'We will teach her how to sing the songs of the dead; for what is remembered, lives.'

They were silent as they walked back down the street, the door to Minnie's old house banging in the wind behind them. Snake led them off the road, through the grass, and into the Wildwood.

Winsome looked up at their approach, blinking at the younger, blonde version of the girl in her arms. She found herself smiling.

The part of Minnie at Morghan's side stepped hesitantly forward, looking around the clearing, taking in the angel, the sow, then glancing back at Morghan, who nodded to her.

In Winsome's arms, Minnie opened her eyes, blinked a few times, then disentangled herself and sat up. Winsome helped her stand, and the blonde girl stepped forward, took her older self by the hand, and stepped into her.

Within a breath, they were one again.

32

THE RED THREAD WAS WRAPPED AROUND HER, ENTANGLING her, she was snared in it, and it was tugging upon her, drawing her down its line, deeper and deeper back into her own past. Erin struggled against it, twisting in her bed, waking Burdock who lifted his head, a frown wrinkling between his ears.

But she stilled, letting go, letting herself drift down the line of her own lives, and Burdock watched her for a moment, sniffing gently, then, when he didn't smell the loch water on her like panic, he sank back down on his bed by the fire and closed his eyes, sleeping, one ear cocked for her.

'Back then are ye, spirit?' Kria asked, knelt at the fire, tucking dried bracken and grasses under a pyramid of twigs. 'Here to torment me with my own imprisonment while ye come and go like a will o' wisp, free and easy as the wind?'

Erin dropped to her knees and shivered. 'What season is it?' she asked.

'Tis winter,' Kria replied. And she lifted her head,

squinting for a moment at the sky, then dropping her head back to her task. 'Coming Midwinter, near as I can tell, though the seasons seem to turn slower and milder here. Where I come from, we would be wading to our thighs in snow by this time.' She sniffed. ''Tis the one blessing of this place that it is so.'

Erin looked around, trying to imagine the valley buried in snow. She shuddered with the thought. 'That would be impossible,' she said. 'If everything was buried in snow.' She blinked at the loch. 'And if the water was frozen over.'

'Then we should starve, for sure,' Kria agreed. 'Without fish, and the tough roots of the plants that consent to grow here, we would perish for certain.' She barked a harsh laugh. 'Although, I would say, perishing is the one certain thing here.'

'But others have gotten out, didn't you say?'

Kria's jaw tightened. 'So the stories tell us,' she said. 'I've not met a one for myself.'

Erin shook her head. 'Why are you here?' she asked. The question she kept coming back to. 'What are they expecting you to learn?'

'I know not,' Kria replied. She lifted her dark eyes to Erin's in a flat glance. 'Everything they taught me wilts in the face of this place.' She laughed again, no humour in the sound. 'I can make fire to keep myself alive, and I can keep the rain from my head, if I've a mind to, and what precious use is that?' She shook her head. 'All tricks,' she said. ''Tis all revealed to be tricks, nothing more.'

Kria cupped her hands, holding them up by her face, ready to make the little spark of flame that was all she had left of her magic.

'Wait,' Erin said.

Kria looked at her.

'Teach me how to do that.'

The cupped hands were lowered, and Kria looked at her empty palms. 'This?' she said. 'But this is child's play – how is it that you do not know how to do this already, you who appears and disappears like a dream from my sight?'

Erin shook her head. 'Where I come from – this magic has been forgotten.'

A frown creased the tight skin on Kria's forehead. 'Forgotten? But it is taught to us priestesses when we are practically babes still at the breast.'

'Not in my time.'

Kria, hunched over the hearth, let her hands drop. 'What magic is done in your time, then?'

Erin scratched her fingers into the damp soil, thinking. Should she talk of cars, and aeroplanes? The magic that let her fly from one part of the world to another in only hours and three meals that smelled of the plastic dishes they were reheated in?

But that wasn't magic, was it, even if it might seem so to someone like Kria?

It wasn't magic, it was mechanics.

That was her world, really. Mechanical things had replaced magic. She wondered how that had come to be – how she had to use a match dipped in some sort of flammable something made in a factory by woman and probably children earning only enough each day for a handful of food – when Kria simply cupped her hands together and brought forth a flame?

She wondered why anyone would choose her world over this one.

Except, of course, in her world, she didn't get taken to a place like this and left there.

'Are they too great of mysteries for ye to speak of, then?' Kria asked.

Erin shook her head, and her hair whipped the skin of her face. 'There's no mystery left in my world,' she said. 'No one does magic anymore.'

Kria's eyes widened. 'What?' She shook her head. 'How does the wheel still turn, then?'

Erin was confused. 'The wheel?'

Kria spread a hand at the land, the loch, the sky, although she thought of the world outside the valley, because the glen, she'd decided, was not on a spoke of the wheel.

'Without the songs, how does the world stay in balance? That is the wheel,' she said, astounded to have to explain such a simple thing. She sat down with a thump upon the thin grass growing straggling amongst the stones. Shook her head. 'Although, outside of here, perhaps fewer see the songs, now. But that is why we must teach them all the more.' She rubbed at a smudge of dirt on her hand. 'Which is what I would be doing now, with my other priestesses, if I had not been condemned to this place.'

Erin didn't know which question to ask first. 'You said see the songs – don't you mean sing them?'

'Ye must see the songs to sing them well,' Kria replied. 'Although, singing them brings on the seeing, so who is to say which way it ought to be?' She smiled, and it felt odd upon her face, the first real smile in many a rising and setting of the sun.

Erin thought this sounded so much like something Morghan would say that she drew in a deep breath. Understanding glimmered for a moment on the far horizon of her mind, then shimmered away to nothing.

'So why are you here, then?' she asked. 'If you would be teaching the songs – which is what? Your magic?'

'They are the truth of the worlds, our songs. They are the way of living, of being part of the wheel.'

'Right,' Erin said, straining to understand. 'So, if that is the most important thing, and the people who know that put you here to learn something – what would that something be?' She blinked. 'It must be along those lines but...more.'

'Do ye not consider that I've thought upon this?' Kria asked, turning away again, losing interest. She was here, where there was nothing important. 'Perhaps I've it all wrong, and it's no honour at all, to be brought here – perhaps that is just a story, a lie. And being here is a punishment, for wrongs done in other lives.'

Erin stared at her. 'I can't believe that,' she said flatly, after a moment. 'We're missing something.'

'Well, when ye have it figured out, let me know,' Kria said, scrambling to her knees and going back to her fire. 'For all I know now, is that here is barren, and it feels a punishment.'

'Yes,' Erin allowed. 'But you can't always trust your feelings, can you?'

Kria barked her bitter laugh. 'If you can't trust your feelings, what can you trust?'

Erin looked down at the ground, confused. 'I don't know,' she said finally. When she looked up, Kria was leaning over her pile of sticks again, eyes closed, hands cupped together.

'Teach me that,' Erin said.

The urgency in her voice stopped Kria and she looked over at the spirit come to meddle away with her mind. She blinked.

'As you wish,' she said. 'Though I will be a little unsettled with the instruction – it's been some time.'

But Erin nodded, enthusiastic. 'I don't care,' she said. 'I want to learn.'

STEPHAN WALKED THROUGH THE DARKNESS TO AMBROSE'S house, his heart alternately singing and despairing. Somewhere in the east, the sun was rising, but it hadn't reached its first fingers of light far over the hills above Wellsford yet, and the forest was silent around him in its white blanket of snow. It would be the winter solstice soon, and they would keep lanterns burning through the longest night to hail the rebirth of the sun. And they would rise with it, unfurling slowly into another season of growth.

Stephan thought he'd never been so busy growing already as he had done the last couple seasons. It had been a tumble of events, one after another to make his head swim. A branch cracked behind him, then fell muffled into the snow. He turned to look, and blinked, feeling someone there, not quite seen, as though they stood in the far periphery of his vision, simply waiting for him to notice them. Inside his chest, his heart started up a loud rat-a-tat-a-tat setting his ribs vibrating.

'Who's there?' he croaked, then cleared his voice. 'Show yourself.'

He blinked. 'Ambrose?'

It wasn't Ambrose, of course, and he knew so. It was the bear fellow; he'd recognised him straight away, only it was easier to think he hadn't.

Stephan breathed deeply of the cold air, filling his chest with it, relaxing his shoulders. Time had moved on, he thought. His life wasn't just in the garden with the plants anymore.

It was here, in the forest.

In the Wildwood.

He swallowed down the sudden flood of spit in his mouth and breathed again. Calming himself. In, hold, out. Slow. Calm. Feet steady on the ground, back straight. Shoulders relaxed. Chin level.

Sharp blue eyes looking.

Deep blue eyes seeing.

His ancestor stepped out of the shadows and pressed a fist to his own heart, bowing his head slightly in greeting.

All the moisture in Stephan's mouth dried. For a moment, there was no feeling in his hands, in his arms, and then he forced himself to copy the gesture of the other.

'I am Finn,' his ancestor said. 'Finn of the Bear, and you are my kin.'

Dazed, head spinning, it was almost all Stephan could do to stay standing. Then he thought of Morghan, and Ambrose, and nodded, found his voice.

'We are well met, Finn of the Bear.' He huffed out a breath. 'I am Stephan.'

'Also called by Bear.'

Stephan remembered the travelling Ambrose had sent him on; he remembered being in the cave, then dancing in a clearing with an old bear fellow – not Finn, but someone else, kin too, an ancestor, and behind them, the great spirit of Bear, paws heavy on the ground as they danced too.

He nodded.

'Come,' Finn said abruptly, turning. 'It is time.'

'For what?' Stephan said, flushing when his voice came out little more than a squawk.

'Bear is the Great Healer,' Finn said, stepping down the snowy path deeper into the Wildwood. 'It is time for you to take the next step in your training. You have learnt already Bear's healing plants, now it is time for more.'

Stephan hurried after him, looking at the man he'd once been in amazement. What was going on, he asked himself?

The snow melted into the ground and vanished. The trees had leaves upon their branches once more. Stephan stared around in amazement.

'Why is it not winter?' he asked, unable to help himself.

'It is,' Finn replied. 'But the seasons are slow here, they only dream they change.'

Stephan didn't know what to say to that, so he absorbed it in a sort of amazement. And then, because he could not help himself: 'Is that why the faerie live so long?'

Finn inclined his head in agreement, and Stephan realised it was also lighter in this forest. The sun had lengthened its fingers over the trees, dipping down here and there to drop strands of pale light between the trunks. He stared

339

around in every direction, knowing his jaw was hanging down, but unable to stifle his wonder.

Small white flowers grew in the dimness of the undergrowth, their blossoms like moonlight. He caught a flash of movement among them and his hare appeared, making him smile in recognition.

Hare hopped to his side, and they both kept pace with Finn, who strode through the forest without hesitation.

'Where are we going?' Stephan asked.

But Finn didn't answer, and Stephan didn't ask again. He simply followed, knowing that was what was required of him.

And soon enough, they came to the clearing he recognised – here he had danced with Bear, stomping their feet along the great golden outline of a wheel while his throat grew hoarse with singing.

Sing our spirits home, Bear
Sing our spirits back to the womb of your cave
Weave our spirits home, Bear
Weave our spirits back to the womb of your care.

Stephan stood blinking in the circle of grass, seeing in his mind again the glory of the golden energy as they danced and wove it together. He breathed deeply, awe and gratitude running with his blood.

His gaze settled finally on the bear fellow, standing gazing at him, a wide, amused smile upon his face. Beside him a group of people huddled together. Stephan glanced across at Finn.

'Who are these people?' he asked.

Finn considered them for a moment, then turned to look at Stephan. 'They have come to seek healing,' he said.

Stephan blinked. 'Who from?' He looked toward the mouth of the cave. From Bear, of course, and he nodded his head in understanding. And from Old Bear Fellow.

But Finn had not taken his eyes from him. 'From Bear, yes,' he said. 'But you are Bear's hands now. You will work on their behalf. Bear Fellow will teach you.'

'What?' Stephan looked wildly around the clearing, as though hoping to find another person that Finn could possibly be speaking to. But there was only Hare who stood on his hind legs, whiskers twitching as he stared at Stephan.

Stephan shook his head. 'Not me,' he said. 'Not me at all. I can't do this.'

'You have done this before,' Finn replied, his voice calm and clear, and he nodded towards the old man. 'All you must do now is remember.'

Stephan wanted to turn tail and run, shaking his head all the way. Run back through the Wildwood, until he regained the path that led through Wilde Grove to Black-thorn House. And there, he'd join Ambrose in some qi gong, and he'd stretch his muscles, and play with the energy between his hands, and brood a little over Erin.

But hadn't going to Ambrose started this? Or led to this? Stephan was confused. It had been Ambrose who had insisted on Stephan learning to travel, to walk in the Wild-wood, venture into the Otherworld. He imagined Ambrose now, the slightly raised eyebrow, and then the drum in his hand. The insistent beat that made him travel, that dug down deep into his chest and beat with his heart, sending him on his way.

He sucked in a deep breath, looking across at the small

group of people gathered there on the other side of the clearing.

'With Bear's help?' he asked, his voice cracking with uncertainty.

'With Bear's help,' Finn agreed mildly.

'And yours?'

'I was hunter, not healer,' Finn replied. 'Bear Fellow will be with you. He will be your teacher from now.'

Stephan blinked at him. 'I don't understand.'

'Bear brings strength and understanding in many ways to those that follow.' Finn looked steadily at Stephan. 'You are a healer.' He nodded towards the clearing. 'Begin,' he said. 'Inside you, there are the songs and the dreams; you must only remember them.'

One of the people broke away from the group, leading an elderly man with her. Glancing over at Stephan, she helped the old man to lie down on the soft grass, then waited.

Bear came out from the cave and sat on their haunches beside Old Bear Fellow, and they waited also.

Everyone, it appeared, was ready.

Stephan stepped forward over the beating of his heart, reaching for the dim strains of a song.

33

Stephan pressed his hands to a woman's abdomen, not knowing how he knew to place them there, only realising that some deep part of him knew it was the right place. She looked up at him, eyes wide and trusting and he wanted to glance away, towards Bear, to check he was doing the right thing.

But there was something there, something deep under the skin, embedded in there, festering. It was maddening, to be able to see it there, and he breathed into the compulsion to draw it out, closing his eyes, working it to the surface of her skin with his mind. Knowing it was coming closer, knowing that he was drawing it out, pulling it from deep inside her.

She whimpered and he whispered to her. 'Just a moment more.'

That was all he needed. Just a moment more. It was almost there. He almost had it.

And then he had drawn it from inside her, a deep,

curving thorn. And from around it came a spill of viscous liquid, a stream of blackness that he drew up into his hands, and into himself, not knowing what else to do, only knowing that it could not stay inside her. He took it into himself, and watched as she cleared, grew healthier again, strength returning to her.

Bear passed a damp wad of macerated wild lovage root, and Stephan coated her wound with it, letting the goodness from the herb seep into her skin, healing as it went. He sang under his breath as he watched the wound heal. Sang a song with words he didn't know, but which wove stories of wholeness and joy, and the strength and compassion of the Great Bear, and how there was a star in the sky to keep them on course while they ducked and wove their lives into being.

The woman smiled at him, rolled away and stood, walked from the clearing.

She had been the last.

Stephan turned to Finn, wiping his wrist across his brow. Then looked across at Bear Fellow who nodded and smiled widely at Stephan as though pleased with his efforts. Next to the old man, Bear swayed and yawned.

He went down on one knee to them both and lowered his head. 'I am grateful,' Stephan said. 'For your lessons, and your help.'

Bear simply looked back at Stephan, then their long snout touched his cheek, and a moment later Bear was lumbering back to their cave, the old fellow following.

'Come,' Finn said. 'You have done well. It is time to return.'

'Return?' Stephan asked stupidly, looking around.

'To your world. You will need time to regain your energy.'

Stephan thought about this for a moment, then nodded. He was exhausted. He could sleep for a week, he reckoned. What he needed, was some of his grounding tea.

A whole pot of it.

But that was at Erin's house, he remembered, getting up to follow Finn back into the forest the way they'd come. He blinked in the dimness of the trees.

Had he really just come here and helped heal a bunch of people?

'Was that real?' he asked.

Finn didn't turn to look at him. 'Was what real?'

'Those people? Were they real?'

Now Finn did turn a curious eye on Stephan. 'What is real and what is not real?' he asked.

Stephan scrunched his brows together. 'You know,' he said. 'Were they like, real people?'

'They are like themselves,' Finn answered. 'And why would they not be real?'

Because you just basically let me operate on them, Stephan answered inside his head. 'But this is the Otherworld,' he said.

Finn kept walking. 'Your question does not matter,' he said. 'What matters is that you remember and become adept once more. You must reawaken your skills.'

Stephan pondered this for a moment. 'Why?' he asked at last.

The question made Finn stop walking to turn and look at Stephan. 'Why?' he repeated.

Stephan shrugged. 'Yeah, I mean, I'm cool with it, of

course, you know – but like, is there a particular reason, or something?'

Finn stared.

'Need,' he answered at last. 'There is need.'

ERIN WAS SCOOTED CLOSER TO THE FIRE, KRIA ALMOST AT HER elbow. There was no flame on the tinder yet, and Erin was frustrated.

'I can't do it!' she cried, flinging herself back onto the stones, then flinching away when she realised she sat almost directly in the spot where Kria would one day lie, her blood spilled to the ground and sky.

'Tis almost the easiest of the songs,' Kria said, looking over at the other, wondering about her lack of ability. To come from a world where the magic was no longer – what did that place look like?

She turned and gazed around her. Like this place, she thought. It would look like this place.

Erin sat up again and moved slightly, opposite Kria at the fire. She shivered again – the breeze from over the water carried a damp chill with it. There was a sound at her right ear, and she turned her head, distracted.

'Have you lit your fire yet?' Macha asked, amusement clear in her voice.

Erin turned and scowled at her. 'Can you do this?' she demanded.

Kria narrowed her eyes. 'Who are ye talking to?'

Startled, Erin turned back to Kria, head spinning. 'You can't see her?'

A searching look around them. 'I see only you, pestering spirit, and myself. As usual,' Kria answered.

Erin looked at Macha. 'Why can't she see you, then?' she asked.

Macha merely shook her head, the beads in her hair clacking. Her long fingers tapped the wood of her staff.

Erin closed her eyes and shook her head, then looked again at Macha. 'Well?' she demanded.

'Well, what?' Macha answered.

Erin nodded toward the fire. 'Can you light it? Do you know how to conjure fire from nothing?'

Macha's gaze did not waver from Erin's face. 'I do not know how to conjure fire from nothing,' she answered. 'But I can light that.'

A deep frown marred Erin's forehead. 'What?' she said. 'That doesn't make any sense.'

'Ye cannot make fire from nothing,' Kria said. 'This is what I've been trying to tell ye.'

'You do exactly that!' Erin said, looking from Macha to Kria. Right now, they were both infuriating.

'Nay. I cannot make something from nothing,' Kria said. 'It is the song, the spark, that makes the fire.'

'Fuck.' Erin hunched down into the grass. 'I don't get any of this.'

'But you do,' Macha said. 'Morghan has taught you how to do this. Kria has shown you it can be done.'

Erin's eyes widened as she stared up at Macha. 'Morghan has taught me to do this?' She shook her head. 'When was that? Because I think I'd know if she'd shown me how to light a fire out of thin air.'

Kria frowned at the invisible person her spirit was talking to. 'But 'tis not thin air,' she said. 'The fire is from...'

'The Song, yeah, I know,' Erin said, then heaved in a deep breath. 'I'm not cut out for this, am I?' she said, deflating.

'You are uncommonly slow,' Macha observed. 'For one with such talent.'

Erin glared at her.

'But then, so was I at the beginning.' Macha nodded towards Kria and smiled.

'I hate puzzles,' Erin said, lifting her hands to tug at her hair. 'Morghan did not teach me to do this.'

'Who is this Morghan person?' Kria asked, leaning closer. This was the most interesting time she'd had since she'd walked down the sides of the glen who knew how many moons ago. All perhaps, a fevered figment of her imagination, but it was better than nothing, that much was certain.

'Morghan is my...my...' Erin cast a glance at Macha.

'Priestess and teacher,' Macha said. 'As she was once mine.'

Erin shook her head again, baffled. 'I don't think she taught me this,' she said. But even as she said the words, something gleamed to life in her mind. She looked across at Kria, then up at Macha.

Macha smiled and the wind blew again, making her braids clack together. Under the grey sky, the blue swirls on her cheeks were bright.

'That exercise we did,' Erin said, slowly, trying again, feeling her way. 'The one where we stood between the sun and the centre of the earth, and the spark...' She closed her eyes.

'We drew the spark in and through ourselves, until we were it, and we were connected.' Erin opened her eyes and looked at the ground. 'I remember now.'

'As you should, since it was only a short time ago,' Macha told her.

But Erin shook her head. 'It was good,' she said. 'But I like the other way better.'

Kria was listening intently, even though she knew she was only getting half a conversation. 'What other way?' she asked.

'Indeed,' Macha said. 'What other way?' Her tone was knowing, amused.

Erin ignored her, following the threads of her own thoughts, blinking. 'My morning routine now,' she said, 'is to go out to the well. There's something special about the wells in Wellsford, although I haven't figured that out yet...' She trailed off for a moment, distracted, then shook her head.

'Anyway. I do this sort of thing there, that Morghan taught Stephan and me right in the beginning. It's kind of like the sun spark thing, but...' She frowned, then shrugged. 'More sideways.'

Kria was fascinated. It had been so long since she'd been with her fellow priestesses. She'd forgotten how much she'd missed their chatter.

'Sideways?' she asked.

Erin shrugged. 'I don't know how else to describe it.' She held up her hands like she was holding a balloon then spread them slowly apart. 'It's like you expand your senses and you can see everything after a while.' She strained to describe it. 'Like, first you can see yourself, standing where you are, and you can feel the water in the well going so deep down into the earth, right? And then you can sort of sense – feel – the garden too, and after a moment, you're also kind of over the fence and you can see inside the forest at the same time you can see the main street of the village, and then if you lift yourself up, it's like being in a hot air balloon and you can see as far as you want to look.' She subsided, shrugged. 'It's all there. Everything's there at once.'

'That's the song!' Kria said.

Erin looked at her, then shook her head. 'The song? How can that be a song?'

Macha stood listening, leaning on her staff.

Kria shrugged. 'The spark – it comes from being part of everything. And the fire – if you're part of everything, then ye can reach for that bit of you that is fire.' She cupped her hands together by her lips, closed her eyes for a moment, then blew into her cupped hands and spread them apart.

The tiny lick of flame fell upon the waiting tinder and Kria grinned, then bent and blew it out before it could take hold.

'You do it,' she said to Erin.

Erin bit at her lip, then cast a quick glance at Macha, who stood watching her, eyes lively. Erin nodded. 'All right, then,' she said. 'I will.'

She sat forward, as Kria had, and cupped her hands in front of her lips. She closed her eyes and took a deep breath. Held it. Let it slowly out, relaxing sideways as she did so, letting her senses spill from her, her spirit loosen and flow. How wonderful it felt to do this, how alive she suddenly was. The air was still around her, but now she did not feel cold from it. She felt as though it flowed through her and was part of her and she was part of it. She felt as though the very molecules of her being were spread apart, with space between them for the world. She was sitting beside Kria's stone hearth, the dried grass tucked under the twigs for tinder, and she was touching the lapping wavelets of the loch as well, and she was reaching out along the stones, towards the small stone building, digging spirit fingers between the stones, reaching inside, then up over the roof and all around in the air.

This was the song, then, as Kria called it. Erin began her search for the spark. She searched for the part of the world that was fire.

But it was not there, and she frowned. She was too amorphous, she decided. Too spread out, a cloud, a mist over the land, and it was all water and air and dampness. Where was the fire? She looked upwards, towards the sun, its rays diffused by the mists above. More water, she thought. Where was the fire?

She looked downwards, into the centre of the earth, digging deep under the soil, but without the sun to attach to, she could not go deep enough.

There was only wetness here in this winter light. Gritty soil, thick mists.

She turned and looked at Macha and reared back in surprise. Looked over at Kria, then back at Macha.

There was fire in Macha. She could see it. The sight made her mouth go dry. There, flickering inside Macha was fire. Everything else was there too, but she could see the fire, bright and fine, burning hot.

She reached for it.

And landed on her back on the stones, her breath gushing from her, head hitting the rocks with a dull thwack.

'Oof,' she said, winded, gasping for breath.

Dazed, she looked up at Macha, and reached to rub the sore spot on the back of her head where she'd hit the ground. 'What did you do?'

Macha's eyes were narrowed, and she pointed her staff at Erin. 'You do not take the spark from others,' she said, then straightened and waved a hand.

'Get out of here.'

34

MORGHAN GAZED AROUND AT THE STONE CIRCLE, SEEING IT AS it would look the night of the winter solstice. She huffed out a breath that blew white into the cold air.

Today she had boots on, and a warm coat. Her gloves were in her pockets.

'What are you smiling about?' Clarice demanded.

'Winsome,' Morghan answered. 'Poor Winsome, horrified at my going barefoot.' She shrugged slightly. 'Although perhaps she was right that day.'

Clarice shook her head. 'I haven't the slightest idea what you're talking about.' She narrowed her eyes at her stepmother. 'You and Winsome,' she said, and her hands fluttered in the air for a moment. 'You're not, like...seeing each other?'

Morghan laughed. 'No,' she said, and cast a sideways glance at Ambrose, who remained bent over at the base of Grandmother Oak. 'I like and admire our vicar very much, but it is only a friendship.'

Clarice followed her gaze to Ambrose and her eyes widened. 'Oh,' she said. 'Ambrose? You and the vicar?'

'There is nothing between us,' Ambrose said, and straightened. 'You and your chatter makes it impossible for a man to pray.'

Clarice gave him a wicked grin. 'She's a very nice woman. It's probably about time.'

'There is nothing between us. Do not tease me.'

'My apologies.' Clarice bowed her head. Then looked at Morghan. 'She started it.'

Ambrose huffed a breath. 'Enough,' he said. 'We are not here to discuss...Winsome.' His face reddened in a dark blush and he turned away. 'What do you envision?' he asked Morghan.

They were there to plan the winter solstice ritual. It was astonishing that already the wheel had turned and that they were here again to celebrate.

'It must echo what I have been shown in the Otherworld,' she said.

'Of course,' Ambrose agreed. 'It is important to find counterparts here to what we are given there.'

Charlie hugged herself in the cold morning. 'It's hard to believe that there might not be any here or there anymore, once the veil is down,' she said and waved a hand at the sky. 'That it might all just be more or less one place again.' She swallowed, nervous at the thought of it.

But Morghan was gazing serenely at the shimmering strands of the web over the stones. In the corner of her vision, lightning still rent the sky and she could hear the booming crash of the waves against the shore as the storm pressed on, but here was the magic, right here all around her. If the veil coming down meant that more would be able to see like this, then she would find a way to bear the chaos that would come with the change.

A profound sense of well-being rose up in her, a flush of feeling that began at her feet and swept up through her, so that every nerve ending tingled and her flesh hummed. She stretched out her arms and opened herself to the sensation, losing the edges of her skin and brimming over them, until she felt alive and bright and as golden as her right hand. Breathing in, the air in her chest was cold and alive and singing.

Morghan opened her eyes. 'Join me,' she said, reaching for the others.

Clarice stepped up and took one of Morghan's hands, then reached for Ambrose's.

In a moment, they were a circle, and Morghan let herself flow through them and between them, nudging up gently against their own spirits and inviting them to see.

Clarice gasped. This was like being in the Queen's realm, but more, and in her own world. She tipped her head back and saw Sigil sitting on a white branch, large eyes fixed on her. The air around the bird shimmered and glowed and she blinked, taking a deep breath, letting herself relax into Morghan's golden seeing.

Ambrose lifted his face to the sky, tears tracking silently down his cheeks as he felt the flow of Morghan's spirit against his own, demanding that he open up, see. He saw himself, tucked up into his study, the fire chattering to itself in the grate while he buried his head in his books, reading and pencilling notes, learning.

Learning so much, so much that was necessary.

But forgetting to live. Inside his chest, his heart welled with feeling.

With longing.

Charlie let out a long sigh and sank into the sight of this glimmering world that Morghan was showing her. Would this be what it was like? Would that she could always see this much!

Everything was alive.

They were connected.

Morghan let her hands drop and smiled at the dazed faces around her. She hadn't been sure she could do that – could make them see too, just for a moment.

'That's what I want it to be like,' she said on a sigh. 'We need to sing this into being.'

The rest of the circle looked at her.

'Well,' Ambrose said, wiping his tears away. 'We'd best get planning, then.'

MORGHAN WALKED INTO THE WOODS. SHE'D SHOOED everyone off after their planning session and now she walked the path through the grove on her own, the snow crunching underfoot. Everything around her glittered with light on ice crystals, and she breathed in the beauty of it, reaching out to trail her fingers through the air, watching the traces of energy from her fingers fluttering like they were ribbons.

Looking up into the branches of the trees, she thought about the plans they'd just made for the solstice ritual and pondered the question that had been constantly on her mind the last few days. How to shine the light of the soul for everyone to see? How to weave the web ever stronger – how to show others that it was possible, that it was necessary?

One person at a time, Ambrose said. But was that all they could do?

Morghan sighed, and yet her lips were still upturned at the beauty all around her. The work she did, it was necessarily one on one. She helped one soul at a time pass from this life to the next. That was what a death worker did.

Not that there had been much time for that lately, with all that was going on. She thought of Winsome again – and inclined her head at her own thoughts. Winsome, Morghan knew without doubt now, would be taking over that aspect of her work.

Which was, she suspected, as it was meant to be.

There was much to teach Erin, and teaching was something she could only do for one or two people at a time.

Morghan stopped walking and closed her eyes, looking at the memory of setting the soul-egg in the bell tower, watching its light shine over the land, reaching out to touch the light from other soul-eggs in other bell towers.

There were others being tasked with the same jobs as she. Morghan knew this, because she was not special, she was not chosen above any others – she had skills, and they were being put to use. Thus, there were others in the same position.

Perhaps, soon, she would reach out to them.

One Grove on its own would become one Grove in a web of them. And the light would spread, would it not?

The world had not lost all its magic. Ideas still sprang up in different parts of the globe at the same time. That was magic, awen flowing freely, inspiration and growth.

But how to make it all explode?

The veil would not come down in a day, she thought. But it must happen, with so much at stake; a reenchanting, a return to seeing.

She did not know how long it would take. What she did know was that it was necessary to begin the work now. The work of the soul could not wait for any of them.

Walking again, Morghan knew she did not have all the answers to her questions yet. But she would keep going, in the flow of her purpose, and she would not waver.

The world could not afford anyone to waver.

The stream pushed against the ice at its border, burrowing in under to continue its rush towards the sea. Morghan bent her knees and squatted down on her heels. Dipped her fingertips into the tumbling flow.

She touched a wet finger to her forehead, her chest, shoulder to shoulder in a blessing that was also a promise.

By sky and root through all worlds. From each birth to each death, my life dedicated.

Standing again, Morghan listened to the burbling song of the water, and the slow dripping of snow from branch to soil. She let the sound seep deep into herself, under her skin, until it was the song of her own body.

'Blessed am I,' she whispered. 'To carry the song of water in this world with me.'

She lifted her face. 'Blessed am I,' she said. 'To carry the song of the wind with me.'

The breeze flattened cold hands against her cheeks.

'Blessed am I to stand upon this ground,' she said, 'where the trees dig deep and join with each other.'

She touched her heart. 'Blessed am I, to carry in me the spark of the world, to feel the fire of its passion.'

There were whispers in the air around her, and she opened her eyes, seeing the faerie man step out of the air into her sight. She inclined her head.

'Maxen,' she said. 'My greetings to you.'

'And to yourself, Morghan.'

'How is the turning of the seasons treating you?' Morghan asked, gesturing at the snow.

Maxen shrugged lightly. ''Tis well enough, and expected, so you'll get no complaints from us. Our fires are warm, as is our food and drink.' He looked at Morghan from under long, dark lashes. ''Tis almost the turning.'

She nodded. 'The solstice. Yes.'

'You've invited us, I hear.'

Morghan smiled. 'And where did you hear that?'

Maxen thrust his hands into his pockets. 'In your circle, where I was listening.'

'You are always invited,' Morghan said with a nod.

That made Maxen grin. 'Well, usually we do just turn up.' He turned serious and gazed past Morghan, at the snowy woodland. 'Things are changing, and I wonder how they will go,' he said.

Morghan turned to walk the paths again. 'Your thoughts?' she asked.

He shrugged at her question. 'People either do not believe in us, or they are afraid of us, or they consider us to be small pretty creatures.'

'Some of you are small creatures.' Morghan cast him a smiling glance. 'And some of you are very pretty.'

'You are in a good mood today, Morghan of the Grove.'

'I am, Maxen.' Morghan sighed. 'I know there is change upon us, and that change is never comfortable, nor the outcome ever certain. I do not know what all my task during it is, and that is something of a concern.' She paused a moment, looking for the right words with which to express what she felt, and what she knew. 'But here are the things I do know...'

She counted them off on her fingers.

'This coming change is a necessity.

'We will keep trying, even when we fail.

'We are capable of extraordinary things.

'We still have our magic, if only we learn to see.'

They walked silently through the quiet woods, breathing in the white scent of snow, listening to the warbling of a lone bird singing in a strand of sunlight.

'I do not know,' Maxen said at last. 'There has been a lot of history under the bridge, so to speak. Our retreat behind the veil was...tactical. I fear humankind's capacity to return to a relationship of reciprocity to the world and its other peoples.'

Morghan sighed. 'As do I, Maxen,' she said. 'And there are so many things happening in the world that I do not know or understand.'

Their feet crunched upon the path.

'But fear cripples,' Morghan said after a while. 'We cannot afford fear. It is the weapon we use against each other and against ourselves.'

They passed out of earshot of the bird's song, and another took its place, this one singing a plaintive love song. They listened to the clear, pure notes.

'Imagine a world without fear,' Morghan said dreamily,

watching the birdsong drift on the breeze. 'There would be no hunger, no violence. No othering.'

'Or there would be more of all of those,' Maxen said, unconvinced.

But Morghan shook her head. 'No,' she said. 'Because to give up fear you must know the truth of your own soul. That you are more than your skin and your fear. That you are more altogether. You shine. And then the next realisation is that as you are, so is your neighbour.'

'Then you'd best find a way to make people see this truth, Morghan. You and all the others.' He nodded to her and stepped away into the air.

Morghan watched it shimmer behind him.

So, there were others, she thought and gazed upwards where the branches of the trees reached for the sky and each other in a web.

That was what was needed, she knew. To reach for the truth, deep within each one, and in each other.

To weave the web.

35

Erin kicked back the blankets, gasping for breath, horrified. She pulled herself up to sit on the edge of the bed and Burdock came over to push his nose into her hand. He'd tried waking her up before, but she'd not paid him any mind.

He needed to go outside. The sun was over the hills.

He was hungry too.

'Burdock,' she said, and her voice was rough, barely a croak. She cleared her throat, glanced towards the window where a long white sliver of light pushed its way between the curtains. 'How long have I been gone?'

It was cold in the room. The hearth was filled with ashes. She stared at it, frowning, for a moment, then reached for her dressing gown. She'd let poor Burdock out.

Poor Burdock was very glad to go out too, dashing from the door in a mad scramble towards his friend the apple tree. Erin tightened the belt on her dressing gown and left the door open a crack. She needed a cup of tea.

Had Macha struck her, she wondered as she filled the kettle? Macha had certainly sent her flying backwards to land unceremoniously on her backside. She put the kettle on the cooker and opened the wood box, picking up the poker, ready to stir the embers back to life.

Their red glow made her pause, lips pursed, brow creased. She'd been trying to make fire. Conjure it out of thin air, for crying out loud! How was she to know what she'd been doing was wrong? She didn't know anything, and it wasn't like anyone was lining up to teach her this stuff, was it? Not properly.

Erin stuck the poker in the wood box and flung the embers about. She fed in the kindling and watched it catch, just like that.

'See,' she said to herself. 'You can't make fire from nothing. It needs fuel.'

She groaned, flinging her head back and baring her teeth at the ceiling.

And besides, Erin thought, wasn't Macha herself, really? So it hadn't been like she was really stealing from someone else, was it? Macha had no right to send her flying like that.

If people would just teach her properly in the first place...

Burdock trotted into the kitchen, came to a halt, and shook himself vigorously, sending snow flying.

'Watch it!' Erin screeched. 'Did you go rolling in it, or something?'

Burdock looked at her, confused by her tone of voice. He dropped his head, hurt. He'd just gone to the apple tree – he'd been a good dog and had waited after all – and the snow was thick out there. Maybe he hadn't been quite able to resist jumping around in it for a moment, but that had been all, just a moment. He slunk over to the wall and looked miserably at his dog bowl. It was still empty.

Erin's phone rang.

Startled, she stared around the room, looking for it.

It was under her bag. She didn't recognise the number on the screen. It was probably her mother, trying something else devious and underhanded to get her to come home.

Well, maybe she just would, for all that. Erin poked at the answer button. Swiped it. Held the phone to her ear.

'What?' she said.

There was a pause before the voice on the other end spoke, and when it did, when Mary from the Care Home explained the reason for her calling, Erin drooped down into a chair at the table, nodded a couple times and agreed to go in. Reluctantly. Only because there was no one else.

The kettle screamed.

She drank her tea as she got dressed, pulling on thick leggings and socks, grumbling under her breath about having to walk into town. Why had her father had to take her car? He didn't need it. He was just trying to manipulate her.

In fact, everyone was trying to manipulate her.

Morghan was trying to get her to learn all this stuff, but she wasn't really teaching her how to do it, she was manipulating her into figuring it out herself.

Which was just pissing her off, Erin decided.

And Macha and Kria and the glen – they could all go to hell. That was how she felt, and she let the feeling sweep through her until she was radiating prickly anger.

Erin dumped her mug into the sink and looked at the kitchen door that led to the garden.

Burdock whined quietly.

She ignored him.

The well was out there, she thought. And she hadn't gone out there and lifted the lid on it and said her prayers over it. She was supposed to do that every morning.

Her hand was on the doorknob. It was brass, and cool under her fingers. She stood deliberating.

Then turned away. Too bad, she decided. She'd had quite the fill of magic and everything that smacked of it for the day.

Besides, she had to get to work. Her day off – which she'd been looking forward to so she could load some of her artwork online – but hey, nothing went to plan, did it?

'And Mr. Roberts is poorly,' she said, mimicking Mary's accent. 'Can you come help out today?'

Well, it was probably better than storming around here. She picked up her coat and jammed her arms into the sleeves. Brooding about Kria. If Kria knew so much about magic and how to sing the wheel or whatever – then why was she stuck in the bloody valley in the first place?

Erin didn't understand any of it, she decided, picking up her bag off the table and slinging it across her chest.

Burdock whined again. Looked down at his bowl. Whined louder.

She wasn't going to leave without giving him his breakfast, was she?

Erin snatched up her scarf and wound it around her neck.

Burdock stared at her. Wait, he thought. She wasn't

going to leave without him, was she? He hopped over his bowls and dashed to her side, toenails clattering on the flagstones.

This was not how the mornings were supposed to go.

Erin grabbed her hat and tugged it onto her head. Then she stuck her feet in her boots and bent to tie the laces. Burdock licked her cheek, trying to make her remember his breakfast.

She pushed him away. 'We have to go to work, Burdock,' she grouched. And shook her head. 'I know,' she said. 'Not my idea either.'

They went through the door and out into the morning, Burdock taking one last glance at his bowl.

Erin walked to the village with her head down, watching her feet, arms crossed, gloved hands tucked under her arms. Her nose grew red in the cold, her eyes watered.

She'd be there in five minutes if she still had her car, she thought.

How could her parents have been so awful as to have those thugs come repossess her car? She rolled her eyes. How could they be so stupid to think Wilde Grove was a cult? How could they think she was such an idiot as to get involved with a cult? What sort of loser did they think she was?

Erin scowled at the road.

And who were her parents to get all righteous, anyway? They'd bought a baby, for crying out loud. Literally. Bought. A. Baby. What sort of people did that?

And to make themselves feel better, they believed the sob story her birth mother had spun them about Wellsford and Wilde Grove.

Even though they didn't know the first thing about it.

And while she was on the subject, Erin thought, what sort of selfish person had her birth mother been? She'd been a real loser. Drugs and who knew what else?

And then getting herself dead. In some stupid meaningless accident.

Erin shook her head. What sort of person went crashing down a flight of stairs anyway? What a pathetic way to die.

She knotted her hands under her arms and stuck her chin down into the folds of her scarf. What was it doing being so cold when she didn't have a car?

She let her mind hop back onto the track of its thoughts about her family.

The only people stupid enough to die falling down a set of stairs, she told herself, were ones getting themselves murdered. She did another eyeroll. What had Charlie said about the way Rebecca had died?

'Thought she was opening the door to the bathroom, opened the basement door instead and fell down the stairs.'

Burdock pricked his ears.

Erin shook her head. 'Wasn't that the epitome of stupid?' she said out loud. 'Who doesn't turn the light on before they step into a room? No one in their right mind goes crashing into a room, even when they know where they are.'

Burdock hung his head back down and pushed on along the snow-strewn road. He shivered and thought about his jacket hanging up in the utility room. Usually he hated that thing, but Teresa always made him wear it when they were out in the snow. He licked at some of the drifted snow on the side of the road, but it wasn't his crunchy biscuits.

It tasted as white as it looked. And it made his lips numb.

Erin wanted to go to The Copper Kettle for a takeaway coffee, but she turned her face away from the welcoming light behind the windows. If she went in there, she'd remember she hadn't had any breakfast, she knew, and then she'd be having a piece of cake to go with the coffee, and she couldn't afford either of them, could she? Not with having had her allowance taken away from her along with her car.

She'd make an instant coffee at the Care Home instead. It was better than nothing. Like, only a tiny bit better than nothing, but beggars couldn't be choosers now, could they?

Burdock followed her into the house, then scooted back outside to the welcome mat and scratched his feet on it and shook the bit of snow off that stuck to his fur. Then he darted into the warm depths of the house before Erin closed the door, and he lifted his nose to sniff.

Scones, he thought, and licked his chops.

He visited each of the people in the house one by one, being careful to get pats and words made of honey from each of them. It made him feel better. He loved coming here. Everyone was glad to see him, and several of the old ones knew exactly where a dog liked to be scritched and scratched best of all. Behind the ears was Burdock's favourite place, but he wouldn't pass up a good butt scratch either – that spot on his back right by his tail? That was some scritchy goodness right there.

And he got some scones. They were warm and buttery, but he didn't mind. Not one little bit. It didn't fill his tummy like his biscuits would have, but it was better than the snow that tasted like white nothings.

The old man wasn't feeling well. Burdock could sniff it on him. There was sneeze inside of him, and something under that too, the dog thought. Something that sniffed sweet, a little bit like Stephan's compost. He stepped delicately onto Mr. Robert's bed, and lay down gently beside the old man to keep him company.

'Burdock,' Erin said, coming in with a steaming cup of tea for Mr. Roberts. 'There you are.' She set the tea down on the table beside the bed and looked at the dog, then the old man. 'I hope he isn't disturbing you. And I'm not sure he should be on the bed.'

Bernie Roberts put a protective hand on Burdock's head where it lay on his thighs. 'Leave him,' he said. 'He's a giant beast, but as gentle as I've ever met.'

Erin dredged up a smile. 'Isn't he, though? And how are you today, Mr. Roberts?' The question was out of her mouth before she remembered the man was probably dying, and certainly feeling lousy.

She just wasn't having a great day.

'Can't complain,' Bernie said, reaching for his cup of tea with a sigh of satisfaction. 'This is just what I needed. A good cup of tea, and a bit of company, if you've five minutes?' There was a tightness in his chest that he knew meant something in there wasn't up to any good, but he was old, and things were wearing out at a faster rate than they could be repaired, and wasn't that the way of things?

Erin shifted slightly on her feet, not feeling in the least in a chatty mood, but she supposed this was her job, after all – making sure the old folk were comfortable. She smiled and nodded.

Bernie saw her smile. 'There we go – and don't you look

a sight better for popping a smile on your dial. Go and fetch yourself a cuppa too. I won't tell Mary.'

Nodding, Erin hid her grimace until she was out the door. Men, she thought. Always telling women they were better if they were smiling and compliant. Her hands knotted together into fists but after a moment she shook them out and heaved a sigh.

'That's a big one,' Alan said as he peeled the potatoes for lunch.

'A big what?' Erin asked, going to the teapot and wondering if she really wanted a cup of strong, stewed tea. Not really, she decided.

'Sigh. Are you having a tough day?'

'Oh, don't worry,' Erin said, turning to make another cup of coffee instead. 'I'll plaster a smile on my dial, and you'll feel better.'

Alan turned to her, potato in one hand, peeler in the other. 'Get up on the wrong side of bed today, did you?'

'Why is it,' Erin snapped, 'that every time a woman shows less than awesome feelings, a man tries to make her feel shit for it?'

'Whoa, take it easy.'

That was too much for Erin. She whirled around. 'No, you take it easy! I'll be any damned way I feel like.' Her hands were tight fists again and she thought if he said one more word she'd scream.

Or cry.

'That's enough of that, Erin,' Mary said, coming into the room and planting her hands on her hips. 'Step out into the garden and gather yourself.'

Erin scowled at her. 'It's cold out there.'

'That ought to snap you out of it double-quick, then.'

Now, Erin narrowed her eyes. 'Snap me out of it?' She gritted her teeth for a moment, shaking her head. 'Why do women have to snap out of it when they express feelings that are uncomfortable for others?'

Mary raised her eyebrows. Erin had been with them for only a week, but so far, she'd been rather good. A little uncomfortable around the old folk, but Mary thought she'd get over that soon, and settle down, learn her way around them.

But something was under the young woman's skin today. She glanced sideways at Alan, who scooted smartly out of the room, still holding his potato and his peeler. She heard him call out a cheery hello to Tilda Sharpe.

'Erin,' she said, turning her attention back to the matter in hand. 'This is your place of employment, and it is a Care Home. It is not the appropriate place for you to express feelings of anger, and nor is it appropriate to act aggressively towards others and make blanket statements to justify doing so.'

Erin stared at her. Her mouth opened. Then closed. She shook her head. 'You can't tell someone to *snap out of it*. I repeat – why do women have to snap out of it when they express feelings that are uncomfortable for others?'

'There is a time and a place for expressing those feelings, and letting others hear and accept them,' Mary said, drawing on her deep well of patience. 'But you must also do yourself the service of being an adult and knowing when that time and place is, and looking at the feelings you're having, determining what exactly has triggered them, and deciding if they're something that needs to be acted upon, or acknowledged and let go.' She looked steadily at Erin. 'If something has happened to you, then I am very willing to discuss it calmly with you at an appropriate time and help you as I can. I'm sure too, that if I am not the right person, then there will be others. Your friends, your family. Morghan perhaps.'

For a moment, Erin wanted to flare up again, especially at the mention of her family. But Mary was right. That wasn't what was really bothering her. Or rather, it was just one thing of many.

'I'm frustrated,' she said. 'About some things that are going on.' She pressed her lips together, then sighed, letting the anger go like a deflating balloon.

'I'm sorry,' she said. 'I'm in a bad mood and I shouldn't be taking that out on anyone else.'

Mary inclined her head, accepting the apology. Really, she thought, it had come more quickly and easily than she'd expected. 'Do you still need a quick trip into the garden to ground yourself?'

Erin glanced out the window, then nodded. When Mary put it like that, maybe it was a good idea. After all, she hadn't done her usual grounding and gratitude routine that morning.

Her eyes widened, and she clamped a hand to her mouth.

'What is it?' Mary asked.

Erin shook her head slowly. 'Oh,' she said. 'I'm such an awful person. I forgot to feed Burdock this morning.' She closed her eyes.

'I was in such a horrible mood, I just forgot about it.'

36

WINSOME LIFTED HER HEAD TO PRAY. SHE WASN'T SURE WHEN she'd begun praying this way, with her face lifted to God instead of meekly looking down at her knees.

But it felt good. It made her feel strong – and shouldn't one feel that way when talking to the creator of the universe?

For, she thought, wasn't she part of it all?

She was back visiting the family to bless the house. Erin, Stephan, and Krista had cleared and cleansed it the day Winsome and Morghan had helped Minnie, but Winsome wanted to go further, blessing the space, bringing warmth and love back to it.

She hadn't practiced what her prayer should be and expected that she would go with one of the beautiful house blessing prayers from the Iona Community. But when she opened her mouth, she found her own words on her tongue, not those of any other.

She prayed from her heart, and it swelled with love as she did so.

'We ask this house to welcome us,

'And we bless it with our presence.

'We ask this house to soothe us,

'And we bless it with our calm.

'We ask this house to comfort us,

'And we bless it with our gratitude.

'We ask this house to cradle us,

'And we bless it with our peace.

'The spirit of this house welcomes us,

'And we honour it with our love.

'The spirit of this house watches over us,

'And we honour it with our love.

'We come and go,

'Here is the place to which we return.

'This house is blessed,

'Roof and beam,

'Wall and brick,

'Window and door,

'Floor and foundation,

'We are blessed,

'Head and eyes,

'Body and bone,

'Hand and heart,

'Love is in us all.

'Here lives the wild spirit of God,

'The bright peace of God,

'The beautiful mystery of God,

'Here in this home.'

Winsome opened her eyes to find that Rosalie had clasped her hand.

'Amen,' Rosalie said.

'Amen,' Winsome whispered on a breath that was more of a sigh. The house felt so much better than that dreadful day when Rosalie had brought her around in a panic. The young people had done a good job cleansing it with the smoke from burning herbs, wafting it into every corner, clearing the stagnant energy and banishing the shadows. Then, they'd rung their small silver bells, another way, Ambrose had said, of breaking up the stagnant energy, but even better, he'd told her, the ringing of bells warded off low-level entities and made the spirit of the house feel welcome and acknowledged. It made the space sacred.

And the house felt so much better.

But that wasn't enough, Winsome knew. It gave them back a clear slate from which to work, but she turned and looked at Rosalie and Natasha. Behind them stood a pale Minnie.

'The house has already been cleared and cleansed,' she said. 'I'm here today to bless it, and to bestow God's blessing on you.' She smiled gently at them, watching their spirits as she did so.

She was getting used to seeing people's spirits – auras. And most certainly preferred the term *spirits*, even though that gave her a bit of the collywobbles too. But it didn't sound quite as New Age, and she was already slip-sliding dangerously into pagan territory as it was.

Her prayer, for example.

As though the house had a spirit of its own.

Morghan, of course, said it did. But like so many houses,

it had been ignored and neglected so long that it had gone to sleep, which, of course, gave space for other entities to walk around as though they owned the place.

Winsome's head spun.

Well, her prayer, along with the bells, had probably woken it up again.

Hopefully.

Because this family needed everything possible on their side. She smiled at them again.

'I want you to begin considering this house as a home, as a sanctuary – your sanctuary.' She glanced at Rosalie. 'I know you already did, Rosalie, as it has been your home for a very long time.'

Rosalie gave an awkward, lop-sided grimace that was supposed to be a smile.

'But to be in a position for this place to be your sanctuary in a time when sanctuary is needed by us all, there are things we need to take care of.'

'Like what?' Minnie asked. She felt confused. On the one hand, whatever the vicar (the Vicar!) and Morghan Wilde had done to her left her feeling clear and sort of hollowed out – like when you finally got over a really bad flu and were out of bed for the first time in two weeks, still wobbly, but everything was bright and you were really happy to be up and about.

On the other hand, and she placed a hand over her stomach, she felt like there was an empty space in her that had been filled before, and she didn't know what to do about it. It wasn't possible to walk around with a hole inside her, an empty space, was it? It had to be filled with something.

Winsome gestured to the couch and armchairs. 'Shall we make ourselves comfy for a minute while we talk about it?'

Rosalie bobbed towards the door. 'I'll make a pot of tea,' she said. Her hands were nervous, and she leapt at the chance to do something with them.

'I'll give you a hand,' Natasha said, unwilling to be left alone with the weird vicar, who wasn't quite like any other she'd met. Not that her and Rog had been churchgoers. More likely to go to the pub really and play the pokies. But still, she was glad the woman was here, and that it was a woman, not some sanctimonious man looking down on her. It would be hard for Winsome Clarke to look down on anyone. The woman was pretty short. But anyway, she was nice. And she'd fixed the bumping and scratching that Natasha had had to work so hard at ignoring.

And who knew? Maybe she'd be able to help with other things too. Natasha rubbed her hands together, then winced and tucked them under her arm. They were red and chapped and she didn't have anything to put on them.

She couldn't seem to stop washing them either.

Tiny sidled out of the room to go find her grandmother and only Minnie and Winsome were left in the small sitting room. Minnie stared at Winsome, gnawing on her lip.

'How are you feeling?' Winsome asked, voice low, warm.

Minnie shook her head and the black hair swung across her face. 'I don't know,' she said. 'I feel weird.'

Winsome raised her eyebrows. The girl's spirit wasn't too bad. Maybe a little ragged around the edges. Someone, she thought, should probably teach the girl the grounding exercises. With a small start, Winsome realised that someone would probably have to be her.

What had she got herself into here?

She could imagine Dean Morton's voice, big and jovial, getting slightly less jovial but even bigger. *That sort of thing isn't done by the Church, Winsome,* he'd say.

But maybe, she thought, it ought to be.

Oh bugger, came the thought on the heels of that one, what am I doing?

First praying in the little pagan temple instead of the church, now getting all set to teach a kid how to become a tree.

She closed her eyes for a moment, hoping Minnie wouldn't notice.

God give me strength, she muttered inside her head. God guide me.

'What sort of weird?' she asked at last.

Minnie shrugged. 'Sort of empty here, you know?' She touched her stomach again. 'And not like hungry or whatever.' Another shrug. 'Just, like, empty.'

'And you're not using the ghost app?' Winsome asked, listening to how steady and clear her voice was as though that were the sort of question one asked every day.

Minnie shook her head. She'd picked up her phone and looked at it several times, thumb almost poised to download it again, but she hadn't.

'Is Morghan going to come back here to see me?' she asked.

'Probably not,' Winsome said, going for honesty. 'She has a full plate just at the moment.'

Minnie looked down at her feet, still in their shabby tennis shoes, crestfallen. 'Oh,' she said.

'But,' Winsome continued, deciding to share the news with the girl now. 'There is something else I wanted to run by you if you're interested. Something of a proposition.'

That made Minnie frown. The vicar was propositioning her? What?

Winsome smiled at her. 'Have you ever been in Haven for Books?' she asked.

The frown on Minnie's face deepened. 'Yeah, of course. It's a great shop. Why?'

'Krista was here the other day, doing the house clearing.' Winsome tilted her head. 'She wondered if you'd like to come help her in the shop a few hours a week.'

Minnie blinked at her. She hadn't known what to expect, but it hadn't been this. 'A job, you mean?' she asked.

'Yes,' Winsome answered. 'I'm not completely sure of hours or anything – you'd have to sort that out with Krista, but she did want to know if you might be interested.'

'Shit yeah!' Minnie clamped her mouth shut. 'Sorry,' she said. 'I mean, yeah. Yeah, I'm interested. Krista is really cool, and the shop is totally fab.'

One small weight lifted from Winsome's heart. 'That's wonderful, then,' she said. 'Of course, I'm quite sure another round of lockdowns are coming our way, but I guess we all must work around those, don't we?'

It was true. They were under Tier Two currently, and she probably wasn't supposed to be inside this house, really. She put the thought aside. Wellsford was self-isolating as much as possible, and they had no cases.

'All right then,' Winsome said. 'Krista is expecting you

whenever you feel up to popping along. You can work out the details with her.'

Minnie nodded. 'That's brilliant, thanks.' And it was too, she thought. Krista was part of the Grove, Minnie knew she was. And the thought of working in the shop had her practically swooning. She couldn't believe she'd been almost ready to nick a deck of cards from there. Her cheeks reddened with embarrassment.

Winsome was taking a deep breath, coming to another decision about the grounding exercises. Stress exercises, she'd call them. Or something. She'd try them out with this family first, and if it went down well, then she'd make a pamphlet or something. Maybe make a video, although putting it online might cause problems.

She did like her position as vicar, after all.

'Shall we see about that tea?' she asked. She had more to discuss with the family yet.

'I was just about to bring this in,' Rosalie said, seeing Winsome come in.

'That's lovely,' Winsome replied. 'How about we sit around the table and have it?' she asked. 'I always find the kitchen is the real heart of the home, don't you think?'

Rosalie looked around hers. It was a bigger room, what with the dining area part of it. She spent most of her time here, usually.

Winsome glanced at the little chip stove. 'It must get nice and warm in here when that is going,' she said, taking in the small armchair tucked beside it.

'It does, yes,' Rosalie said and glanced out the window where it was snowing again. She had the bar heater going but the room was still chilly. She stopped herself from yanking her old cardigan tighter around her chest. She didn't want the vicar to know she was cold.

'I can have a load of wood delivered for it, if that would help,' Winsome said, hoping Morghan wouldn't mind her volunteering some of the Wilde Grove supplies. 'There's nothing worse than being cold when it's snowing outside.' She shook her head. 'And the price of electricity these days.'

Rosalie looked mournfully at the little stove. 'That would be very welcome,' she said. 'How much would it cost?

'Oh,' Winsome said. 'Nothing,' she said. 'There's a supply we can dip into when there's a need for it.' Morghan and Ambrose wouldn't mind, she thought. She'd ask Ambrose that afternoon. 'These are the times when we need to take care of each other, not just as a family, but as a wider community – no matter who we are, or what faith we follow.'

Rosalie squeezed her eyes shut. It was all she could do to nod dumbly and search for her voice. When she found it, there was little more than a squeak.

'Thank you,' she said. 'We haven't been using it lately, but it warms so much better than the electric fire.'

'Good,' Winsome said. 'That's one thing sorted, then.' She glanced around the table and smiled. 'Let's have some of that tea, shall we?'

With a cup of good hot tea in her hand, Winsome got down to business. 'Now, she said, having had the run down on this from Morghan and agreeing completely with all of it, 'the thing is, we want to avoid a repeat performance of the situation of the other day.' She carefully didn't look at Minnie, because really, it wasn't just because of Minnie that all the trouble had happened.

Tiny shook her head vigorously. 'I don't want to see any of those bad fairies again,' she said.

Rosalie placed her hand softly over her youngest grand-daughter's. Natasha turned away, looking resolutely at the wall. She pretended to listen for Robin to wake up. Surely he would soon? Perhaps she ought to check on him.

Make sure he wasn't dead from the virus. Natasha gripped the edge of the table, knuckles whitening.

Minnie wasn't listening. She was thinking about working at Haven. How amazing was that? Her dad – or the spirit who'd told her he was her dad – had said nothing good was going to happen to her while she lived with her Mum and Gran, but that wasn't true, was it? Sure, they were still stuck in this tiny house where there was no privacy, or much of anything, really, but she had a job!

She'd be able to get a pair of new boots.

She'd be able to get a new skirt, or the material to make one. Perhaps she would dust off her grandmother's old sewing machine after all, ask her Gran to teach her how to use it. She cast a cautious glance at her grandmother, thinking about it. Maybe her Gran wasn't so bad, she knew the vicar after all, and the vicar knew the leader of the Grove here in Wellsford. Minnie wanted to shake her head every time she thought about that. How weird it was. Morghan Wilde had said they were friends, that she and the vicar worked together.

Minnie was about busting to know what sort of work they did together. Except, she guessed, she sort of did. Because hadn't – and here she glanced over the table to watch Winsome speaking – hadn't the vicar been part of getting rid of the entity that had been attached to her?

She had. That's what they worked together on.

Minnie had never heard of a clergywoman and a...a... priestess working together.

It was blowing her mind, thinking about it.

The world was a lot stranger than she'd ever thought it was. What sort of witch had Morghan said did spirit journeying or whatever?

A hedge witch, that was it. That was what Minnie wanted to be. She wondered if that was what Morghan called herself.

'Now,' Winsome said. 'The key to not having a repeat of the...disturbance...here, is to help you all settle in together and find a way to live harmoniously together in this house, and to cope as best as you can with these difficult times we're all going through.' She glanced over at Minnie who was, as far as she could tell, away in her own little world, eyes round, face bemused.

Krista had been an angel to offer the girl a job.

'So,' she continued. 'I know it is very difficult to have you all squeezed in here together, when you're used to far more independence, so what measures can we take to make you more comfortable?'

It was Tiny who piped up. 'You can get Grandma a comfy bed.' She frowned, a tiny pucker of lines between her eyebrows. 'I'm sleeping in her bed and it makes me feel bad because she's just on a camp bed and there's nothing cheerful in her room at all.'

'Oh, sweetheart,' Rosalie answered, touched. 'I'm all right. You don't have to worry about your old Gran.'

'But we all should,' Winsome said. 'We need to care for each other, not so much in the way that we ourselves want to be cared for – but in the way that each of us needs.' She paused a moment. 'I don't know if you've heard of the what's often called The Golden Rule. *Treat others the way you want to be treated.* But I subscribe to a slightly different version of that.' She cleared her throat a little. 'Treat others the way they need to be treated.' She smiled around the table.

'Because we've all different things we need, and we can't assume that everyone needs the same things we ourselves do.'

37

ERIN PUT DOWN A BOWL OF BISCUITS IN THE SMALL ROOM OFF the kitchen of the Care Home and stroked Burdock's back as he lowered his head and crunched them up. Mary had let her run down to the grocer's and pick up a bag of his favourites.

'I'm sorry, boy,' she said. 'I've been awful this morning. I wish you could have told me you hadn't had your breakfast.'

Burdock picked up another biscuit and broke it up between his teeth. It was so good, he thought. Now he'd had biscuits and scones. This was going to be the best day ever, after all.

Erin shook her head. 'I wish I hadn't had my head stuck so far in a hole that I didn't think about you,' she corrected. After all, it was hardly Burdock's responsibility to remind her to do her job. She sighed. 'It's just been a crappy morning, that's all.'

She patted the dog again, happy that he was wagging his whip of a tail and bulldozing his way to the bottom of the bowl. Now, to go back to Mr. Roberts and apologise to him too. She had a feeling she'd been a terrible grouch to him as well.

'Hello Mr. Roberts,' she said, coming in and looking at the old man in the bed. 'I'm sorry I didn't get back with a cup of tea to have a chat.'

He'd been a big man once, she thought. He had that look that big men got, once they started aging. You could tell that once there'd been muscles and strength.

'It's all right,' Bernie said. 'Your Burdock kept me company until just a minute ago.'

'He had to go and have his breakfast, I'm afraid,' Erin said, setting down fresh cups of tea for them both. 'I was a terrible person this morning and forgot to feed him.' She drew breath, let it out. 'He's making up for it now.'

'Ah,' Bernie said. 'That accounts for the swift exit.' He coughed, then thumped his chest. 'And we all forget things such as that when a mood gets on us.'

'Maybe,' Erin said.

Bernie eyed the girl. Just a slip of a thing, she was. Looked a terrible lot like her grandmother though. A great deal.

'Sit yourself down,' he said, nodding towards the chair beside the bed. 'If you've a minute for a chat with an old fella like me?'

Erin smiled behind her mask. 'I've got a minute or two,' she said.

'You're Teresa's granddaughter, aren't you?'

She nodded. 'Did Stephan tell you that?'

Bernie laughed, then coughed again. 'S'cuse me,' he said

when the coughing bout subsided. 'Got a frog and a few tadpoles in the old chest today.'

'Shall I get the nurse for you?'

He shook his head. 'I'll be good as gold for a sip of this tea,' he said, and picked up the mug, eyeing Erin over the rim. 'Stephan didn't tell me – I can see it for myself,' he said. 'You're the spitting image.'

Erin managed her first genuine smile of the day. 'You knew my grandmother?'

'I did,' Bernie said. 'Same shade of hair. Same temper too, I'll warrant.'

She shook her head. 'You know they did scientific studies and disproved that redheads have bad tempers.'

Bernie put his tea back down and guffawed. 'I deserved that, my girl, I'm sorry.' He narrowed his eyes. 'Teresa though, she could be a bit sharp with her tongue.'

Erin let herself grin. 'You sound as though you're speaking from experience.'

'I tried my hand at courting her for a time,' Bernie said, letting himself drift back to the memory of his youth. 'She was a year or two younger than me, and friends with my sister. She wasn't much interested in me, though.' He laughed quietly so that he wouldn't start coughing again. 'Told me she couldn't possibly step out with a bobby as I was then. Said a witch couldn't marry a policeman.'

Erin's eyebrows shot towards her hairline. 'She was that open about being a witch?'

'Our Teresa was not one for subterfuge or making allowances for social proprieties. Which was why she would have made a lousy policeman's wife.' Bernie tapped a finger on his mug of tea. 'We were required to be exemplary members of the community then, you see. And needed to get along with all sorts, be accepted into the front parlour of every house, when you were a village bobby.' He sighed. 'Of course, village policing didn't last too much longer after that. They consolidated everything, you see.

'But your grandmother wasn't the marrying kind at all, really, and I think we both knew that.'

'But she did marry, didn't she? Or how did she have my mother?'

Bernie took a sip of the tea. It was nice and sweet, just the way he liked it, and it made his throat feel better. 'She never married your granddad. Never even lived with him. Were a bit of a scandal around some quarters, but as she never cared what was whispered about her, everyone was required to get over it and move on.'

'Wow,' Erin said, sitting back in her chair and thinking on it. She sipped her own tea. 'So she was a bit of a rebel, my Grandmother.'

'All the women in her family were, I reckon,' Bernie said. 'Her father passed on quite young, and she and her mother Lizzy lived there in Ash Cottage ever afterwards, bringing up Becca between them.'

'Becca,' Erin repeated, her voice suddenly flat. 'My mother.'

'Now, she was a rebel if ever I've seen one,' Bernie said, thoroughly caught up now in his reminisces. 'Except she was the sort who didn't have a cause, if you get my drift. It was more like she was born angry with the world.'

He looked over at Erin and reached out, patting her hand with his age-speckled one. Physical distancing be damned, he thought. He was on his way out, and nothing could hurt him now. And who knew – his mouth quirked in a smile – maybe he'd get to try his luck with Teresa Lovelace again on the other side.

'She gave me up for adoption,' Erin said, turning her head to stare out the window. It was snowing again out there, a light drift of flakes that flecked the air like miniature white stars. 'Even though she knew my grandmother wanted to keep me.' Her voice was rough, as though it was her with the cough, with the rising tide in her lungs. 'She asked my parents to give her money for me.'

The snow outside was too pretty for the story on her lips. It danced suddenly in a gusting breeze, swirling and catching the light.

'She sold me, essentially,' Erin said. 'And spun a tale about needing to escape from a black magic cult.'

Bernie was watching Erin's face, feeling worse for the girl with every word she spoke. 'A black magic cult?' he broke in to ask.

Erin lifted her shoulders in a tight shrug. 'Crazy, huh?' she said, looking at Bernie for a moment, then dropping her gaze to her cooling tea. 'And even crazier, my parents – my adoptive parents – believed her.' She shook her head. 'They still believe her.'

'A black magic cult here in Wellsford?'

'They think Wilde Grove is a cult,' Erin said, and there was no inflection in her voice now.

'Well, that's crazy,' Bernie said. 'Hasn't someone told them that?'

'You'd have to force them to listen,' Erin said, finding the old man surprisingly easy to talk to. 'I guess they don't want to believe anything else, because then...' Her voice turned bitter again. 'Then they'd have to acknowledge that they'd essentially bought themselves a baby, not rescued a poor unfortunate from the grip of evil black magic practitioners.'

Bernie's bushy eyebrows rose to where his hairline had once been. 'What are your parents like?'

'Very unhappy with me,' Erin answered.

'Sure,' Bernie said. 'But are they good parents – have they been good to you?'

Erin swallowed as Burdock came into the room and dropped his head onto her lap. She played with his hairy ears. And nodded.

'Yes,' she said. 'They have been. I've not wanted for anything, I suppose.' Then decided to qualify that. 'Or, not anything material, I guess.'

'Well off, are they?'

Erin nodded. 'But they're dead against me living here in Ash Cottage.' The now-familiar anger smouldered inside her. 'They want me at home where they can keep me under thumb. I'm letting them down, coming here and doing...well...'

'Black magic,' Bernie finished for her, with a smile. 'Not everyone can fathom the charms of a place such as Wellsford, my girl.'

For a moment, Erin felt desperate. 'I wish I'd grown up here with Teresa.' She was suddenly sure that if she had, then she wouldn't be having this problem with Kria. She was sure she wouldn't be having it at all. She could only imagine what her life would have been like if she'd grown up in Wilde Grove.

Like she had been supposed to.

Why hadn't it gone that way? Why had her mother given

her away – make that sold her – to strangers, and why had she had to grow up with strangers, far away from where she had been supposed to be? Was it some sort of glitch? It must have been a mistake.

'Watch out,' Bernie said. 'Your mouth is drooping again.'

'I don't feel like smiling,' Erin said, and Burdock lifted his furry eyebrows and gazed up at her. She pressed her thumb idly between his brows, and he sat down, the better to be close to her.

'There's no point brooding on that which can't be changed, girl,' Bernie said. 'We can't change things that weren't our doing, for starters.'

'It's all wrong, though,' Erin said. 'I should have been born here and grown up here. My mother should have kept me or let me grow up with my grandmother.'

'But then you wouldn't have all the wonderful memories of growing up with your family.'

Erin shook her head. 'It doesn't matter. It's a question of what is right.'

Bernie raised his eyebrows at the statement. The arrogance of youth, he thought.

Things can be changed, or they can't. If they can't, then they had to be lived with.

Made peace with.

Because carrying the grudges with you did no good for anyone.

Erin was still deep inside her own grievances. 'Did you know my mother?' she asked.

'I did,' Bernie answered, wondering where this was going to go. Maybe he ought to tell the girl he was tired. He was tired; it wouldn't be a lie.

He didn't say anything, though. Just waited. It seemed, really, the least he could do. And he had no other pressing appointments. A slight smile lifted his lips. Not yet he didn't, anyway.

Erin sighed. 'I hate the way she died, and it doesn't make any sense, you know. I realised that this morning.'

Bernie answered slowly, repeating her words. 'Doesn't make any sense?'

She shook her head. 'No – listen. Charlie told me she was around at some newish boyfriend's place, right?' She glanced at Bernie, waiting for him to agree.

He nodded, wondering where this was leading, hoping it wasn't leading anywhere. Fearing it was.

'Were you a policeman then?' Erin asked, changing track unexpectedly.

'I was.'

She chewed on her lip for a moment, thinking. 'So, anyway,' she said. 'Charlie Beckford – you know Charlie, right? She lives here in Wellsford.'

'I do,' Bernie answered. He reckoned he knew everyone in Wellsford, and most everyone in Banwell. Charlie and Martin lived on Martin's family farm. The land had been in his family for at least a couple hundred years. It was like that around here. Not many people moved in or out of Wellsford. Not until the last few decades anyway, where it seemed all the young people were born with restless feet and souls.

Probably this virus would change that.

Erin nodded. 'Well, Charlie told me how it happened, you know? How my mother died?' Pausing, thinking, getting her ideas in order, Erin rested a hand on Burdock's warm back, stroking him slowly.

'She said what happened was that my mother, Becca, opened the basement door instead of the bathroom door and fell down the stairs.' She blinked. 'My mother hit her head, on the railing, or the steps, or something, and was knocked unconscious.'

Bernie nodded. He knew the story.

Erin took a sip of tea. It was cold, but her mouth had turned dry.

'So her boyfriend called an ambulance, right, and she was rushed to hospital.'

Bernie watched Erin's face. It was a hard story.

Erin blew out a breath. 'She never regained consciousness. She died when they were operating on her head to relieve the bleeding or swelling or whatever.' She looked over at the old man in the bed.

'God,' she said. 'I'm sorry – I shouldn't be going on about this. You're tired and not well, and I'm just blabbing on about things that happened years ago.' She pushed Burdock away and got up. 'I'll let you get some rest.'

He was tired, that was the bother of it. 'Perhaps I will have a bit of a nap,' he said.

Erin picked up the tea things, the cups rattling in her hands.

'But come again later and we can pick up where you left off, all right?' Bernie said. 'I want to hear what you've been thinking.'

'I'll come again,' Erin said. 'But it's just rubbish, that's all. Don't mind me.' She headed for the door, Burdock at her heels, then turned. 'Can I get you anything?'

Bernie shook his head and watched Erin bustle out of the room.

He was tired. Sometimes, memories could be exhausting. He remembered Teresa, and he remembered Becca, remembered being the one to break the news of her death to Teresa. They'd called him up, asked him to do it, since he was local, knew everyone.

They'd also said it had been just an accident.

But Bernie had always wondered. Just like he expected Erin was wondering now. She was a bright girl; he could see that.

And really, he asked himself. Who barges into a room without turning the light on? Especially in a house they don't know very well.

In any house, really. He thought, not for the first time, about his own habits.

No, he'd come to this conclusion before.

Becca's death was odd. There wasn't any question.

38

'TEACH ME HOW TO MAKE FIRE,' ERIN SAID, LOOKING ACROSS the stone circle at Morghan. The snow had stopped, but it was cold and she'd pulled her cloak about herself, her breath puffing white in the morning.

The sun of a few days ago was a distant memory.

Kria and the valley was not, however. Nor was her humiliation at Macha's hands.

Morghan raised her eyebrows. 'Make fire?' she asked.

Erin nodded. Explained. 'Kria can make fire drop from her bare hands,' she said.

'Really?'

Erin thought of Kria cupping her hands and repeated the gesture in the stone circle. 'Like this,' she said, bringing up the tight bowl of her hands to her forehead. And then opening them, spreading them wide.

'The fire falls from her palms like magic,' she said. 'She makes the flame from the spark, she says.'

Morghan was interested. The girl was able to do this in

the Waking, not just the Otherworld? She'd seen many hard-to-believe manifestations of magic in the Waking, but not fire like this, not yet.

'Tell me about this spark,' she said.

Erin tried to recall exactly how the conversation had gone. 'I don't remember the details,' she said. 'Something along the lines of being connected and singing the right song and reaching for the part of yourself that was fire and bringing it forth.' Put like that, she knew it was impossible she'd ever figure it out. Any of it.

But Morghan was nodding, as though she understood. She did understand. It made immediate sense to her, although she was sure it would be quite the trick to do these days, not because it was impossible, but because it would take a great leap to overcome the conditioning that such things were impossible.

Now impossible.

'We have forgotten that so much is possible to us,' she said, musing upon it.

'Well,' Erin said. 'It's a neat trick, but I guess we don't need it anymore. We invented matches and...' She paused, considering. 'And whatever there was before matches.' What had there been before matches? She'd never wondered that before.

Maybe Macha was right, and she was uncommonly slow.

But if Macha was right, then she was also talented. Maybe one day she would be able to pull off such a thing as to conjure fire out of thin air.

'Do you think,' Erin asked, 'that if I learnt how to do it, I could solve this Kria problem?' She paused. 'Do you think it's possible to learn to conjure fire like this, now? Like, here and now, in today's world?'

Morghan nodded without hesitation. 'I have seen many things,' she said. 'I have done a great many of them.' She and Grainne had done a great many. 'It is absolutely possible. So much more than we believe is.'

Morghan moved out of the circle of stones, Erin trailing after her. It was time for Erin to finish her initiation, she decided. Once and for all.

'Where are we going?'

'Somewhere warmer,' Morghan said, her boots crunching on the snow as she headed further into the rocky hills.

Towards the cave. Not the small one where she went to do her own travelling, but the larger, where Ambrose had been taking Stephan. Not that Stephan needed to go there to travel to the Wildwood anymore apparently. Her lips curved in a smile as she thought of Ambrose's excitement in recounting Stephan's tale of healing.

The Great Bear had chosen well, she thought. And so a healer was being retrained. A new generation relearning the Old Ways.

She glanced back at Erin.

Maybe the young woman would learn to conjure fire with her hands. It was not impossible. She felt suddenly the glimmer of Ravenna within her and knew that the ancient lifetime stood only a step to the side.

Should she take that step, she wondered?

'Take my hand,' she commanded Erin.

Erin blinked at the outstretched fingers. She couldn't think of when Morghan had ever touched her except occasionally during prayer. They weren't praying just now. They were walking. She didn't even know where.

She touched her fingers to Morghan's and saw Morghan's lips tilt in a smile, and then she opened her own mouth.

'Wha?' she asked, the trees spinning suddenly around her in a dizzying circle. 'Wha's happening?'

'Move with it,' Morghan's voice said to her. 'We are stepping sideways for a moment.'

Her voice was calm as always and Erin grasped hold of it as the trees blurred around her and the ground under her feet shifted. As she shifted.

'We are stepping sideways and back,' Morghan said. 'Macha will catch you.' There was a slight pause. 'And you will pay attention.'

Pay attention? Erin closed her eyes, stomach heaving with the unexpectedness of the shifting. She was not slipping backwards in time in her sleep, in her dreams, not this time. She was not lying on her sofa grasping the red thread. This time she was being thrust back, the snow and dirt and stone under her feet giving way so that...

She tumbled.

Sideways.

Down.

Back.

And opened her eyes.

Morghan stared at her. Except it wasn't Morghan. The eyes were dark, the hair darker too. Erin blinked, looked down at herself, the movement setting her stumbling. Morghan – not Morghan, the other – watched her without moving. Erin flailed a hand out, touched a tree, righted herself and stood there trembling, looking down at her body.

It wasn't her body. She closed her eyes, the world still spinning. How did this work, she wondered? How did this happen?

Nothing about herself was familiar. Or not...exactly. She recognised herself. Recognised that she was related to this body.

It was Macha's form that she saw when she looked. It was Macha's hand that she pressed to her thigh, feeling the coarse fabric of her dress under her palm.

She glanced up, and saw the woman who was Morghan, or would be Morghan one day, looking impassively at her.

'What is your name?' Erin croaked at her.

'I am called Ravenna,' she said.

'But you're Morghan too.'

Ravenna – Morghan – Ravenna inclined her head.

Erin blinked in Macha's body. 'If I'm here, where is Macha?'

A slight smile. 'She is there also.'

But Erin looked around and did not see her. Then realised that of course she would not see her standing there among the trees. She was in Macha's body and there could not be two bodies. She looked for Macha inside herself instead. And found her there, standing as though at the back of the room, in the shadows.

Except there was no room inside Macha's head. It was instead a spacious landscape, and Macha stood on a far, green hill, hair waving in a breeze.

'Can she come closer?' Erin asked.

'Need she?' came the answer.

Erin frowned.

Morghan watched her, feeling Ravenna's thoughts drifting right under her own. They floated along the same current.

'Come,' Morghan said, turning back towards the stone circle. 'Let us do what we came here to do.'

This was planned, Erin questioned? How powerful was Morghan that she could nip back and forth in time like this?

A thought wafted towards her as though on a breeze. *As powerful as you are to do the same.*

Erin shook her head. She did not go hopping back to the glen with its great deep loch by choice. Given the choice she would never have gone to the place.

She shivered. Never.

Erin stopped walking and stood swaying slightly instead, her mouth open in astonishment. Here were the standing stones again, just as she knew them.

Almost as she knew them. She glanced across at Morghan, seeing Ravenna, her heavy hair braided with shells and bones, her cheeks tattooed with swirling patterns, the eyes dark with knowledge as she leaned on her staff.

Erin realised why Morghan had dressed the way she did at the Samhain ritual. She was dressed as Ravenna. Why, she wondered? Why would she have done that? It was confusing.

But then, pretty much everything was confusing. She felt Macha's laughter and dropped her head.

Curiosity, however, got the better of her and a moment later she was looking again, for how could she not? She didn't know what year it was, but it wasn't winter and

Grandmother Oak looked sprightly. She peered closer at the tree and realised it wasn't the same tree at all – their oak had been planted in the same place, but it wasn't the same tree.

How far back in the past had she fallen? Further back than Kria? She had no answer for that.

One of the women in the circle turned and gestured for Erin to join them. Erin wanted to shake her head, because she was not Macha and she didn't know if they knew that, and because she had no idea what they were doing.

Well, she guessed they were dancing. Much like the Grove had danced at Samhain. How long had groups like theirs been gathering to dance like that?

And what was it about dance? Erin swallowed, allowing herself to be drawn into the group while Morghan watched. She looked down at her feet as she tried to follow the steps around the circle, then finally opened her mouth.

'What are we doing?' she hissed to the woman next to her.

Blue eyes looked back at her in surprise. 'We are weaving and honouring the weaving. Macha, are you all right?'

Erin nodded her head dumbly. She wasn't Macha, but she didn't think this was the time or the place to say so. Instead, she concentrated on the dance again, which was simple enough really. Round and round in a circle, touching a stone and turning. A circle, she thought. Then, a star. She looked upwards at that thought.

And gasped. Above them, shimmering in the warm sky was the weaving. That was the only way to describe it. Like the trails a sparkler left in the darkness, it crisscrossed overhead.

Hadn't she seen this, glimpsed it for a moment at Samhain?

She glanced across at Morghan, and wanted to ask if this was something that had to be danced into being, or...

There was movement in her mind, from Macha, and excitement.

Or what? Macha asked, stirring.

Erin touched one of the stones. It was not as pitted as it was in her own time. It was taller also, and straighter. She turned away, stepped across the circle to another stone and touched it with her fingertips. The stone was warm under her hand and humming. She wanted to press her palm to it, lean into it and put her ear to it, listen, but the dance moved her on, and she looked up at the weaving again, the pattern that shimmered above them in the sky between the stones like a map.

Or what? Macha asked again.

Erin blinked. She'd lost track of her thoughts. Or what? What had she been on the verge of realising?

Morghan watched the dance from behind Ravenna's eyes, seeing the tracing of the web over the stones, seeing how tall and straight the stones were. One was chiselled with a design that was no longer there in her own time, lost to the ravages of the years. She stood there, her hands wrapped around Ravenna's staff, and under her hands it was a living tree still, its roots diving deep under the soil to wind away to touch a whole network of such roots, and dipping down further, deep in the earth to anchor there. So, she was part of the web of the earth too.

All things were connected, she thought, and watched

Erin dance and weave, her young body – Macha's young body – gleaming with spirit, full to the brim with its vitality.

Here was magic, Morghan thought. Dancing the web into seeing. Dancing the spirit into strength.

All around her, the very air hummed with life. With consciousness. With magic.

How she wished her world were still like this. She closed her eyes for a moment and the golden threads of the web hung behind them. She corrected her words, for she had misspoken.

Her world was still like this.

Her wish was for the people to see it.

What would that take, she wondered? How to make everyone realise they could experience the worlds and everyone in it like this?

It was her constant question.

Something drew her attention away from the circle. A movement in the woods. A calling. She recognised it.

And knew it wasn't for her. She'd been called long before.

Erin. The Lady was waiting for Erin.

Macha's name was being called and Erin turned her head to look at Morghan. Was it still Morghan, or had she returned to their own time and left her here? Dry panic closed her throat, and she broke away from the dance.

'Morghan?' she asked, hearing Macha's voice.

Ravenna nodded and Erin pressed a hand to her pounding heart.

'Come with me,' Morghan told her. 'You are being called.'

Erin frowned, looking around, not understanding. 'What?'

'This way.'

She followed Ravenna's body, still unused to her own, and they ducked under the trees on the rim of the clearing and entered the woods.

It was darker under the canopy of trees. Erin blinked in the dimness.

'Remember,' Macha told her, and then there was the shifting sensation again, and Erin gasped, closing her eyes, opening them, seeing that she was herself again, herself wearing the thick grey woollen cloak, and under it the green dress that Lyndsay had woven and sewn for her, and under that, the linen dress and her underwear, fleece leggings, strong waterproof boots. And in front of her, Morghan walked again, grey hair cascading down her straight back, her cloak black over a long grey tunic.

'Morghan?' she croaked. 'What are we doing?'

Morghan glanced back at her, lips twitching in a smile. 'Answering the call,' she said.

But Erin shook her head and stood still, refusing to walk any further along the trail. 'No,' she said. 'I don't know what is going on and I'm not going anywhere until I do.'

Morghan stopped and turned fully to look at her. For a long moment, she was silent. When she finally spoke, her voice was low and cool as a breeze.

'I cannot tell you the things you need to know, Erin,' she said, looking at the way Erin's white fingers clutched at her cloak, and how her dark eyes were shadowed under the hood.

Erin shook her head.

'The truths are best experienced, and then given words,' Morghan said. 'I have been showing you, over and over.' She lifted a hand, waved it at the trees. 'This world,' she said. 'You must see it the way it truly is. You must see it with the eyes of your spirit – the way Macha and her priestesses do. The way Kria was taught to but refuses. The way I have shown you.' She blinked.

'Now,' Morghan said. 'You are being called.'

Erin stumbled after her, questions withering and dying on her tongue.

And was brought suddenly up short.

Morghan melted back into the trees. She would stay there, while Erin went on ahead. This part of the journey was only for her.

Erin stared at the fox standing on the path in front of her. It looked back steadily at her through amber eyes, whiskers twitching. It had fur a shade lighter than Erin's hair, and a sharp, cunning snout.

Erin glanced around for Morghan, but she was alone on the path. Alone that was, except for the fox.

'You're the one I've been seeing,' she whispered. 'Out of the corner of my eye. I've been drawing you.'

The fox tipped its head to the side, eyes bright and intelligent. Then, with a swoosh of its bushy tail, it turned and trotted away down the path.

Erin stared for a moment, uncertain. Was she supposed to follow the animal? What was she supposed to do? She looked around for Morghan again, but she was nowhere to be seen. Erin was on her own, except for the fox.

Fox turned and looked back at her, impatient for her to follow. When Erin took a tentative step towards her, Fox turned and continued on. They had places to go. They had people to meet.

Erin's heart suddenly lightened. This was Fox! Fox, who had slipped in and out of her drawings, and her dreamings, and her imaginings. Here was Fox at last. She followed her, knowing suddenly deep inside that she must, that this was how things worked, that spirit walked with spirit, and never alone.

The forest grew around her, not just woods now, but becoming deeper and darker. Fox's fur glowed red in the dimness and Erin looked up at the trees but could not see the top of them. Their trunks were tall and straight and so thick she could not have put her arms around them. She did not know what sort of trees they were.

Only that they were ancient.

They reminded her of the well. Somehow, the well and the trees, they connected the worlds, she thought.

The path curved upwards, higher and higher, and on one side the trees slipped down into a steep valley – nothing like Kria's; this one was green and brown and heavily wooded, fragrant with the scent of leaf and soil and magic.

And then she was not walking anymore, but falling, tumbling over the edge, and Fox was falling with her, paws in the air, back curved, tail a white-tipped flash in the darkness. They fell together, fell down and down and impossibly further down, through the great dark forest filled with trees and stars and more trees and more stars, vast in every direction.

Erin looked up as she fell, and a giant face leaned over and looked back at her between the trees. It opened its mouth and laughed and laughed and laughed.

Erin gaped at it, a dizzy shock of knowing going through her – this was her own soul she was looking up through the great trees at. This was her own soul gazing down upon her.

Not an aspect of her soul, no, it wasn't just that. This was the sum of herself. Erin and Kria and Macha and a hundred others in their entirety.

And it laughed and laughed and laughed, delighted with her, delighted with everything. Erin stared up at it, and it felt so big, so close, and yet so far away, and amused. Amused with her, with everything, and in that amusement, and laughter, and delight, Erin felt warm and valued, accepted, and celebrated, held in its laughter.

With a puff of its breath, she was blown back onto the path, and tumbled to the ground, disoriented, not knowing for a moment, which way was up, which way was down, which way was sideways.

Perhaps they were all the same direction.

Fox went up to her and poked her sharp nose into her hair as if to tell her to get up. She listened, found her feet, and fell in behind Fox once more. Her heart thudded against her ribcage as she walked behind Fox and realised she was back in the woods again.

But which woods? The Grove in Wellsford?

She didn't think so.

The woods in Macha's time?

She wasn't sure about that either.

Looking around at the trees, her heart beat like a drum, louder and louder, and suddenly it didn't matter where she was, or when, or even how.

What mattered was that she had reached out and touched a great mystery. She had seen the face of her own soul. She had discovered that she lived in a universe that was vast and awesome in its joy.

Elation flooded through her and she picked up her feet and ran, Fox flying along at her side, white paws barely seeming to touch the ground, white tail flashing.

This was the way to live, she thought! This was the way to be!

Back and forth in time, up and down in space, the beating of her heart to tether her, and her kin racing at her side.

Morghan had been right all along, she thought. She was never alone – how could she be alone when she was part of that great laughing face that had beamed down at her?

She was a tree, a star, a gleam in a soul's eye.

She was alive. A small running creature in a huge world. A vital, beautiful creature in a world that was marvellous with magic.

Something blocked the path, and Erin came to a panting halt, staring up at it. Her blood pounded and rushed between her ears, and her heart squeezed and expanded in her chest.

Not a something.

A someone.

She was so tall, Erin thought. As tall as a tree, she thought, and squinted her eyes at the brightness. She was as bright as a star, glowing so brightly white that Erin could not make out who she was.

But Erin knew what she was.

She knew that immediately and heard her soul laughing again. Here was the ancient goddess. Gleaming with white light, and so tall, as tall and straight as a tree.

Was this the Lady of the Ways? Erin thought it must be –
she recognised antlers in the dazzling brightness. The Lady
wore antlers on her head, and suddenly, she was bending
over Erin, and touching her staff to Erin's forehead, as if
putting her mark on her.

Claiming her.

If she wished to be claimed.

Erin knew there was a choice. She felt it within herself,
and the question welled up inside her – did she wish to
accept the invitation?

Morghan had, she knew, and Selena before Morghan.

Macha had, and Ravenna.

Perhaps every Lady of the Grove. Every priestess of the
Grove.

This goddess, or another. But this goddess was inviting
her now.

Erin's head nodded the answer, voice stuck somewhere
down deep in her chest. She nodded again, dumbly.

Elen of the Ways touched her again, then held something out and Erin lifted her hand, feeling the creak of her
human bones, the blood in her veins.

The goddess dropped something into Erin's hand, then
straightened, dimming the forest around her with her
brightness. The antlers were like branches from her head,
and a moment later she was gone, and Erin stood alone on
the path again except for Fox, blinking, her sight dazzled.

She opened her hand and stared down at the diamonds
glittering on her palm.

39

Stephan shook his head. 'Everything has changed this year,' he said. Then shook his head again. 'Everything. I mean, first Teresa crossed over, and then you came, and then my life was turned upside down.'

'You make it sound as though my coming here turned your life upside down.' Erin sat at the table where she'd been playing idly with her runes, still too shaky from the day's events to do much more than sift them around. She'd been trying to learn the symbols and their meanings so that she wouldn't have to look them up in the book all the time. Her mind kept wandering however, to the corner of her eye where Fox lurked. To the vision of Elen of the Ways in the Wildwood.

To the dance with Macha,

To Kria.

To Stephan. She looked up at him and her chest swelled with the looking. She wanted to get up and cross the room to him, lean against his chest and dig her fingers into his curling black hair. He still hadn't had a haircut and it was almost shoulder length now. Just right for running her fingers through.

'Why are you looking at me like that?' Stephan said over the sudden rush of blood in his veins. He licked his lips and thought of the time he'd kissed her and wondered why they hadn't done that again.

That and more. So much more.

Erin didn't speak. She didn't trust her voice. Instead, she gave in, and got up unsteadily from her chair, wincing when it scraped against the flagstones, the noise grating inside her head. She crossed the kitchen in four steps and shook her head at him.

'Don't move,' she said.

Surprised, he held his hands up. He'd been leaning against the cupboard door under the stairs, holding a cup of tea and just rabbiting on like he did.

Erin closed her eyes, and leaned against him, feeling the lean hardness of his chest against her breasts. She breathed in the scent of him, her chin tucked down, head on his shoulder. He smelled of soil, she thought, breathing in the slightly musky scent of him. Of secret burrows in the earth, where animals lay together in pairs, paws on fur, muzzle to muzzle.

'Can I put my arms around you?' Stephan asked, his voice hoarse.

Erin made herself shake her head. 'No,' she answered, but she turned slightly to the side and pressed one of her own hands to his heart. It leapt and bounded under her touch.

'Why not?' he asked, aching to circle his arms

around her.

She shook her head again. 'I can't,' she said. 'I can't go where I want to go with you yet.'

Stephan was silent for a moment, digesting that titbit. He cleared his throat, feeling her warmth and softness against him as an exquisite torture. 'Where do you want to go with me?' he asked, mouth dry, heart pounding.

She sighed a little. 'Everywhere,' she said eventually, and lifted her face to look at him, taking in the black stubble on his winter-pale cheeks, the long lashes that fringed his startlingly blue eyes, and she looked at his lips. She touched a fingertip to them, the lightest of touches, just the merest brush.

'Everywhere we've ever been, everywhere we've yet to go,' Erin said, and her breath was warm against his chin, his lips.

He swallowed, desperate to lay his hands on her back, her neck, her cheek.

'But?' he croaked.

She rested her forehead against his cheek for a moment, then touched her lips to the spot and stepped reluctantly back from him.

He was suddenly cold where she'd been. She'd been so warm against him.

'But I have to get out of the valley first,' she said. 'I have to find my way to a place where I can do that.'

He didn't understand. 'Why is that necessary before we can...you know?'

She sat back down at the table and looked at him, her

eyes serious, deep. 'Because I'm in pieces,' she said. 'And I want to be whole when I'm with you. I want to meet you on equal footing.'

'We are on equal footing,' Stephan said fervently.

But Erin shook her head. 'Not yet,' she said. And sighed again. 'But soon. I think I've almost got it.'

'You have?'

'Almost.' She looked back at the table, scooped up the runes and dropped them in a stream into their bag. 'It's complicated, isn't it? Living properly?'

Stephan thought about it for a moment. 'Yeah,' he said. 'And no.'

Erin swirled her fingers among the stones. 'I'm afraid of losing you,' she said, not looking at him but gazing out the window where the largest raven stood on the hedgerow.

'But you don't have to be!'

Erin shook her head, wanting him to be quiet and he was. 'I'm afraid of losing you because Kria is too much part of me still, and she is so alone. She has been abandoned there, and I feel it. I feel her pain and her desperate need.'

She pulled out a rune and lay it face down on the table. Put her hand back in the bag that had belonged to her grandmother. So many connections.

So many strands.

She thought of the web they'd danced at Samhain. She thought of the weaving she'd danced in Macha's body, thousands of years before.

She drew out another runestone.

'I'm going back to her tonight,' she said. 'To Kria.'

Stephan stepped forward, wanting to argue with her,

about Kria, about all of it. She would never lose him, he wanted to tell her. Couldn't she feel the bond between them? He could. The energy swirled around them whenever they were together. He could feel it. He could almost see it.

Clarice had said he was almost impossible to be around because of it. Because of the energy. It made her drunk, she'd said. Drunk and wanting. And then she'd asked about Krista again.

He didn't say any of that, though. Instead he made himself sit down at the table and look at her. 'Do you want me to stay while you go back?' he asked.

She shook her head. 'No,' she said. 'I need the quiet of being alone to prepare. I'm getting to be an old-hand at it, I'll be all right.' She glanced away to where Burdock snored in front of the stove. 'Burdock will wake me if things get too much. He seems to have a second sense about it.'

Burdock's ear twitched at the mention of his name, and he thumped his tail twice, but he was warm and comfy, and his stomach was nice and full from dinner. He went back to his own dreaming.

Erin pulled the third and last stone from the bag and put it down on the table next to the others. Stephan watched her turn them over and they both gazed at the symbols etched on the stones.

'Wow,' Stephan breathed out. 'That's some drawing.'

Erin looked them over, then reached for the book. She shook her head. 'I don't know them well enough yet.'

Stephan pointed a finger at the first one she'd drawn. She'd put it in the middle of the row. 'This one is *Dagaz*,' he said. 'It kind of means *day*, and hope and happiness.' He looked up at her face and she met his eyes for a moment, then dropped her gaze back to the book.

'Here is *Dagaz*,' she read. 'When the sun rises on a new day, we greet the dawn with hearts open and ready for our spirits to be filled with joy. For only the open heart has space for hope, and only with hope can we be happy.'

She looked at the words on the page for a long moment, drawing in their meaning. 'Well,' she said. 'I guess that's some sort of message.'

'I'd say so,' Stephan nodded.

Erin felt her heart lift just thinking about it. There was hope, she realised. There was always hope. And help. Hope and help. She smiled.

'What's the next one?' she asked.

'Which one did you draw next?'

She looked over the top of the book at the stones and pointed to the one that reminded her of a fish, or a crossed ribbon. 'I know this one,' she said, relieved to be remembering something from her studies. It had been hard to concentrate on anything lately, because of not sleeping well, because of her dreams of the glen and loch and Kria.

'*Othila*,' Stephan said.

'Right,' Erin agreed. 'But I'm not entirely sure how to take its meaning.'

Stephan touched the stone. It was cool under his finger. 'What does the book say?' he asked as he thought about it.

'Well,' Erin said, looking back at the page. 'I mean, it's straightforward enough.' She trailed off. 'I guess I'm just afraid of it.'

Stephan looked up at her, gazing at her face. She had

such beautiful eyes, he thought. 'It's your inheritance,' he said, glancing down at the rune. 'That's what it's talking about – your inheritance, your tradition, your history. Like, taking your place in the Grove – that's your tradition.' He shook his head. 'I think it's really spot on.'

'Yeah,' Erin said. 'I know you're right. It's just really in your face, you know?'

'Would you rather have drawn a spread that just kind of pussy-footed around things?' Stephan asked. 'I like that it's so meaningful and direct.'

Erin nodded and looked down at the book.

'Here is your inheritance: the tradition of your soul,' she read. 'The time has come to step into your blossoming and to determine upon which tree you are growing. Know as you become, that you are not the first and nor will you be the last, but like every soul in your lineage, you are essential for the health of the tree upon which you grow.'

What tree was she blossoming upon? One of the Wilde Grove trees, of course. She thought of Macha, of Kria, of herself, and all the others she'd been between. It was so clear to her that here was her lineage, and here was her tradition.

Why then, was she still afraid?

'What's the last one?' she asked.

Stephan smiled at her. Picked up the runestone and held it up to her. 'This,' he said, 'is *Wunjo,* and it means joy.'

'Well,' Erin said. 'I guess that sounds pretty good.' She looked at the other two runes. 'What's the difference between happiness and joy, do you think?'

Stephan had wondered the same thing once and asked

Teresa about it. He remembered her reply now. 'Your grand-mother told me that happiness was the perfume of the rose, and joy was the rose.'

Erin raised an eyebrow.

'Well, you know,' Stephan continued, grinning. 'The smell of a rose is great and all – wonderful, in fact, some of those old varieties have an amazing scent, not like a lot of the new roses that are grown for looks more than scent...' He trailed off, seeing Erin's other eyebrow rise to meet the first. 'Right. Well, where was I?'

'The smell of a rose is lovely,' Erin contributed.

'You bet,' Stephan said, then added with a sly grin, 'especially those old tea roses.'

Erin narrowed her gaze and he laughed.

'But anyway, I think she meant that happiness is a feel-ing, you know? It doesn't last, it isn't really tethered to anything – hell, half the time I reckon my feelings aren't even related to what I'm doing or anything, they just get triggered from things I'm not even aware of.' He paused for breath. 'So, joy then, is the rose.'

'The rose.'

'Yeah. Not just a feeling, but a whole state of being.'

Erin nodded slowly. 'Sometimes,' she said, 'especially when I'm drawing, or doing one of Morghan's exercises – you know the one, where you kind of stretch out over the land and see it all?'

Stephan nodded.

'Sometimes when I'm caught up in that, this amazing sensation just kind of sweeps over me. This incredible sense of well-being and it's more than just a feeling, I think. It's like I know suddenly that the world is a much bigger and a much more interesting place than the way I usually see it.'

Stephan was suddenly excited. 'Yeah! I get the same sensation sometimes, and I always wish I could hang onto it longer, because everything is suddenly brighter and I always get real sure that I know a lot more than usual, and that the world is really a place that makes sense.' He drew breath, grinned again. 'And all that,' he said. 'Right?'

He ticked a fingernail on the table. 'I bet that's why Morghan and Ambrose have us do that exercise. So we will experience that sudden joy.'

Erin nodded, reached out and touched the back of Stephan's hand. 'I bet that's it too,' she said. 'And try to hang onto it.'

Stephan turned his hand over, held onto Erin's fingers. Nodded.

Erin liked the feel of his hand around hers. 'Do you think that's what my soul was feeling when it was looking down on me and laughing?' she asked.

'Experiencing, not just feeling,' Stephan said. 'And yeah, I do, now that you've said that.'

She nodded. 'Experienced. That was why it was laughing so much. Because it was filled with joy.' Erin breathed deeply and looked back down at the runes. 'Are these saying that if I step forward into my new life, claim my rightful inheritance, I'll get to experience that joy as well?'

Stephan glanced at the row of runes on the table then looked back over at Erin. 'I think that's exactly what they say,' he told her.

She flicked through the book to find the page for *Wunjo*.

'Here you are no longer bud nor blossom,' she read.

'Now, between sky and earth, at the meeting of both, you are the fruit of your labours, and you are ripened in the sun. Now you are flesh, and seed, and the great cycle continues. Now in joy, you are eternal.'

She put down the book and looked at Stephan. Nodded.

'Yes,' she said. 'That's exactly what they say.'

40

ERIN BURROWED DEEPER IN HER BLANKETS, TUCKING SLEEP around her, and holding the red thread in her hands. Outside, the wind blew, rattling against the window, and in the grate, the embers glowed, crackling gently. Burdock sat on his bed, watching as the spirit fox slunk into the room, a dark red blur that smelt not of fox, not properly, but of something that made Burdock wrinkle his nose and lift his lips in a silent growl.

Magic, he thought. Soil and stone and water and wind. An uncanny combination in one thing.

He watched it, squinting as it slipped up beside the bed where his person lay tucked in a tight cocoon of blankets. What was old Foxy up to?

Nothing. The spirit fox sat down and stayed sitting and Burdock yawned, the fire warm against his flank. He grew tired of watching, and anyway, those spirit animals never did anything but skulk about. He got up and stepped around in a dainty circle, then lay down again with a contented groan. His bed was soft. His bed was warm. His stomach was pleasantly full, and dreams awaited. Good dreams of pats and tickles, and long romps up and down hills. Burdock closed his eyes and stepped into his dream skin.

Erin tumbled down into her dreamings as well, holding the thread in her hands, knowing it would lead her back to Kria, because to dream was to open doors, and this one she knew. She knew the way.

The deep metallic tang of the loch filled her lungs and the air over it was chill with the taste of snow. She opened her mouth and let the air fill it as though to eat it and rolled around the taste of it in her mouth. Cold, like ice, like snow, like a thousand things over a thousand years that were cold, white, icy.

The light was low. Dusk, she guessed, looking up at the sky. Or dawn, perhaps. Dusk, or dawn, she couldn't tell which.

Where was Kria?

From where she stood on the stones of the shore, there was no one in sight. A glance over at the hut and Erin moved towards it. Perhaps Kria was in there, sleeping on that hard narrow bed of furs.

But she was not there, and Erin stepped out of the empty building, drawing the hood of her cloak up over her ears, for the wind had begun a keening over the water and she had remembered to dress warmly in her dreaming.

Or perhaps it was not the wind. Erin cocked her head to the side, listening.

The keening continued, wavering up and down, despairing.

Kria. It was Kria.

And Erin knew where she was.

The side of the glen was stony, the dirt loose around the crumbling rocks, held together only by the tough grey grass. Erin pulled herself up, grabbing handfuls of their tussocky leaves, then stepping along the narrow trail, hands out for balance.

Hurrying, hurrying.

There was something blocking the entrance to the tiny cave. Someone.

It was Kria.

Erin knelt down, feeling the gravelly dirt under her knees. 'Kria?' she said.

The keening cry was loud in the cave. It cut off abruptly at Erin's arrival.

'Go away,' Kria said. ''Tis better to be alone, I think, than haunted by spirits that come and go when you cannot.'

'I'm sorry,' Erin replied. 'I came here to help, but I don't think I've been much use.'

The whites of Kria's eyes gleamed in the dimness. Beneath them, her mouth stayed shut.

Erin wriggled further into the cave, thrusting away the shudder of fear, mindful of the bones laid out at the back wall.

'What are ye here for now then?' Kria asked, unable not to. 'To have conversations with invisible spirits?'

'No,' Erin said. 'Or at least, I don't think so.'

Kria shook her head and wiped her wet cheeks with the heel of a hand. 'Ye speak in riddles,' she said. 'And I've not patience for riddles.'

'I was going to come to this place,' Erin said after a moment. 'Even if you weren't here.'

Kria remained silent. In one closed fist, she held a small bone from a finger. The smallest she could find.

'Where do you think she is now?' Erin asked, looking over where she knew the skeleton was, and trying not to shiver at it lying there on the cold dry dirt.

'Not here, that's for certain,' Kria said grudgingly. 'And a sight better off she is for that fact.'

'But where has she gone, then?' Erin said.

Kria looked over at her. 'The Summerlands is where we hope to go after our deaths,' she said. 'For a spirit, ye are very dense.'

'So I keep being told,' Erin said dryly. 'So I keep being told.'

She sighed. Tried again. 'But doesn't a spirit have to be sung over?' she asked. Stephan had told her about how he and Morghan had sung Teresa over. How he'd seen her leave Ash Cottage, a shining spirit with her Lynx kin on her heels. 'Aren't there songs for this?' she asked. 'There must be. You said there are songs for everything.'

'I never,' Kria said.

'Well, perhaps not,' Erin agreed. 'But you made it sound like there are.'

'I will not sing over her bones,' Kria said, and began backing out of the cave.

'You cry over them,' Erin said, being brutal. 'Why won't you sing over them?' She followed Kria from the cave.

Kria whirled around on her, long thin braids of hair flying. It was dawn, the day was lightening, the sun hauling itself up into the mists over the glen.

'I will not sing over her bones because who will do the same for me?' She spat in the dirt. 'Let me tell you who will sing over mine – no one. No one will see the spilling of my blood, and no one will sing the songs that will show me the way home.'

There was only the sound of Kria's ragged breathing then, and somewhere, the lonely sound of a gull flying in the path of the sun. Erin lifted her face to the sky to look for it.

'I flew once as a gull,' she said. 'I called for my kin and first Raven came and looked at me, and then a seagull took his place and lent me his wings.' She blinked. 'We swooped out over the ocean together and I never wanted to do anything else but be a seagull.'

Kria stared at her, silent. There were streaks of dirt and tears on her cheeks, so that the tattoos there were only the faintest blue lines.

'I think Gull came to me not because he is my spirit kin, but because he is yours,' Erin said.

Kria looked away. 'I have no kin,' she said.

'I thought everyone did,' Erin answered.

Kria shrugged her thin shoulders. 'Not those who come here.'

'Why?'

Now Kria gripped her elbows in her hand. The small bone dug into the flesh of her palm. 'They can't come to this place.'

Erin looked around. The light was as grey and seeping as the mist. Below and to their right, the loch had turned a deep green that made Erin long for something she didn't even know the name of.

'Why?' she asked again. 'What keeps them out?' She gazed up at the mist overhead, where in the distance the speck that was a gull still flew. 'Not the mists, obviously – they still fly here.'

'Those be birds of flesh and blood, not spirit,' Kria said.

'I would think,' Erin said slowly, threading her fingers together under her cloak, 'that spirit birds would have an even easier time of entering this place.'

Kria stared at her a moment, eyes flicking uncertainly to the sky and back to her face. Her expression hardened. 'What would ye know? Nothing about anything to my mind. Ye be here only to torment me.'

'I'm not here to torment you!' Erin shook her head and lowered her voice, looking down at her feet. 'I'm here to get you out of here. Get us out of here.'

Kria riveted her gaze on Erin. 'What?' she said. Then laughed, a rough, joyless sound that bounced off the side of the valley so that the mist coughed it back down at them. 'And do tell me how it is that ye plan to get me out of here? And I have seen that ye be not stuck here forgotten and doomed as I.'

This wasn't going in any way as Erin had planned, insofar as she'd planned. 'You're too stubborn for your own good,' she said, shaking her head, feeling the familiar despair creep over her. She took a breath and tried to shake it off.

'You've given up,' she said.

Kria laughed again, turning to go back down to the loch. 'And who could blame me?'

Erin's mind worked desperately. 'The people who sent you here? I'm sure this isn't the outcome they hoped for.'

Kria's steps slowed and she cast a creaking glance back at Erin. 'What do ye know of their intentions?' she asked.

'Only what I can surmise,' Erin answered.

A slow blink from Kria. 'And what would that be, then?'

'Where I come from...' Erin started.

'Where you yourself have admitted there is no magic anymore!'

She nodded. 'Some of us are trying to change that,' Erin said. 'And so, I'm being taught things.'

'Not among them though, how to make fire.' Kria's words were mild, disinterested now. She was looking down at the loch and thinking about the depth of the water, how silent it would be underneath that rippling surface. Like another world.

A world where there were fishies and...

Shadows and who knew what else. In her dreams something large and sinuous rose from the loch in the dead of the night and she shrank back against her furs, burrowing down deeper into her bed, whimpering like a child.

Under the surface of the loch was not where she'd meet her end, she knew. The old water dragon living there would eat her soul and clean his teeth with her bones.

'You're not listening,' Erin said.

Kria turned to her. Then turned away again. 'It's time to eat,' she said flatly.

Nor, she knew, would she lay herself down in one of the caves that pockmarked the sides of the glen, as the other whose bones she had found had done. She had not the strength – or was it patience – to lay herself down and wait for death to find her in the darkness.

She would die under the sky, under the mist that

426

trapped her. It made no difference to her that this pesky spirit had come to torment her. The conversation she had with it inside her head – it did nothing to change anything, except to make her wish all the more fervently to be done with this place.

She would die looking up at the mist, and if anyone were to find her, they would see her staring skull looking at them, accusing them. And that would be right.

'Where are you going?' Erin asked, stumbling after her. 'What are you doing now?'

Kria ignored her.

'Wait,' Erin cried, because there was something about the stiffness of Kria's back that made her breath catch in her lungs, that made her dizzy with dread. 'What are you going to do now?' She reached for Kria, lunging to catch hold of the threads of fabric Kria had wound about her to keep out the chill.

And she gasped, for her hand passed right through the material. Right through Kria's arm, the elbow bones nothing under her fingers.

Erin stopped still, her body rippling with shock. She was nothing more than a spirit here – Kria was right to call her that.

There was nothing she could reach out and do, nothing she could touch and change.

She only had her voice, the power of her words, and what power was that, when she could barely manage to arrange her thoughts in the right order, and when Kria would not listen anyway?

'Kria!' she screamed, and her cry was echoed by the sudden shrill call of a gull. 'Kria! Wait!'

But Kria wasn't listening anymore to the voice in her head. She gazed up at the mist, spread thick over the sky like thunder made solid. It was a far cry from the delicate strands of weaving she had been used to seeing in her previous life as a priestess. Back when she had sung the songs of the world and danced the weaving of the same. Back when life was golden and lovely and filled with hope.

Her mouth curled down at the sight of the hated gull. 'Come here!' she screamed at it. 'Come to me, you hoary, hated thing!'

It came to her, like they always did when she made them. Wings flapping frantically against the chill of the air and the fire in her gaze. It came to her, eyes rimmed in yellow, staring, for certain hating her all the while it had to obey. She saw its gaze and knew it hated her.

Just as she hated it, this gull with the freedom to come and go, to fly through the mists and away.

Erin fell to her knees, hands going to press the scream back into her mouth.

She shook her head. No. No. No. This wasn't how it was supposed to happen. She thought back to standing on the hillside, high up over the ocean with Morghan, and how the gull had come to her, its bright eyes, its feathers thick and white, and she crammed her fingers into her mouth, as though to shove her cries right back down her throat.

'No,' she moaned around them. 'Don't. Please don't.'

But Kria didn't listen to anything but the snapping of bones as she wrung the neck of the gull. Its head hung loose from its body in her hand, swinging gently as she panted over it, closing her eyes for a moment, then snapping them back open.

Kria turned to stride back down to the water's edge. She began to shiver from the cold.

Erin crawled to her knees, stony grit digging into her palms. She tripped on the skirt of her dress and fell, clawed herself back up, her hood falling back so that the mist could soak her hair.

'Wait,' she called. 'Wait for me.'

And oh goddess, she thought, scrambling down the hillside. Oh, goddess, that gull had come to Kria when she had called it to herself.

Come because Gull was her kin.

And Kria had plucked it from the air and snapped its neck. And even – yes, it was true – though Kria had to eat, had to find sustenance, the sacrifice of her own kin for her brought Erin to tears.

It was horrible.

And it was beautiful.

And oh goddess, Erin thought, it was awful. This was no sort of initiation when it did this to a person. To make them thankless.

She fell again, digging her fingers into a tuft of tough grass and hauling herself to her feet again. Her body jerked and lurched as she went after Kria, and tears made her cheeks wet, the cold air slicing against them. She wiped her nose, choked out a sob.

'Kria!' she screamed. You've gone crazy, she wanted to say. Being alone here has made you lose your mind.

And Erin couldn't blame her for that. She couldn't find any words of recrimination inside herself for that. She could only cry.

You're not alone, Morghan said over and over.

You'd never really be without me, Stephan said. Even if we were not here together.

You're not alone, Morghan said again.

Erin pressed her palms to her temples, stopping her hurtling run down the hill and stood straight so that the wind could bluster about her, flattening her cloak against her, battening it around her ankles.

And Elen leaned down and touched her staff to Erin's forehead, as if putting her mark on her.

Erin's fingers were cold against the hot skin of her forehead. She closed her eyes, and the world fluttered and streamed around her. World upon world upon world.

Her voice was small, ragged, as she repeated the words she'd been taught.

'May the strength of your heart be with me wherever I go.

'May I be guided through the wilderness,

'Protected through the storm.

'May I follow your path

'Through the eternal forest.

'May healing and blessing be mine.

'May compassion be in my heart

And in my hands.'

She took her hand from her face and looked at them, holding her palms upwards. Prayers, she realised suddenly, with a certainty that settled and nested in her very bones, were spells. As she uttered them, so the universe shifted so that she also lived them.

That was why Morghan made her pray. They were casting spells over themselves. Bringing the world into alignment.

Bringing themselves into alignment with the world.

She closed her eyes and Elen dropped something into her palm and Erin closed her fingers around the gift. Diamonds. The most precious stone.

The most valuable gift.

She'd been given the most valuable gift.

Erin opened her eyes, held her fisted hand to her heart for a moment and breathed deeply, then set off down the hill, leaping over the shrubs clinging to the stony ground, skidding around the tough little spikes of grass.

She didn't call out for Kria.

Kria had forgotten how to listen.

And listening went together with the singing.

Kria squatted upon the stones not six strides from the water's edge. She held her knife, preparing it to cook the bird over her fire. She put the bird down, looked at its blood on her fingers and closed her hands together, smearing the gull's blood over her hands with something as close to satisfaction as she ever felt.

Erin came up beside her, stood watching, shaking her head. 'Don't,' she said.

Kria shifted, her bones grinding together under the scrawny leather of her skin and she sucked in a deep breath of air that smelt of blood and the rawness of cold water.

Tucking her skirts about her knees, Kria leaned forward over the circle of stones that was her outside hearth. She brought her hands together, concentrating on drawing from herself the spark of fire. There was little enough spark left in her now – now that she was no longer connected to the great fiery flow of sun and earth, now that the mist separated her from them. Soon enough, she knew, she

431

would not be able to draw fire from herself like this anymore.

Soon, she would have none left inside her.

But that was a day she would not allow to come. It couldn't. She couldn't bear it to come to that, to take herself off to a cave, to lie there and wait for death, nothing left inside her.

Kria dropped her hands and the tiny lick of flame fell on the waiting lichen in the rough stone circle. She stirred a hand over it, feeding it air to breathe and grow fat upon.

Erin stood and watched, hands clasped tight enough to turn the knuckles white with pressure. The wind gusted up against her, bringing with it the taste of loch water. She swallowed it.

'Don't,' she said again.

Kria lifted her head and squinted at the sky, the dead bird back in her hands. She stared at the endless granite clouds that reflected on the water in front of her. The wheel, she thought. It turned and turned and turned again, and all she was to it was a small speck of something caught in its great grinding. She was broken up against days that were shortening into tight knots and there was rain coming, and the wind was gathering to come sweeping down to churn the water of the lake, the great dragon under its waves thrashing its tail about.

She turned her head and looked at the stone hut, baring her teeth. She despised having to seek shelter in there, looking at blocks fashioned into shape by a man's hand. A man she would never meet, and did she want to? Not the one who had built this prison for her, and others like her.

Not that one. But another perhaps. A softer one, who

would hold her to his breast and touch her in ways that made her feel...

Anything but this isolation.

Abruptly, it was decided. This would be her last meal.

Kria thrust the skewer through the few soft feathers left on the gull, through the cooling flesh, and set it over the flames. She would turn it a few times until it was cooked, and she would sit there in front of the fire and eat it, even when the rain came. Rain was water and could be diverted so that it did not fall on her.

Was there enough spark inside her left to do that? Precious little enough for the fire.

The bird dripped grease upon the flames which spat back, hissing. Kria stood up.

Erin reached for her, dropped her hand. Reached for the egg on its leather thong around her neck.

'Don't,' she repeated.

Kria looked down at her hands, the ones that had plucked the gull from the sky, broken its neck. Her hands. The only one's whose touch she'd felt for so many turns of the moon she'd lost count. They were still damp with the gull's blood and she planted them over her eyes and cheeks, fingers splayed, painting her skin red. Through the mask, she looked baldly out over the water for the first time in many turns of the sun and thought about taking her life.

The water was cold enough to claim her breath, should she wade out until it lapped at her thighs, and then deeper still so that her feet lifted from the stones under them and she floated under the sodden bowl of the sky.

She would only have to wait. For the water to fill her lungs, drawing her down to stare sightlessly at the dragon that would swim by her, nosing against her with its long, scaled snout.

A gull flew overhead and cried out, making her wince at the pained and angry sound. Perhaps it was mad that she was roasting one of its kind, or perhaps it was just worried for itself, flying by mistake over this goddess-forsaken valley.

Erin lifted her head and watched the seagull track its way across the mist overhead. Its underbelly was a soft white, webbed feet tucked up neatly towards the tail. She remembered flying, the sound of her wings against the sky, the weightlessness.

The water would not do. Kria could not bring herself to wade out into those unwelcome depths. The loch would take her like an offering, dragging her down as though she were its due, and there was enough left of her not to want to be a sacrifice to whatever lived under its surface.

She had tried, when she was still only days here, to make her offerings to this water, but it had been indifferent, too large, too deep, too foreign, and she had stopped, begun turning her face from it.

The wind blew up, whipped down into the valley from the clouds, whistling from one steep side to the other, its voice like a knife in the air. Kria turned from the water and gazed up the shore behind her, seeing the grey stones blend into the sparse soil, everywhere empty, everywhere made of nothing.

Her eyes looked straight past Erin. The spirit was not real. Only a dream, only a torment.

They had brought her here to learn to see. And now she saw.

She saw her future, spreading out into interminable days and nights of isolation in this scrubby, stony, ugly land.

She had not proved worthy. She had failed the initiation. They had left her here and she had shrivelled. Closing her eyes, she felt the first drop of rain on her head, and unthinking, she waved a hand and was dry, the rain falling to darken the stones in front of her instead. Behind her, the fire spluttered and she lumbered back around to contemplate it with eyes gritted and wild behind her hair.

'Let's sit down,' Erin begged. 'We can eat together and talk.'

Perhaps there was no point to eating after all, Kria thought. She was not hungry. She had failed. This day, she thought, she finally decided. She had failed.

Beside the fire and the bird on its spit, staining the stones red, was her knife. Its blade was still sharp. The only thing she took care of. Thinner than it had been previously, but still sharp.

Sharp enough.

'No,' Erin said, leaning towards her. 'No.'

She would die by her own hand, Kria decided. She would not be taken by the water; she would not lie in the belly of the earth waiting fruitlessly to be born into the next world. She would die raging against the mist.

The knowledge of her failure filled her and strangely, instead of sitting in her organs like a heavy, tumorous mass, it was weightless, made of air, and she rose onto her toes as though she might fly like the gull and make it past the mists after all.

The knife was in her hand, the handle stained as red as her hand and the masked prints on her face. She stepped away from the dead bird, waving a casual hand as she went, the fire going out in a quiet exhale of heated air.

Erin fell to her knees, covered her eyes, shaking her head. 'No,' she wailed.

The sky was above Kria, but the gulls were gone. Lying on her back, she gazed upwards, the mist at the corners of her eyes as though death was already milking them over.

It was so cold here in the valley. She longed for warmth. For something warm and human.

She longed to take something of herself and transform the place.

The knife touched her naked stomach and sliced into the flesh stretched thin between her bones. There was nothing warm in this place except her own organs, and with her other hand, she touched them, brought them steaming out into the air.

The knife touched her throat then and drew a red line across it and her eyes stared up at a passing gull, watching it fly beyond the mist.

41

Ambrose frowned over the pages of the story of the Prince with the Golden Hand. It was full of symbolism, but he wasn't sure it was getting him any closer to answers for Morghan. He pushed it away and leaned back in his chair, stretched, and gazed at the fire blazing away in the hearth.

The shortest day of the year was drawing to its early close. He looked out the window, to see the trees gathered close around the house, the shadows hanging from their branches like dark cloaks.

What a year it had been, he thought, turning back to the warmth of his study, where the shelves of books and note-books brought him a comfort of their own. This was where he was at home.

Although, he thought. Spending time with Stephan was surprisingly gratifying. The young man was jumping ahead in his training by leaps and bounds. He had slipped into the Otherworld like he had always been walking there.

The veil was coming down, Ambrose thought, the

knowledge intruding suddenly. The veil was coming down, and the Grove – and all others like it, and every individual possible – had to step up and walk through the coming days and years with strength and conviction.

The path, like the story of the Prince with the Golden Hand, was never clear. Just as it had been that night so many years ago, when he had met and chosen his own fate.

A log shifted restlessly in the grate and Ambrose stretched his legs out under his desk, sinking down into the memory.

He had been more than a hundred miles away from Wilde Grove then. Hadn't even known about it. Ambrose smiled slightly – was that possible, he thought? That there was a time when he hadn't been here in the Grove?

It seemed impossible now. And the thought that he might have ended up somewhere else, that too was unbelievable.

No, he thought. You step onto the true path of your life, and it leads you where you need to go. Which is what he had done, all those years ago. He closed his eyes, listened to the low singing of the fire as it licked at the apple tree logs, filling the room with the scent of their sweetness.

He'd been working protection magic at the boundaries of his house, he remembered. Not Blackthorn house, but something much more ordinary. Just a lad of twenty two, then. Stephan's age. And the magic he'd been doing, he'd been just tripping over his own feet, really. Trying it out. His room had been full of books already, by that point, by that night, he'd been out doing it, actually doing the stuff his books were teaching him.

He'd been elated. He remembered that feeling with a

smile. Finally, he'd thought that night, there he was, not just reading about magic but outside doing it. Because you could read about it until the cows came home, but magic was an active thing, it was something you did, experienced.

Ambrose opened his eyes and gazed around his study again, lingering over the untidy piles of papers and books everywhere. Yes, he thought, nodding. It was good to be out with Stephan.

Doing the magic. Being the magic.

That night he'd been outside under the clouds that glowed orange with the lights from town – and how he'd longed then to see the stars, to glimpse the true sky – and he'd been walking the boundary, putting a sort of bubble around the place, if he recalled correctly.

Then it had happened. He'd stepped from one world to another, from his ordinary life into something quite different. His extraordinary life. Instead of the tiny suburban lawn, he'd been surrounded by trees. Just like that.

Through the trees, there had been a path. Ambrose sat forward and placed his palms on his desk, then reached for the scrying mirror, looking into the black obsidian depths of it and seeing that night again.

He'd stood still, rooted to the spot, staring down the path. Not knowing what was happening.

The path had curved not far ahead, and he'd not been able to see around the curve. Only a few paces deeper into the trees.

For a moment, he'd glimpsed a figure at the curve of the path. A horned man.

A horned god, his antlers rising white as though with moonlight.

Follow me, he'd said, and Ambrose had heard the voice in his head, low, made of wind.

Follow me and I will take you where you need to go.

The vision had faded then, but Ambrose had answered the invitation anyway. He'd stepped onto that path and started walking along it.

He'd never seen more than a few steps ahead – he still didn't see more than a few steps ahead, but he knew he was on the path that was right for him, and hadn't he always been shown the way?

Ambrose stood up. It was true. You might never get a glimpse of more than the next few paces, but if you walked the path anyway, the gods and your kin showed you the way.

So it would be with the Grove now. They would continue the work they knew they must do, and the way ahead would open for them. Life was a journey of strength, of trust.

And of knowing that there was a greater pattern of which you were a part. And although you might see only a strand at a time, you knew the pattern was there.

His front door opened, and Ambrose stepped out into the hallway.

Morghan closed the door behind her and pushed the hood of her cloak back from her face. She leaned against the door and looked at him.

'Are you ready?' she asked.

Such a simple question, he thought. He shook his head. 'No,' he answered. 'Never.'

Morghan's face bloomed into a radiant smile. 'Me neither,' she said. 'Not ever.'

Ambrose reached for his own cloak and picked up his drum from where it waited for him.

Ready or not, he knew, they would follow the path meant for them.

'READY?' STEPHAN ASKED ERIN.

She squeezed her eyes shut for a moment, blew out a breath, wanted to shake her head. She nodded instead.

'I guess so,' she said.

'Burdock, old man,' Stephan said, turning to the dog who thumped his tail against his cushion by the fire. 'We'll be back to give you your breakfast, all right?'

Burdock thumped his tail again. They were going out into the gathering dark and they weren't taking him, but it was all right, because he remembered his other person doing this. She had given him pats and extra treats to keep him company and stepped out into the dusk and come back later, tired and stinking of magic.

So he guessed he'd be all right, on his cushion by the fire, two biscuits stashed under the bed for later, in case he wanted a snack. He wrinkled his nose, watching the spirit fox sweep under his mistress's cloak and decided he'd be much better staying put.

'Okay,' Erin said. 'Let's go before I lose my nerve.' She blinked at the view outside the window. The moon was only in its first quarter phase, and it was tucked behind the clouds anyway. It would be no help showing the way once the sun sank completely behind the hills. Stephan pushed open the door, and she stepped out into a chill gust of wind, making the unlit lantern in her hand swing.

'It'll be less windy in the woods,' Stephan said, closing the door gently, touching the wood with his fingertips and whispering a quick word of thanks to the house for keeping Burdock safe while they were away.

Erin was silent. There had been no new snow, thank goodness, although she was absolutely sure they'd still be standing here getting ready to do this even if the snow was swirling down in a white curtain from the muddy sky.

Stephan stepped up beside her and they walked in silence across the yard to the path leading into the woods, to the stone circle and beyond.

This evening, they were going beyond. The words shivered inside Erin's head as she thought them.

'Are you all right?' Stephan asked. Erin had been pale and silent when he'd arrived, and he couldn't help himself – he kept asking.

She nodded, then tucked her chin down into the warmth of her cloak and tried to watch where she was walking. Inside the grove, it was almost dark, and quiet.

'It's so quiet,' she said.

Stephan looked around. Nodded. 'It's like the world is holding its breath,' he said, and his own breath puffed thin and white in the air. 'It's always like this at these times of the year. Like at midsummer, the days are so long you feel like they're stretched almost to breaking point, and you're just waiting for them to tip over, you know?'

Erin did kind of know. She loved the long summer evenings, when the light turned golden and the air was warm enough to feel like life was one long dream.

'And at this time of the year, I guess it's the same, just the other way around. The days are short and sort of fragile, like they could break at any time.' He pushed himself up the hill, eyes adjusted to the dimness. They had to get there before it got too dark to see, despite the lanterns they carried. Those were for later. 'It's the nights that feel never-ending, like the darkness will never fall away again.'

'But of course, it does,' Erin said, her voice heavy in the cold air, sinking towards the snowy ground like stones.

'Yep, it does. We'll keep vigil tonight, and the sun will return, and the wheel will turn, and the days will grow longer.' Stephan took a deep breath, feeling the weight of the rucksack on his back, in which was his bearskin and mask. The long winter hibernation was coming to an end.

'Don't you ever feel stuck in this never-ending cycle?' Erin asked suddenly, turning to glance at Stephan in the gloom.

He looked at her in astonishment. 'No. Do you?'

Erin didn't know. She didn't know why she'd even asked. Well, that wasn't true. She'd asked because of Kria. Kria who had been brought up to live by the cycle of wheel, and yet, threw herself from it.

Erin closed her eyes for a moment, took a few steps in the vision of Kria lying upon the stony shore of the loch, her dark blood seeping into the ground. She took a deep breath, turning her mind from the metallic tang of it, and snapped her eyes open.

'It's so big,' Stephan was saying. 'When it comes down to it, the cycle of seasons, of lifetimes, it's so big.' He was thinking as he spoke, as they trekked up towards and past the stone circle, making for the cave.

'Big?' Erin asked.

'Yeah. That's what I reckon. Think about it for a

moment...' He cast around for a way to explain the vague idea forming in his head. 'Like, when we do that exercise, you know the one?'

'Which one?' Erin asked, head down, watching her feet as she walked.

'You know, we really gotta come up with names for all this stuff,' Stephan mused. 'The one where you sort of expand and spread until you can see really far, until you're really part of everything around you.'

'That one,' Erin replied. 'That's actually my favourite.' It always made her feel better. Peaceful and exhilarated at the same time. Connected, she guessed. She wished Kria had been able to do it.

But Kria had been angry, and hurt, and lonely. She'd believed the stories about the glen, hadn't trusted the truth of her training to show her the way.

Erin swallowed and her throat clicked dryly.

Stephan waved the lantern in his hand and it clanged and rattled. 'Well, you know what I think?' he said. 'I think that the biggest part of that exercise is being present, you know?'

'Present?' Erin nodded. Yes. He was right. Relaxing into being where you were like that, there was no room for worrying about the future or brooding on the past. You just had to be exactly where and when you were.

'Well, when you do that – when you're really present like that – this is what I find anyway, then the present stretches, you know? It's actually really spacious.'

'Spacious?'

'Yeah. Big enough to live your whole life in when it comes to it. Like...' He frowned, losing track of how to say what he was thinking. 'I don't know,' he finished. 'It's just like the present moment is much bigger than we really think, and when we're inside it, really inside it, like we are when we're being super mindful, it just seems like it encompasses almost everything.' Stephan closed his mouth.

'This stuff is so hard to express,' he sighed. 'It's like you have to do it, and then you know it, when usually we try things the other way around.'

Erin agreed with that.

42

E RIN DIDN'T WANT TO GO INSIDE THE CAVE. S HE STOPPED dead outside it, looking in and feeling a deep unease spread down into her bones. She shook her head.

'I don't think I can,' she said. 'I've had a bad time in caves just recently.' But then, she'd had a bad time outside caves too.

Stephan reached out to touch her shoulder. 'It's okay,' he said. 'There will be a fire going inside, and it'll be quite cosy, I promise.'

She raised her eyebrows at him. Cosy was the last way she'd describe any cave, even one big enough for five of them to sit in together. Erin shook her head again, looking up at the way the hill hung its stone eyebrow over the entrance. She could feel the weight of the hill already, and she wasn't even inside.

'I don't know what's wrong with me,' she said. 'But I don't want to go in there. It's like I'll be swallowed whole if I go inside there. It's just wrong.' She turned slightly away and shivered. 'What if the roof collapses or something?'

'This cave has been here for thousands of years,' Stephan replied, astonished. 'It's not going to collapse.'

'What if there's an earthquake?' Erin said.

The bearskin on Stephan's back was growing heavy, as if it wanted out of the bag and onto his back properly. The cave called to him. He wanted to crawl into the womb of the hill.

'Come on,' he said. 'We have to go in.'

Erin pushed her hood back and looked at him. The light was dying around them, her face in shadows. 'It's too heavy,' she said.

'What's too heavy?'

She cast a glance at the mouth of the cave. 'The hill. The stone.'

Stephan looked helplessly at her, not knowing what to do. 'I'm going to go get Morghan,' he said, and ducked into the cave before Erin could respond.

She turned all the way away and stared back down the track into the trees. They stood silently, black limbs on white snow. It was stark, and somehow glorious. Something shifted, nosed up against her and she stepped back, startled. There was nothing there.

A hand touched her shoulder briefly then withdrew. 'Stephan tells me you won't come inside.'

'I can't,' Erin said.

Morghan stood beside her and gazed out over the fast-fading day. 'I never liked going inside caves either, to be truthful,' Morghan said. 'Or any dark, tight space, really. I still don't like tight spaces, but I've made my peace with caves.'

Erin glanced at her, taking in the long dress, tied at her waist as Ravenna had worn it, the loose hair, the spiralling designs drawn on Morghan's cheeks. She shivered again, remembering Macha.

Macha, who stepped from the trees to join them, her red hair gleaming in Erin's mind.

'How did you make your peace with them?' Erin asked.

Morghan's calm face gazed out over the dimming view. The Shining Ones were abroad tonight, she thought, seeing them wend their ways through the trees. They would keep vigil too, the faerie, and wait for the rebirth of the sun.

'I asked the earth to welcome me inside her,' Morghan said. 'I asked for her protection.'

Erin looked at her.

Morghan watched Maxen climb onto a rock and perch there, drawing his flute from a pocket. When he set to playing, his tune wound in and out of the wind and spread out like the last fingers of dying light, low and mournful.

'What's that sound?' Erin asked, looking around and seeing only shadows.

'It is a faerie whistle,' Morghan said, smiling over at Maxen. 'Played by a master. He is singing the light from the world.'

'Singing,' Erin said, but her voice was low, private.

'Yes,' Morghan agreed anyway. 'Come,' she said. 'You have been in one womb of the world, and now you must enter another. We are always being reborn.'

A frown. Then Erin remembered her tumble down into

448

the well. 'I've become less brave along the way,' she said suddenly.

Morghan looked at her kindly. 'There's a saying,' she told her. 'No less true, metaphorically, for being something of a cliché – that the darkest hour is just before the dawn.'

'Is this my darkest hour?' Erin said.

'Today it is.'

Erin had turned and was looking at the cave. There was a wobble of light from within it. Someone had lit the fire Stephan had said would be there. She took a deep breath, sighed.

'Do I have a choice?' she asked.

'There is always a choice,' Morghan said.

Erin's lips twitched. 'But?'

'But one choice means slipping into the flow of a meaningful life, and the other will have you fighting the current the whole way.'

'I guess we go with flow, then,' Erin said.

'We follow the path,' Morghan agreed.

'Yes,' Macha whispered. 'We follow the ancient way, for it is our soul's path.'

Erin's scalp prickled and under her cloak, she rubbed her arms. She looked at the wide, low mouth of the cave.

It is a womb, she thought. Something pressed again against her skirts and she looked down, seeing – sensing – Fox there, and that helped. Fox at her side. Morghan at her side.

Another glance, as the faerie music whooped and floated on the breeze.

Macha at her side.

The only one missing was Kria.

449

The womb of the world, she thought. Where you go to be held, nurtured, reborn.

Morghan spoke softly. 'Mother Earth, we beg of you to hold us in the warmth and safety of your belly.'

Erin closed her eyes, aware of Macha watching her. Uncommonly slow, Macha had called her.

'Mother Earth,' she whispered. 'Hold me in the depths and safety of your body. I am small and slow, but inside you I will grow stronger.'

Morghan nodded and touched Erin gently between the shoulder blades. On a deep breath, Erin ducked her head and stepped inside the hill.

The only light was from the fire, and it was small, sending miniature shadows dancing around the rough walls of the cave. Stephan looked up at her as she stood in the entrance and he smiled at her.

He had his bearskin wrapped around him, and Erin gazed back, looking at the sharp claws on the ends of his bear paws. The mask was on the top of his head, the muzzle tipped toward the roof of the cave.

To his right was Ambrose, but not the Ambrose of the books and pens and notes and stories. Erin's lips curled into a smile at him, the heavy fur he wore around his shoulder, the feathers woven in his hair, the tattoos drawn on his face. She glanced back at Morghan, who nodded her forward and then took her own place in the circle.

'We are well met, Erin,' Charlie whispered, reaching out a hand to grasp Erin's as she sank down on the ground in her position in the circle.

'Charlie,' Erin said, then drew breath. Charlie was resplendent in a fur cloak of her own, and Erin reached out a tentative hand to touch it. Not real fur, of course, but in the low light of the fire, Charlie looked half...

'What sort of skin?' she asked.

Charlie smiled. 'Beaver,' she said. 'And who is your kin here with you tonight?' she asked.

Erin did not have a fur to wear. She licked her lips and knew she could answer anyway. 'Fox,' she said. She touched a hand to the strand of her hair where she had tied a feather. 'And Raven.'

Charlie's smile widened.

Ambrose began beating softly upon his drum, the rhythm soft and haunting. Erin could still hear the flute's haunting song outside, sounding far away, like a dream.

Stephen threw a handful of herbs onto the fire and sat back as they burned, letting loose a cloud of fragrant smoke. He curled his paws around his bear snout and drew it down over his face.

Morghan hummed for a moment, then lifted her voice in a wordless, chanting song that swelled inside Erin's chest as though filling up all the space beneath her ribs and soaking out through her skin.

The song, inside the cave where they would keep the fire burning through this, the longest night, had no words, and yet, it did. Erin closed her eyes against the smoke and let the song flow through her veins.

She heard Macha join in.

She heard Charlie, on her other side, sing the wordless song of the world too.

Opening her eyes, she looked across at Stephan, but he had curled himself into his skin, tucking his bear nose between his paws. She closed her eyes again, listening to the beat of the drum, to the lilting wind of the flute, the chanting song. She listened to them with her ears, and her skin, and her blood, and all her organs.

She listened to it with her spirit, and it danced and spun, and she swayed where she sat, because the song of the world was inside her, and she was inside it.

There was a small, tight ring of stones, and inside them, a pyramid of kindling waiting for a flame. Erin cupped her hands together and held them against her face. She closed her eyes and let her spirit loosen and flow. She filled the cave, the rock, felt the grass growing on her back, felt the secret flow of underground rivers in her veins, and down deep, she felt the heat of the earth and reached for it at the same time she reached outside into the crisp air of the winter night, the longest night, where the air was silver and glossy from the moon in the mist, and she took that light into her, warming it, reaching for the spark, for the song, for the part of the world that was fire, for the part of herself that was fire.

And it was there. The spark that came from being part of everything, and the fire that was inside her, because she was part of everything.

The tiny flame fell upon the waiting tinder, caught, climbed, grew.

There were bones laid out in the back of the cave and she bent over them, the song in her ears. She reached out a finger and touched the curving scythe of a rib, the flat plate of a hip. She looked down at the tiny rows of finger bones, splayed out in the dirt, and knew one was missing.

But that was all right, Erin thought. She knew where to find it.

Outside the cave, it was night, a swelling moon caught tight in the mist over the glen, silvering the air. She stood and looked out over the loch, watching the clouds reflected in the deep water, seeing something stir the surface for a moment, a great long shadow, then disappear.

And there on the shore, there was Kria, her skin as white as the moon, as the mists. Erin's boots crunched on the moon-spun grass as she picked her way down the hillside.

She hummed as she walked. Her heart beat in time to a faraway drum.

Kria stared sightlessly up at the sky beside the ruins of her fire and the charred remains of a seagull. Erin dropped to her knees beside her and touched the smooth face.

This time her fingers did not pass through Kria, but she felt the cold skin under them. She smoothed Kria's hair back from her face, pulled Kria's clothes back tightly around her ruined body, then lifted her own head and looked around.

There, where Kria had left them, was the pile of feathers she'd stripped from the gull. Not all of them for the wind had claimed some, but enough. There were enough. Erin picked a handful, and knelt back down, smoothing Kria's hair and humming as she rewove her hair, fastening the white and grey and black feathers into the braids, careful not to get them sticky with spilled blood.

She hummed as she wove, and remembered flying on the wings of the seagull, how the water had looked far below them, how the wind had sounded against the steady beat of their wings, how sharply their eyes had seen all around as they circled and swooped over the liminal space of earth and sea.

She sang and imagined Kria's spirit, flying now with the seagull, up over the sides of the valley, through the mists that were cold against their feathers, pushing through into the clear night sky, where the stars waited like diamonds in the cupped hand of the heavens.

There. The feathers were wound into Kria's hair, and Erin reached up to touch the feathers in her own hair for a moment. Raven's black feathers, which she'd found on her doorstep, as though left there for her. Along with one long grey one, from the raven that sat on her windowsill and sometimes invited themselves in to sit on the back of a kitchen chair, watching her with their knowing eyes.

There was one more thing to do, and Erin traced her fingers over one of Kria's hands, unfurling the fingers from their fist and plucking up the tiny bone that rolled free. She tucked it away in her pocket, then bent and kissed the cold fingers, returning them to Kria's side.

Erin scrambled to her feet, then bent down and scooped her arms under Kria's body. She knew she'd be able to pick the girl up, and she did, lifting Kria's spirit gently into her arms so that Kria's head was cradled against her shoulder.

She weighed less than a leaf on the breeze. The seagull feathers fluttered behind them as Erin turned back the way she'd come. Her boots crunched again on the stony soil. The smell of the loch was on the breeze and she breathed it in as though it was a secret she wanted to taste.

She wondered about the creature swimming in its depths.

But she wondered for only a moment before she reached the small, pursed mouth of the cave, breathed deeply, looked down for a moment at Kria's pale face looking up at the sky from the crook of her elbow, and then she bent down and entered the cave.

Somewhere, deep inside the rock, there was the steady beat of a drum, like the heartbeat of the earth she crouched inside, lying Kria down beside the delicate bones of the other woman.

Erin spread Kria's hair out around her, tucked her chin down to hide the red slash across the throat, and looked at her for a moment, before backing out of the cave.

The air outside was cold against her face, inside her lungs. Something moved again in the loch, sending wide rippling waves out to each shore. Erin listened to them lapping up against rock and stone, then stepped once more out onto the path.

Macha stood to one side of the stone hut, her red hair blowing in the breeze, the beads in it clattering gently together, but Erin ignored her. This wasn't the time for words, for conversation, and they both knew it.

The skins on the bed were jumbled, but Erin brought them outside into the silvered night and picked through them, choosing the finest and folding and smoothing them over her arm. It was too dark inside the hut to hunt for anything else that might do honour to Kria, but Erin didn't think there was anything there anyway. She hadn't seen anything.

Kria had deprived herself of every comforting, of seeing any beauty. She had clung to her abandonment, to the fear and the stories she'd been fed. She'd not looked, questioned, kept to her training, cracked open and *seen*.

Erin skirted around the body on the shore and took the furs back to the cave. The breeze, blowing up over the loch

455

and through the narrow ravine of the glen, lilted and swept from side to side like the lilting notes of a flute played by a dark and mysterious faerie man.

Outside the cave, Erin hesitated, breathing in the cold air. She turned and looked back down at the loch shore, seeing Macha standing there, leaning against her staff, and for the first time in a while, the woman's presence strengthened her.

They were here to do what was necessary.

Many things were necessary, Erin was discovering. And most of them were not easy.

She slowed her breathing, ducked her head, and went back inside the cave.

The drum beat steadily. The flute whistled, lilting up and down in its song.

Gently, quietly, Erin drew the finger bone from her pocket and reached over to place it back where it belonged, putting it on the grey soil near its mates. She sighed over it, then went back to the fur blankets, spreading one over the bones of the unknown woman, who once upon a time, a long time ago and in a place far away, had brought herself here to this cave, to lie down and hope for rebirth from this small womb in the world.

Erin spread the second over Kria, tucking it about her spirit's shoulders as gently as if Kria were her child. She spread Kria's hair, so that the seagull feathers gleamed white and black and soft, soft, pearly grey in the flickering light.

Sitting back, Erin looked down on the spirit and bones, and heard the beating of the drum like a heartbeat. She pressed her hands to her chest and reached out from there for the song that would sing them over, that would take them home.

And it was there. Erin recognised it, realised she'd been carrying it in her heart the whole time, that perhaps everyone did.

She sang it, and it smelt of trees, the song, of the scent of their sap, their leaves, their nuts. It was the song of the trees, for she was a Lady of the Forest, and a Lady of Death. Why did those two go together, she wondered for the briefest of moments, but it was a wondering for another time. They did, just as she knew there was also a song of the desert as there was a song of the forest, so many songs, so many lives, so many deaths.

So much life, and so she sang of renewal, of the turning of the seasons, of the eternal wheel of the world.

Outside the cave, the low tune of the flute wove in and out of her song, and together, they sang Kria and her companion from one world to the next, the song like a sigh of the wind in branches, the beating of wings, the humming of bees, the laughter of children.

She sang the turning of seasons, she sang the longest night into its dawn, she sang the stirring of petal, thinking for a moment of Stephan, and the stretching of root. She sang of soil and seeds and bears waking and yawning in the new dawn. She sang of foxes slipping through the night, glimpsing the moon between hurrying clouds. She sang of the strength of ravens, and women standing straight and tall in the night before green and deep water that stirred with a great beast within.

She sang Kria onto a small boat, and the boat took her across the waves to an island of healing, beyond which stretched the Summerlands, and she sang the song that welcomed Kria there, sang an egg into her hand.

She sang Kria's soul home.

And then, she went outside, down the hill to where Macha stood in the same place on the shore, looking at her. Erin said nothing, instead, she knelt down beside the cold body and reached into her own pocket, drawing out this time not a bone, but a smooth brown acorn.

Reaching for Kria's curled fingers, Erin tucked the acorn into the cold palm, then stood again and looked around the valley for one last time. She glanced over at Macha.

Macha raised her eyebrows, then stepped over beside her and they looked up the length of the valley together, the deep water of the loch at their backs.

'Well?' Macha asked. 'Have you learned to see?'

Erin thought of the acorn she'd just pressed into Kria's palm. The song was still inside her, and the acorn, and the acorn burst forth into life. She nodded.

'This place is beautiful,' she said.

And so it was. And as she looked about it, great trees sprang upwards along the steep sides of the glen, the branches of the beautiful Scots pines reaching out to each other, their roots digging deep into the earth, spreading out in an intricate web. Overhead, the mists cleared, and the stars shone, brilliant like diamonds against the sky.

A bird sang, something low and sweet.

Erin gazed out over the forested valley, feeling her heart swell. She touched her fingers to the crystal egg hanging on its leather string around her neck.

'Did I do this?' she asked.

'You saw it, and you sang it into being,' Macha answered.

Erin turned and looked at her. 'Is it time to go now?' she asked.

Macha smiled. Nodded.

And Erin stepped forward into the trees, Macha at her side.

Behind them in the loch, the water stirred, and a dragon rose to the surface, the water streaming from its thick hide as it unfurled and stretched its great head into the air, bringing what had been so long hidden out from the depths.

43

WINSOME SAT IN HER KITCHEN NURSING A CUP OF TEA. SHE'D slept poorly, tossing and turning on a wave of dreams that seemed to chase her through the night, hot on her heels. She'd woken with the blankets twisted around her and her skin slick with sweat that cooled too rapidly in the pre-dawn air of her bedroom.

She put the cup down and sighed, thinking she'd go upstairs and get dressed, think about what to do for the rest of the day, how to keep her service to the community going under the stress of yet another lockdown, this time so close to Christmas.

There was someone moving outside on the road when she drew her bedroom curtains and looked out.

A hooded figure, holding an old-fashioned lantern in their hand, the light from it warm and yellow like a glow worm in the early morning darkness.

Another light caught her eye, and beside it swam into view another figure, head down, lantern swinging.

And four – no five – more, coming from the direction of the main street.

The windowsill was cool under Winsome's hot palms. Below, in her front garden, the grass was covered in snow.

The figures with their small, silent cluster with lights swinging in the darkness disappeared from view. Winsome pressed her hand to the glass, leaning forward to peer downwards to where they had vanished.

She suspected there would be a trail of footprints in the snow beside the church grounds, leading into the woods.

Suspected? She knew.

She closed her eyes and the lantern lights swung behind her lids. Warm and yellow. Miniature suns.

A gasp escaped her lips and Winsome threw herself away from the window and down the stairs, snatching up her coat and shoving her feet into her boots. Her heart beat like a hammer when she bent down to tug on the laces.

'What are you doing?' she asked herself, and she waited a moment for an answer.

It didn't come, unless she could count her hand on the doorknob as it, and she pushed the door open and stepped out into the darkness that preceded the dawn.

She knew the way they were going; she didn't even have to follow their footprints. For a moment, she looked back at her own, leading away from the kitchen door. Behind the door, the light was on, and the empty room looked lonely.

She didn't want to go back there. Winsome turned for the trees instead, slipping between them like a wisp, wishing she'd brought a torch to light the way.

But she hadn't, and gradually, her eyes adjusted, and she

could see the way well enough to stop from walking off the path and into the trees.

Her head was full of hissing static. Go back to the vicarage, it hissed inside the white noise. Go back where you belong.

But her feet kept carrying her on through the woods, over the boundary between Wellsford and Wilde Grove, and she shivered as she stepped across the path from one place to another. Shivered and held her coat tighter around herself.

Winsome stopped at the edge of the clearing, looking in astonishment at the gathering around the stone circle. There was a lump in her throat, and she swallowed it down, her breath coming harshly. Almost, she wanted to sink to her knees, but she straightened her legs, locked the joints upright, and stood there, clasping and unclasping her hands.

Under the hoods and cloaks and furs, she recognised most of the people gathered around the circle. She recognised them, could have said their names, and yet, they were different. She blinked.

More.

Their faces in the golden lights glowed, and their lips curved in smiles about things she thought she could only guess at. She lifted her own face to the lights – everywhere there were lights, hanging from the trees, a night sky of stars strung from tree to tree.

A hand touched her elbow. A hooded head bent down to look at her, and she recognised Rima, Charlie and Martin Beckford's daughter in law. She smiled into Winsome's dazed face and held something out to her.

It was a lantern, and Winsome stared at it, noticing the simple tins into which the outline of the sun had been pierced, so that it glowed from the candle burning within. She took it in numb fingers and Rima led her over to the outer circle, behind the ring of stones. Rima's hand held her shoulder for a moment, then let go, and Winsome watched the young woman walk back to take her place in the circle.

Over the rushing of her blood between her ears, there was the slow beating of a drum, and Winsome wondered if that had been playing all along and she'd mistaken it for the sound of her heart knocking against her ribs. She looked down at the lantern in her hand, then upwards again, to the web of lights.

She remembered Morghan's words. *How to shine brightly in this darkness? To weave the web ever stronger?*

Where was Morghan? Winsome dragged her eyes away from the stars in the dawn and looked for her. She didn't see her. Or Ambrose. She closed her eyes.

The drum beat steadily on.

And there was a flute, whispering through the woods. She heard it and listened and was captivated. It was a sigh, a leaving, a whispering, a prayer.

There was movement around her, and Winsome opened her eyes, saw that the ring of people she stood with had turned to step around the circle, holding their lanterns out. She stumbled a little in her boots, her limbs wooden, uncertain, and then she was moving with them, around the outer circle of the stones.

How long had the standing stones been there, she wondered? How many times had they seen gatherings like this?

Inside the circle of stones, another circle of lanterns began to move, in the opposite direction. Around and around they went, slowly, in a dazzle of light, and now, joining the otherworldly sound of the flute, a harp played, each sound and strand of music like light in the last minutes of the longest night. She moved in time to the music that sounded like forests growing, and mountains dreaming, and oceans singing, and lovers reaching for each other.

And she realised she was humming along with it, and so was everyone else, and the lump in her throat was gone now, and the air in her lungs was cold and scented with snow and soil.

A voice rose over the humming song, over the music of flute and harp, over the muffled heartbeat of the drum.

'We weave the worlds together. We come together here to do this weaving to bring peace to the heart of our community, so that our song vibrates ever outwards and inwards.'

Winsome blinked, holding her lantern. Her circle changed direction, began their slow swaying dance the other way, their lanterns held higher towards the sky.

A voice close by called out, startling Winsome.

'Hail and welcome to the spirits of this land, this circle, this grove. Hail and welcome to the gods we serve, with whom we walk our paths. Hail and welcome to our honoured Neighbours, with whom we are grateful to share this grove. Hail to our ancestors, who have walked this circle before us, wearing a path for us to follow, and whose love and tears we carry in our hearts, burden and blessing, both. Hail to all those here, seen and unseen. Hail and welcome!

To all those who come in peace be welcome to our weaving. Hail and welcome!'

Winsome lifted her face to the sky, and for a moment, she thought she saw what could not possibly be there, a great glowing web that stretched across them all, reaching and connecting everyone. For a moment, she did not step, but felt she floated.

Then their stepping changed, and they were dancing, the two circles mingling, weaving in and out. Winsome's head cleared, grew heavy, cleared again, and she breathed in and out, and was not positive that everyone she passed was human.

For a moment, she caught sight of a familiar face, the pale brow dreamy under the heavy black hair. Minnie looked at her, eyes widening in shock, and then she was gone and Winsome laughed.

She should not be here, she thought about herself.

The dancing turned, started the other way, weaving an unbroken path. She held her lantern higher.

Another voice lifted to the lights overhead.

'We call peace into this space. We call for peace so that inside that peace we may hear the voices of our souls and our gods and sing back the light so that the wheel may continue to turn.'

Winsome listened to the words of the call, and the wordless song of her fellow dancers, and over it the sound of the harp and the flute, and under it like a heartbeat, the drum, the drum, the drum.

'In peace, may the voice of spirit be heard,' another voice called into the light and dark of the circle. 'May there be peace in the east. May there be peace in the south. May there be peace in the west. May there be peace in the north.'

There were others gathering around the edge of the dancing weaving circle now, Winsome saw.

Spirits.

These were the faerie of the Otherworld, she thought. And the veil was coming down, and she could see them.

They shone. The Shining Ones, Morghan had called them. Winsome looked down at herself, at her thick woollen coat, her gloveless hand holding the lantern.

Did she shine too?

The voice rose again in its call. 'May there be peace throughout all the world. May all who gather here, seen and unseen, be blessed by the spirits of sea and sky and soil. May the worlds always be acknowledged, may we walk in each, honour each, receive the blessings of each.'

A sigh from everyone in the circle.

'World upon world upon world.'

Winsome repeated the words. 'World upon world upon world.' The words were like salt on her lips and she licked them. There were more worlds than she had imagined.

Which of them did she belong in?

This one?

She blinked and wove in and out with the other dancers, casting glances at the Shining Ones as she moved.

All of the worlds? Did she belong in all of them?

'I call the spirits of the South – the fire of our hearts, the passion that burns and keeps the worlds alive, spirit of Dragon, guardian over the treasure of our own bright gold, the gold of our eternal beings, whose purpose never tarnishes. I call you to be with us, to surround us with your protective breath of fire. Hail and welcome!'

Winsome stopped moving and the circle danced on around her. She swayed where she stood, dazed.

'Oh my god,' she whispered.

From another part of the dancing circle, another voice lifted over the music that was playing inside Winsome's very veins now.

'I call the spirits of the water – those who hold the memory of the ages within you. I call the spirit of the whale, ancient and wonderful, who dives to the deepest depths, whose songs bind each to the other, who swims through the ages. We are blessed by you, we call you, hail and welcome!'

Winsome lowered her head and looked as though through water, feeling the rush of it around her, carrying her away.

Carrying her home?

Where did she belong?

Carrying her home?

The image of the whale rose before her, and she looked into its ancient eye, swaying, swimming.

Another voice.

'I call to you spirits of the North. You spirits of the earth upon which we walk, she who gives birth to us, grows us from seed, feeding and watering and tending us. I call upon the spirit of Bear - bless us, dearest one, Bear, with your nurturing wisdom, calm and fierce, with your great power of healing. Hail and welcome I call you!'

Winsome found herself moving again, stepping along with the others, the lanterns bobbing and weaving, leaving streaks of honey light behind her eyes. She lifted warming fingers and found a smile upon her lips. Inside her, something swelled, broke forth in a song that heated her blood.

She belonged. Here and now.

'I call to you, spirits of the East. Spirits of air whose breath fills us, who offers wings to our prayers. I call to you, spirit of Hawk with your gift of far-seeing vision, to you, spirits of the eastern wind, who beat upon the door to my heart, to the waking spring, to everything that unfurls and reaches to grow, and to you, Rising Sun, I call you to be with us so that we may be with you.'

The circle stopped and lanterns were raised to the eastern sky.

The flute hushed. The harp.

Only the drum beat on, getting louder, stronger.

Above the horizon, a streak of light. The first light of dawn.

'Rising Sun,' Morghan said, coming down from the cave to meet the dawn. 'Bringer of light, giver of strength, we have waited through the darkness for you. We have held on through the longest night. We have wavered and wailed and cried for you and held on, our faith in seeing your face again.

'Rising Sun, bringer of light, giver of strength.'

Morghan stepped into the circle, seeing the dim light of the dawn strengthen, lengthen its fingers over the hills, reaching for them.

'The seasons are long,' she said. 'And we have been waiting for this glimpse of the risen sun, knowing that now the season of darkness is over, our work begins again. We must look for life, within us, within the land, and we must tend what we find, with compassion and diligence. That which we wish to grow, we must plant. That which we wish to grow, we must cherish.'

Morghan looked around at her grove. 'Thus it always is when the wheel turns from the season of death to the season of new life.'

She fell silent for a few minutes and watched the eastern sky lighten, feeling inside her the ancient turning of the tides. The light threaded up through the clouds, and they were glorious even while the sky was murky with weather, the ground weighted with snow. There were few visible signs of the coming season of growth, she knew, but inside the trees, the sap was stirring, the knuckles upon their branches that would become buds were swelling, and their song was soon to be not of dreaming, slumbering winter, but the celebration of spring.

'The wheel turns,' she said, as she said at each of the eight rituals they held at the circle, as she always had. She was aware of Ravenna deep inside her, the woman she'd once been, who had in her own time stood in this very spot, watching the sun rise higher over the hills, spilling its light towards them to show them the way.

'The wheel turns, as it always has, in cycles. Once, many ages ago, we gathered here to mourn the turning as the world moved away from what we knew to be the truth.' She repeated the words, her fingers tight around her staff, the dawn air cold against her cheeks, her eyes radiant as she gazed towards the brightening horizon. 'A veil was falling, separating ourselves from the world of spirit. Humans were turning their faces away from their true selves, and their true kin, and holding themselves above it all, master upon the earth instead of grateful equal.'

She'd said that before, during Samhain, but now, Morghan had more to add. The season was well and truly changing. She drew breath, and looked around at her Grove, at the familiar faces, each turned toward the sun, its light growing upon their faces.

She saw Winsome there, tight in the circle, holding a lantern, and her next words died in her throat.

Well, she thought. Here was something she hadn't foreseen, and it brought a smile to her face. She closed her eyes, recalled the words she needed to say.

Ambrose's drum kept its beat, a slow, powerful pulsing.

'We could not stop it then,' she said. 'We could not stop the veil falling over our eyes, our knowing. But tides always turn, and circumstances call us to their service once more. The veil is lifting from our seeing and the worlds will once more belong to all of us.' She lifted a hand and gestured to those outside the circle of her grove mates, bowing her head to the faerie who had joined them.

Those in the circles shifted on their feet. Their breathing came quicker, lips parting. Winsome thought of the entity who had tricked Minnie. She thought of the flocking darkness, and she pressed a palm to the wool of her coat.

Minnie heard the words feverishly, her heart keeping double time to the drum, and something swept over her, a sensation of being in the right place. Of taking her place. She straightened, lifted her head.

Morghan took a long breath. Listened as harp strings were plucked, the notes pure and winding about the cool morning air. The strains of the flute wove in and out of the melody.

And underneath it all, the drum beat time.

Beat the pulse of her heart.

'The veil thins,' she repeated. 'This is the year of the Bear, of great healing, of coming out from the darkness of the cave, of the womb, and being born into a new world.' She paused. 'A new world where much will change, and where we will need all our courage.'

Stephan pricked up his bear ears and raised his bear paws to the sun, drawing its light down to himself. He had been asleep in his cave all the long winter, he realised. All the long winter of his life so far – but now he was awake.

He danced where he stood. The dance of the bear, of healing, of the courage of the heart.

'This is our great Belonging,' Morghan said, feeling the words well up inside her. 'This is the world we must claim – the one to which all belong, no matter what skin they wear. The world will be led back to its sacred balance, and we will walk by the side of the Shining Ones as they reclaim it, and we will lead our kind by example, with integrity, compassion, and unfailing kindness.' She sighed quietly at the beauty of the morning, the white of the snow, the dark of the trees, the shimmering colours of the people gathered there with her in ancient ritual.

Erin sighed too, looking around the circle with the gaze she had brought back from the glen. With the song she had found there. She saw each of them gathered there under the spreading rays of the reborn sun, each of them brilliant with their spark inside them. Bringing her hands up to her face, she cupped them together, and reached

471

inside herself, reaching for the connection with the world that was there.

And finding it. World upon world upon world where she belonged.

She spread her hands and gazed at the diamonds there.

They glittered in the rising light.

PRAYER OF THE WILDWOOD

Blessed water, blessed earth, air, fire.
Spirits of the north, east, south, and
    west.
I greet you, in peace and blessing.
I am called to weave the world
    with you.
I am called to keep the weaving safe.

JOIN THE GROVE

Subscribe to the Wilde Grove mailing list to receive free books, prayer cards, oracle cards, updates, and more. Be the first to hear about promotions and discounts.

Be part of the magic behind the books.

www.katherinegenet.online/join-the-grove

ABOUT THE AUTHOR

Katherine has been walking the Pagan path for thirty years, with her first book published in her home country of New Zealand while in her twenties, on the subject of dreams. She spent several years writing and teaching about dreamwork and working as a psychic before turning to novel-writing, studying creative writing at university while raising her children and facing chronic illness.

Since then, she has published more than twenty long and short novels. She writes under various pen names in more than one genre.

Now, with the Wilde Grove series, she is writing close to her heart about what she loves best. A Spiritworker, Druid, and polytheistic Pagan, Katherine is a member of the British Order of Druidry.

Katherine lives in the South Island of New Zealand with her wife Valerie. She is a mother and grandmother.

Made in the USA
Middletown, DE
09 August 2023